ADVERSE REACTION

ADVERSE REACTION

A NOVEL

TERENCE MIX

Auctorem House
276 5th Ave, Ste 704-2591
New York, NY 10001
www.auctoremhouse.com
Phone: 1 888-332-7718

Published by Auctorem House: 02/21/2025

ISBN: 978-1-965687-10-9(sc)
ISBN: 978-1-965687-11-6(e)

Library of Congress Control Number: 2024920529

CONTENTS

CHAPTER 1 1
CHAPTER 2 11
CHAPTER 3 26
CHAPTER 4 43
CHAPTER 5 55
CHAPTER 6 67
CHAPTER 7 82
CHAPTER 8 94
CHAPTER 9 103
CHAPTER 10 114
CHAPTER 11 121
CHAPTER 12 130
CHAPTER 13 138
CHAPTER 14 144
CHAPTER 15 149
CHAPTER 16 156
CHAPTER 17 160
CHAPTER 18 164
CHAPTER 19 172
CHAPTER 20 179
CHAPTER 21 186
CHAPTER 22 192

CHAPTER 23 196
CHAPTER 24 200
CHAPTER 25 207
CHAPTER 26 212
CHAPTER 27 217
CHAPTER 28 226
CHAPTER 29 231
CHAPTER 30 235
CHAPTER 31 241
CHAPTER 32 247
CHAPTER 33 258
CHAPTER 34 265
CHAPTER 35 274
CHAPTER 36 282
CHAPTER 37 290

EPILOGUE 301

CHAPTER 1

Saturday, July 11

She did not know it yet, but the events of the day were about to send the life of Niki Burroughs careening out of control.

At the moment, Niki's red BMW F10 sped along the northbound number one lane of the 405, the speedometer needle flirting with the 75-mph line. The lane was running clear, and every minute or two, she would cast a glance at her rearview mirror, hoping to catch sight of a black and white before it got a fix on her. The dash clock now displayed the time at 12:12 p.m.

It had taken longer than expected to reach this point, and Niki was now considering dropping her six-year-old son off at Alicia's and skipping lunch entirely. After pushing it back by three hours, it would not sit well with the Dohertys if she showed up late to their one o'clock meeting.

Niki caught Randy's reflection in her rearview mirror. He was buckled up in the back seat and intently working over his coloring book. It would not be an easy decision. Between Randy's schooling, the irregular and frequently late hours of her own schedule, and classes at Harbor Junior College, Niki and Randy spent little time together. Not quality time, anyway, where they could sit and talk about matters other than homework, chores, and scheduling. Weekends were also her busiest days for showing homes. But months ago, Niki took a stand when she pronounced Saturday mornings as their own private hours, the Doherty appointment being one of the rare exceptions. Her routine was to spend an hour or two playing with Randy at the house and then heading out for a leisurely lunch at a local fast-food restaurant. But that was before her world turned upside down a few hours earlier. Today would have to be condensed into 20 minutes at McDonald's – and now, maybe even that would have to be scrubbed.

⸻ ● ⸻

Reggie Allerton had reached his limit. "Goddamn traffic," he growled as he clenched his teeth and crushed the accelerator to his International six-wheeler, charging ahead another 3 car lengths.

He was a rugged man, solidly packaged, yet surprisingly handsome in spite of a three-time loser for a nose, a souvenir from a high school football game, and two barroom brawls. Over the past twenty minutes, he crawled a half mile from the Wilmington Avenue onramp in Carson, where he had entered the Interstate. He had left the Carson warehouse of Ginther's Pilsner with a full load of beer, stacked high with over three hundred cases of cans and bottles and a half dozen kegs. Now, he was on his delivery route to various locations throughout the South Bay area of Los Angeles County, falling further behind on his schedule by the minute.

Saturdays were usually light-traffic days. There were days he could frequently slack off and enjoy an hour or so at the Red Stein Tavern in Torrance. For the past several months, his pattern had been to hit the Stein at about one o'clock and break for a steak sandwich and a couple of beers. It was the third stop on his route, and although Ginther's only approved a 30-minute break for lunch, Allerton had found it easy on Saturdays to stretch it another half hour and still complete his prescribed course on time.

But over the past five weeks, the one hour at the Stein had grown to an hour and a quarter, then to an hour and a half, and finally last Saturday to a full two hours. After the sandwich and swilling down an initial stein of Ginther's, Allerton found himself locked in a contest of skill on one of the four pool tables in the back of the tavern.

And it took little enticement to pick up chalk and cue. Many local patrons were of the opposite gender, and several were quite attractive to the recently separated father of three. One in particular – "Monica," she had told him – had walked up to Allerton while sitting with his sandwich and challenged him to put up ten if he dared to break a rack with someone in a skirt. It was surprising to the truck driver that he had been so quick to accept since he had never fancied himself skilled at the game and was certain that he would walk out of the Stein at least ten dollars lighter for the experience. Yet, recalling her inspecting eyes and the slight and somewhat defiant smile that tickled at his loins, he fully understood his motivation. It had been five months since his separation from a wife who had grown to be a stranger.

From the elevated position in his truck, Allerton could see in the distance a set of amber lights twirling from several emergency vehicles, apparently at the site of an accident another half mile away.

Finally, traffic began to clear in the two inside lanes to his left. The outer lanes, however, were still fully blocked. If he was going to escape the gridlock, he would have to change lanes. He hit his blinker and checked the side-view mirror. For a brief moment, there was a surge forward in the number 3 lane and a slight opening in the traffic. Allerton immediately hit the gas and nosed into the lane – then slammed on the brake pedal as it just as quickly closed.

"Shit!" he said, slamming his hands on the steering wheel. "Shit, shit, shit, shit!"

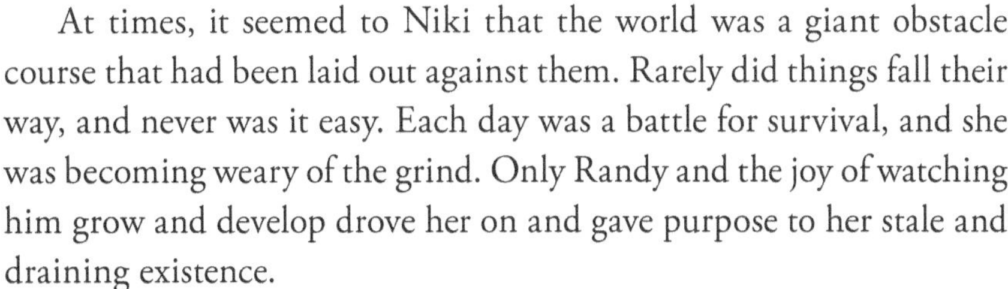

At times, it seemed to Niki that the world was a giant obstacle course that had been laid out against them. Rarely did things fall their way, and never was it easy. Each day was a battle for survival, and she was becoming weary of the grind. Only Randy and the joy of watching him grow and develop drove her on and gave purpose to her stale and draining existence.

Nikifora Burroughs, nee Leondopoulos, led the exhausting and stressful existence of a single mother trying to succeed in the greater metropolitan area of Los Angeles County. Struggling with the ups and downs and sporadic income of a real estate agent in a fluctuating market, Niki also carried the financial burden of her father's Parkinson's disease and the economic needs of her young boy. At times, the monthly billings from the nursing home, compounded by the ever-present costs of clothing, babysitting, food, utilities, mortgage payments, household maintenance, and automotive repairs, seemed overwhelming.

Yet she had always found a way to survive. Short-term bank loans have averted financial ruin on many occasions, as have timely commissions. It was mystifying to Niki how, at the bleakest times, an escrow, seemingly plagued by insurmountable problems, would close or a cash buyer would step out of nowhere to rescue her from disaster; so often that more than once, she had pondered the possibility of influence from a higher plain. Out there in the ethereal cosmos of the universe, had there indeed been a divine power ordaining the course of her life?

Not a chance. Not to the mindset of one Niki Burroughs. In fact, it ran against the grain of her stock. Commitment and resolve were the tenets by which she forged her life. The larger the problem, the more she dug in her heels. She had the determination of a prizefighter, her best friend Alicia had once told her. Not the fancy-footer who jabbed and parried, but the slugger who always bounced from the ropes, time and again pounding away, gradually transforming defeat into victory. Niki was always coming back, always finding a way, because destiny was in her own hands and her achievements would be of her own making – as long as she was in control and her life planned to the last minute.

Niki was a striking woman, a head-turner with hair pulled straight back into a ponytail and as black as midnight on a moonless night. Her complexion, satin-smooth in texture, tended toward the dark of her Greek ancestors and, when accented with the right colors and wardrobe, added an exotic allure to her attractive features. Though, if the truth were known, Niki hated her coloring, seeing it as an ethnic brand, and she went to great lengths to avoid the sun and its darkening rays. Her figure was equally appealing, petite in structure, with full yet firm breasts, that as a developing young girl, were a source of taunting and embarrassment but now were found as useful equipment in a male-dominated society. When the need arose, Niki was not beyond displaying and accenting that with which nature had blessed her – and for which she religiously exercised and dieted to maintain.

Yet the physical characteristics that lingered long after a meeting with Niki Burroughs were her eyes. Deep brown, seeming almost black at times, they were perpetually alive with energy, sparkling with life. Adaptable and variable in use, they were the most effective instruments in the arsenal of a woman who found an equal facility in using them to melt the coldest of hearts or intimidate the boldest of adversaries.

At the moment, those eyes were taking in the clear number one lane ahead. She was determined to spend lunch with Randy – no matter how short it might have to be. So she pushed the speed up to eighty.

⸺●⸺

"Roll in a minute off schedule, and you're out the door," were the supervisor's last words. The line had been drawn after the customer complaints began to trickle in. During the recent heat wave, the markets and taverns ran short on inventory. Many orders had been doubled over the past two weeks, and still, the beer was selling out. Empty shelves and kegs meant a loss of revenue. In a market dictated by the thermometer readings, the products had to be available when demand was high, or consumers went to optional retailers – as well as brands. Thus, the virtue of patience was also in limited supply. At other times, customers seldom notice a late arrival, even by an hour or two. But for the past two weeks, they seemed to be looking down the street ten minutes after Allerton's expected delivery time.

Now, of all times, this blasted accident had to pop up on the San Diego Freeway, and Ginther's would give little consideration to the delay it imposed. Unless, of course, Allerton gave up his lunch stop – a concession he was unwilling to make. Although the risk of losing his job was high, after last Saturday, the Stein offered too much promise. It was a risk worth taking.

Opportunity suddenly opened again in the number 3 lane, and Allerton was quick to react. Experience had taught him to move fast and decisive in heavy traffic. Once he entered a lane, the smaller vehicles would yield, not wanting to challenge the large truck. In an instant, the accelerator was to the floor, and the six-wheeler and its 13,000-pound load began to move forward behind the laboring engine. For a few agonizing seconds, the line of vehicles from behind began to close in on him again. But this time, Allerton kept his foot grounded, refusing to look at the sideview mirror, preempting all others from the space he would shortly be occupying. Even before he was halfway over, Allerton could hear from behind a piercing screech of braking tires and a simultaneous blast from a horn.

"Fuck you, Mac!" responded Allerton as he hoisted his middle finger to the sky. He was now up to 18 miles per hour and selecting his next move to the adjacent number two lane to his left.

———•———

As usual, the headache was back. It always seemed to be around, even when she was not experiencing its pain. It just sat there below the surface, lying in wait, looking for its opportunity at the first sign of stress. It ebbed and flowed like the oceans of the world, at bay, dormant, yet threatening, while Niki's ever-present pills ran their course. Then, it rises again, at times only nagging and irritating, and at others, it is like a raging storm dictated by the frequency and intensity of the disrupting events of the day. It had been her constant companion since she was 14, and at the moment was creeping up her neck into the base of her skull.

Niki fumbled through her purse with one hand until she located her favorite bottle. Then, using her thumb, with the dexterity of a card shark, she forced open its plastic cap and turned over the container, jostling out a couple of enteric-coated tablets. In the blink of an eye, she had popped the pills into her mouth and forced them down her throat with a hard swallow. She had followed this procedure so many times before it was almost an unconscious act.

Up ahead, a good mile distant, traffic was beginning to congest. A pair of brake lights suddenly illuminated, then three more, a dozen, and then a sea of them came into view. Niki promptly dropped her speed to 70 and urged to curse out loud, but instead bit her lip, mindful of the 6-year-old in the back seat.

An accident, she thought, could only be an accident. Damn!

As she closed in on the mass of vehicles, she rapidly considered – and dismissed – the option of leaving the freeway. The lanes to her right were loading up, and the next off-ramp was almost upon her. There was little chance she could negotiate her way over in time. Besides, the surface streets would take her forever to reach Lomita. She slowed another five miles an hour.

A glimmer of hope loomed before her. The two inside lanes were apparently open, the number one moving faster than the two, which was absorbing most of the converging cars and trucks from the outer lanes. If she stayed where she was, she just might be able to slide through with little delay. She had slowed now to 60 and continued to reduce her speed. A blue Camero, 200 feet ahead in the same lane, was now entering the congesting traffic and decelerating. It approached and began to pass a large truck to its right, which had just charged over from the number three lane and was blinking its direction, announcing it had not yet completed its move. Sweeping across its back, in bold red and black cursive letters, were the words "Ginther's Pilsner."

Not about to be saddled behind a slow and obstructing beer truck, Niki instinctively punched the accelerator, and the F10 surged on, rapidly closing the gap between it and the Camero.

—— • ——

Allerton leaned forward in his seat, cradling the steering wheel, as the six-wheeler continued its assault on the number one lane, quickening its pace, holding position, and waiting for the opening that would soon be presenting itself. His eyes were riveted on the side view mirror. In another moment, the Camero would be by him, and he would finally ne be through and on his way to the Stein.

For the briefest moment, he thought of her flowing red hair, her lips, full and moist, and her breasts hanging openly in her T-shirt as she leaned forward, lining her shot, and her tight rear end as it protruded and provoked, and her eyes, wild and communicating her want and her need. He thought of her manner and her subtle hints and invitations that, with each succeeding Saturday, had become increasingly open. He thought of her naked and begging on a king-size bed in a neighboring motel, as he had dreamed of for 7 days, and he felt reckless and uninhibited and longing and hungering and impatient.

Suddenly, without thought or caution, as the Camero slid by, Allerton pulled the steering wheel hard to his left, not consciously registering the red vehicle that now filled his mirror, but only a face that soon would symbolize the nightmare of his life.

The two competing forces instantly came together in a deafening impact that some, up to a mile away, thought was an explosion.

In a millisecond, the International's left front fender had buried itself into the right rear panel of the car, propelling it in a clockwise rotation, as the resulting collision shattered glass, ripped at metal, deformed frames, flung bodies, and catapulted the smaller BMW sideways, out of control, at 73 miles per hour. At the same moment, Niki's shoulder slammed against the door, and her head careened off the driver's side window, numbing her senses, as she helplessly clung to the steering wheel while a multitude of colors flashed by, her car nearly completing a full revolution before impacting with the concrete median barrier. Unspent, it was propelled sideways off the wall like a toy car as its tires folded under and the wheel rims bit into the asphalt, throwing the BMW onto its side, and it began to roll and roll and roll until rocking on its roof with one final reach to come over on its side, but stopping short, settling back, and finally baring its belly.

Silently, it lay, as all else seemed to stop, save for its four wheels, which continued their rotation as if to remind all of the recently completed events that preceded. It was 273 feet beyond the point of its initial meeting with the truck.

Niki's first thoughts were of a dream. She was screaming as she was whipped out of a world of reality, void of relation or balance or control or senses. A world where up was down and down was up – a world without pain, feeling, or anguish, as she was pounded and pounded into a series of nondescript obstacles, while confined within her small and nondescript world.

Then it was over – and the dream gradually and unalterably became a reality. At first, there was the buzz, as if she had just finished off the last of five wine coolers, insulating and euphoric. It was warming and comforting, and she attempted to cling to its security. But in moments, it was replaced by the anxiety and shock and fear that it had all really happened.

She blinked her eyes several times, trying to focus and get some sense of bearing. Her breathing felt impaired, and she shortly began to feel pressure against the back of her head and her chin burrowing into her chest. There was also now an appreciation of compression onto her left shoulder, and she reached up with her right hand. Or was it down? Niki suddenly came to the full realization that she was upside down and somewhat suspended by her lap belt and shoulder harness. Her head was down against the partially collapsed roof of the F10. She looked out, and above, at the asphalt of the northbound number one lane and the sprinkling of glass pebbles that covered it.

A whimper broke the silence.

At that very moment, she felt a rush of unimaginable terror and desperation. She twisted her head to her right and came face to face with the bottom rear seat that had somehow become wedged between Niki and her son. She attempted to scream his name, but it only came out as a muffled gargle, as if speaking with a throat full of mouthwash. She tried again with the same frustrating sound. Tears flushed her eyes. She had to reach him. With her right hand, she grasped at the bottom of the steering wheel – then tried a similar feat with her left. Pain suddenly shot through her forearm with the searing intensity of a knife penetrating all of its skin, muscles, and ligaments. She instinctively looked up at the inner portion of her left arm. Four inches down from her wrist, she beheld the white, jagged edge of a bone. It had breached the surface of the skin and reared itself, dripping a crimson red, as the distorted limb hung helplessly before her – and the anesthetic buzz again returned.

Desperately, Niki tried to cling to consciousness, unwilling to leave, absent knowledge of her son's well-being. She hung there, sustained only by hope, as she began to sense the full-bodied aroma of beer, at first weak, then stronger and stronger, until it seemed presented directly to her nose.

She also now heard footsteps approaching, increasingly louder, initially a distant staccato tap on the pavement, then crunching through the glass as they neared the car. Niki was now almost in a dreamlike state but still had the presence to hear Allerton's voice as he kneeled and peered into the other side of the overturned vehicle.

Niki's last memory was of the truck driver's words, hopeful and laden with anxiety. "Are you all…Oh Jesus, God, no!"

Then came the scream that rang out over the gathering of vehicles and onlookers that no one present would soon forget.

Among the debris, shattered glass, and a scattering of toys and crayons in what was once the back seat area of the BMW was a vision that would be seared in Allerton's memory banks until his death – a small six-year-old child curled up in a fetal position, leaning against the back of the rear seat, whimpering, tears flowing from his closed eyes, clutching at his right thigh with both of his hands. But it was what he viewed below those hands that sent him into near hysteria.

Nothing existed below the thigh – nothing but a bloody stump.

◆━●━◆

CHAPTER 2

Tuesday, July 21

The two men in suits looked up from the conference table at the tall, athletic Adonis. He stood grinning with apparent amusement. At six foot three and 190 pounds, he was somewhat imposing to the surprised lawyers. He wore only a T-shirt stenciled, "I survived the road to Hana," and a pair of loud shorts. Leather sandals added a further touch of defiance. Trisha O'Brien, a fresh and wide-eyed court reporter, sat patiently behind her stenographic machine, quietly taking it all in.

"Morning, gentlemen," grinned the casually dressed man. His musculature was trim and defined, with a tan that told of many hours under the sun. In some ways, the body didn't quite go with the older and more mature features of the face.

"Mitchell? My God, is it you?" The older of the two attorneys was clearly shocked.

Mitchell Redden extended his hand. "Hi, Sandy, welcome to the South Bay."

Sanford Goodman pulled his slightly obese body up from the chair and took his firm handshake. "What's it been, four years? And what have you done to yourself? I mean, you look so…healthy."

Redden chuckled. "Let's say a very long time. I dropped the pounds when I cut back on booze and stopped abusing my life."

Goodman shook his head. "I saw your name on the door, but I thought somebody forgot to take it down or it was some kind of a rental suite. You actually back in practice?"

"Can't you tell?" smiled Redden, extending his arms to display his wardrobe. At the moment, he preferred to sidestep the question. He wasn't quite sure himself.

"So, are you sitting in on this thing? I thought this was Blaylock's case." Goodman's question came with a tinge of concern. He was never one for confrontation and had often questioned his choice of personal injury defense work. Redden, on the other hand, carried a fighter's reputation – at least the Redden of four years ago.

"Just pinch-hitting. Harry had a matter come up in Orange County – an *ex parte* or something." Redden winked. "Relax, Sandy. I won't get in the way."

Redden turned to the younger lawyer, a clean-cut man in his early thirties. He was short and wore frameless glasses. "Hi! Mitch Redden," he said, again reaching for a handshake. The young man's features seemed vaguely familiar but held no importance. Perhaps one of a thousand faces he had seen before that had been washed away by time and a need to forget.

The young lawyer rose, hesitated, then replied, "Geoffrey Rothenberg," and accepted the shake. He was noticeably uncomfortable with the meeting. "So…Mitchell Redden, a name out of the past."

Redden examined the face closer. "Have we met before?"

"No," said Rothenberg. "Not that I remember." It was a lie. Their paths had crossed briefly nine years earlier. "But your name just came up the other day."

"It's always nice to be remembered," said Redden.

"Yeah, well, some of the older guys at Barry, Klein were wondering where you had disappeared to."

"Let's keep it our secret," smiled Redden. "I wouldn't want to create any illusions that I am actually down here having a good time."

Redden continued to ponder Rothenberg, seeing an image of himself fourteen years earlier. He was a recent graduate of Boalt Hall from the UC Berkeley campus and was out to cut a wide swath of victims in the civil trial courts of California. His was an ego born of intellect, a high standing in class, a glib tongue, and looks to assure he'd be a natural charmer in front of any jury. Energetic and ambitious, to some, his manner smacked of arrogance, while to others, his actions and attitude were only a reflection of confidence in his own skills. A member of Law Review and Moot Court champion in law school and captain of his debate teams during his undergraduate years, Mitchell Redden, was considered by his contemporaries and teachers alike as a "can't miss," a natural for a successful practice as a civil trial lawyer.

Then came disillusionment.

Heavily recruited during his senior year, Redden had no sooner completed the State Bar exam than he found himself firmly entrenched in a cubbyhole office in one of the old, prestigious law firms of San Francisco. But rather than standing in a courtroom with a trial brief and witness list in hand, Redden became lost in a labyrinth of associates whose opportunities for trial were dictated by the pecking order on the firm letterhead. The credo was simple: serve your time, wait your turn, and patience will be rewarded. Then, too, was the dress code, the homage to the senior partners, and the general regimentation of each and every facet of the practice of law.

Not one to fit anyone's mold, nine months later, Redden was out the door looking for something different and hopefully better. No, the closest a young lawyer in a major law firm ever came to a courtroom was appearing on a law and motion matter, and the only opportunity to confront a witness under oath was in the quiet and non-dramatic confines of a law office during a deposition.

"How's Chester doing? I figure he'd be pressing for senior partner by now." On its face, the question seemed innocent enough, but a discerning listener would have detected a slight trace of sarcasm.

"Ray Gillingham, you're talking about? He prefers 'Ray.'"

"I know. That's why I always called him 'Chester.'"

Rothenberg slowly nodded an understanding. "I had heard you two did not get along." Barry, Klein & Nance had been one of Redden's many stops before ending up in Redondo Beach.

"Chester and I? Sure, we got along. Just a little bit of friction here and there."

"I heard it went beyond friction."

"Not really a problem. Chester just took everything a little too seriously. Tell me," he said, changing the subject. "Did he ever manage to talk ol' man Klein out of that corner office? Last I heard, Klein's only coming in once a week now. Can't imagine that Chester would let that waste of resources slide by."

Rothenberg stared at Redden for what seemed the longest time, then said, "I think you should be directing these questions to Ray Gillingham." There was something about Mitchell Redden that left Rothenberg uneasy. His manner was light and casual, but Rothenberg could not shed the unnerving feeling that he was being used. The young lawyer glanced at his watch and said somewhat anxiously, "Look, I hope you don't mind, but I'm a little pressed for time. Maybe we could get on with this deposition. I presume the client is ready to go?"

Redden again broke into a smile. "Sitting patiently in my office. I'll bring him in." Redden started to leave the conference room, then stopped at the door. "Hey, you're not going to drag this thing on all day, are you? I've got a volleyball tournament at one-thirty. I'll need to be out of here by one."

"I don't know. We'll see how it goes. This is not your average rear-end auto case, you know."

Redden's face grew stern for the first time, and he fixed his eyes on Sandy Goodman and said, "My God, you defense guys will complicate even a rear-ender. Is there nothing sacred?"

Goodman laughed. "That's how we justify our existence," he said. "Obscure and confuse. *Boy,* do I like this job."

Rothenberg, however, was not finding any amusement in the exchange. "Why don't we get on with it," he said. "If need be, we'll break for a couple of hours at one. That way, you can play your *game...* and I can do my job."

Rothenberg had made his point, which was not lost on anyone present. Redden immediately took a step toward the younger lawyer, telegraphing imminent confrontation, his steel blue eyes set and piercing.

For the briefest moment, Rothenberg seemed to stop breathing. Then, as if someone had just thrown a switch, Redden flashed another smile. "I'll be back with the client," he said. With that assurance, Redden turned and was gone, marching down the hallway to his office.

Welcoming the exit, Rothenberg eased himself back into his chair. Angered and perplexed, he was having a difficult time assessing Redden. What was his angle? Perhaps it was some kind of strategy for the forthcoming deposition. Did it have anything to do with Ray Gillingham? The wheels kept turning, but nothing made sense except for one unequivocal fact – he did not like the lawyer from Redondo Beach. "Is this guy for real?" he asked to no one in particular.

Yeah, he was for real, thought Goodman. But then he saw everything from a different perspective. What had started out as another morning dragging through yet another boring deposition had now become a form of entertainment. His curiosity had also been whetted. Rumors had persisted about what had happened to the famed Mitchell Redden. Some said he had gone to the bottle, whereas others observed that he had become a religious fanatic, preaching on the beach to anyone who would listen to him. Another theory was that he had fully retired from the practice of law and was living on an isolated island in the Caribbean. Or was it Hawaii – or the South Pacific? Yet, all speculation aside, no one had seen Redden inside of a courtroom in well over four years. Not surprisingly, Sandy Goodman was savoring every moment and, for the first time, was looking forward to the remainder of the day. He would let Rothenberg have his run-in with Redden while he settled back and enjoyed the entertainment.

"As you will find out," Goodman said. "Mitchell Redden does not give quarter. If you take a swing, be prepared to duck." He then quickly added, "But you'll have to admit, he does have style."

Rothenberg leaned back into the thickly padded conference chair, not prepared to acknowledge Goodman's observation. What Redden had was an utter disregard for protocol and professionalism, thought the young lawyer. He was also brazen and an outright insolent ass. But what really grated at Rothenberg was that he was actually welcoming the absence of Redden and the release of tension that followed his departure.

In his relatively young career, Rothenberg had already taken well over a hundred depositions. During this time, he had learned his craft well. He was always well-prepared, his questions were precise on the issues, and he was thorough and probing. Above all, he was aggressive in his approach, no matter who sat on the other side of the table. Yet, here he was, after a brief encounter lasting no more than five minutes, actually feeling anxiety over what was about to take place. He reached for the hot pot of coffee on the table, poured himself a cup, and took a sip. It was at this point that he became conscious for the first time that his stomach, his thighs, his arms – indeed, his whole body – seemed coiled like a tight spring waiting to be released. He took a deep breath and slowly exhaled.

Rothenberg began to reassess the conference room and its furnishings more closely. When he had first arrived, it appeared tastefully decorated and comfortable, though nothing he would have selected for himself. The contemporary look pleased Rothenberg, with generous displays of chrome and glass and accents in black. It was clean, sterile, and somewhat simplistic, with a straightforward look that left little to speculation. It also symbolized Rothenberg's approach to his vocation – simple and direct. No one would ever have to guess where Geoffrey Rothenberg stood on an issue.

The same, however, could not be said of Redden's law offices. Eclectic would be a better description. The conference room had a certain openness to it, with panels of beveled glass framed in bleached white oak, offering a direct view from the adjoining hallway. A matching white oak conference table was the centerpiece of the room, large and richly finished, sitting boldly in the middle of the conference room as if it had been carved out of a large block of wood right there on the spot. In the center of the back wall was a large painting of Bora Bora, with Mount Otemanu and its prominent monolithic peak and surrounding lagoon. It was accompanied by a series of black and white and colored photographs of surfers and volleyball players, many including Redden in various action shots. Against one side wall leaned a bicycle; the other a surfboard. Along with its light tan carpeting and a scattering of pastels, the suite radiated a feeling of warmth and casualness, appropriate for a law office sitting directly across the street from broad sandy beaches and the blue Pacific Ocean.

A good ten minutes later, Redden led Felix Sanchez was led into the conference room. He was short, with a slight build and sharp pointed features. His eyes were dark and pleading, his manner and movement submissive. He conveyed a history of one subjected to domination throughout his life. This was a man who had grown to accept his lot without resistance. If asked, Sanchez would say he knew his place and wanted life simple. Anything was better than starving in the hills of Guatemala.

"Felix, this is Mr. Goodman…," said Redden, indicating with his head, "…and Mr. Rothenberg." Sanchez, seeming terrified about the experience, tentatively gave a quick nod of acknowledgment to each, his movement impaired by the cervical collar that snugly embraced his neck. Redden then herded him around the conference table until he stood opposite the two defense lawyers. "These are the enemy," he announced. "Keep this table between you at all times, and remember, a moving target is hard to hit."

Sanchez's eyes immediately widened, and he looked up appealingly at Redden. He had somehow been drawn into a mystifying legal system in a foreign land, supervised by lawyers who took delight in transforming English into another language. He was nervous and confused and resenting his cousin Hector for persuading him to seek out a lawyer to begin with.

Redden eased the client down into a chair and winked at him. "Just kidding," he smiled. He wore a smile often. It was part of his grace and smoothness and would frequently shield what was going on inside. His eyes settled on the men across the table as he continued to speak to Sanchez. "These two will be complete gentlemen throughout this deposition. They are each a professional, and I'm sure they would not for one moment consider being abusive or in any way try to take advantage of you."

The small man from Guatemala comprehended little about what was being said. But, of course, it mattered little to Redden since the targets of his remarks well understood the admonishment. And Goodman took little offense to it. It was Redden's style to poke and weave – to keep his opponent off balance, always guessing. He had seen it before and wanted nothing to do with it anyway. Today, he was there as an observer, nothing more. Rothenberg, on the other hand, became flushed with anger. The remark was out of line. This was an adversarial proceeding, and he was there to take advantage whenever and wherever he could. He was not about to be branded unprofessional for simply doing a good job for his client.

Rothenberg straightened himself up in his chair and tapped his fingers anxiously a couple times on the table. He then leaned forward, about to fire off a retort – and caught himself, not about to be drawn into a verbal battle. He was being baited, subtly and with finesse, but would not be distracted like a first-timer right out of law school. Instead, he turned to the court reporter and said, "Why don't you swear the witness. We don't want to keep this man from his volleyball game."

O'Brien asked Sanchez to raise his right hand and proceeded to administer the oath. When she had concluded, she tapped some words onto her stenographic machine, stopped, offered a nod to Rothenberg, and then took a fix on his lips. Her hands were poised over the keys, ready for the first of his questions.

But the words did not come. Rothenberg blinked a couple times, shifted uncomfortably in his chair, and then, for the longest moment, stared at Redden, searching for the right verbiage to set him in his place for the duration of the deposition. Those words, however, refused to come to his aid.

Redden sat patiently and exchanged the stare. After what seemed an eternity, he leaned toward Sanchez, and with a smile seen only in his eyes, offered, "Be my guest." He then brought up a current edition of *Sports Illustrated* and began reading, seeming indifferent to what was taking place as a teenager on an iPhone.

This was even more perplexing to Rothenberg. Was this some form of strategy or the supreme insult? Was it a subtle attempt to distract, or was Redden totally unconcerned about the effectiveness of his questioning? In reality, it was neither. Apathy more accurately defined the temperament of the man thumbing through the magazine.

He was there out of necessity, a commitment extracted from him by Harry Blaylock, his sole tenant, confidant, associate, oldest and dearest friend, and unequivocally the only one capable of bringing him to a judicial proceeding of any form or importance. Redden was simply there as a representative of the plaintiff. He was totally resolved not to be a participant in the deposition itself and had clearly communicated this to Harry. If anything of an emergent nature arose, he would salvage the problem. Otherwise, he was only in the room to hold the client's hand.

But that did not mean he lacked an agenda.

Four years, eight months, and 12 days earlier, Mitchell Redden had suddenly and without notice walked away from one of the most lucrative and promising practices in Los Angeles County. This action followed closely on the heels of several large and media-grabbing verdicts, all within a relatively short period of time. In 22 months, he pulled in 9 awards totaling 55 million dollars. For two consecutive years, he was named "Trial Lawyer of the Year" by the Consumer Attorneys Association of Los Angeles. Three of the verdicts had been taken away by the trial judges on motions for a new trial, and four others, which had survived the post-trial motions, had gone up on appeal. The remaining two had later settled for a combined total of eleven and a half million dollars. The net fees, after costs and taxes, had been used to purchase a small two-story building on the Esplanade in Redondo Beach and an annuity paying Redden $10,000 a month for life.

Then, one day, he locked the doors and walked away.

When Redden reopened those doors, 5 weeks to the day before the deposition, he did so with considerable misgiving. Though unappreciated by Rothenberg at the moment, the man across the table was only a shadow of the high-charged lawyer whose prowess in the courtroom had become almost legendary. On this day, he was a man indifferent to protocol and void of purpose, a man whose singular goal was to kick back and enjoy the good life with a minimum of effort and acrimony.

"Thank you for the invitation," was the best that Rothenberg could quip as he now directed his attention to the apprehensive witness. To his surprise, the admonition and preliminary series of questions went without incident. Only after the first 25 minutes of questioning did Redden open his mouth, and then only to express an innocuous objection that the question was "vague, ambiguous and unintelligible." What made it even less threatening was the curious refusal of Redden to look up from his reading material as he stated the legal grounds against the question. Out of deference to Redden's apparent passiveness, Rothenberg reframed the question and continued his next inquiry.

And so it went for the next fifty minutes. Every five or ten minutes, Redden would throw out an objection without his eyes leaving the page, and Rothenberg would accommodate and rephrase and proceed to the next question.

But as time rolled by, the young lawyer found himself increasingly and inexorably drawn to sneaking a glimpse of Redden, hoping to detect a peek or some other sign by his opponent that this was all a ruse. Redden could not possibly be absorbed in an article and still have the presence of mind to attack the text of his questions. He was also becoming more and more preoccupied with the exact form of each inquiry. Was it clear and concise? Was he articulating properly? Was it grammatically correct?

By the time Rothenberg had concluded the first hour and fifteen minutes, all pacing had abandoned him. His questions were broken and disjointed, frequently repeated on his own volition. He was angry, frustrated, distracted, disorganized – and almost to the point of calling a restroom break to recapture control of his emotions and professional demeanor. The thick accent of Sanchez also did little to help his plight. Only through concentration could one hear and understand the testimony of the Hispanic witness, and the ability to concentrate was simply not available to Rothenberg. Finally, after stumbling over another of a series of unwieldy questions, and out of utter desperation, Rothenberg stopped, pondered the table in front of him for a few moments, stood, reached over for the pot of coffee, poured a cup, and took a long slurping sip.

Goodman could not have been enjoying himself more. This was nothing short of pure entertainment. In just a little over an hour, Redden had reduced the arrogant and contentious Geoffrey Rothenberg to a babbling fool – and with nothing more than a few well-placed objections. Even after a lengthy layoff, Mitchell Redden was still the master strategist he had remembered him to be. Bravo! Well done! And to such a deserving lad. Goodman didn't care much for Rothenberg and never had. If only he would smile – just once.

The distinctive sound of Rothenberg's coffee break now caught Redden's attention, who had been deeply analyzing all of the post-All-Star pennant races. He innocently looked up at Rothenberg, truly not appreciating the effect of his objections and indifference. "Run out of questions?" he asked.

Rothenberg inaccurately saw it as a jab. "Hardly!" he snapped. "Take note, counselor. I'm just warming up."

"Just asking," said Redden, somewhat defensively.

"Since you insist on being obstreperous," continued Rothenberg, "it would seem we're going to be sitting here the rest of the day."

"Obstreperous?" Redden arched his eyebrows and gave a quick shrug to Goodman, bewildered by the sudden antagonism. "And for this, I'm gonna be punished, huh? All Day?" Redden slowly shook his head. "No, I don't think so. Come one o'clock, and we're out the door. Gone. For the day."

Rothenberg checked O'Brien to ensure he was still on the record. "I'm giving you due warning, Mr. Redden. Break this deposition prematurely, and I'll be in Department 37 next week, asking for an order and sanctions. On that, you have my promise."

The veteran broke into another smile. Having been distanced so long from rules, procedures, deadlines, notices, motions to compel, sanction orders, and the tactics that filled the day-to-day existence of a civil litigator, it all seemed so silly. Conformity was no longer part of his life. He now chuckled and added, "Rothenberg, you're so full of shit." And then let go a loud, hardy laugh, shook his head a couple more times, leaned back, and dove into another article.

It was as if someone had suddenly slammed a fist under Rothenberg's ribs. His back arched, and his jaw dropped, and with utter shock, he glanced first at O'Brien, then at Redden, then at O'Brien, and again at Redden. Had it been said - on the record? Was this whole morning really happening? Such callous disregard for professionalism deserved an articulate reproach that was both stinging and eloquent. And he longed to deliver it; if only he could grasp the amorphous and elusive words that had usually been at his disposal. But instead, he stood steaming, silently cursing Redden, muzzled by his own emotions.

At this somewhat dramatic moment, Mary Ellen Dovinowitz stuck her head in the door. "Hope I'm not interrupting," she said. "But it didn't look like you were much busy anyway."

Redden briefly examined the huffing Rothenberg and then looked back at his secretary. "What you got, Mary E?" Redden always played with names, and Mary Ellen was an easy target.

"You wanted to know when that call came in. I've got them on hold."

"Be right there," he said. Redden popped up and tossed the magazine onto the table while Mary Ellen disappeared back to her desk. "Be back in a flash," he said as he stepped over to the open door. He then stopped and turned back to the two lawyers. "You know, this could be a while, so… don't wait for me. Gotta get this thing over by one," he winked to Goodman. Without another word, Redden stepped out the door and was gone.

And Rothenberg's mouth was again open. Had Redden truly committed the unpardonable sin of abandoning a client in a deposition? Always an opportunist, Rothenberg was not about to let the occasion slide by, though his first thought was to proceed with caution. Perhaps Redden had recalled their brief and distant meeting after all and had devised some cunning scheme out of revenge. Perhaps he was being drawn into a circumstance to compromise his own ethics. Yet he had to act fast and felt confident about the propriety of his intended course of action.

Rothenberg again sat down and addressed O'Brien. "Let the record reflect that Mr. Redden has left the room and invited counsel to proceed with the deposition. He also expressed that he had no estimate on the length of his absence. Thus, in the interest of expediency, it is my intent to continue with this proceeding." Rothenberg briefly hesitated and looked over at Goodman as if seeking his approval as well.

Goodman just shrugged.

"Did you speak with Mr. Redden before the deposition?" asked

Rothenberg of Sanchez. He would go right to the jugular. Such opportunities were rare and fleeting.

"Yes," nodded Sanchez.

"Did you discuss certain facts about your case with him?"

"Discuss?"

"Yes. Talk with him. Tell him how the accident happened. Where did you work? Where did you come from?"

"Yes."

"When you came to this country?"

"Yes."

"How did you get into this country?"

Sanchez was now noticeably concerned about the line of inquiry and hesitated with his answer.

"Did you talk about this?" persisted Rothenberg. "What did you tell Mr. Redden about how you got into this country?"

"Lawyer Redden, he say you not suppose to ask me thees. What we talk. He say you cannot ask me thees queschone."

Rothenberg leaned forward, his voice taking on a harder edge. "Mr. Sanchez, you *must* answer all questions. Absent a proper legal objection, you could be sanctioned by the court for your refusal to answer."

Sanchez had no understanding of the legal threat, but it sounded quite frightening. Still, he held his ground. "Lawyer Redden say you ask bad queschone. Not to trust you. Cannot ask what we talk. He say thees priv…priv… How you say? Priv…"

"Privileged!" The word impulsively shot out of Goodman's mouth, surprising even himself. He immediately recognized it had torpedoed Rothenberg's game plan, but he was not bothered by this in the slightest.

"Si, preevliged. Tha's the word!"

After glaring at Goodman for the longest time, Rothenberg finally, in total frustration, began pursuing another line of questioning.

The three-plus years at Barry, Klein & Nance had turned out to be one of the more unpleasant periods in Redden's life. Not initially. As a young associate who had already bounced around through four law firms between San Francisco and Los Angeles, including a two-year stint with Harry Blaylock, it brought stability to his life. He now began to broaden his trial experience considerably. By pure number, a trial attorney for a personal injury defense firm saw more jury trials than his counterpart would ever hope to see. Defending insurance claims was a high-volume business, and frequently, Redden found himself taking a verdict on one case and selecting a jury the next day on another. The innate talent that had been lying dormant for so many years gradually began to blossom. He also liked and enjoyed all the other associates and junior partners of the firm – save for one.

Hired two weeks earlier than Redden, C. Raymond Gillingham had always been a thorn in his side. He was not Redden's fellow associate. He was his competitor. Achievement and political positioning within the firm, and the power that went with them, were Gillingham's obsessions. Everything else was a means to those ends. And as Redden's successes in the courtroom began to mount, the relationship between them began to deteriorate inversely. Redden was a threat. By the time both made junior partner at three years, they were simply tolerating one another and keeping their distance. After the partnership, the true depth of Gillingham's devious side began to manifest itself, and one day in particular, brought Redden to detest him.

Redden had not been easy on the young Rothenberg and had not intended to be. As much as he wanted to bury the past, there was little he could do to hold himself back. He harbored no grudge against Rothenberg. He seemed to be a jerk, but what did Redden know. Working under Gillingham could turn *anyone* into a jerk. No, it was nothing personal. Redden was simply sending a message to his old friend Chester.

⸺•⸺

Redden looked down at the phone on his desk and the blinking light. Was he ready for this? Was he moving too fast? He had now tasted the practice again, ever so slightly, and the taste was bitter. Beneath the care-free façade of Mitchell Redden was a man with a scarred past. He had left the legal profession for a reason – a reason that still hung over his head. He had been pulled reluctantly out of retirement with considerable reservation. Opening the doors was the easy part. But now, phase two was waiting at the other end of the blinking light.

He picked up the receiver. "Hi, this is Mitch Redden."

"Oh, yes," said the voice. "This is Nurse Richmond at Long Beach Memorial. We spoke earlier."

"Yes, ma'am."

"I have that patient now. Niki Burroughs. She would like to speak to you about possible representation – for her and her injured son."

CHAPTER 3

Niki Burroughs hung up the receiver to the phone next to her hospital bed. Mitchell Redden will be there the following day to discuss possible representation.

At the moment, Niki was reclined like some abused and discarded puppet, with cables elevating her left arm, held together by two brightly polished pins, and another set cradling her casted left leg. Across her forehead was a sprinkling of minute scabs, none more than a quarter inch in width. Above her left eyebrow and fortunately close to the hairline was an irregular L-shaped laceration, three-quarters of an inch in length, which was still held together by a series of neatly aligned dark sutures. About her eyes and upper cheeks, one could see a number of resolving contusions in various shades of blue, gray, and yellow, as well as the attendant swelling that had not yet fully dissipated. Her facial features resembled one who had recently concluded a fistfight – and lost.

She had now taken the first step to rehabilitate her life, to restore some sanity to a world that had been devastated in a matter of seconds only ten days earlier. For the first time since the accident, she allowed herself to revisit a day that was to change her whole life – and would live forever in her memory.

— ● ● —

Absolutely nothing had gone right all morning. The temperatures had only dropped into the upper seventies during the night. A record for Los Angeles, she was sure, but would have to wait for the Sunday edition of the *Los Angeles Times* before her suspicion could be confirmed. Still, the heat and its opportunity for a record overwhelmed her thoughts as she tossed and turned throughout the night until succumbing to exhaustion somewhere between three and four a.m.

Then she had overslept.

Niki Burroughs never slept beyond the hour she was to arise. Back in the formative years of her youth, her brain had been programmed to kick into its awakened state at a preset time determined necessary the night before. This was the way it had always been, even when retiring at a late hour. And so reliable was this phenomenon that she rarely, if ever, set the alarm on her bedside clock. Niki could not recall a day in recent years when she had overslept. But this particularly frustrating, angering, and upsetting Saturday morning, it had happened.

At precisely 9:53 a.m. Niki opened her eyes and stared at the illuminated diodes of her digital clock, briefly processing her surroundings and the circumstances that existed at the moment. It had taken less than three seconds to register the importance of the hour. In exactly seven minutes, she had been scheduled to meet Mr. and Mrs. Edward Doherty at their residence in Palos Verdes Estates, a good 17-minute drive from her home in Lomita. The Doherty house was to be a new listing, the first one she would place through her broker in five and a half months. Over the past half year, the real estate market has gone flat, and the last thing Niki needed at this time in her life was to lose a prospective listing to another agent.

Like a suddenly surprised cat, she had sprung from her bed and rushed for the phone in the kitchen of her small three-bedroom house – and sprained the small toe on her right foot in the process.

As Niki had raced unthinking through the doorway of her bedroom, her leg had swung on an arc only slightly too wide but sufficient to abruptly stop her outermost toe from its high rate of speed, while the rest of her anatomy had tumbled forward, leaving her sprawled on her back as the world spun around at a thousand miles an hour. After the initial wave of pain and dizziness had passed, she had struggled up and limped to the telephone, cursing the weather and the fates – until the presence of Randy had captured her full attention.

He had been standing there in the living room with his mouth open, having just caught some words that most certainly had added to his limited but growing vocabulary. He would no doubt be seeing their way around Lomita Elementary School, to the great consternation of all teachers and staff.

After a hurried and unavailing stab at an apology and explanation of the inappropriate use of such words, Niki finally placed her call and rescheduled the appointment to 1:00 p.m. It was the only other hour available that day to the Dohertys – which necessitated another change in the day's slate of events.

Seventeen months earlier, Niki's widowed father had been placed in a nursing home, afflicted with an advanced stage of Parkinson's disease. Over the ensuing months, his condition had further deteriorated to the point where he now mostly stared, seldom reacting or acknowledging, his attention seemingly fixed on an imaginary spot on the wall, with his hands incessantly trembling as if in need of a warm blanket. The end was drawing near to the life of Stavros Leondopoulos, a reality both painfully and increasingly evident each Saturday afternoon as Niki and Randy kept their near-ritualistic visits at the appointed hour of 1:00 p.m.

A woman of considerable, if not obsessive, organizational skills, not until today's series of unanticipated events had thrown the ordered life of Niki Burroughs helplessly and unalterably askew had she missed a 1:00 p.m. visit with her father. Determined to salvage the day, she had promptly laid out Randy's clothes and then carefully dressed, encumbered by the throbbing and swollen toe. It had taken little time to abandon any idea of wearing hose and anything other than flat sandals, a grating concession to one as fastidious in her dress code as the young real estate agent. She would see Stavros early, enjoy a short lunch with Randy, and then meet the Dohertys at the agreed-upon

time. Effectively, she switched the two meetings and would be back on track for the day shortly.

As Niki eased to a stop in the small parking lot of the Golden Age Nursing Home, she was beginning to feel better about the disconcerting chain of events that morning. Under the circumstances, she had handled it well. A twenty-minute ice pack on her toe helped to keep swelling to a minimum and taping it to the adjacent toe had a splinting effect that reduced movement. Then, to ease the pain and dissipate the inevitable headache that greeted her each morning of her life, she had taken three of her tablets – one extra for the toe, she had justified to herself. The voicemail on her phone had been loaded with an array of frantic calls, though none truly urgent, and each would easily be dealt with in the late afternoon following her meeting with the Dohertys. Now, after a shortened 25-minute visit, her day would be realigned to the structured agenda in which she found solace and comfort so badly needed in her harried life.

Before exiting the car, Niki checked the clock on the dash. She was still on her revised schedule. It was 11:53 a.m.; enough time remained to perform any necessary repairs to the hastily thrown-on makeup back at the house.

"Ready to see Grandpa?" she asked while applying some lipstick in front of the rearview mirror.

Randy had long ago lost interest in spending what seemed hours in a small room with sickening smells and a wrinkled, frail old man with whom he felt little attachment. He was Mommy's daddy, he had been told, but Randy could recall a little conversation with him and had no memory of the days when Stavros Leondopoulos still had the strength and coordination to crawl on the floor with his little *agonas* and laugh at the funny sounds that came out as grandfather attempted to teach grandson a few words of his Greek heritage.

"Do I have to?" This was not how Randy wanted to spend his Saturdays.

"Yes, you do. It'll be a quick visit today, Honey. But he *is* your Grandpa."

"I know..."

Niki's face became slightly somber. "We have our obligations, Honey. We are family. When someone is seriously ill, his family should always be there." Niki dropped the lipstick in her purse. Then, after a contemplative stare at the one-story nursing home added, "Besides, I doubt that we will be doing this much longer. Okay?"

"Okay, Mommy," Randy said with resignation.

"Then let's go."

The two of them climbed out of the car and were on their way. Niki was at a brisk pace, and Randy was doing his best to keep up. By the time she had reached the double glass doors of the entrance, Niki realized that she was alone. She turned and saw that Randy was a good twenty feet behind.

"Sorry," she said. "Mommy's in a big hurry today."

She spoke apologetically but felt no guilt. Randy would have to make his own way one day, and she saw him as part of some form of a training program for that time. When it came, her son would be ready, both physically and emotionally.

"That's alright. But you had a head start. I'll race you back, okay?"

Niki allowed herself a momentary smile. "Sure, as soon as we finish our visit with Grandpa. But this time, I'll give *you* a head start."

"No, I can win fair." Randy was always trying to prove himself, which was pleasing to Niki. The dangling carrots and extra pushes along the way were paying off. Randy, too, would be a survivor.

"Then fair and square it will be. Let's go see Grandpa."

She pushed open the doors, and the two of them made their way through the empty lobby. Niki rarely saw visitors in the sterile-looking reception area or, for that matter, anywhere else in the facility. The Golden Age Nursing Home was nothing more than a staging area for the soon-to-be departed. A place where guilt-ridden relatives shoved away their problems into twelve-by-fourteen cubicles somewhere in Long Beach, there to be forgotten while tended to by others for a monthly stipend. At least, that's the way Niki saw it. It was also her resolve to set herself apart from the others whose faces she had never seen – although, in some way, she shared the sense of culpability she condemned them for, but for a different reason.

Niki had indeed tried her best. She had interviewed, inspected, and assessed five different nursing homes – some better, some worse – before settling on Golden Age. Cost, however, was a factor over which she had little control, and in the end, Stavros was in the best nursing-care facility she could afford. Then there were the visits. For 17 arduous months, in spite of all the difficulties and distractions, Niki had always been there, even in recent days when her presence seemed more an act of contrition than a benefit to the patient. Lately, it was difficult to detect if Stavros was cognizant of even the most rudimentary functions of elimination, let alone the presence of his daughter of twenty-five years. But the guilt she carried long preceded any admission to a nursing home. It was something that had hounded her for years and only worsened with each stage of deterioration in Stavros' condition.

The two of them traveled the long hallway to the nursing station, hand in hand, as had been their practice. Through each open doorway they passed existed the frail remnants of what once had been a healthy and energetic human life, full of hopes and dreams, not unlike those of the young mother from Lomita. To now see these unfortunate souls awaiting the rescue of death served as a reminder to Niki of what lay ahead in the hopefully distant future. She tried to avoid looking but was still drawn to catching a glimpse, thinking perhaps the images would somehow change – though, of course, they never did. On this day, she gripped her son's hand a little tighter, trying somehow to draw on his youth as if to insulate her from the surrounding morbidity.

They both arrived at the counter unobserved for a brief moment. Lillian Bronson, a nursing aide, was studiously reviewing a series of physician's orders, preparing for rounds that should have started over two and a half hours earlier. Liz Heilman, another NA, sat positioned in front of a panel of monitors that held little interest for her. The principal focus of her attention was instead a magazine resting in her lap. She would read or scan something of interest, then briefly glance up at the monitors as she turned to the next page. The screens reported the vital signs of three patients hooked up at the other end of the equipment, each nearing the end of his or her stay at the home. On the far side of the square island, a good 15 feet away, Louise "Burnie" Burnfield, the charge nurse of the day shift, seemed to be quietly engaged in a heated discussion with another nurse. Though they could not be overheard, their animated movements telegraphed that all was not going well at the moment.

Not one to wait much for anything, Niki cleared her throat and said, "Excuse me."

Only Burnfield and her debating partner turned. Both seemed surprised about the two early visitors, and Niki thought she heard a "shit" under Burnfield's breath.

The charge nurse approached them, rapidly transforming from a state of obvious agitation to the artificial pleasantness that greeted Niki each Saturday. The obliging smile, the instant sparkle of the eyes, the slight tilt of the head as she listened to the inquiries and the concerns, and sugared voice with its repertoire of canned phrases were all disturbing to Niki and viewed as a form of condescension. She had been tempted several times to express her thoughts on the subject but judged it to be a certain act of futility and a waste of valuable time in her world of expediency. So Burnfield was tolerated – just.

"Ms. Burroughs, you are early today." Although a stalwart of the feminist movement, Niki's insistence on the title was only out of a desire to distance herself from a painful marriage that ended several years earlier.

Niki leaned on the counter and returned the smile. "Hi, Burnie," she said reluctantly. Niki detested the sugar-coated nickname but generated her own measure of sweetness when it worked to her advantage. "Look, I know I'm a little early on visiting hours, but my whole world turned upside down this morning. I'll just be a few minutes, I promise."

Burnfield now shifted to a contrived frown. "Oh, I am so sorry. I hope it won't be a problem, but we do have our rules."

Niki maintained her smile, though now with more of an effort. "Burnie, I really need your help this morning. Help and understanding. I have no other time all day, not a minute." She paused for a moment, hoping to see a change in the tightly-held frown, but saw nothing to give encouragement. "I'll be ten, fifteen minutes tops, I promise."

Burnfield still held the frown and slowly shook her head. "It would be quite impossible, Ms. Burroughs. Administration has made it clear to the whole staff. Visiting hours are one to six, and no exceptions. My hands are tied, really."

The smile was now gone as Niki geared for a more assertive tack. "Then let me speak with someone in administration. It is important that I see my father this morning."

"I'm sorry. Today is Saturday, and administration is closed. There is absolutely no one here to talk to."

"Then gimme a name, a phone number. I'll make the call myself."

"I know how frustrating this must be for you, but we cannot give out home phone numbers and are absolutely forbidden to call administration or staff physicians at home except in an emergency. Now you can understand that, can't you?"

Niki stared for a moment at the same patronizing frown. Not one facial muscle had changed – and anger began to simmer inside for the first time. "No, I can't! Since you ask, I will tell you that I absolutely cannot understand why you are so insistent on denying me the right to see my father."

Burnfield now began to exhibit some nervousness, and Niki was able to get the attention of the two nursing aides as well. "As…as I explained," stammered the charge nurse, "it's the policy of the home. I'm sorry, but…uh, it's just going to be impossible to let you in until after 1:00 p.m."

Behind Burnfield the hands of a wall clock pointed to 11:28. Niki's world was closing in on her again, and the somewhat portly nurse with the full and wrinkled cheeks represented yet another obstacle in this frustrating and aggravating day. Niki's dark eyes pierced a hole right through Burnfield as the anger had now reached a full boil. "I'll tell you what will be impossible, *Burrr*nie. That will be to stop me from marching in there at this very moment and seeing my father." Niki began moving past the counter with a confused Randy clinging tightly to her hand.

No sooner had Niki taken 3 steps when Burnfield was out from behind the counter and at her side, trying to keep pace and plead her case. "Ms. Burroughs, would you...would you please reconsider what you're doing? This can be very disruptive to the whole wing. There are... well, there are reasons for these rules." Intent on not being dissuaded by Burnfield or anyone else who might choose the task, Niki ignored the now desperate pleas of the charge nurse. "This...this will break up the scheduling of our rounds," continued Burnfield, beginning to flutter her eyes, her composure totally broken. Not in 23 years of nursing had her authority been so challenged, and she was ill-equipped to deal with such a contingency. So it was nothing short of an act of a desperate woman who shouted, "Ms. Burroughs, please!" and reached out and grabbed Niki by the arm.

This unexpected invasion of her person brought Niki to an abrupt stop. Physical contact was to be only by permission. That rule was inviolate – no exception – since the last day Niki and her abusive husband had any form of a relationship with one another. The scars were deep and permanent, both physical and emotional. No one, but no one, would ever be allowed to physically abuse her, and an older woman wearing a nurse's uniform was no more exempt from this boundary than the man who created it.

Niki's eyes, confrontational and afire with anger, examined Burnfield's hand, then slowly moved up to the nurse's face. And for the briefest moment, the older woman felt physically threatened. It was terrifying, she would later relate – as if someone had been peering in at her soul. It was thus no surprise to all present that Burnfield immediately dropped her hand to her side, much like an obedient servant responding to a command from her master – though Niki had yet to utter a word.

For the next few moments, the two principals of the altercation stood in place, grabbing for emotional control, trying to fathom how matters could have escalated so fast and so far. Finally, Niki coldly admonished, "I would suggest, Mrs. Burnfield, that you continue with your agenda for the day...and I continue with mine. I will be out of here in 15 minutes, as promised." Burnfield just stared, not responding. "I presume you have nothing further to say on the matter?" added Niki.

Burnfield fluttered her eyes a couple more times, focusing again on the problem at hand. "Some explanations will be necessary," she said. "I am so sorry. If only you could have waited…"

Niki instinctively looked down the hallway to her father's open doorway, and suddenly, they all came together. In an instant, she brushed by Burnfield, rushing to the room and even releasing her grip on Randy so as not to slow her down. By the time she had reached the entrance, a plethora of horrible visions had raced through her mind, none of which prepared her for what she was about to see.

Death had been imminent for Stavros Leondopoulos over the past several weeks, and Niki had grown to accept this – and, in many ways, welcome its arrival. Yet she had wanted to say her goodbyes and had prepared the words she would deliver in her father's final hours. There were things that needed to be said. There were unsettled, painful, and lingering things that she had evaded and postponed, which Stavros had never allowed her to speak about. In the end, captivated in a non-responding body, he would have unwillingly heard – and just maybe even forgiven. Perhaps his degenerating brain cells would deny access to all external communication, a definite possibility that Niki had considered and dismissed. Her overriding guilt and need to purge herself of earlier transgressions dictated that somehow, in some way, whether possessed of his earthly consciousness or by the soon-departing spirit, as long as Stavros was alive, he would hear and understand.

Had that opportunity now been denied her? Niki braced herself for what she was about to observe.

As Niki passed through the doorway, she was immediately overwhelmed by a stench that filled the room. A curtain hung from the ceiling, shielding her from the view of her father. But the odor had a definite familiarity to it – there was no mistaking the distinct smell of urine. The room was thick with it.

This was now even *more* puzzling as she took a couple of steps forward and gripped the curtain in anticipation of throwing it back – and then hesitated. Had Stavros, in the throws of a terminal series of convulsions, unleashed the contents of his bladder all over the bed? Had he then been ignored in deference to the needs of the living until he could be taken away? Was he now lying there, his body contorted in some grotesque bundle of muscles and bones? Did she really want to remember him this way?

Niki slowly drew back the curtain and beheld her father – and was relieved and, at the same time, incensed at what she saw.

Stavros was alive. Just as she had left him a week earlier, he lay in the bed with his trembling hands holding one another. His breathing was slow and rhythmic, not labored or in any way distressed. His mouth hung open, displaying crooked and discolored teeth while loudly drawing in and then expelling the air. Though his eyes were open, his lids were partially dropped, and Stavros Leondopoulos was in a deep and seemingly restful sleep.

But there were distressing differences. His face was peppered with gray and white stubble that almost camouflaged the rugged lines running along his gaunt cheeks and no doubt represented a seven-day growth. Small remnants of food clung to his decaying teeth, leftovers from his last several feedings, the most recent of which still sat on a roller-equipped table shoved aside in the far corner of the room. Likewise, the upper sheet and blanket evidenced the hastily-administered-then-forgotten meals, soiled with soft foods and consumable liquids about the area of his chest and hung loosely over the lowered side railings. Niki pulled them back and was struck by an even stronger odor. The bottom sheet was stained and still wet from urination.

Niki dropped the sheet, spun around toward the open doorway, and glared at Burnfield, who had just been joined by the nursing aide, Bronson. "Who is responsible for this?" she screamed. Neither responded, uncertain what to say. Niki took an aggressive step forward. "I want answers, Burnfield, and I want them now. Not tomorrow, not in an hour, not in 5 minutes, but now. Tell me this instant how something like this could happen."

Burnfield entered the room, as did Bronson, who was pushed by the charge nurse with an arm-load of sheets, pillowcases, and a blanket, and began to work on the bed. "I know it seems inexcusable, and…and it is, but we have tried, we really have," said Burnfield. There was now genuineness to her voice and manner, and it communicated concern.

She was also near tears. "I have never felt so helpless. We've been short for over a week. Two out on vacation, then bang, three out with the flu. At the same time. It's really been a battle all week…"

"You have no backup? You mean to tell me you have no backup?"

"Yes, we do…did," Burnfield corrected. "They are covering the two aides on vacation. And there's usually another pool that we draw from, but they were also caught short. Ms. Burroughs, we have been trying so hard, you've got to believe me." Ruth Hoskins, the RN who was deeply involved in the debate when Niki arrived, came through with a gurney and pushed it alongside the bed.

"That's it?" said Niki, barely noticing the arrival of Hoskins, who was now assisting Bronson in moving Stavros onto the gurney. "Two nurses on backup? For the whole nursing home, two nurses on backup?" Her voice rang with incredulity.

"Believe me, I'm not any happier about it than you are, but it's budgetary. That's all they give us. We're budgeted for two on-call and beyond that, we must go to outside services, which are not always that reliable. It is not nursing, believe me, Ms. Burroughs, it is not our fault." Burnfield then tentatively added, "I wish you would complain to administration, Ms. Burroughs, I really do."

Behind Niki, unobserved, Bronson was efficiently changing the sheets, pillow case, bed pad, and blanket while Hoskins was administering a sponge bath to Stavros on the gurney. Niki's anger was now well under control, and she selected her words quite carefully as she said, "I'll tell you what. I'll do even more than that. I *will* go to administration and I *will* complain. I think that's a very good suggestion, and I'll do it Monday, bright and early. I guess I'm safe in presuming somebody will be here on Monday?" Her question was laden with sarcasm.

"Yes, ma'am, they open at nine."

"Good. But I'm not going to stop there. I'm sure you'll also be happy about that. My next visit will be with the Department of Health or whoever else licenses this sorry excuse for a nursing home. And before I'm through, I can promise you this, there will be a full-blown investigation into this whole matter. *Then,* we will find out if it's nursing, administration, or anyone else in between. But, of course, nursing will have no problem with that because *none* of this," she said, indicating, "has anything to do with the efficiency of your nursing staff." Niki glowered at Burnfield, awaiting a response that was slow to come.

"Uh,…no, ma'am."

"That *is* what you said?"

"Yes, ma'am."

"Good. I wanted to be sure about that. And there is just one final point I would like to make." Niki waited again until Burnfield's eyes, which had been nervously dancing around the room, made contact with her own. Conviction was best communicated through the eyes. "If you ever at any time see or hear that my father's care is being neglected, I want you to call me. Day or night, just call me. You have my home number, my work number, and the number for my cell phone, and I will always have my cell. That is all I ask. Call me, and I'll do the rest. Am I making myself clear?"

"Yes, ma'am."

"Good. Then, as long as I have not received a phone call from you – and I don't want it from anyone else – then I can go about my very busy life totally comfortable with the thought that my father is in *your* hands and getting the best nursing care possible? That is our understanding?"

"Yes, ma'am."

"Good." Niki waited again until she had Burnfield's eyes. "Because I will be making spot visits from time to time, and if I ever again find that Stavros Leondopoulos, my father, has been abused, neglected, ignored, or in anyway maltreated, it will be my goal, my *mission* in life, to see that *you*, Mrs. Burnfield, never again put on a nursing uniform! Have I made my point?"

Burnfield, fuming inside, bit her lip and then angrily said, "Yes, ma'am," promptly turned away and rushed out of the room.

Niki stood for a moment, staring at the vacated doorway, then punctuated the brief silence with a final "Good." She was on a high, proud of the efficiency with which she had encountered the problem, stood her ground, vanquished the ostensible enemy, and then secured her position. It was indeed something to savor – until her gaze dropped down to Randy.

The small boy was just outside the room. He made no noise, neither openly crying nor sobbing, but quietly stood there staring up at his mother with tears streaming down his cheeks from his big brown eyes. In so many ways, he looked like his father, with the shock of blonde hair that always seemed to be falling onto his face, no matter how many times she ran a comb through it, and the slender features with his mischievous and knowing smile that telegraphed a maturity beyond his years, and his light complexion and sprinkling of freckles. However, for the brown eyes, which Niki saw as the only physical marking of the Leondopoulos lineage, he was no doubt his father's son, handsome and personable. He would one day be stealing away young girl's hearts just as Scott had done to her so many years earlier. He was a perfect young lad – except for his right leg.

Randolph Taylor Burroughs had been born with a proximal femoral focal deficiency, a congenital absence of the femur and fibula, effectively leaving his right leg about one-half the length of his left. The tibia, his remaining long bone that normally would have acted as his shin, had been loosely joined at the hip to a malformed socket, later replaced by an artificial joint. His right foot, which had little articulation with the bottom of the tibia at birth, had been amputated at the age of two to accommodate a prosthetic device. At six years of age, he was a veteran of two major surgeries. The device itself, which allowed Randy to walk, did so while producing a pronounced limp, and in combination with the hip joint, affected a definite list to the right while standing.

Seven hours later, Reggie Allerton would learn of the birth defect in the emergency room of a local hospital. Upon being informed, the truck driver would collapse onto a chair and weep.

Randy now stood, like a picture right out of a poster for the handicapped, tearing at his mother's heart as she was suddenly overwhelmed by a sense of guilt she could no longer avoid.

Niki hurried over to Randy and swept him up in a tight embrace. In her arms, he felt so light, so small and helpless. She buried her face next to his and whispered, "I'm sorry, Honey – so sorry for this whole lousy day." She tried so often to be tough, to condition him for a world that would never be easy. He was fatherless and handicapped and would encounter many frustrations and cruelties, as he already had, and could ill afford to be weak. Yet, at times, such toughness was impossible.

Niki still clung tightly to her child as she recalled the circumstance and turned back toward the room. To her surprise, the scene had totally changed. In a matter of minutes, the room was transformed into a model of cleanliness. Stavros lay in the same position in bed but was now tucked in with fresh linen and a clean blanket, as well as a bright new gown. All food and dishes had been taken away, furniture rearranged, and the roller-equipped table sat neatly next to the bed with a fresh pitcher of water and a small stack of plastic glasses on top. Hoskins was gone as well, and Bronson, the only reminder of what Niki had first walked into, was leaning over the bed, finishing a shave of a few remaining whiskers. Niki approached the bed as Bronson took the last few swipes and blotted away a couple spots of shaving cream. It was as if the whole shocking scene had never really existed. Stavros was just as she had seen him so many Saturdays before – and would have seen him again had she arrived at one o'clock.

After gathering up the shaving gear, Bronson stopped in front of the two of them before leaving. "I am sorry," she said. Then, after checking her watch, she added, "It's 11:42. He's due for lunch in twenty minutes. I'll brush his teeth after he eats, but only if it's okay with you." Niki inspected the aide's eyes for a moment and sensed concern. Bronson was quite worried. Perhaps she, too, was a victim, thought Niki, and she gave her a nod of approval. The nurse then hastily left the room.

Niki let Randy slide to the floor, then reached over and shook her father's shoulder. "Steve, it's me!" she said loudly. Since her first year of high school, Niki had always called her father "Steve." Used at first in an effort to "Americanize Pappa," it later became a symbol of her own stubbornness when she finally came to grips with the futility of her endeavors. Bullheadedness was not unique to Stavros in the Leondopoulos household. "Come on, Steve, it's time to wake up," she said, shaking again. Stavros continued to snooze.

"Stavros Leondopoulos, ene ora na xepneses! Ehies epieskepthes! Oh,

micros agonas sou ierthe etho na se thie." At times, speaking Greek seemed the only way to draw his attention anymore – that and announcing the presence of Stavros' grandson. Finally, he stirred and widened his eyes, momentarily staring at Niki and Randy, then at his usual spot on the wall.

Niki knew she had little time left and thought it best to let Stavros know she could not stay. "Steve, listen to me." She then resorted again to Greek. She would be returning more often, she promised him, even during the week.

Niki took hold of Randy's hand, preparatory to leaving. Why did she continue this silly charade, talking to a man incapable of listening? Even if he understood, had he really earned such devotion and dedication? Stavros Leondopoulos had been a hard man, difficult to understand, resistant to change, and unwilling to forgive when remission was all that would salvage their relationship, which had been clinging to a thread for some time. After all, had she not herself forgiven him?

She leaned over and kissed the old man on the cheek. *"Se agapo, Pappa."* As impulsive as the kiss, Niki told Stavros she loved him. It was a surprising act and expression, confusing and unexpected. It had been years since she had communicated any affection to her father, another mystifying highlight in their strange love/hate relationship – and another unusual occurrence on this bizarre and extraordinary day. Niki inspected the features of her father one final time, and then took her son by the hand, and hurriedly left the room. It was 11:50 a.m. Enough time still remained for a quick lunch at a McDonalds with Randy and then all afternoon to restore some order to her life.

Little did Niki know that the sequence of events, which found their birth in the early hours of the day, and then gathered momentum through mid and late morning, had yet to run their course.

⸻ ● ⸻

As Niki sped along the 405 Freeway, she recalled the short race with Randy back at the Golden Age parking lot. "I guess you're kind of proud of yourself, beating Mommy," she smiled, maintaining her vigil on the lanes ahead and the rearview mirror.

"Yeah," said Randy, intently working over a large coloring book sitting on his lap. Then, after thinking about it further, he added, "But you let me win."

"You think so, huh?"

"Yeah." Randy looked up from his book, now sporting his patented smirk. "Mommy, kids can't beat grownups. They're too big."

"Not true. Kids are quicker and unquestionably have more energy."

"But you have longer legs."

"Yes, but we can't always move them as fast as we want to. Today, I'm wearing a skirt, and then there are my very, very sore toe. See, for kids, things have a way of balancing out."

"They do?"

"Cross my heart. Especially for kids with problems." Niki always avoided the use of the word "handicap."

"You mean my leg?"

"That's right. Every kid who's born with a problem is given something else to make up for it. You were born with a short leg but also with one of the smartest brains at Lomita Elementary. You just happen to have some pretty speedy legs, too.... You won fair and square. Honest."

Randy now beamed – and his mommy was more determined than ever to keep her date with the boy of her dreams.

A blue Camaro, 200 feet ahead in the same lane, was now entering the heavier lines of traffic and decelerating. It approached and began to pass a large truck to its right, which had just charged over from the number three lane and was blinking its direction, announcing it had not yet completed its move. Sweeping across its back, in bold red and black cursive letters, were the words "Ginther's Pilsner."

⋯━●━⋯

CHAPTER 4

It was a hospital, nothing more. True, it had grown. Long Beach Memorial Medical Center has been a fixture in the Long Beach community since 1907. It expanded from a small general hospital over the years to a large multi-specialty facility. Its brown and beige seven-story structure was always in a state of growth. A new wing, a parking structure, an additional room for some new form of therapy – it was always something. But Redden had not remembered it quite this big.

At the moment, he was sitting in the hospital parking lot, grasping for enough motivation to climb out of his Porsche Cayman. It was 1:20 p.m. He had found a number of matters to occupy himself with for most of the morning and was now twenty minutes late.

A number of men and women could be seen weaving their way through the parked cars and up the steps into the lobby. These, no doubt, were friends and relatives, well-intentioned visitors whose attendance at the moment was for the laudable purpose of providing love and support to the injured and diseased. Mitchell Redden, on the other hand, was there for only one reason – business. This was strictly a money-making enterprise. For a brief moment, Redden considered kicking on the engine and heading back to the office. It would be ever so easy to empty his drawers and drop a note on Harry's desk. But instead, he grabbed his briefcase and joined the others, making their way into the hospital.

Inside, he moved quickly through the crowded lobby and took the elevator to the fourth floor. Alone and away from the office now, there was no smile, no brightness. The pretense was gone, replaced by a self-imposed resolve to remain low profile. It was the way things had to be. He pondered an earlier day when such a case would have brought him charging down these halls like some kind of white knight. A single parent and her crippled child were devoured by a reckless truck on a freeway; it had all the elements to anger even the coldest of juries. To the old Mitch Redden, it would have been a showpiece, a vehicle to display his talents and further enhance his reputation. But not now; now it was just a case, and one that no doubt would lead to a quick settlement without the need to ever set foot in front of a jury.

At the nursing station, he turned left into the east wing and proceeded to search for room 413. The hallways were alive with staff and patients, some in wheelchairs, others on crutches, and still others with casts of various sizes, lengths, and locations. Each side of the hallway was outfitted with a long, wooden railing offering support for anyone in need. There was little doubt that he had arrived at the orthopedic ward. Yet the soft pastel colors and the carpeted hallway added warmth that almost seemed out of place.

As Redden approached the open doorway to 413, a physician, who had been charting entries on a small table folded down from the wall, momentarily inspected the lawyer's briefcase, shook his head a couple times, and then returned to his chore. Redden just bit his lip and stepped inside.

Niki Burroughs' voice over the telephone had been strong, with conviction and purpose, and had not prepared Redden for what now lay before his eyes. Indeed, Niki's description of her injuries had been vague. But between the cables, the casts, and her battered face, there could be little question that this woman had sustained major injuries.

The value – and complexity – of the case had just escalated another notch.

At that moment, Niki's eyes were closed, and Redden hesitated at the doorway. He couldn't shake the feeling of being an intruder. The patient sharing Niki's room had rolled over, facing the wall, and was apparently asleep as well. Redden approached Niki's bed. "Excuse me," he said softly, hoping not to awaken the other patient.

Niki's eyes immediately opened, blinked a couple of times, and then stared directly at Redden. "Mr. Redden?"

"Call me 'Mitch.' I hate formality."

"Then it's 'Niki.'" She extended her right hand, which Redden gripped lightly and shook as if it were a fragile vase. She smiled with amusement. "It won't break," she said.

"Just being cautious."

Wide awake, Niki's eyes now had a surprising vitality to them. For the first time, she fully assessed the man she was about to entrust with her future security. Redden was wearing nothing more than slacks, an open-collar short-sleeve shirt, and loafers – without socks. On the floor next to him sat his briefcase. "Not exactly what I expected," she continued. "You somehow don't fit the image of a famous trial lawyer."

"Fame can be misplaced, and the image is artificial. I prefer to be myself."

"My next-door neighbor told me that you were one of the best. She believes everything she reads in the newspapers, and apparently, you have hit the press a number of times. Personally, I'm a little more skeptical than my neighbor. I only believe about half of what I read and give guarded weight to the rest. I just want to know that you're the genuine article and not a bunch of flash with a good press agent."

Redden folded his arms and studied the floor. He had little inclination to be a salesman. For what purpose? This was all an accommodation for Harry. He studied her face again. "I'd suggest that you forget the clippings and go with your instinct," he said.

"I'm not after publicity."

He nodded. It was certainly a reasonable request. "What *are* you after?" he asked.

"I simply want a lawyer with commitment – someone who will place the interests of my case ahead of his own."

"I have no problem with that."

She paused while in thought. As she was finding out, she had not prepared well for the interview. Her only other experience with a lawyer was during her divorce, during which he did all of the talking. She had thought Redden would somewhat take charge, but it wasn't happening. "Maybe you could tell me about yourself," she urged. It seemed a good place to start.

"Well, let's see. I'm a forty-year-old lawyer who was admitted to the California Bar 14 years ago. I am experienced in personal injury litigation and…and, I guess I don't really have much more to add." Redden was unmotivated and felt cumbersome about the issue of his recent experience, which was more or less nonexistent. He had been away too long.

"You're not a man of many words."

"Not at the moment."

"Look at me. Look at my face…my arm. Look what has happened to me."

Redden obliged.

"My face is scarred for life. My arm is held together by two pins. I have multiple fractures in my leg, broken ribs, a punctured lung, and a spleen that went out with the trash. My son had two bad fractures in a leg that was of little use to begin with. Our lives have been destroyed, and I want Ginther's to pay for this."

Redden could sense some pressure building. "Oh, they'll pay, and big. In four to six months, Ginther's will be handing over a very substantial check, maybe even sooner."

"I don't want sooner," she said with conviction. "Nor am I interested in substantial. I am interested in full value, something in seven figures. I am prepared to go all the way with this, and I want a lawyer who feels the same." She seemed a woman out for vengeance, a dangerous element in the prosecution of a personal injury lawsuit. Such clients were irrational and seldom satisfied with the result.

"Absolute top value on your case could take a couple years," he said, probing her resolve, "and probably a trial. No one pays top dollar until you are about to select a jury, and sometimes not even then."

Niki gathered herself, painfully, straining, and leaned forward as much as allowed by the wires and tubing. "I am told you are the man," she said, her voice rising to an uncomfortable level. "I am told you can mesmerize a jury, and bring in verdicts that make others pale in comparison. I am prepared to wait however long as necessary. But I don't want to compromise. I want maximum value. And if a trial is what it takes, then let's take it to trial. I do not want compromise." The complexity of the case escalated another notch.

The patient in the adjacent bed stirred and let out a slight moan, prompting Niki to cut short her plea. Redden's attention was also drawn to the small figure as he rolled onto his back and then sat up, rubbing his eyes. It was Randy, who, for the moment, was trying to make sense of what was going on. "Mommy, who's the man?"

"Sorry, Honey," she said. "Mommy got a little loud. This is Mr. Redden. He's a lawyer, and he is going to help us."

As Redden looked into the big brown eyes of the small boy, the charge suddenly became more compelling – though he now knew the course he had to follow. The lawyer with the casual clothes stepped forward and shook the boy's hand. "Hi there. I'm told that you are Randolph Taylor Burroughs. Is that true?"

The six-year-old boy nodded his head. "Uh-huh."

"That's quite an impressive name. Sounds like a famous writer, maybe even a lawyer."

"'Randy.' I like 'Randy.'"

"Then that's what I'll call you, but only if you call me 'Mitch.' Is that a deal?"

"Uh-huh." The two shook again.

"Good," said the stranger named "Mitch," who at the moment was revealing the engaging personality that had won over so many juries in the past, though it was neither contrived nor fabricated to sell a prospective client. When Mitchell Redden released his charm, it flowed naturally, with genuine enthusiasm. It was honest, the same honesty that had captured the support of every juror who had ever voted him a verdict. "I also understand that you hurt your leg pretty badly."

"Yeah. You wanna see my cast?"

"I sure do."

No sooner had Redden let go of the words than Randy's sheet was down, displaying a cast that extended the full length of his shortened stump. From top to bottom, it was covered with several dozen autographs and good wishes. It appeared that every nurse and doctor on the floor had given it a go, as well as a good number of patients with the physical capacity to find his or her way into the room. There was little doubt that Randy Burroughs had become the floor mascot. Redden feigned shock at the sight. "My God! I've never seen so many signatures in one spot in my life." He then looked up to see a felt pen extended in his direction. "You want me to sign, too?" he asked.

Randy nodded, sporting a bright grin.

"Gee, I don't know if you've even got a spot left."

"Here," said Randy, pointing to a rare virgin area of the cast.

Redden took the pen and began to write.

Niki lay enjoying her son's enthusiasm. He had been up and around on crutches for the past three days and would have been discharged, but for the fact that his mother and sole guardian was still confined to the hospital. In spite of it all, he was a growing and energetic boy and needed space, activities, toys, and peers, not the restrictions of a small hospital room. That he remained uncomplaining and quiet brought pride to his mother – and a good share of guilt as well.

"The fracture at the upper end extended into the artificial hip joint and required surgery," she said. She had seen equivocation in Redden's eyes just before Randy awoke and sensed a need to impress him further with the severity of the injuries. "The fracture at the bottom of the tibia extended completely through the bone. Probably broke when his prosthesis was torn off." Her dark eyes glistened from the welling tears. "It ripped open the bottom of his leg. He was bleeding…quite…" Her voice trailed off.

Redden stopped writing and stared at the cast.

"The truck driver…when he arrived," she continued. "He apparently looked inside, I guess, to see if he could help. He…he saw Randy's shortened leg. The prosthesis, it was detached, laying somewhere." Niki stopped and took a deep breath. "Well, it's something I try not to think about."

After returning the pen to Randy, Redden stood erect. The case was a perfect script to further propel his career and reputation. It was a dream case and had every element needed to capture the passion of a jury – even a client eagerly pressing for a trial. There was just one problem. He was handcuffed. Under no circumstances would he be allowed to step in front of a jury – not without disastrous consequences.

It was time to walk away.

Redden stepped over to Niki, pulled some tissue from a box on her nightstand, and handed it to her. She accepted it and dabbed at the moisture in her eyes.

"I can't accept your case," he said.

"My God, why not?" she asked pleadingly.

Going in, Redden's skills had been beyond reproach, her questioning notwithstanding. And though seemingly uncertain and equivocal in purpose, there was something about Redden's easy and unpretentious manner that broke down all barriers and attracted a confidence that in his hands, all would be right. In the few short minutes since his arrival, Niki found that she was quite comfortable with Mitchell Redden. He was to be the one, her salvation, not just from the myriad of problems arising from the accident but from the financial quagmire that had become her life. A major settlement with Ginther's was to be a doorway to a better life, and Redden was the man who would take her there. But now, with a few simple words, he had shattered her hopes. "But why?" she repeated. "What's wrong with our case?"

"Not a thing," he replied, his eyes searching the carpeted floor, unwilling to meet hers. "It's not the case, it's not you." Redden paused, drew in a breath, and then tilted his head slightly as he finally met her dark eyes, summoning all the resoluteness he could muster. "I'm not the lawyer you're after, Niki. Not anymore. It's impossible. I'm not prepared for this, not now, maybe never."

"That makes no sense. Your reputation, you're one of the finest. How could you not be prepared?"

Redden held up his hand, signaling that there would be no debate. There would be no explanations beyond what had been given. The options available had been limited by others years earlier, and this particular client and her particular case did not fit the agenda. She was demanding and insistent, a headstrong woman who could not be controlled and had her own vision of how and when her case would be resolved. This, by itself, would have eliminated her from consideration. His control over the case had to be absolute, or this new undertaking would never work.

"I'm sorry," he said simply. "It just won't work." Redden cast an uneasy glance at Randy, turned, and headed for the door, resenting the phone call and the visit and Harry Blaylock for convincing him to take another stab at the practice of law.

"Please! Mr. Redden...Mitch, I'm begging you."

The words caught Redden at the doorway and stopped him in his tracks. He briefly pondered the wisdom of not ignoring her plea but instead turned back to face her.

"I'm desperate," she said, the tears now cascading down her cheeks. "I know there are other lawyers, but I have no confidence in anyone but you. I'm sure whatever your problem is, it can be worked out. I'm begging you, please reconsider."

"You don't understand," he said. "I've been away. For a long time. Longer than I had thought. I'm not the lawyer your friend read about."

"Please," she repeated as if she had not heard a word he had said.

Redden took a step back inside to make his point but instantaneously recognized that it was a mistake. It was becoming a debate against this woman and her cause. It was one he had little hope of winning. "You're not getting my point," he hopelessly insisted. "I have not been inside a courtroom in over four years..."

"I don't care."

"I don't have the same edge, the drive, motivation...I am not the same lawyer."

"I don't care."

"I haven't opened a law..."

"I don't care," she interrupted. "I don't care, I don't care."

He now looked pleadingly at her – and she knew at that very moment she had him. His position was founded on a false premise. Sure, he might currently lack drive and stumble along the way for a while. The battery had to be recharged, and the motor ran for a period before it would start hitting all cylinders again, but it would happen. Unpolished though he might be, beneath his apparent indifference, beat the high-powered engine of one of the premier trial attorneys in the state. This was something he could not take off like a coat – and Niki knew it. She was also convinced that she would have him up to speed in no time at all.

But there was one monumental problem. The real reason for his reticence, known only to Redden and one other, could never be shared. And in playing the hand he had been dealt, there was little else he could say. At the moment, she had him trapped. His commitment to avoid any trials, however, was unalterable.

"You have now informed me of all your deficiencies," she added, "and I am telling you that it makes absolutely no difference."

"I would have to have total control over all decisions on your lawsuit…if I was to accept your case," he added as if that decision had not already been made.

"I agree…"

"Listen! Hear what I am saying. I want there to be a full understanding of what this means. I and I alone will call all of the shots on what needs to be done on the case. This also includes if and when to settle and how much to take. I give the orders, and you follow them. If we reach an impasse, then I walk away, and you find yourself another lawyer – without debate."

Redden's words had a certain authority to them that rang of a pronouncement more than a proposal. And their desired effect was swift. Niki's sail suddenly went limp as she pondered the alternatives. Such terms were absolutely unacceptable, but she also was not about to let Redden walk out the door without a signed retainer. "Without explanation?" she asked.

"I would give my reasons, but it would not be a matter for discussion. These are the only conditions under which I could ever accept your case."

"Then I agree."

"You sure?"

"Positive."

Across the room, Randy lay in a state of confusion, still gripping the felt pen that Redden had returned to him. The lawyer smiled at the small boy and walked back to his bedside. "I guess you've got yourself a lawyer," he said, extending his hand. The two shook again, this time with more animation and spirit. "Tell me about yourself," asked Redden, pulling up a chair. "Tell me all about Randy Burroughs."

For the next thirty minutes, Redden questioned his new client, digging and probing, yet with delicate sensitivity, frequently falling back on self-deprecation to ease his way through. "Lawyers can really be dummies," he would often preface a question before exploring an uncomfortable area. By the time he had finished, Redden had not only learned of Randy's perception of the accident and injuries and suffering but also his schooling, grades, friends, chores, hobbies, interests, challenges, disappointments, intellect, personality, and character. In a matter of minutes, an abstract victim named "Randolph Taylor Burroughs" had fully blossomed into a real, living boy.

As always, Redden had made a thorough study of a client at the outset of his representation, and this one, in particular, gave him cause to rejoice. At the appropriate time, he would drag the claims manager for Ginther's insurance carrier down to his office and shove him into a room with Randy. The thought of this child in front of a jury would strike terror in his heart. Within a week, an offer would be on the table. which would be difficult to ignore.

Niki intently observed the interview of her son, appraising the skill of the man whose services she had just secured. She marveled at Redden's thoroughness and the ease at which he could draw out a candid and open dialogue with a six-year-old child. Her confidence further grew as she again noted his warm, personable manner of expression and control of his voice. And not for a moment was it lost that this lawyer, with the straw-colored hair that hung a little long to the back of his neck, the strong square jaw that evoked power and determination, and the finely-etched lines that added maturity to his eyes rather than the aging that fostered their presence, was as attractive as any man she had known in years.

All in all, Mitchell Redden was quite a package, and she had just brought him down like a deer trying to escape across a meadow.

Niki wiped away her tears with a fresh supply of tissue, and a smile of satisfaction settled across her face. She had drawn on her emotions, and it had worked. The master manipulator had found Redden's weakness: compassion. Like everything else, it would be catalogued away. When the need arose, it would be used again. Redden would take her case exactly as far as she would want him to take it.

After a final pat on the hand, Redden's attention turned from Randy to his mother, whose smile had been exchanged for a despondent gaze at nothing. Like a surgeon, Redden dissected the entire accident into seconds, from Niki's approach on the freeway to her final seconds of consciousness. In detail, he reviewed with her the traffic accident report prepared by the California Highway Patrol and obtained by Niki only a day before her call to Redden. He discussed each point of impact, demonstrated by the deposits of dirt from the wheel wells and the scrapings and other markings on the highway and median barrier. He read to each witness statement to her, cross-checking each one with the other and her own recollections for the inevitable inconsistencies between the various historians. He also related the rambling and incoherent statement taken from the truck driver, not for its value but to convey the conscience and feelings of a faceless nemesis. Allerton, in his own way, was also a victim of the tragedy, and a full appreciation of his remorse was essential if Redden had any hope of dissipating his new client's anger.

They talked about her career in real estate and the income loss brought about by the injuries, which were also described again in greater detail. Redden recorded everything onto a yellow legal pad, from which he would later dictate a memo for their file.

Two full hours later, Niki signed a contingent fee retainer agreement and several medical and employment authorization forms. Redden informed her that he would be sending over a professional photographer to snap a series of shots of their injuries, and she should not be modest or embarrassed. Absent the photos, three years down the line, no one would likely appreciate the severity of the injuries and what human flesh looks like when subjected to severe trauma.

Finally, they said their goodbyes and Redden eagerly made his way back to the parking lot. He dropped into the Porsche, and for a moment, stared back at the hospital glistening under the hot sun of July.

It was done; step number two was completed. For the first time in over four years, he had made a commitment, at least one with some permanency and enforceable in a court of law. He kicked on the engine, but his eyes refused to stray from the edifice. Had he gone too far? It wasn't supposed to happen this way – not this soon, not after only 5 weeks. There was only to be a trial period of smaller, uninvolved cases, the cervical and lumbar sprains, and strains of the world, the whiplash injuries that every claims adjuster from California to Maine had cut his or her teeth on. Whether from an auto accident, slip and fall, or any other negligent cause, such injuries were easy to evaluate and easy to settle – uncomplicated and quick.

So why did this woman and this child have to come along right at this moment in his life? Why had he agreed to come to the hospital? Why had he signed them up on a retainer? Perhaps he had yearned to confront the matter rather than hide away in a small, obscure corner of the world. Wasn't it his nature, after all? It was, but it could never be. What he yearned for was what he had given up – what he could never have again. With this case and these elements, the maximum recovery – what Niki demanded – could only be found in a courtroom with an emotionally charged jury, a place in which he could never again set foot.

CHAPTER 5

The two-story structure at 1624 Esplanade had been originally constructed as dental offices. The 5,000-square-foot building sat directly across the street from a broad sandy beach, with blue curling waves and a backdrop of the Palos Verdes Peninsula to the south. It was new, stylish, and appealed to the affluent, middle, and low-income patients alike. For those unfortunates searching for relief from their dental miseries, it offered the smell of fresh salt air and the serenity of the ocean.

For 23 years, Matthew Turner's oral surgery and dental practice flourished. Over his head in patients, he hired three dentists and a half-dozen dental hygienists. When he ran out of room on the first floor, he moved his residence out of the second and expanded his offices to the upper floor. Then, at the peak of his success, scandal rocked the South Bay. A patient accused Turner of molestation while under an anesthetic. Complaints from three additional patients followed. In a matter of weeks, the patient pool had dried up, and the operation shut down. Turner lost his license and moved out of state, abandoning the building, which no longer had a mortgage by then.

Several real estate agents attempted to locate Turner, who had vanished somewhere on the East Coast. Although property taxes and insurance on the building were paid semi-annually out of a trust fund, no one locally had any idea where the former oral surgeon had settled. Neither had his divorced wife nor younger brother in Seattle. Matthew

Turner had severed all ties with his past and disappeared from society, leaving a deserted building at 1624 Esplanade as his only legacy.

A year passed, and the vacated building began to show signs of neglect. First, a few scattered newspapers found their way up against the full-height windows of the lobby. With all utility and maintenance services terminated, plants died, and weeds took over the property like a cancer running rampant. Fed by the prevailing ocean breezes, dust blanketed the property, and white crusty rings from the salt-laden damp air covered the windows and their frames. By the second year, graffiti began to appear, and a couple of the upper windows were broken by vandals. Because of complaints from neighbors about the appearance of the building, police began to patrol the property more frequently. This substantially reduced the defacement but did not stop it. Three years later, the police ousted a commune of seven vagrants out of the building who were attempting to use it as a home. Neighbors continued to complain and circulated a petition to have the building condemned, but no one was disposed to pursue it further when city officials rejected the plea.

Matthew Turner died in a small town in Virginia. During probate proceedings, the administrator of his estate discovered several bank accounts totaling over three and a half million dollars and an office building all the way across the continent in Redondo Beach, California. Renovations were started approximately twelve months later with funds from the estate, including replacement of windows, new roofing, and a complete paint job. The building was simultaneously put up for sale. After another year without a satisfactory offer and under pressure from Turner's brother, the property was set up for a probate sale in the Los Angeles Superior Court. Mitchell Redden, having recently settled two major cases, saw one of the legal notices in a newspaper, inspected the property, and outbid three other potential buyers in court.

Redden moved in after restoring the second floor to its earlier living quarters and altering the first floor from a series of small examining rooms to a larger reception room, a conference room, a secretarial bay, a coffee and supply room, and three large lawyer offices. The exterior stucco walls were also repainted from a sterile off-white to soft beige with blue-grey trim. The large planter boxes in front of the building were stuffed with an array of plants and flowers. An electronic gate was also added to the underground garage to not only add security but also to exclude surfers and others attracted to the beach during the summer months and other hot days of the year when parking was at a premium. Once again, the building had a new face and another fresh start.

Four months later, Mitchell Redden became part of its history – two owners and two failures. From the moment he locked the doors for the final time, he carried that burden. Not overtly, but subtly, almost to a subconscious level. It was never the subject of conversation; he never cursed of it, and with some effort, he rarely thought about it. But it was always there. Failure had not been a frequent visitor in Redden's life. Stull, there it was, leaning over his shoulder, whispering in his ear that at the moment of his greatest successes, all of his resourcefulness, money, and talent were not enough. In the end, he had to walk away from a profession he excelled at and cherished. Failure was not only a fact; it was a monumental disaster that had altered the very course of his life. And when Harry was pleading his case and urging his return, though Redden would never concede its influence, the thought of the vacated building at 1624 Esplanade and its symbolism of failure was a significant driving force in Redden's acquiescence. History was to be changed.

⸻ ◆ ⸻

On the way back from the hospital, Redden drove by the scene of the accident. He always went to the scene, even after it had been exhaustively investigated. It gave him a feel for what had occurred and offered insight into the weaknesses of each case that he would have to respond to in court. In this particular instance, however, it required no expenditure of time since it was on the route back to his office.

In an effort to reproduce the facts leading up to the impact, Redden approached the scene at the same speed as Niki had, then slowed for the same approximate distance, then accelerated to the point of the initial collision. He imagined a small pickup truck ahead of him as the

Allerton truck, but on a larger scale with its directional signals flashing away, warning of the driver's intentions. He considered Niki driving the accelerator to the floor at this point, attempting to squeeze by the scene of the earlier accident. As he suspected, though the case against the truck driver and Ginther's was strong, a jury might well find Niki had her own degree of responsibility for the accident.

Upon returning to his office, Redden began calling the eyewitnesses listed on the traffic accident report prepared by the CHP. Five names had been listed, each giving a slightly different version of the same accident, but everyone corroborated that Niki Burroughs had the right-of-way and that the truck had pulled into her lane of travel.

It seemed a very straightforward case. Every witness implicated the truck driver as the primary cause. Only the issue of contributory negligence remained unsettled, but it was sufficiently important that he attempt to tie down the witnesses in a light most favorable to his client. Any degree of negligence on the Niki's part would have the effect of reducing her award. Besides, what else did he have to do? Burroughs versus Allerton was the only case in his office.

By 5:30 PM, Redden had reached four of the 5 witnesses and had tape-recorded further statements from them. Two, who had implicated Niki with excessive speed, were easily discredited by Redden's gift of persuasion. One conceded that he had seen Niki's BMW only a fraction of a second prior to the initial collision and would have had inadequate time to make a valid and accurate estimate of her speed. The other witness acknowledged that it could have been another car he had seen since he had not witnessed the actual impact. When Redden concluded the last of the calls, he hung up the receiver and stretched his arms as a final signature to a day that was both challenging and draining.

Redden stood and, as he had done so many times before, stared pensively through the window at the sprawling Pacific Ocean. Though late in the day, the sun had yet to position itself over the far horizon. As if to endorse the ancient mariners who had named her, the sea sat glistening like some tranquil mountainous lake. He stepped over to the sliding glass door and slid it open. The fresh salt air immediately attacked his nostrils and awakened his senses. The call of the seagulls, the pounding of the surf, and his brethren at play had not been quite so vivid since his return.

He turned back inside and pulled a diet cola from a small refrigerator near his desk, snapped it open, and stepped outside onto the balcony. The effervescence of the drink added to the feeling of rejuvenation as he swallowed almost half the can. Redden's mind drifted again to Niki Burroughs and the dilemma she presented. He thought of the image that confronted him at the entrance to her hospital room and the endearing enthusiasm of her six-year-old boy as he recited a list of near-impossible goals. The indomitable spirit of youth had always been a perplexing observation to a man who had spent his career addressing the tragedy of others. With considerable trepidation, he had stepped back into his profession, planning a menu of light and inconsequential cases. Instead, he was handed one of substance. Would he be up to the challenge? Could he pull it off? How could he possibly prosecute the case with the energy and conviction of a trial lawyer and at the same time sidestep the forbidden arena of the courtroom?

Redden's concentration was suddenly broken by the sharp sound of a closing door. He stepped back inside and glanced at his watch. It was 5:48 PM. "Harry, is that you?" he called out through the open doorway to his office. He closed the sliding glass door to better hear the reply.

"Who'd you goddamn think it was, your fairy godmother?" The unmistakable, grave voice of Harry Blaylock rang out like a school alarm whenever he reached a state of irritation, which was quite often.

Redden followed the voice to the entrance of the adjoining office. Blaylock was inside, loading up a briefcase. "Where have you been?" Redden asked. "Haven't seen you around for a couple of days." Without waiting for the reply, Redden took another long swig of the drink and leaned against the doorjamb.

Blaylock looked up for the first time. "I'll tell you where I've goddamn been," he said, not backing off a decibel. "I've been on a goddamn freeway, is where I've been. Two fucking days of exhaust pipes is where I've been."

"You sound a little upset." Redden was amused. Blaylock *always* seemed upset, but it was rarely deep, and a smile was never far away.

He seemed at odds with the world. Nothing was ever right, and he was perpetually unloading his frustration on whoever was handy. Yet he was tolerable because, just as quickly, he would turn and laugh at himself.

Harry snapped his briefcase shut and began to nod his head. "'Upset,' you say? Well, let me see. I leave Santa Barbara at two, fly through Carpenteria, hit Ventura by two-thirty, and in an hour, I'm sailing past Thousand Oaks. I mean, I'm cruising at a low altitude. Then disaster. I hit the Valley, and it's gridlock. In half an hour, I move two miles. By the four-oh-five, I had almost three hours invested and no relief in sight. It's a goddamn parking lot from the one-oh-one to Wilshire, and I don't have the fucking ticket to get out!"

"So you went to see Jesse."

"Don't change the subject. I'm on a roll." Harry's mood was beginning to lighten up. With the flare of a bullfighter, he pulled off his coat and raised both arms to the ceiling. "Check this out! Gunga Din with body fat. I got water pouring out of me like Niagara." From the armpit to the waistline on either side of his blue pinstriped shirt, he was saturated. At this point, he is even managing a smile.

"Get the picture, Mitch. The kid needs a big car, so who does she call but the old man. Going on a run up the coast with a bunch of her sorority pals. Got a short break from summer school. So in drives Harry with the old Buick, and out he goes in an under-sized Hyundai and … tah tah," he announced, like an introductory blast from a trumpet, as he joined his hands over his head and clumsily twirled with little tip-toe steps like a 250-pound ballet dancer, "…noooooo air conditioning!"

Though a good three inches shorter than his younger counterpart, Harry Blaylock was unquestionably a big man. He was thick through the chest with broad shoulders and hands that would swallow most others when greeted with a handshake. Time and an appetite for rich foods had also not been particularly kind to his abdomen, which protruded like a seven-month pregnancy and was largely responsible for his exclusive use of suspenders. The consummate image instantly conjured up memories of an elephant rotating on a pedestal at a circus.

Redden could no longer hold it in and doubled over in laughter.

"I mean, catch this sight," he continued. "Here's this fat old man stuffed in the front seat of a toy car covered with every kind of decal imaginable. This gal must've cleaned out the Student Union. And here he is, sweat dripping out of every pore of his face, which is a fucking vin rose red…"

"…and no doubt cussing up a blue streak," offered Redden.

"Cussing! I must've shut every window for ten miles, some of them with as much air conditioning as I had. But catch this, Mitch. Here I am, putting along at 5 miles an hour, hanging over the steering wheel, 'cause the goddamn seat was designed to go back for a tall midget. Now tell me that everyone who took in this sight didn't think I was pedaling a delivery for Toys R fucking Us. Tell me. You're goddamn right. I'm upset."

Redden is so weakened by laughter that he stumbles over and collapses on an over-stuffed couch in the back of the office. Meanwhile, Harry tosses his coat over the back of a chair and begins walking out of the room. "Now gimme a goddamn beer," he added, which was more of an announcement of where he was going than a request for refreshment.

The departure gave Redden a short time to consider the trip to Santa Barbara. In a minute, Harry was back twisting off the cap of a bottle of beer. Redden wiped a tear from his eye and asked, "So I understand that you went up to visit Jesse?" Blaylock's 20-year-old daughter was a junior at the University of California at Santa Barbara. He made a point of visiting her once a month, though he never stayed longer than overnight.

Harry did not immediately respond. Instead, he pursed his lips as if analyzing the question and made his way over to his chair behind the desk. Apparently wanting to avoid the subject, he inspected the beer like some prized possession, took a healthy swallow, belched, and smiled. "Yeah, I went to see Jesse. Went up on Tuesday. And with the same goddamn traffic, but in a little more comfort."

Redden's smile transformed into a look of puzzlement. "Tuesday morning, as in yesterday?"

Harry had yet to drop into his chair, sensing that it was not a time to relax. He put the beer on the desk, hooked a thumb in each suspender, as was his habit, and slowly shook his head. "I knew this conversation was gonna happen. I knew it, but I sure as fucking hell wasn't looking forward to it."

"You lied."

"You're goddamn right. I lied."

"So yesterday there was no *ex parte* hearing in Orange County."

"A complete figment of my imagination."

Redden inspected his old friend. Harry Blaylock was a weary-looking man, appearing a good 10 years older than his proclaimed age of 58. Baldness had nearly taken over his dome, save for a few resistant strands of hair combed strategically over the top. A crop of silver hair crowned each ear, which Harry let grow a sufficient length to tie behind his neck in a little tail. Although he had developed more than his share of lines about his forehead and face, it was in the eyes that most revealed his fatigue. Deeply set, with wrinkled bags, one could see many years of pain and turmoil. Blaylock was a man who was again trying to put together a legal career – and a life. At a time when one would have expected financial security and contemplation of possible retirement, Harry's practice had been reduced to picking up the crumbs that other lawyers preferred to ignore. A default divorce, a simple will, and an occasional judicial appointment for a misdemeanor criminal matter were the staples of his practice. His clients were low-income people struggling to make ends meet, capable of paying only a few bucks a month against their bills. Harry Blaylock was a failure, both professionally and personally. Redden carefully selected his words, wanting to communicate anger but not injuriously.

"I don't like being manipulated. I don't like it at all."

Harry picked up the bottle again, inspected it, and finished it off. "Okay, Mitch, let me have it. Both barrels, right in the face."

Redden leaned forward on the couch and ran both hands through his hair. True, he was angry, but he was not about to explode. It would be tantamount to kicking a puppy dog. He took a deep breath and glared again at Harry. His bright red suspenders and matching bow tie seemed to be glaring right back at him. Redden could not recall ever seeing Harry without a matching set of suspenders and a bow tie. He must have had twenty sets of them.

"You lied to me, Harry, you goddamn lied. You're not supposed to lie to your friends."

"That's it?" Blaylock bunched his lips in a prissy pucker and continued a couple octaves higher, "You lied to me, Harry. You're not supposed to lie to your friends." He then angrily snapped, "Is that fucking it? For Christ's sake, get pissed off. I conned, I manipulated, I used. I got you to cover a deposition under the pretext of needing to appear in court. C'mon Mitch, get angry. Gimme some of the goddamn Redden fire that you're famous for."

Redden promptly rose from the couch and began pacing. "Don't provoke me, Harry," he waved.

"Why not? *Somebody's* gotta do it. You'd been in the office for over a month and hadn't even stuck your head out the door. Twelve call-ins and not one signup."

"They weren't good cases. I did not agree to open my office again to sign up a bunch of dogs."

"Shit they weren't! You didn't sign up the goddamn cases 'cause you're too fucking terrified to be a lawyer again." Blaylock moved out from behind the desk. This conversation had been waiting too long to take place. "You walked away without a word of explanation. 'It's private,' you said. So okay, I respected that. Not once did I push you. You wanted some time away. By three years, I figure this has gotta be more than a little burnout. Still, you don't wanna talk. I'm thinking, this guy's my best friend. Why won't he open up to me?"

"I've had enough," announced Redden, holding up his hand as he exited the room and sought refuge in his own office.

Blaylock was close behind, not to be denied. Not again. "C'mon, goddamnit! Talk to me. What happened? What in the fuck is going on? You're back, but you're not. Something has happened to you…"

"Get out, Harry!"

Blaylock refused to back off an inch. "You won't go to court. You won't sign up cases. You won't talk. You dress like a goddamn beach bum…"

"I said get out," snapped Redden, his face beginning to flush. At this point, he had fully retreated behind his desk. He was cornered, both literally and figuratively. Out of utter desperation, Redden brought his hand crashing down on the desktop and screamed, "Get out of here, damn you!"

Harry rounded the desk. His face was a foot away, leaning toward Redden, his teeth showing like a snarling dog. "I'm not leaving 'til I get a fucking answer. Unless, of course, you would like to try and *throw* me out."

Redden's white-knuckled fist rose defiantly, trembling, separating the two men by inches. "You son of a bitch..."

"You don't have the guts to use that any more than you have the guts to be a lawyer." With those stinging words, the scene suddenly froze, and neither man was moving or speaking, not knowing his next move. Then Harry, as if to release them from their purgatory, began to shake his head. "Then again, maybe you don't deserve to be a lawyer."

Redden had finally reached his limit. "You're not one to sit in judgment," he fired back.

Harry Blaylock instantly deflated. The fight was gone; all drive sucked from his body with the utterance of a few well-placed words. His eyes sagged, the pain obvious. "Well...," said Harry, briefly clearing his throat, "I wanted you to come out swinging. I guess I expected something a little bit higher." Harry took a couple of steps backward and then turned to leave. "I...uh, got a depo' in the morning...on Sanchez. I'd better get on home..."

"Harry, I'm sorry," said Redden, taking a few tentative steps after his friend.

Harry stopped at the door and looked back. "No. You're right. I'm the last one around here to be making such a judgment. Your reasons are your own. It's a private matter, and I should stay out of it." With that pronouncement, Harry disappeared through the door, retrieved his briefcase, and was gone.

Since Redden had reopened his doors, Blaylock had been a tenant of the law office on a time-for-space arrangement. In return for his overhead costs and use of Redden's secretary/receptionist, Harry was to cover depositions and court appearances, as well as any legal research that Redden deemed necessary on any of his cases. The association thus supplied a mutual need for both men.

Their relationship, however, went back many years earlier. Redden had drifted into Los Angeles after bouncing from job to job in the San Francisco Bay area, unable to find direction in his life, a man no longer with a focus or ambition. After his initial disillusionment with the practice of law, he had even considered chucking it all and seeking out a new vocation. Only a family tradition of lawyers and the insistence of a dominating father kept him pursuing a career chosen by his family long before he was even old enough to read.

Redden's inability to succeed didn't stop with the legal profession. Two failed marriages, neither of which lasted longer than 18 months, only added to his increasing lack of self-respect. His first marriage, during law school, turned out to be more a relationship of convenience than love. His second was to a career-minded woman who rejected the role of a housewife and the restrictions of rearing children. Indeed, Redden had always considered it fortunate that no children had resulted from either marriage. However, as he recently sailed into his forties, he often found himself pondering the meaning and value of such a relationship at this point in his life.

In need of a change, if only a geographic one, Redden had moved to the Los Angeles Basin after three wasted years in San Francisco. The transition had effectively and symbolically severed the controlling strings of his father, leading to a somewhat estranged relationship. And Redden, to his own surprise, welcomed it with open arms.

It was at this point in time that Harry Blaylock took Redden under his wing and channeled his God-given talents toward a career he had been born and bred to fulfill. Harry had many failings, but he was quick to recognize talent. He was also a byproduct of the school of hard knocks and held a wealth of practical knowledge on the art of survival – and the means of dealing with those in the profession who considered the rules of professional ethics as an obstacle course rather than a guiding light. Since those early days, Harry found himself gradually assuming the role of Redden's surrogate father.

The pain of the run-in with Harry prompted Redden to turn his attention back to the sprawling sea outside his office. It had always been calming to behold its waves, incessantly churning and pounding, as they had been from the very beginning. Somehow, whatever problem brought him to take in its view would be washed away, its importance dwarfed by the unfathomable power of nature. But not this time – not this dilemma.

Redden's eyes glistened from the welling tears. "I did sign up a case…," he uttered softly, "you cantankerous old bastard." His private torment could never be revealed to Harry Blaylock because Harry Blaylock was his private torment. Redden's unexplained departure from the practice of law and Harry's burdening past were inextricably woven together. One could not be explained without a discussion of the other.

Yet Mitchell Redden owed his career and his successes to the same man who brought about his agony. It was one of the cruel incongruities of his past. Life was ambiguous, with undefined borders, sullied heroes, and tainted role models. Redden wanted to hate him, as one might have a thorn buried deep in his foot, but he felt only love. The human spirit was, after all, fallible and flawed, and Harry Blaylock was no exception. Though he had stumbled and fallen more often than most, Harry was, in the end, a battler, fighting his way to respectability when others would have drifted to alcoholism or worse. It was what Mitchell Redden admired most about his former mentor. Why had he hurt this wonderful old man?

Grief suddenly transformed into anger, which again rose to a near-explosive state. "Damn it!" he screamed out as his shoe found a handy trash container and drove it and its contents flying across the room.

CHAPTER 6

Thursday, July 23

It had not been a pleasant morning for Harry Blaylock. At the moment, he was sitting at a large conference table in the prestigious Century City offices of Barry, Klein & Nance. Harry detested Century City. He despised the tall, sterile buildings that rose boldly into the west Los Angeles skyline. They symbolized the establishment and its unchallenged power that had been hanging over his shoulder his entire career. He resented the look of opulence, which was distanced and detached. Harry always felt like an outsider whenever he visited. He never quite fit in.

Then there was the parking. No doubt it would require a roadmap to find his car, which was presuming that he could pick out his daughter's Hyundai among the fleet of Japanese cars in the cavernous underground parking structure.

Harry also detested the firm's wide hallways, carpeting that almost swallowed his shoes, and paintings and sculptures that adorned the walls and reception room. Seven years earlier, the partners had voted to invest the firm's revenue in artwork, looking to appreciate its assets and, at the same time, elevate an image created by backroom political deals and high-volume lawyering. Though elegant in appearance, Harry saw the offices as a museum and referred to it as such to anyone within earshot.

It was also not lost on him that payment for such trappings dictated a very aggressive billing practice for the firm, which in turn equated to a never-ending trail of paperwork from Century City and a corresponding extra burden of work for Harry Blaylock. The firm had to be responsible for the death of more trees than every logging company in the State of Washington combined. But above all else, he detested Geoffrey Rothenberg, who sat across the expanse of table smugly, with an insolent look of pleasure, while Harry struggled with his next question.

"As you approached the intersection, were you aware of the color of the traffic light?"

Rothenberg began shaking his head. "Mr. Blaylock, the question is again vague and ambiguous. By 'aware,' do you mean he saw it? Did someone tell him, or had he judged it from some earlier timing? And what intersection are we talking about? Is it really so difficult to pose understandable questions?"

"The same intersection where he smacked my client, of course. Did he see it, observe it, perceive its color at some point before arriving at the intersection and hitting my client." Blaylock, who normally ran at a high level of irritation anyway, had been fighting for well over an hour and a half to keep the lid on his temper.

"Much better," observed Rothenberg, condescension dripping from each word. He turned to his client, authorizing him to provide an answer.

Marvin Litvig, bespectacled, with a slender and orderly face, momentarily pondered the question, seeming to analyze it from 25 different directions. "Yes," he finally said.

Blaylock considered the labor he had invested for one brief word and then again pushed ahead. "How far back were you…when you first saw it, that is?"

Rothenberg exhaled to demonstrate his growing impatience. "Objection. How far back from what? The signal? The intersection? The car that was 'smacked' by my client? Vague and ambiguous – again."

"Well, let's see," said Blaylock, a smile forcing its way through the anger. "We were talking about a traffic light. *That* seems like a convenient point of reference. Why don't we pick that one?" For the first time he had thrown back a little sarcasm. He rarely had time for rancor in a deposition. All it succeeded in doing was prolonging and distracting, and he had no inclination to do either.

Rothenberg nodded to his client.

"One hundred and fifty feet."

"You sure?"

"Yes."

"Positive?"

"Asked and answered," snapped Rothenberg. "Instruct the witness not to answer. Ask your next question."

"I'm presuming that was an estimate?" Harry had intended it as a question, but neither the witness nor his lawyer reacted. Instead, they both sat stone-faced as if no one had even spoken. "Let me phrase it differently. Was this an estimate?"

After a pause, Litvig said firmly, "No, it was not."

In all of his years, Harry Blaylock had never seen a witness so well prepared and rehearsed. It was as if he was speaking to a machine. He would ask a question, there would be a momentary delay while it computed and processed the inquiry, and then would spit out a reply. In some ways, Harry was more fascinated by the efficiency with which the deponent responded than the content of his answers. After all, the case was nothing more than a garden-variety fender bender.

"Not 160 feet, not 140 feet, but one hundred and fifty feet… exactly?"

"You get one answer per question, counsel. Instruct not to answer. Ask your next question." Rothenberg's tone was becoming increasingly abrupt and acerbic.

"Well, then, enlighten me. How is it you were able to arrive at such a precise distance?"

"I measured it," said Litvig after another delay.

Harry's features transformed into a look of utter astonishment. "You measured it?"

Again, the silent stare.

Harry's smile was now genuine. "I must tell you, I am a little confused…"

"Apparently." Rothenberg continued to dig. Tension between the two lawyers escalated another notch.

Blaylock's eyes locked onto Rothenberg as he continued his questioning, barely missing a beat. "Then perhaps you could enlighten me. Did you, upon seeing the signal, stop and pace it off?"

"No," said Litvig, unruffled by the provoking question.

"Then when did you measure it?"

Another pause. "Yesterday," he said.

Now, it all made sense. Rothenberg had been so fanatical in his preparation that he had the client go to the scene and reconstruct the accident. It was almost flattering to Blaylock, who rarely had a case of any importance, that a big Century City law firm would give so much attention to his lawsuit. In fact, it was downright baffling. "Do I understand correctly that yesterday you actually went down to the scene and attempted to recreate the accident?"

Litvig immediately turned to Rothenberg. It was clear that this subject had been the topic of an earlier conversation between them. Rothenberg's eyes glowed with pleasure. "I'm sorry, counsel, but I'm going to have to cut you off at this point."

"For what reason?"

"Attorney work-product privilege."

"What you are telling me is that you were with him?"

Rothenberg leaned back and began exploring the question somewhere on the ceiling of the conference room. "You presume correctly, counsel," he said. "I was with him, and what took place was at my direction and under my supervision. Thus, everything associated with that event is privileged, and you are not allowed to question him about it."

Blaylock's voice took on a sharper edge. "You can't do that. You can't have a witness research the facts in order to give an opinion, then cut off any questioning after rendering the opinion – even if it *is* at the direction of a lawyer."

"It's the law," said Rothenberg.

"The hell it is! If there was any privilege to begin with, which I seriously doubt, it was waived the moment you allowed him to give an opinion. Now I want an answer to my question. Tell me," he said, directing his question to Litvig, "tell me exactly how you went about measuring the distance between you and the traffic light."

Litvig again looked at Rothenberg, who was about to deliver the blow he had been waiting for. Blaylock was right on the law, but it meant little difference to Geoffrey Rothenberg. Blaylock never followed up on anything. He was a sloppy lawyer with a bad reputation, and in Rothenberg's mind, he did not belong in the same room with him, let alone in the same profession. He thus had little concern about the matter being brought in front of a judge. But that issue had nothing to do with what was taking place at the moment.

Rothenberg had been humiliated at Blaylock's office. His pride had been damaged. That night, he had experienced little sleep, reviewing over and over what had taken place and engineering how he would exact his retribution. The deposition with Harry Blaylock had seemed the right vehicle. Though he would have preferred having another shot at Redden, given his history, he might never have been presented with that opportunity. Blaylock, on the other hand, would shortly be at his office and had considerable vulnerability. He also had the right client. Litvig was intelligent and disciplined and would follow instructions like a marine just out of boot camp. Rothenberg would make the deposition one of absolute misery for Blaylock. Kind for kind. In some fashion or way, the message would get back to Mitchell Redden. He was equally adept at playing the game and was not about to forget what had happened and crawl into a hole.

"Counsel, you know little of the law," said Rothenberg. "That's quite evident after agonizing through your laborious questioning this morning. It is unfortunate that a man with your obvious years has not picked up some skill along the way. But your question still violates the attorney work-product privilege, and I am not about to let you invade it. I would suggest that you move on to your next line of questioning." Rothenberg's eyes stared confrontationally at Blaylock.

The court reporter's face flushed in embarrassment. She was middle-aged and thought she had seen it all, but she was obviously taken aback by the remarks. Sandy Goodman, attending his second deposition on the case in three days, likewise seemed to be considering the option of crawling under the conference table. Ten minutes after they had started, he began to appreciate what was happening and why. But unlike the entertainment on Tuesday, the day's experience had been uncomfortable. For some incomprehensible reason, he had always liked Harry Blaylock. In fact, it was only because Litvig had claimed that his brakes had failed that Goodman's client had even been brought into the lawsuit. Like Harry, he, too, had a number of questions for the defendant.

Harry's eyes dropped to his notepad, which contained a scattering of incoherently scribbled notes. He had taken more than his share of abuse over the years, most of it justified. So much so that the acidity of Rothenberg's remarks barely penetrated his crusty exterior. Harry Blaylock was barren of pride and ego, characteristics he had shed along his torturous path to maintain his sanity. But there was something about Geoffrey Rothenberg and the moment that seemed to dictate some form of action.

Without a word, Harry stood, took off his coat, placed it over the back of his chair, and then stepped over to the window that seemed to lay all of Century City and Beverly Hills at his feet. For a good two minutes, he simply stood taking in the view, his thumbs characteristically hooked on either side of his suspenders. They were blue and sported a scroll weave of reds and golds that would have looked more at home at a yodeling contest in the Swiss Alps.

Harry finally turned to Rothenberg and said, "Let me speak to you outside. It'll just take a moment." Surprisingly to Rothenberg, Blaylock's features had taken on a calm quality and even detected a slight smile. Perhaps this would be a plea for mercy. He accepted the invitation, and the two men stepped into the hallway.

Blaylock crossed his arms and leaned against the wall close to Rothenberg as if he were about to relate a secret. It was at this point that the younger lawyer began to get a sense of the size of his opponent. Blaylock stood a good six inches taller. Even as Harry hunched over to draw close to him, any view of Rothenberg would have been completely obstructed from behind.

For the first time, a tinge of anxiety began to creep up Rothenberg's spine.

Down the corridor, an attractive brunette was busily typing on her computer. She was facing toward Harry and sensed someone was staring at her, and she looked up without altering her rhythm on the keyboard. Seeing the warm, pleasant features of the older man, she smiled. Harry returned the friendly acknowledgment over Rothenberg's shoulder as he spoke in a voice just above a whisper.

"Counsel, I know I carry around a lot of baggage from the past, and I guess most of it isn't too flattering. So it's not exactly surprising that you're having a difficult time with this. And if you don't love me, that's okay 'cause I don't really give a rat's fuck." From the tenor of the conversation, Rothenberg could sense that things were not exactly heading in the direction he had anticipated. "But a word of advice," Harry continued. "You may have noticed that I removed my coat. Now, with the physique of an over-ripe pear, I am sure you can understand why this rarely occurs and only then out of absolute necessity. But since I just got it out of the cleaners, the last thing I need right now is to get a bunch of blood splattered all over it."

Rothenberg's stomach instantly twisted into a knot, and he took a defensive step backward. Blaylock was still smiling, and his eyes had not moved an inch from the legal secretary. Rothenberg wanted to be amused by the exchange, but something told him that he had little to laugh about.

"Now I know I am not very smart," Harry said. "But if you want to grandstand for your client, I'd suggest you find a fucking auditorium someplace. It will no longer be at the expense of Harry Blaylock – not without serious consequences, anyway." The secretary was now beginning to blush and losing her concentration. "I guess I am probably asking a lot of dumb and confusing questions. But I'd suggest that you, well…that you simply state your legal objection and keep your fucking personal remarks to yourself." Blaylock momentarily switched his eyes over to Rothenberg but didn't change one muscle of the smile on his face. "Know what I mean?"

Rothenberg took another step backwards. His face was ashen, and his eyes now telegraphed a genuine fear. The challenge had come unexpectedly and had caught him off guard. He stood silently, frozen and indecisive, unwilling to engage in any dialogue that might further provoke the animal from Redondo Beach. Indeed, had he been familiar with Harry's pugilistic history, he would have understood that this was not an idle threat. Harry nodded toward the conference room door, inviting Rothenberg back inside. The young lawyer hesitated for a moment and, without once uttering a word, reentered the room.

The remainder of the morning went smoothly and without incident. Other than three or four occasions when he succinctly stated his legal grounds, Rothenberg remained resolutely silent, even ignoring Litvig more than once when his eyes begged for more direction. Goodman's questions were brief, and he eagerly left upon conclusion.

Geoffrey Rothenberg's world had been thrown askew. Threats of legal accountability had been a part of his professional existence since being admitted to the Bar, and he had paid his share of economic sanctions when his exploits had met the displeasure of a judge. But this was different. Physical violence had always been an abstract item that had happened to others, whether as something he had read in the press or through rumors that had surfaced around the county courthouse. As it was, the experience was almost paralyzing. After Blaylock had concluded and began stuffing his briefcase with his notes, Rothenberg hurriedly said goodbye to his client, excused himself, and then vomited his breakfast in the executive washroom.

Redden and Blaylock. They deserved one another. Neither belonged in the legal profession and Rothenberg, now more than ever, was committed to bringing that about.

No sooner had Harry marched ten steps down the interior corridor when squat yet imposing figure stepped into his pathway. He had slipped out of an adjoining office, but his movement was so swift that he seemed to appear out of nowhere. He stood defiantly, with his arms crossed and sleeves rolled up to the elbows. His tie had been loosened and the top of the shirt unbuttoned, though the size of the neck suggested such an achievement would have been next to impossible anyway. His teeth clenched tightly on a long, unlit cigar.

Harry stopped in his tracks. He had not seen Raymond Gillingham in several years.

Gillingham pulled the cigar from his mouth, rolled and inspected it a couple times in his fingers, then said, "Now you weren't gonna sneak out of here without saying 'hi,' were you?" He smiled, but in a sinister way that instantly put Harry on guard. This was not to be a friendly chat.

"Naw," responded Blaylock, "sneaking is not my style. But I had thought of blowing a little gas as I paraded by your office."

"Indeed," said Gillingham, smugly nodding an acknowledgment.

"I choose to call it a form of free expression," said Harry. "I think of myself as an unpretentious sort." After casting a quick glance at a few pieces of ornate artwork along the wall, he added, "But I guess living in a museum, as you do, you'd find it a little difficult to grasp what I'm talking about."

"I suppose so." Rather than a concession, Gillingham considered his reply more of an affirmation of their respective stations, both societal and professional. "Look, I have a few matters to discuss with you," he said after a pause. "Perhaps you wouldn't mind stepping into my office."

Harry shook his head and pushed on by. "I think not," he said. Whatever was on his mind, nothing good would ever come out of a conversation with Ray Gillingham.

"I would recommend that you hear me out," said Gillingham. His voice left little doubt of his sincerity. "The consequence of being ignored might prove…well, let's say somewhat embarrassing."

The words brought Harry Blaylock to a stop. By the time he turned to respond, Gillingham had returned to his office, not for a moment doubting that Blaylock would be right behind. Gillingham seldom had to deal with failure or rejection. Few were inclined to confront his power and wrath – even an irascible rebel from Redondo Beach.

Harry stepped inside the large, exquisitely decorated office, intent on maintaining his bravado. "I was overcome with curiosity," he said. "I had thought I was pretty much beyond embarrassment, but then one never knows."

"Just trying to get your attention," smiled Gillingham, who had already assumed his chair. He sat behind a large mahogany desk that was surprisingly uncluttered. On it sat a telephone, an outbox tray with a file and dictation tape, a small clock encased with Waterford crystal, and what appeared to be a dossier on some unfortunate dupe of Gillingham's latest vendetta. It sat in the middle of an immaculate desk mat. The top of the desk glistened with spit-polish luster.

Harry couldn't help but inspect the rest of the room and was instantly taken by the order of everything. It was as if the office was a layout for a magazine ad. From the cherry wood paneling to the library shelves of venerable law books to the credenza and its crystal decanters and cognac glasses to the parquet flooring and large Oriental rug to the glass-top cocktail table and crystal candy dish of Jelly Bellies, everything – every piece of the entire ensemble – was exactly where it was supposed to be. Only Gillingham's suit coat, casually thrown over the arm of a leather brass-buttoned chair, hinted that someone was actually using the room. Raymond Gillingham had a reputation for twelve-hour workdays and virtually no life away from his professional existence. The office just did not go with the man.

"If I was summoned in here to be impressed," announced Harry, "you're in for some big-time disappointment. My tastes lean more toward low-budget modern. I prefer to funnel my money into my stock portfolio. No kidding. My tax man would have a coronary if I did something like this."

"Sit down, Harry." The tone was instructive.

"No time. Got a power luncheon with my state senator. He's pushing me for a seat on the appellate bench." Blaylock, totally enjoying himself now, scanned the office one more time with an animated frown. "You don't actually work in here, do you?"

"Neatness and organization are the building blocks of success," said Gillingham, but not defensively. It was one of several tenets he enjoyed quoting at every opportunity. He then scowled, "I said 'sit down.'"

"Fuck you!"

Gillingham lifted the dossier from the desk and opened the cover as if to be reassured of what was inside. "I have in my hands the complete professional biography of one Harry Leonard Blaylock," he began, leering over the top of the folder. "It holds every intimate fact of your tainted and defiled past, not to mention considerable insight into what portends for the future…if you catch my meaning."

For a brief moment, Blaylock absorbed the thinly veiled threat. Chester Raymond Gillingham III was a man of considerable intellect, graduating at the top of his class at Cornell. He was thorough, to the point of obsession, and absolutely prepared for every task he undertook. But his dark side uniquely set him apart from the rest. He was deceptive, untrustworthy, and absolutely ruthless, with an ends-justifies-the-means philosophy for just about every challenge he encountered. Power and status were the ultimate objectives of his career, and to achieve them, he had evolved into the consummate political animal. He had moles and other connections extending from the state legislature and the Governor's office to the local bench and key committee chairmanships of the Los Angeles County Bar Association – of which he was a former president. Largely through well-placed political contributions, not only was he the first to learn of prospective judicial appointments, but he also enjoyed a direct pipeline to the Governor himself, who frequently solicited Gillingham's input before making a selection.

Over the past several years, principally through the efforts of Ray Gillingham, Barry, Klein & Nance had become a major player in state and local politics, a fact not lost on most trial and appellate court judges in the state. At year's end, he would finally be considered for senior partner, with a likely change in the name of the firm that had remained the same for the past 17 years. Beyond his political influence, Gillingham took the greatest pride in the extensive resume he maintained for anyone and everyone who had or might have some association with Barry, Klein & Nance. His computer was stuffed with a variety of facts and rumors – much of a tabloid nature, both publicized and confidential – on clients, judges, politicians, lawyers – including those within the firm – and just about anyone else who might prove useful to Gillingham. An absolute priority on his list of musts was to be the first with the news, especially when dirt was about to be thrown on someone's job, career, or reputation. Ray Gillingham always carried a big stick – but he rarely walked softly.

"What's your point?" Harry sounded less recalcitrant, now aware that *he* was the unfortunate dupe.

"My final word on the subject – sit down, Harry." He again smiled, but there was an unsettling calm to Gillingham's voice. He was like a lion slowly circling his prey, waiting for the initial show of weakness. Watching others submit to his demands was one of life's great highs, and it was all the more gratifying when it followed a contest of will. But he had to avoid histrionics and displays of anger. It was only when a few calm and carefully chosen words brought an opponent to his knees that he reached his greatest exhilaration.

As a final act of defiance, Harry sat down in the brass-buttoned chair with Gillingham's coat and leaned back to ensure it would be well-pressed. He crossed his legs and glared back at his host.

"I understand your friend is back in town," began Gillingham, not about to reveal any reaction to the maltreatment of his favorite suit.

"I have many friends."

"Debatable, but we both know who we are talking about."

"Not in the slightest."

"Mitchell Redden, of course."

"Oh, Mitch! Well, I'll be damned. So he's really back, huh?"

"When did he open his doors?"

"Beats me. Maybe you oughta give him a call."

Gillingham began reading from the dossier. "'Blaylock, Harry Leonard. Born 58 years ago in Greenfield, Indiana. Attended Southwestern Law. Nights. Took 5 years to complete. Passed the California State Bar Exam. Four attempts.' And…let me get to some of the more interesting details," he added, following his finger down the page. "Oh yeah… 'Suspended from the practice of law. Nineteen years ago. Misappropriation of client funds.'" Gillingham shook his head disapprovingly. "Dipping into the ol' trust account, huh. Now I understand how you built up that stock portfolio. Let's see… 'Suspension lifted five years later.' Then there's something about a criminal conviction for forgery, 9 months in County – a good criminal lawyer – probation, and so forth. Shall I continue?"

"Five weeks ago," said Blaylock, grudgingly.

Gillingham stood, poured himself a small amount of cognac into a snifter, and swirled it around several times under a discriminating nose. He then took a sip and stared intently down at Harry. It was his way of demonstrating that he – and he alone – would control the pace of the discussion. Like Mitchell Redden, Gillingham had not set foot inside a courtroom for the past few years, but for entirely different reasons. The power game was played from business offices and conference rooms, not through the time-consuming ordeal of a jury trial. Yet he had a presence about him, both in word and manner, which could be intimidating whenever he wished it. And that was exactly what he was after at the moment.

"Enough of the games," proclaimed Gillingham. "Where has he been?"

"Away. For the past three years in Hawaii. Holed up in some run-down beach house on the island of Kauai. Before that, he took a tour of the world. That's all I know," said Harry with resignation. "He didn't exactly keep in touch."

"Why is he here? What brought him back to Los Angeles?"

"I guess I did."

"Explain," demanded Gillingham. His face was square and blunt, and his forehead ran halfway to the back of his scalp. His jaws, full and unresisting gravity, were like the jowls of a bulldog – which had earned him that distinctive appellation around the office, though never to his face.

Harry was half-tempted to growl at him but considered it ill-advised. Instead, he merely offered, "I tracked him down. Took almost a week. Then we talked." He hesitated, feeling as if he was breaching a confidence. "He, uh…wanted nothing to do with practicing law. He said he was finished."

"And you talked him out of retirement?"

"You might say that."

Suddenly, Gillingham threw his head back and heaved with laughter. For a good minute, he enjoyed himself and then smiled, "A private joke. At the appropriate time, I'll share it with you."

"No need," said Harry, pulling himself out of the chair. "But now that you've had your laugh, I'll be on my way."

"I'm not through," stated Gillingham, no longer sporting the smile. Harry stood motionless and simmered. "How did you pull it off? How could someone with your obvious deficiencies talk Mitchell Redden out of a committed retirement?"

"I guess I'm gifted."

"You're playing Russian roulette, Harry…and you just might be in the wrong chamber." The words had their desired chilling effect on Blaylock. "You had to have something – a piece of information, a hold, something he couldn't fight. I want to know what it is."

"I'll tell you what it is," said Harry. "It's *friendship*, you bastard. Something you'll never have or even comprehend." He paused, and his eyes fell to the floor. "I couldn't cut it anymore. Clients were down to a trickle, and my overhead was eating me alive. I simply asked him for help." Harry fixed his eyes again on Gillingham. "I told him I needed him."

"How touching. Just one final question. How far is Redden taking this…this new career? I want to know his intentions, everything he has told you, every detail, where he is going with this."

Harry shook his head. "No way," he said. He began walking to the door – then added over his shoulder, "Do what you want with your legal profile. I'm outta here."

With a confident air, Gillingham inspected his cigar again and shouted out, "Word is that one of the local papers is doing a where-are-they-now story on some interesting legal screw-ups of the past."

Harry stopped at the door but refused to turn.

Gillingham continued. "I guess 14 years is not so long that everyone has forgotten. Given a little cooperation here, I might be persuaded to place a call and kill the story."

Gillingham now had Harry's full attention, who turned and said, "You're full of shit. There is no such story floating around, and we both know it."

"Perhaps not, but there *will* be."

The vice was tightening on Harry, and with it, all of his energy to resist. He took a step toward Gillingham as if to emphasize his point of view. "Not even *you* have the power to force a newspaper to violate one's right to privacy. Fourteen years is too long. If one word is printed about Harry Blaylock, I'll own the fucking newspaper and everyone else involved with this blackmail."

Gillingham eased himself down into his chair. He reclined and gnawed a couple of times on the end of his cigar. It was never lit and was used as a pacifier. It had been four and a half months since his last cigarette. "Mr. Blaylock, you're threatening me," he smiled.

"I'm telling you that a newspaper would never write such a story."

"Harry, you should know by now I always cover my bets. Past criminal activities are only protected by the right to privacy when the activities are no longer newsworthy. And that means the perpetrator must be rehabilitated. Check out *Briscoe versus Reader's Digest*. You'll find it good reading."

"Fourteen years, and I've served my time. Nine months in the county and five years away from the bar. Not so much as a complaint since I was reinstated. I would say I qualify as rehabilitated."

"Harry, Harry, Harry," said Gillingham, shaking his head. "That simply isn't true, and I *know* we can both agree on that."

Harry's head hung in full defeat. There indeed was one other matter, something more recent. He had not forgotten the incident, of course – only that Chester Raymond Gillingham III had been a beneficiary of the news. For the first time, he found himself at the mercy of the bulldog – and painfully unloaded what he knew about Mitchell Redden's planned agenda.

⚫

CHAPTER 7

Tuesday, August 4

The Chevrolet Monte Carlo rattled to a stop at the curb. Demonstrating a mind of its own, the engine continued to kick over several times, defying the fact that the ignition had been turned off and the key had been removed and held in the hand of its driver. Alicia Wexler was steaming. She had been after her husband for weeks to take the old tank in for a tune-up. Now, she had to sit there in utter embarrassment while the engine ran its course and then finally died.

She turned to her passenger with a sardonic grin. "You're in need of a car – why don't you take this one?"

Niki Burroughs just smiled. She had other matters on her mind.

"Really." insisted Alicia, not quite sure if she was truly joking. "Take the damn thing. Better yet, I'll pay you. That's it. I'll pay you five hundred bucks; all you have to do is take the title and keep the thing out of my sight for the rest of my life."

Niki shook her head, "No thanks." Up to this point, she had resisted viewing her small three-bedroom home. It had not been touched in almost three weeks. "No, I think I've got all I can handle," she said as she inspected her front lawn for the first time. The grass, overgrown to the point of being shaggy, was blanketed with an array of leaves. Hundreds of green, brown, and golden leaves lay scattered indiscriminately across the lawn. Dirt, debris, and more leaves covered the walkway to her front door. Only the entrance porch seemed to rise above it all and offer an escape from the sea of neglect.

She had missed the payment to her gardener – a good two weeks before the accident – and he had quit without notice while she was hospitalized. Alicia had broken it to her only the day before their discharge. She hadn't wanted to upset Niki until she had her strength back. Great timing. The bastard, he just couldn't wait. But then, that was the pattern, wasn't it? Men running away. Niki hadn't held a boyfriend longer than 9 months since her divorce. Of course, she was always falling behind on payments. Maybe the gardener had just reached his limit.

"Let's go!" urged Randy from the back seat.

No sooner had Niki opened the door than Randy sprung out like a racehorse at a starting gate. Not even the encumbrances of crutches and a missing prosthesis were about to slow him down. "Yeah!" he screamed as he sent leaves flying, swinging his leg pendulum-style, plowing a trail to his front door. By the time Alicia grabbed the two small suitcases from the trunk, Randy was anxiously waiting on the porch for someone to open the door. "C'mon, Mommy, hurry," he urged.

"Be right there, Honey," she said, not sharing in her son's excitement. Niki stood with crutches of her own, her left leg and arm still in a cast. While most of the facial swelling had subsided, residual bruises were still quite evident, as were the scabs and scarring across the forehead. She stared apprehensively at the front door, not looking forward to what awaited inside.

"It's gonna be alright," assured Alicia. "Really. We'll have the place cleaned up in a few hours, and Frank will take care of your yard when he gets home from work." It had been their plan to have it raked and mowed shortly before Niki's arrival, but her discharge had caught them somewhat by surprise, and they had been burdened by an array of their own time-consuming chores.

Niki offered no reply or acknowledgment. She simply fixed her eyes on the door and began pushing herself along the pathway blazed by her son. Alicia followed until they reached the porch. They took a key from Niki, unlocked the door, and swung it open.

Randy was the first one to enter. "Eeeau!" he screamed out as the odor reached them from the kitchen. "Gross!" Always the investigator, Randy rushed into the kitchen and began inspecting the source of the smell. The breakfast dishes of three weeks earlier lay in and about the kitchen sink. The previously identifiable food had been replaced by a green fuzzy mold and an army of ants trailing from the sink, along the counter, down to the floor, and out through the bottom of the door to the garage. It appeared that every ant in the neighborhood had been called in for the feast. Niki followed her son, took in the view, and then continued with the rest of her tour as Alicia waited in the living room.

The remainder of the house was also in disarray. Beds were unmade, and clothes were strewn about – in both of their bedrooms. A towel and bathmat were in a pile on the bathroom floor. And on the sink counter was an open tube of lipstick, a mascara case, a can of hairspray, underarm deodorant, a toothbrush and tube of toothpaste, and a curling iron – still plugged into the wall outlet. "Damn it!" she exclaimed as she gave the cord a hard tug. Her electric bill was about to take a turn for the better. Back in the living room, toys were all about the floor, and Randy had already found a small tank and was putting it through maneuvers.

Niki eased herself into an over-stuffed chair and hoisted her leg onto the matching ottoman. On the table next to her sat a vase with dead flowers. She ran her fingers through a layer of dust on the table. For a moment, she examined the accumulated dirt on a fingertip, and tears began to well in her eyes. Alicia had deposited the two suitcases in Niki's bedroom and now approached her next-door neighbor.

"I know you're down, Niki, but it's gonna be alright."

Niki shook her head. "No, it's not."

"Hey, c'mon. We'll have this place squeaky clean inside of two hours." Alicia tried forcing a smile, but it didn't come easily. The room was heavy with depression.

"It's not the dirt, Ali."

"Then what is it?"

Niki only shook her head.

"Talk to me, Niki. C'mon. What's going on in that pretty head of yours?" Alicia sat down on the floor, pulled her knees up to her chest, and drew herself closer. Now, Niki was looking down at her.

"Nothing ever turns out right, does it?" Niki's question was rhetorical, but subconsciously, she wanted to be talked out of the thought. The light of hope was still burning inside, just flickering but still there. "Really, Ali, this is a pretty shitty world when you get right down and think about it."

Alicia could only offer a shrug and a bewildered furrowing of her brow.

Niki's eyes drifted away. She was waxing philosophical, and it mattered little who was around to hear her. "I mean, sure, there are good days here and there. Even the cursed get a few crumbs now and then. But just dare allow yourself to catch a moment's breath – and wham, something bad reaches out and pulls you right back." Niki inspected the dust on her finger and painted it across her otherwise white and clean cast. "I'm not a negative person, you know. Sure, I'm a little bitter, but I don't dwell on my losses. It's just that I can't remember a day that wasn't all uphill."

To Alicia, the brief interlude of reflection was both discomforting and intriguing. Niki Burroughs had never been open about her life before her arrival in the neighborhood. She knew about Niki's unsuccessful marriage to Scott and her infirm widowed father but little else. At times, a revealing fact would seep into their conversations, though the revelations seemed to be more on a need-to-know basis than a desire to open up to her neighbor.

Though they were the best of friends, in many ways, Alicia was as much an outsider as a stranger casually passing by their homes on the sidewalk. A few days went by when the two of them did not see one another. Yet they coexisted on a superficial plain, never exploring confidentialities and the feelings behind them. At the moment, Niki was giving a dissertation of some depth, and Alicia shied from any comment for fear of breaking the spell.

"There was a time, Ali. Seems like a hundred years ago. Life was a little bit kinder." Niki was a thousand miles away. "My mother was a stabilizing force in my life, all of ours, really. Steve was the pusher, always working. 'Got to provide,'" she said in a deeper voice, thick with accent. "That's what he would say, 'Got to provide.' But Mamma, she would keep him on track. If he was not home by seven, he would not get dinner. We would eat. The two of us. Right on time. Then everything else went right into the garbage." Niki smiled at the memory. "I mean, *nothing* from dinner would be left. Steve would come dragging in at some late hour, and all he would find was a bunch of shiny, clean dishes with no dinner. And it wasn't easy for Mamma, you know. We didn't have a lot, and throwing away good food was a definite sacrifice. But it was her way of making a statement. Steve was stubborn and would always do things his own way. He was the head of the family and knew best. The macho shit, you know. But when it came to his stomach, Momma had him right by the balls. I'll tell you, it was a rare night when Steve would come home after seven."

She closed her eyes as if a medium were reaching out for some departed spirit. But rather than embarking on a séance, Niki was bridging time, focusing on days left untouched by memory. Never one to look back, she had severed all ties with her distant past, the early years when life had a different perspective fostered by the innocence of youth and the affection of a loving mother. She had found that visits to those days only brought on pain of their loss and burdened her resolve and drive.

"After dinner, we would sit around and talk. The three of us. Some nights, Pappa would sit back in his easy chair and light a pipe. You know…those were the best nights of all." Niki was now laying herself bare. It was also the first time Alicia had ever heard her refer to Steve as "Pappa." A tear escaped Niki's closed eyelid and slid down her cheek. "He had this silly old pipe, all scratched and stained, with a bowl so caked with ashes and nicotine that you could barely stick a pencil in it." She smiled with fondness. "Quite disgusting, really. But that old pipe was just loaded with stories. All about Greece, of course. And between Mamma and I, we could never figure out just where fact would end, and fiction took over. But it really didn't matter. I'd be curled up at his feet on the carpet, questioning the accuracy of the latest escapade of this incredible Greek boy, who we always assumed was Pappa, though he would never say. And then he would look down at me…"

Niki's eyes suddenly popped open, and her narration stopped. With the speed of light, the past became present, and dreams became reality. Her eyes drifted down to Alicia, who had assumed Niki's role on the floor and Niki her father's in the chair - unwittingly re-creating a time etched deep in her memory. And for a moment that seemed to suspend time, Niki sat agape, reaching for the sense of what had just taken place. Then, just as quickly, her eyes flushed with tears, and she pleaded, "Why did she have to die, Ali? Why? Why did she leave us that way? It just wasn't fair!"

"What way, Niki? How did she die?"

Niki's response was only a shake of the head.

"How did your mother die?" The follow-up was expressed weakly, with little expectation of a reply. History had taught Alicia that when her next-door neighbor withdrew from a discussion, it was a closed issue.

"My headache is back," said Niki. Though she was staring down at Alicia, there was again a distance in her gaze. "Could I impose on you one more time?"

Alicia exhaled her frustration and said, "Sure, Niki. What ya need?"

"Water…a glass of water would be wonderful."

It wasn't a minute, and Alicia was back with the water. Niki had not moved, nor had her empty eyes disengaged from their fix on the floor. She looked up at Alicia almost mechanically.

"Thanks, Ali," she said.

She fumbled for a moment in her purse, found the bottle, performed her ritual of dexterity, and then popped three pills in her mouth and followed it by downing almost half the glass of water. "Now I wait," she added with a forced smile.

"When are you going to do something about those headaches?" Since Niki and her young child had moved in almost two and a half years earlier, Alicia had noted her ever-increasing dependence on the small blue tablets. What had started out as a couple of pills once or twice a day had evolved into a frequent scene of Niki throwing three of them in her mouth virtually every time they found themselves together.

Niki shrugged. "Just one more thing that has plagued me most of my life. Thank God for my pills," she said, holding up the blue-and-gold-labeled bottle as if proclaiming it the wonder drug of the ages. "Aspirin won't touch my headaches, and they eat away at my stomach. But not my babies."

"C'mon, Niki. Don't you think you should get to the bottom of this? Your headaches seem to be getting worse."

"My headaches are the product of a stressful life. The day my stress ends, so will my headaches."

"You can't know that."

"I know that three years ago, my doctor ran a battery of tests and found nothing."

"Nothing?"

"Nothing. Not even a brain."

"You and the scarecrow. I could have made that diagnosis myself."

"See, all I need to do is find the Wizard, and everything will be fixed."

It did not escape Alicia that their banter had drawn them away from their original topic of conversation. "I don't believe you," she announced.

"You don't believe what?"

"I don't believe you had a battery of tests three years ago, or ever. You don't believe in doctors."

"Sure I do."

"No, you don't. You don't trust them, and you don't need them. You've told me that a thousand times. The only reason you were in a hospital is because you were taken there by ambulance – and probably against your will. So don't give me this shit about a battery of tests."

Niki considered the observation and the demonstrative nature of her neighbor. Alicia Wexler was petite, short, and spunky, a pixie of a figure who was frequently given to blasts of verbiage at a machine-gun pace, arms waving, exploding with enthusiasm, as if to compensate for her diminutive stature. She was a shade over five foot one and tipped the scales at 97 pounds. Her blonde hair was cropped short, which hugged her slender face with individual tufts that casually curled in a way that added to her elfish appearance. With her long and lanky husband, they cut quite a contrast as the classical Mutt and Jeff couple. She was also a devoted friend who was always there. Following the hospitalization, Alicia stopped the newspaper and had been picking up Niki's mail and delivering it to her at the hospital. And not once had she failed in her vigil of daily visits.

"So, you think you have me figured out," said Niki, a smile ever-so-slightly emerging.

"Oh, Christ no!" said Alicia, flinging her hands. "That challenge would have sent Freud off like a babbling idiot. What I do know is that you're as stubborn as a mule and wouldn't call a doctor if you were on your deathbed. So, stop pulling my chain."

The smile was now prominent. "Okay, Ali. But I *would* have had a battery of tests three years ago if I had been blessed with a little bit of time."

"Well, old friend," said Alicia, jabbing a finger at the two left-sided casts, "let me break it to you gently. Time is gonna be an abundant commodity around this household for the next month or two."

"I'll look into it, I promise," assured Niki.

"Sure you will," responded Alicia with absolute skepticism. "But right now, I've got to go check on the kids." She leaned over and gave Niki a hug, assured her that she would be back in fifteen minutes to tear into the mess, and then rushed out the door.

Through the screen door that had just slammed shut, Niki could make out Alicia's figure rapidly disappearing through an opening in the hedge that separated their two lawns. One minute she was there; the next, she was gone. Alicia never walked. She flitted. And though, her perpetual motion was unsettling at times, at the moment, Niki felt uplifted. Enthusiasm had a way of rubbing off.

Alone with her thoughts, she began to ruminate about her circumstances. After all, they had both survived a near-fatal accident and were now out of the hospital. Escrow was about to close on two small homes she had sold shortly before the accident – meaning payday. Enough to keep her going for the two months she predicted she'd be out of circulation. Any necessary shopping or running around would be covered by Ali – a further imposition, though one she would make up for when she got back on her feet. And yes, time would indeed be available. Maybe, just maybe, it might give her the opportunity to bring some sanity into her life, to take inventory of where she was at and where she was going. Finally, there was the lawsuit. It singularly represented the most meaningful hope for a happy future. Maybe things were not quite as shitty as they first seemed, after all.

On the table in the adjoining dining room sat a neat stack of the day's mail, exactly where it had been deposited by Alicia. Niki was suddenly inspired. She pulled herself up from the chair and struggled with her crutch across the room, adeptly sidestepping a couple of toys in the process. She sat down at the dining room table and began sorting through the mail. Nothing, however, proved of any interest to her. Twelve pieces equated to 7 bills and five advertisements addressed to "Resident." None got opened.

Motivated to expend some energy but not yet prepared to take on the bills, her eyes drifted to the other end of the table. An edition of the *Los Angeles Times* sat neatly folded, inviting any interested party to bone up on the news of the world. Had it only been three weeks, or had she been absent for months? It came to her at this moment that, in a somewhat deepened state of depression, she had shut off contact with the outside world. No TV and no newspapers. Not even an old copy of the *National Enquirer* had found its way into her room. Other than laying there feeling sorry for herself and conversing with Randy, her time had been pretty much taken up with four or five paperback novels.

Suddenly, she was overwhelmed with a hunger to bring things up to speed. If she had been presented with the opportunity to reorganize her life, it had to start with acquainting herself with what was going on. She reached over and pulled the paper in front of her.

What she saw gave her a start.

At the top of the front page, just below the title of the paper, was the date, "Saturday, July 11." It had not been Alicia, ever considerate and insightful, who had placed the newspaper there for her reading pleasure. It had been Niki herself, only moments before her rush out the door on that fateful day. And there it sat as if suspended in time, ready to present the news of that date no differently than if the morning of July 11th had only started just thirty minutes earlier with a shower and a hot cup of coffee.

A prominent article on the front page identified the ongoing battle between Israel and the Palestinians. Another piece on the same page explored the relationship between Western journalists and the dangers facing local Muslims assisting them in the Middle East. Neither captured her attention.

She flipped through a couple of pages and noted a story describing Hezbollah's power in Lebanon and a political force to be reckoned with. Again, no interest. Everywhere she looked, there seemed to be a story about violence, death, and destruction throughout the world. North Korea was developing nuclear weapons. Iran was again committed to continuing with its enrichment of nuclear material. At times, it seemed to Niki that the world's leaders saw violence, or its threat, as the only efficient means of overcoming their national challenges. Was the world insane?

She continued to turn the pages, perusing each small headline, browsing for a story of interest and finding none. With each succeeding page, her enthusiasm continued to wane. Each article was either a visit to another tragedy, boring or irrelevant to the future course of her life. And after all, it was stale news anyway.

Then, a small headline leaped out at her as if it had been suddenly illuminated: "HEADACHE PILL LINKED TO BIRTH DEFECTS."

Niki simultaneously found herself drawn to the story and terrified at what she might encounter. She now found it absolutely incredulous that she had never drawn a possible relationship between the deformity borne by the boy crawling about her living room and the pills she had been swallowing since shortly after puberty. Not even once had the thought touched her consciousness. Yet there it was in black and white. Headache pills and birth defects: two realities that had consumed her life over the past six years. Reluctantly, she began to read.

> "A strong association has been found between the maternal use of phenylpropylene and limb-reduction congenital malformations. So reports the New England Journal of Medicine following a

two-year study sponsored by the National Institutes of Health. The drug, used by hundreds of thousands as a headache medication over the past 12 years, was found to have a three-fold increased risk for infants born without all or a portion of one or more extremities when compared to women taking placebos. Representative Virgil Ritner, chairman of the House Government Operations Committee's Subcommittee on Inner-governmental Relations and Human Resources, demanded an immediate investigation…"

Niki dropped the paper and found her heart pounding in her throat. Across the small living room, sitting on the dusty lamp table, stood her colorful bottle of Phenatol. She rose, knowing what she would find but hoping against the odds. She stepped forward, and pain instantly shot through her leg, causing her to almost collapse and catch herself against the wall. She had forgotten her cane.

But she was not about to go back for it, so she placed her weight on her right foot and tried hopping in the direction of the chair and table. Her lower lip trembled, and she uttered in a barely audible voice, "No." With the fifth hop, she lost her balance and stumbled forward, breaking her fall with the cushioned ottoman. "No," she said again, slightly louder. She crawled over it and reached out for the bottle, sensing neither Randy's pain not eyes as he stared at the inexplicable acrobatics being performed by his mother. Extended across the ottoman and her easy chair, Niki anxiously read the label.

The principal ingredient was given as phenylpropylene .

Her hand slowly dropped away, clutching the Phenatol, as she met the perplexed eyes of the boy with half a right leg. The anguish of guilt was now overwhelming as she began to shake her head in denial of the obvious. "No, no, no," she cried, then let go with a shrieking, "Nooooo!" and flung the bottle across the room, spraying bright blue tablets out of the capless container. A dam of tears let go, and she began to convulse with uncontrollable sobbing.

"Mommy, what's wrong?"

The inquiry of the now-frightened boy went unheeded.

"Mommy…?"

Unable to summon a reply, Niki brought herself upright on the ottoman and extended an inviting arm to Randy. He crawled over to his mother with tears streaking down his cheek, though he did not understand why. As he reached her, she leaned over and clutched him.

"Oh God, forgive me," she said.

It was an impassioned plea, yet something she would never extend to herself – something she would carry to her deathbed.

CHAPTER 8

Monday, August 10

With two casts and a crutch and a six-year-old boy doing little better, Niki struggled through the entrance door to Mitchell Redden's reception room. Twice, her arm cast thudded against the door, and after holding it open for Randy, the large paneled barrier sought its revenge on the tip of her crutch as Niki was a little slow in bringing it in after her. She cursed at her handicap, this time not caring who might overhear, not even Randy. She then instructed him to grab a seat and a big magazine with pictures and hobbled over to the open reception window.

When it came to pumping work out of a computer, Mary Ellen Dovinowitz was a magician with few peers. When typing from dictation through a set of small earphones, her eyes would fix on the screen with hypnotic intensity. So deep was her concentration that Redden frequently found himself yelling out to grab a moment of her attention. On one very frustrating day, he had even reached across and turned off the transcribing unit. Yet it was her hands that showcased her talent. They glided across the keyboard with such quickness and grace that the muted clicking of the keys seemed to run together like the patter of rain. When she hit her pace, she was on a high. Operator and machine would become one, and Mary Ellen Dovinowitz would depart into her own special world.

Niki stood and stared for a lengthy moment, more surprised at going unnoticed after her clamorous entry than to marvel at the obvious skill of the secretary/receptionist.

"Excuse me," she announced.

Still, she went unnoticed.

"Hello!" Niki anxiously added, this time leaning over the counter and waving a hand as if to hail a cab.

This finally captured Mary Ellen's attention, who instantly stopped and pulled off her earphones. "Answers to interrogatories," she shrugged as if this would explain her preoccupation. "Can you imagine? Two hours of typing a client's answers to stupid interrogatories and I'm off in Never-Never Land. Quite a statement, huh?"

Niki nodded her head, not knowing how to respond and not having the foggiest idea of what she was talking about. "I'm here to see Mr. Redden," she said with a hint of uncertainty.

"Of course. Mrs. Burroughs, right?"

"*Ms.* Burroughs," Niki corrected.

Mary Ellen rose from her chair and faced Niki. "Duly noted," she said with an approving smile. "And I'll not make that mistake again." She found Niki's name in an open appointment book and entered the title above it in bold letters. The respect for the client was instantaneous. "Please have a seat, and I'll let Mr. Redden know you are here. He shouldn't be too long."

With the same deliberate gait, Niki joined Randy on a large couch and eased herself down next to him.

Behind the reception counter, Mary Ellen could be seen placing a call on the intercom, presumably to Mitchell Redden. Niki gave her a quick once-over for the first time. She appeared older, perhaps 48, yet attractive with aristocratic features. She had the high cheekbones and slender nose of a high-priced model set against striking pale blue eyes. Her posture and grace of movement added to her sophistication to the point where she seemed almost misplaced behind a secretary's desk.

Yet there was a sense of sadness about her. Mary Ellen's hair was obviously dyed, one or two shades too dark, and styled for a younger woman. Her makeup was also somewhat excessive, adding artificiality to her otherwise engaging appearance. She was a woman past her prime, refusing to give in and age more gracefully. No doubt a stunning lady ten years earlier, Mary Ellen Dovinowitz was clinging to her past, certainly in dress and possibly in social life as well. Perhaps what tugged at Niki's heart was that she was peering at a vision of herself 20 years into the future, a lonely, aging woman. She indiscriminately grabbed a magazine and jumped into the first article that drew her attention.

Twenty minutes later, Redden was buzzed over the intercom. "Hey, you've got a client out here," said Mary Ellen, her voice barely heard. "Anything you want me to tell her?"

Redden leaned back in his chair, considering his limited options. Mary Ellen always knew when waits began to shift from expected professional delays to irritating impositions. "Yeah, uh…just say I got tied up on a lengthy call, and I'll be with her in a minute."

"Oh, that's creative," she needled and then broke off the call. She was always rescuing Redden, even when his career was in full swing. Although he exhaustively prepared for his trials, Redden was never one to focus on the day-to-day problems of running a law office – that was left to Mary Ellen. She also had more knowledge of legal procedures and street savvy than most lawyers gained in their first 5 years in the business. It was little wonder that she was the first one Redden went after when he made the decision to reopen his doors.

The phone call that morning had been unsettling. Perhaps that was why he had delayed the interview, even though he did little more than stare at a blank legal tablet on an uncluttered desk. "It involves the cause of Randy's defect," Niki had shared, "why he doesn't have a leg." When he had pressed for more details, she had put him off. She had preferred to discuss it at his office. He then had reluctantly consented to the meeting. Yet he had a sense of where it was all going. He had represented clients before in drug product liability cases. One of them had suffered from tragic birth defects, and most of the lawsuits had ended with mixed results. Redden knew quite well what he'd be facing and the problems it would create. He reluctantly stood, stared one more time at the legal pad, and then went out to meet Niki Burroughs and her young son.

After greeting the two of them and a short chit-chat with Randy, Redden returned to his office with his new client, leaving the boy under the watchful eye of Mary Ellen. This was Niki's idea, and Redden could not have been happier with the decision. He was quite aware of what had to be done and how the interview would likely end.

As Niki entered, she noted, somewhat expectedly, the informality of the office. A volleyball lay conveniently in the corner, next to Redden's desk, and through a partially opened closet door, she could glimpse a surfboard. Several surfing photos were displayed on a paneled wall, including a few of Redden. As before, his dress was casual. This time, however, she avoided commentary.

Redden assisted Niki into one of the two client chairs and returned to his seat across the desk. But as he was about to launch into his opening comments, he caught himself. Niki's crutch lay against the arm of her chair. Her face, though clearly on the mend, still carried the battle scars he had seen earlier. Yet she sat erect, resolute, assertive, with one arm extended over the desk. In her hand, she held a clipped-out newspaper article. "Read it," she requested. "I would like you to read this before we talk."

Without comment, he took it from her and spent a couple minutes perusing its contents. When he was through, he looked up and nodded pensively. "Interesting reading," he noted.

"I have been eating this stuff since I was fourteen," she said.

"You're suggesting that this phenyl…pro…propa…lane is somehow related to Randy's leg defect?" The stumbling was designed to distance him from any level of expertise with drug cases. "I just don't see it," he added.

"You just don't see it! Two and two doesn't add up to four anymore?" Niki whipped the now-empty bottle of Phenatol out of her purse and placed it on the desk. "Phenatol contains phenylpropalane. It's loaded with the stuff. I consumed it daily throughout my pregnancy with

Randy. It causes limb-reduction defects, and my baby was born with a limb-reduction defect in his right leg. How could you possibly not see it?"

Redden stared at Niki, still uncertain how he was going to justify not exploring the merits of the case. Without a word, he reached over, picked up the bottle, and began to read its label.Slowly rotating the bottle, he analyzed each word, looking for an out – something, anything, to comfortably send her on her way.

And there, at the bottom of the label, he found his escape route.

"I'm sorry," he said, shaking his head. "But I can't take this any further."

"Well, why not? What can there possibly be on that label…"

"Brookhurst Pharmaceuticals," he interrupted. "Phenatol is manufactured by Brookhurst Pharmaceuticals."

"So…"

"Brookhurst was and is a client of Barry, Klein, and Nance, a firm I used to work for a few years back. There'd be a conflict of interest, a violation of the Rules of Professional Conduct. I'd risk a suspension, maybe even disbarment."

"Then I'll give up my rights. I'll sign a waiver, just like we do in real estate."

"I would also need one from Brookhurst, which is as likely to happen as Brookhurst accepting the results of this study. Ain't gonna happen," he added with casual finality.

"I…I can't accept this."

"You'll have to."

"No, there's got to be another way, some way around this."

There was, but Redden was not about to give it to her. He was now back on his feet, shaking his head at the floor. "Niki, you have no idea. These lawsuits are near-impossible to win." He now found her eyes. They were afire with determination. "It's a battle of experts," he continued, knowing his quest was a hopeless cause, "with the pharmaceutical company holding all the chips. They have access to the finest scientists from around the world and provide most of them with the grants and aid needed to support their research."

Redden began to pace back and forth, staring at Niki as if she was a juror. "Their wealth is incomprehensible, and they use it to attract not only the top scientists but also the best legal talent around. Then there's the nature of the litigation itself. It's complex, time-consuming and expensive. Drug product cases, all of them, involve, at a minimum, a journey through a mountain of scientific papers, charts, graphs, articles, statistics, letters, memos, and numerous other confusing and esoteric documents, sometimes numbering over one hundred thousand pages, all to review, digest and comprehend. Then there's the FDA, with its multitude of regulations. 'Look,' they will say, 'we have the FDA stamp of approval. We have researched our drug for years and spent millions to evaluate its safety. The FDA, after being provided with every page of our research documents, is convinced that the drug poses no risk beyond what is listed on our labeling.' It's a convincing argument, Niki, and sells almost every jury that hears it." The words came almost as an outburst, sounding a bit like a pitch from a used car salesman pushing something he wasn't sold on himself.

Niki still sat defiantly. "You said *near*-impossible to win."

"You're not listening to me."

"Really, how could it be that difficult? We have the study. It says Phenatol causes birth defects – *limb-reduction* defects, I might add. It was sponsored by the National Institutes of Health. So how could it be that difficult?"

"Because for every study like the NIH paper, Brookhurst will point to five others that establish the drug's safety. This is not how you want to spend the next two or three years of your life. It's a dead end, Niki."

It is now Niki who is being frustrated. But she is not yet through. "Bare with me a moment," she said, struggling to her feet. "I'll be right back."

Within two minutes, she was back with Randy and sat him down in the other client chair – then immediately began removing his prosthesis. "When Randy was two, they had to amputate his right foot," she said while working on the straps. "It became necessary because the foot was useless, and the leg would better accommodate his prosthesis."

Redden was already aware of this but chose to remain silent. He would let Niki complete her presentation, as it would serve no purpose to cut her off. This time, she would not succeed in convincing him to make another injudicious decision.

Randy had been advised earlier that this event was likely to occur, but he was nevertheless uncomfortable about displaying his "problem." His mother had also insisted that he wear shorts rather than his preferred long trousers, another concession which he was forced to accept. "I know it will be embarrassing," she had acknowledged. "But unfortunately, it may be necessary. Just trust me on this. Someday, when you're older, you'll understand why this was necessary." Of course, what really sealed the deal for Randy was pizza at Chuck E. Cheese, a promised first stop after leaving Mitchell's office.

"Look at it!" Niki urged as she withdrew the device and displayed Randy's stump. "Look at it and tell me that this should go unpunished."

"Niki, I can understand your anger…"

"Can you? Can you really? Try walking around with the guilt, knowing that you spent nine months sticking pill after pill into your mouth while your little baby was inside you, trying to grow his little fingers and toes and feet and legs. Try living with the thought that rather than being the protector of this precious little being, you were throwing all of these drugs down your throat without once considering the consequences to your baby. Try looking at that handicap day after day, knowing that the only reason he will have to carry this burden for the rest of his life is because of something that *you* did. Just think about it, Mitch, think about it for one straight hour of the day, and then tell me you can understand my anger."

"You're right, Niki. Unless I personally experienced your plight, I could never fully comprehend the level of your suffering – nor your anger. I am not unsympathetic, believe me."

"But you still won't help me…"

Redden shook his head, still holding to his game plan. "No, it's not that I won't help you. It's that I *can't* help you. My hands are tied, as I explained."

"The conflict of interest…"

"That's right, the conflict. My hands are tied," he repeated.

"You're telling me," she persisted, "that it is beyond all of your ability to figure out a way around this? You're telling me that if you bothered to take a day or two to give this a lot of thought – which you are apparently unwilling to do – there is absolutely no possibility of coming up with some other option?"

Niki's fiery eyes were fixed on Redden, waiting for his response.

But unlike their meeting at the hospital, this time, Redden was just as committed to his course of action as Niki was to hers. "That is correct," he responded without hesitation.

Niki immediately began reattaching Randy's prosthesis. "Then I see no further reason to remain a client of this office. So, if you don't mind, I would like my file."

"Of course, but I will first need to have it duplicated. My secretary will mail it to you by the end of the day." This was not what Redden wanted. This woman and this child needed help, and he wanted to provide it. Indeed, it was what he had been trained for. If only he was at liberty to disclose the forces that had taken control of his life. No, it was not the conflict of interest that dictated walking away from this case. It was something much more complex and insidious. "Before you go," Redden offered, as Niki finished attaching the prosthesis, "I would like to provide you with some names, some very good trial lawyers who have experience in drug product liability."

Niki stood and assisted Randy to his feet as she pondered the offer. "No, I think not," she said. "I would like a clean break, and I am certain I will be able to find a very good lawyer on my own."

Redden nodded. "That, of course, is your choice."

"Yes, it is," acknowledged Niki. "And I'll not burden you again." With that final comment, the two of them hobbled over to the door and exited Redden's office.

As the door snapped shut, the lawyer in the casual clothes momentarily surveyed the two empty client chairs, mentally noting that they were symbolically reminding him that he again had no clients. Here he was, back to square one, as if the past two weeks had never existed. How easy it would be to walk out the door and fade again into an existence that had been his life for the past four years. "A never-ending vacation," he had described it. No stress, no obligations, no responsibilities, no deadlines, no schedules, no complications – only absolute freedom to do what he wanted, when he wanted. And Harry… well, Harry was welcome to use his office building rent-free. Redden would even extend a loan to bail him out of debt. And if he was never repaid, well, so what?

How easy it would be… if only the past two weeks had never occurred.

CHAPTER 9

Friday, September 18

It is Friday night, and Friday nights are spent getting acquainted with available young ladies at Ricardo's. Several weeks have passed since Niki and her son walked out the door, and Mitchell Redden's life is finally evolving into some sort of routine. He is again taking control – well, partially. No longer does he see himself as a twig being swept down a charging river. Now, he is treading water, waiting for the first opportunity to head for shore. He is again practicing law and has even signed up for a few small cases. Dating has also entered his life if one defined a weekend pickup at a singles bar as a date. It was the way he wanted it; no attachments and no complications. Freedom from involvement was essential. As Redden saw it, he had nothing to offer but a dubious future.

To regard Ricardo's as a singles bar would be to miss the intent and vision of its owner. If one were to ask Richard Smith what he did for a living, he would respond that he was the proprietor of a family restaurant, a place where home-style cooking and friendly faces were the order of the day. Yet this was only his vision. Few restaurants with high overhead survive on a food menu alone, and Ricardo's, plopped right in the middle of Redondo's King Harbor, was no exception. Expanding his bar and introducing live entertainment had infused new life into Smith's floundering business a few years earlier. It was the "weekend warriors" who had saved the day, he would confide to close friends – the singles crowd on Friday and Saturday nights and the boating set on Sundays, though it never set well with him that his cuisine could not survive on its own. Unlike The Watering Hole down the road, Ricardo's attracted an older group of followers, many of them coming off of unsuccessful marriages.

Outside, the sun was just setting on the horizon, silhouetting the boats in the marina below. Naked masts of sailing craft formed rows of pickets that seemed to fill all of King Harbor. Lights were beginning to illuminate a number of the cabins of various yachts as owners and guests discussed the day's events both on the decks of their crafts and the docks they were tied to. It was a scene that played out every day of the week and captured in full view through each large bay window at Ricardo's Restaurant and Lounge.

At the moment, Redden was staking his claim on a blonde who had seated herself next to him at the bar. She had arrived with her girlfriend about fifteen minutes earlier and had immediately launched into a discussion about college football. Her father had been a starting quarterback at UCLA until he blew out a knee in his junior year. As far back as she could remember, she had been fed a steady diet of football facts, figures, stories, and strategies – especially involving college ball. Within ten minutes, Redden was convinced that this gal knew more about football than Knute Rockne did in his prime. Since exchanging their names, he had been waiting for her to come up for air.

"So, I take it you like football?" Redden thought he'd slip in a little humor while his companion stopped to sip at a chardonnay. To be heard, he had to speak up. Between the live three-piece band and all the chatter, reading lips was almost a necessity.

"You're kidding, right?" She had a pretty face with deep blue eyes that widened as she gushed with enthusiasm. He guessed that she might be pushing thirty.

"Katie, is it?"

"Yeah, Katie Marshall."

"Katie, do I look like the kind of guy that would be pulling your leg?"

She smiled as she took a hard fix on his eyes. "Well, I had my hopes."

Redden digested the comment for a moment and then nodded. "That does present some interesting options."

Katie swung her legs down from the bar stool and stood next to Mitchell. "So…big decision. What's your best option? You gonna spend the whole night trying to go up the middle, which can be a big waste of time, or maybe…," she winked, "just take a chance and go for the touchdown." She then added, "Gotta go pee," and took off for the ladies' room.

Had that much changed in four years. or was this woman a true anomaly? Women were more aggressive these days – that much he knew. They wanted equal standing with men, which was reasonable, but many also disdained the chivalry of old and had no interest in traditional courtship. That belonged back to Mom and Dad, not to the modern-day woman. If she wanted something, she went after it. But this fast? Something told Redden that he might want to dig in his heels a bit.

As he sat on the bar stool, watching Katie disappear into the ladies' room, someone tapped him on the shoulder. "So it's blonde week, is it?" The unmistakable voice of Mary Ellen turned Redden around to come face-to-face with his secretary. This was no surprise as he sees her at Ricardo's frequently. "No, I don't discriminate," he said. "I'm an equal opportunity bachelor."

Mary Ellen shrugged as she watched the door to the ladies' room close. "Well, you can do better. I've seen her in here before. Comes in with her friend and leaves with a guy. Just in here to get laid." Nothing that interested Mitchell Redden ever met with Mary Ellen's approval, having more to do with her lengthy and well-hidden longing for Redden than his taste in women.

Redden took a sip from a light beer he had been nursing for the past half hour. "You could be right. But that description might cover half the people in this room, don't you think?"

"Fact is, I got a hot one on the line myself. Claims to own a boat in the harbor. Wants to show me his dingy. I told him to put it on display, and we'd see how he'd measure up. He laughed but assured me he was talking about a boat."

"Sounds like a good lead."

"Yeah. Probably married, but that's alright. If he's good in the sack, maybe I'll see him again." Mary Ellen always seemed to be testing Redden. Maybe one day, he would try to dissuade her from a life of promiscuity. "But what about her?" she asked, nodding back over her shoulder at the dance floor. "Which half does she fall into?" Mary Ellen was then off to the ladies' room herself.

Through the crowd, Redden spied Niki dancing with a young partner who seemed more preoccupied with his good fortune than keeping in step with the music. It was Niki, but not the same woman he had last seen over a month earlier. Gone are the leg cast and crutches, as well as the swollen and discolored face; a short flesh-toned cast on her left forearm was the only hint of the event that had brought their paths together. Gone also was the drab and loose-fitting wardrobe, replaced now by clothing designed more to entice and provoke, clinging and revealing what nature had blessed her with. Her hips, swaying with the slow-driving beat of the music, sensual, suggestive, are the focus of attention of several others around the room, men and women alike.

Katie returned from the restroom and spied Redden, inspecting the competition. She decided to avoid comment. "So, what do you think?" she asked, climbing back onto the bar stool. "Interested in a little game of football?"

"Sounds attractive."

Again, the smile. "You have no idea."

For what seemed the longest moment, the two of them just stared at one another as the music pounded rhythmically with the strobe lights across the room. She was attractive, no doubt about that, and her perfume had an allure that challenged his judgment, not to mention the "V" in her dress that revealed just the right amount of cleavage, all coalescing to solicit him off the bench and into the game. But something told Redden that it was all happening too fast, that he needed a time-out. She was exactly why he was there, yet it was just too easy.

Redden glanced over at Niki a couple of times, his interest – and curiosity – now stimulated. She had returned to her table alone. A couple other would-be suitors approached her but were turned away. Another song started, with more invitations and rejections. Redden decided to give it a shot himself if only to get a closer look and an answer to a few puzzling questions.

"Tell you what," he said to Katie. "I see a client of mine that I've been trying to reach for weeks." He nodded in the direction of Niki. "Just hold my seat, and I'll be right back." Redden was off before getting a reply, negotiating his way to the other side of the room.

"Life and its little surprises," said Redden as he approached her table. "Glad to see that you're on the mend."

Niki smiled, but only to be cordial. She had no intention of conveying either interest or desire for an extended conversation. "I'm getting there. One more cast to go."

"No, it's dramatic. You're looking…well, quite beautiful." Up close, he was even more taken by her attractiveness and was finding it difficult to conceal his interest.

"Thank you," said Niki, again being polite, but this time without a smile.

"Never seen you in here before."

"My first time."

"So then, what brings you to Ricardo's?"

Niki is looking up at Redden, yet there is coldness in her gaze. "A broken date. I was to meet him here at seven, but he bailed on me."

"The man's a fool."

"Said his boss dumped a big assignment on him at the last minute."

"He should've quit."

She nods. "Perhaps."

"But you came anyway."

"I had to eat."

Niki showed little inclination for chit-chat, and Redden ran out of subject matter. "Could I interest you in a dance?"

"No thanks. I'm sitting out a couple."

Having crashed and burned, Redden now seeks a comfortable way to disengage. "Well, just wanted to say hi. Maybe some other time," he offered as he stepped back from the table.

"Perhaps," was her final comment.

After weaving his way back to the bar, Redden was pleased to see that Katie was still hanging around. "So where were we?" he asked while reassuming his seat. He had a live one, so why waste his time on a Greek with issues, pretty though she might be. All she offered was an opportunity to further complicate his life.

"Football."

"Oh yeah, my favorite sport."

"So you up for the game?"

"You don't waste time, do you?"

"The more time I spend on recruiting, the less I have for playing the game. So what's it gonna be, big fella?"

He considered her proposition for a few moments, uncertain where he should go with it. "Tell you what," offered Redden. "Before I cozy up behind the center, I like to know my teammates. Maybe we could spend an hour or so getting better acquainted." Over Katie's shoulder, Redden could not help but notice that Niki was back on the dance floor. Perhaps she had changed her mind about sitting out a couple of dances. Perhaps – but then again, maybe it was nothing more than retaliation. He resolved to forget it.

Katie nodded and smiled. "Sounds like time well spent."

Over the next hour, Redden began to invest some effort in getting to know Katie. After all, she was his for the taking, and he vowed to get his horns trimmed if given the opportunity. Five months of celibacy had just been too long. He had even managed to pry a few personal details out of her – she was a divorced medical assistant with two pre-teen children – before she had launched again into football. Ohio State was the team to watch, so take the Buckeyes over Texas on Saturday and lay the points. Watch for Arkansas to bounce back after being blown out by USC. The Trojans were strong again, but they did not have the same offensive power and would not be in the running for the BCS. But watch Louisville this year. They're gonna surprise a lot of people…

"Hold on! Time out!" Redden pleaded, forming a "T" with his hands. "You have any interests outside of football?"

"That's a silly question," she smiled.

"Okay, beyond football and sex?"

"Sure do," she said, dragging Redden from the bar. In no time at all, they were out on the dance floor, bouncing with the rest of the crowd.

Dancing had never been one of Redden's strong suits. At slow speed, he could hold his own. He wasn't Fred Astaire, but he could avoid stepping on toes. It was when the music picked up tempo he began having problems. He was out of his element. He could fake it for a while, bobbing and weaving with the rest of the crowd; then, he would invariably find himself out of beat – and a source of amusement for his partner. Yet, at the moment, he was holding his own. He had actually found a rhythm and was keeping up with the music. He even began to throw in a few creative movements here and there, taking cues from others on the floor; an extra spin, a gyrating hip, arms thrown in the air. He was now seeing himself as a star in the remake of *Saturday Night Fever*.

Then *she* danced onto the floor – literally.

Niki was in dance mode from the moment she placed her foot onto the flooring, as she spun with both hands in the air and began to drive her hips sideways at her partner, who likewise appeared skilled at the art and answered with reciprocating movements of his own. And if this was not intended to be a grand entrance, it certainly had that effect. The new couple on the floor became the center of attention as if two dance instructors had been unleashed to show how it was done. Other couples – including Mitchell and Katie – continued their own feeble efforts while taking in the performance of the evening.

Within moments, Redden was struggling again to keep in sync with the music. What had seemed so easy only moments earlier was now proving impossible. Twice, he stopped and then started again, only to become another uncoordinated lawyer who had no business on a dance floor. Still, he refused to give up, each time shrugging at Katie, who was taking great delight in his dismal effort. Embarrassed though he might be, he was not about to leave the floor, at least not while Niki remained on stage.

He couldn't take his eyes off her.

Then they had nearly collided, with neither of them offering a comment or gesture – unless, of course, one considered Niki's penetrating eyes as a form of communication. For a good half minute, she stared at Mitchell, not smiling or speaking, her dark eyes never leaving his, as she swayed and gyrated to the beat of the band. She was mesmerizing and distracting, and Redden couldn't purge from his mind that there was something going on between them.

Something, but what? He didn't have a clue.

This, of course, did not go unnoticed by Redden's partner, who moments later was dragging him back to the bar. "You ready yet for football?" she asked, somewhat impatiently.

"Not quite," responded Redden, who ordered up another set of drinks. He was not quite ready to leave. Not yet. Not until he had a firm understanding of what was taking place between him and his former client.

But thirty minutes later, Niki had totally vanished from the room. She was absolutely nowhere. Her table had been vacated, except for her half-filled drink, and she was not on the dance floor or anyplace else in the large room that accommodated the cocktail lounge and dancing area. From his perch at the bar, he inspected table after table, but no, she had not moved to a new location. Another twenty minutes passed, and he gave up on any idea that perhaps she had snuck off to the ladies' room.

Niki Burroughs was gone.

By now, Katie had seen enough and was writing Redden off as a lost cause. It was nearing eleven o'clock, and her choice for the evening had been more interested in surveying his surroundings than demonstrating the slightest attraction to her. It was time to vacate for greener pastures. Without further thought, she slid down from her stool.

"Well, see you around, big guy."

"Hey, where ya going?"

She flashed a brief smile and a quick wave of her fingers. "Obviously, nowhere with you." With that, she began making her way through the crowd, charting a new course and hoping to salvage a disappointing evening. Redden's eyes followed her until she disappeared into a small group clustered on the opposite side of the room, after which his attention drifted back to Niki's table.

And there she was, sipping her drink as if she had never left.

Redden decided to give it another shot. In fact, his departure from the bar was almost simultaneous with his discovery. It was as if his legs had engaged before his brain had computed whether he should take another stab at reestablishing a relationship.

Again, he approached, and again, she was staring up at him, but this time with a slight grin. "Well, if it isn't the Gene Kelly wannabe."

"You noticed."

"It was hard not to."

"I thought I might be able to talk you out of a lesson."

She was now warming up a bit – the chill factor was definitely gone. "You don't give up, do you?"

"It's not my nature."

"And it's not mine to waste my time." Her grin broadened to a full smile. "No, I'll pass. I'm not one for hopeless causes either."

"I'm sure you're right, but I'd be willing to give it a go."

There is a pause. They are at a point where their relationship could go in two different directions – a definite improvement. Two hours earlier, they were almost beyond speaking to one another.

"Have a seat, Mitchell," she invited. "I'm sitting out for a while. I guess my body isn't quite up to speed yet."

It exceeded the speed of sound, he thought. "Given what you've been through, it's a wonder that you're even out there dancing. How are you doing?"

"Better – much better, actually."

"And Randy?"

"You wouldn't know he has been in an accident. He's now back in school, of course."

Redden was running out of small talk and knew they would be covering some uncomfortable ground sooner or later. He wanted to explore a possible relationship but did not want to be pressed into service again. Was one possible without the other? He would soon find out.

"So, have you found representation yet?"

"No, I'm going to represent myself. I've already paid a lawyer to file both lawsuits."

"Not a good idea, as you will soon find out. But let me help you out here." Redden gave her the names of two lawyers who might be willing to represent her, especially if the auto case was part of the package. They were both experienced in drug product litigation and not intimidated by it like most of the others. They are also good at what they do, and either one of them would be an excellent choice.

To his surprise, not once did Niki suggest that Redden would be the better choice.

As the evening progressed, Niki and Mitchell exchanged personal histories, all the way from childhood into adulthood. They were actually becoming acquainted. Niki even discussed her marriage with Scott Burroughs. She was wed right out of high school. They were both 18, and she was two months pregnant with Randy. At the time, she had high expectations of college, but then along came the pregnancy and the need for a full-time job. But Niki was not about to give up on her dream. She put away half of her salary in anticipation of pursuing her college education when the baby had reached preschool age.

Then came Randy's birth, and Scott could not come to grips with the deformity, somehow seeing it as a reflection of his own imperfection. He began to spend more and more time away from their home until one day, he just left – along with all of her savings. She hadn't seen him since.

"Last round!" The announcement that the last round of drinks was available and Ricardo's would soon be closing caught both of them by surprise. Redden checked his watch and was shocked to see that it was 1:00 AM – and a quick scan of the room revealed that it was almost empty.

He offered to walk her to her car, and Niki accepted.

Outside, the two of them approached her car in the near-empty parking lot. It is a new Ford Mustang – a rental. Although her BMW had been "totaled," she had yet to find a replacement. It was still surprisingly warm outside, and Redden was carrying his sports coat in his arms. Standing next to her car door, Niki looked up at her escort. They had yet to exchange a word since leaving the restaurant.

"Well, I guess I'll see you around," he offered.

"I guess," she said.

Redden caught a reflection of the moon in her eyes, which were illuminated by the spill of light over his shoulders. He was tempted to lean over and kiss her, but as he hesitated in a brief moment of indecision, she unlocked the car door, sat down in the Mustang, and inserted her key in the ignition. She then closed the door and rolled down the window.

"It turned out to be an enjoyable evening," she said.

"We'll have to do it again sometime." Sooner rather than later, he thought.

Niki twisted the key. But rather than kick on, the engine turned over and over without starting. Twice more, she made the effort, with the same result.

"Goddamn rentals!" Niki was furious.

"I guess I'm taking you home," said Redden.

The rental car agency could worry about picking up the car in the morning.

CHAPTER 10

The silver Porsche glided to a stop in front of Niki's house. Redden turned off the engine and sat for a moment in silence, staring at his passenger. It was just more of the same, as neither of the two had spoken a word in the twenty-minute drive from Ricardo's. Both had been giving a lot of thought to what was going to happen next and how it would play out in their respective futures.

Niki decided to break the moratorium. "Could I interest you in a cup of coffee?"

Redden hesitated, then said, "I just might take you up on that." He again sensed that his life was flowing along an uncertain path but resolved to submit to it and play out the hand he had been dealt – at least for the moment. The two exited the car and entered the house.

"Have a seat," said Niki, motioning to the couch, "I'll put on a pot. Shouldn't be long." She slipped a CD into the stereo system and entered the kitchen. Classical music instantly filled the room.

Redden dropped onto the couch. "Classical music. I'm impressed," he said to the open door to the kitchen.

"Oh, I'm full of surprises," she responded, without elaborating.

"So, where is Randy?"

"Next door. My neighbor is babysitting."

Redden gave the living room a once-over as a grinder did a number on a batch of gourmet coffee beans in the adjacent kitchen. It was small but had a cozy warmth to it, with an array of knickknacks, photographs, plants, and flowers. The furniture appeared inexpensive but comfortable. For a brief moment, he thought of his teen years in San Francisco, sitting in front of a roaring fireplace while his mother worked her wonders in the kitchen. Had it really been over two decades? He had written to her several times during his four-year sabbatical, often sending postcards. They were all addressed to his mother and usually ended with, "Say hi to Dad for me," which was more for her benefit than to communicate with his father. They had not spoken since he had moved to Los Angeles County.

As the aroma of fresh-brewing coffee filled the living room, Niki exited the kitchen, announcing that she was on her way "to freshen up a bit."

Redden had never been close to this father, which was perplexing to most of their close friends. But his mother understood. Alexander Redden was simply an enigma, a man who rarely shared his inner thoughts. He was also a formal man who insisted on his family abiding by a set of rules and schedules – and he had at least one for every occasion. Dinner would be served each night promptly at six; it was only to be served in the dining room, including weekends, with all members properly dressed, even Alexander – who always wore a suit; each would then discuss the past events of the day; Mitchell and his older sister were limited to one hour of television in the evening – only if their homework was completed - and two hours per day over the weekends; all other leisure time was to be spent reading; breakfast was served at the kitchen table each morning, again with all in attendance, no exceptions, when each would discuss their intended plans for the day. And so it went. Yet it was not that the rules were necessarily bad – each was well-intended – it was that they were strictly enforced with little room for deviation. Only the most extreme set of circumstances would justify an exception.

The regimentation, of course, took its own toll on Mitchell's relationship with his father. But what sealed their eventual estrangement was Alexander's distance and detachment. It was a rare day when the older Redden shared his personal views with his son – unless it involved the practice of law. From as far back as he could remember, Mitchell's father had been grooming him for the day he would become a member of the Redden law firm. Mitchell recalled how he had resisted the idea – his passion had been baseball. But he eventually accepted the will of his father.

The stirring, driving beat of Ravel's *Bolero* suddenly intruded on Redden's reminiscence and prompted him to focus on the source of the classical piece, although the music came at him from the four corners of the room. He recalled the movie *Ten* when Bo Derek introduced Dudley Moore to the same composition from the famous French composer. Fiction was soon to be repeated as fact.

A movement to his right drew his attention to a figure standing in the hallway to the three bedrooms. It was Niki – and he finally understood what was going to be happening next.

Her timing had been perfect. She stood with her back to the hallway, wearing a short negligee that cut low over her breasts and extended only halfway to her knees. The light from behind outlined her trim, rounded figure in the somewhat transparent clothing. Redden's heart rate began to escalate. The vision left him speechless, having been caught by surprise. Even on the drive over, he had not considered the possibility of such intimacy; maybe it would be a kiss, but nothing more. It was too early in their relationship if indeed there was even going to be a relationship.

Without uttering a word, Niki began to approach him with slow and deliberate steps and, without breaking stride, reached up to the back of his head and pulled him down to her open mouth. As he opened his own, her tongue darted in, exploring, massaging, penetrating his oral cavity, stimulating his senses in a way he had not thought possible, as the rhythmic beat of *Bolero* filled the room and consumed his capacity to hear. He was more determined than ever now to accept the will of the gods and embraced her with both of his arms.

One of Niki's hands dropped from his head to his waist and then lower and lower until she felt the hardness she was after. Without hesitation, she began to massage him, slowly, up and down, her fingers softly kneading. So subtle was this movement that she was well into her effort before Mitchell realized what was taking place, at which point he pulled back his face and stared down at the beautiful Greek woman with dark, hypnotizing eyes. Niki reciprocated his gaze but continued her manual exercise, not slowing a beat. She knew what she was after, and tonight was the night. He was hers for the night and would not slip away. And that was not about to happen, as Redden was well beyond the point of no return.

Within moments, their clothes had been flung indiscriminately to the floor, and their bodies merged, making love wildly, physically, the excitement and energy seeming to feed on itself. The couch, though convenient at first, was quickly abandoned for the less restrictive playground of the carpeted floor. Out of deference to Niki's injuries, Redden initially held back. Still, she she continued to attack, urging him on, until he thought of her not as a frail partner but as a counterpart to an erotic adventure. Investigating all options, they rolled over the floor, alternating the lead, first her on top, then him, then her again, then both sitting up with Redden's back against the ottoman. With each change of position and location came a squeal of pain as her battered body tried to protest the ordeal, which only spurred Redden on, whether misreading the cause of the emissions or just simply out of indifference.

Eventually, somehow, some way, they ended up in Niki's bedroom, neither recalling how they had arrived, but both appreciated the comfort afforded by the soft, pliant mattress. Within minutes, out of utter exhaustion, they had both collapsed and fell into a deep sleep.

⸻ ● ⸻

Saturday, September 19

The first rays of sunlight through the east-facing window caught Redden square in the face at exactly 6:38 AM, which was what the digital clock on the nightstand recorded as he blinked awake and inspected it while shielding his face. So quick had they fallen asleep that neither had given any thought to pulling the drapes. A check on his sleeping partner confirmed she was still sound asleep, with a sheet pulled well up over her head.

At this point, that Redden became aware of two eyes peering at him over the foot of the bed. He smiled and waved at the six-year-old visitor, somewhat uncomfortable at being caught in bed with his mother but not knowing how else to extricate himself from the uncomfortable situation.

A small hand waved back, although the edge of the bed continued to hide Randy's face as would a bandit's mask during a holdup.

Redden put a finger up to his mouth to suggest remaining quiet while he searched the room for something to cover up his nudity – at least until he could locate his clothing. Nearby, on the floor, he spied a blanket that had been discarded as they had scrambled into bed a few hours earlier. In one quick movement, he slid out from under the sheet, grabbed the blanket, and wrapped himself up like an Indian.

Hand-in-hand, the two of them exited the bedroom, and Mitchell closed the door. Randy was clad in his pajamas with a fully attached prosthesis. Redden then began to pick up various items of clothing throughout the living room while his new host followed him about, enthusiastically pelting him with questions.

"Hi, Mitch!"

"Hi, Randy."

"Where have you been?"

"Oh, around."

"But I haven't seen you. Why haven't you been over?"

"Been busy. Lawyers have lots of things to do."

"What kind of things?"

"Oh, going to court, research, those kinds of things."

"You going to court on *my* case?"

This one was a little more difficult. "Not yet, but we're working on it." After segregating Niki's negligee onto a convenient chair, he nodded toward the guest bathroom. "Let me get dressed, and I'll be back in a flash."

"You gonna live with us for a while?"

This one stopped Redden in his tracks. He turned and said, "No, just visiting overnight," and disappeared into the bathroom. When he reappeared a minute later – fully dressed – Randy was still standing there waiting for him.

"I'm gonna make you breakfast, okay?"

Redden knew it was time to leave, but there was absolutely no way he could decline the offer. "Sure," he said and followed Randy into the kitchen.

Randy poured two bowls of cornflakes – each with a generous supply of sugar – followed by milk and then led Mitchell to the kitchenette, where they sat and began eating. Between mouthfuls, Randy continued to chatter. He related his prowess on the Little League field – T-ball, where the baseball was placed on a "T" to be struck by the batter. He can't run very fast, so he had to hit the ball hard. He assured Redden that he had even hit a home run.

With Redden in tow, Randy next led him into his bedroom and, with pride, exhibited his collection of model fire trucks, also pointing to a number of paintings and photos of similar vehicles on the wall. He is going to be a fireman someday when he grows up. The impossibility of this dream had its impact on Redden, who sensed an overwhelming urge now to distance himself from the house and its two occupants as soon as possible.

Just as Redden was about to leave through the front door, Niki emerged, dressed in a robe and slippers.

"I guess we never did get that coffee, did we?" she smiled.

"Still being heated, but after six hours, I wouldn't encourage its consumption. How are you feeling?"

"Like I've been dragged by a horse."

"What we'll put ourselves through for a few moments of…" Redden caught himself as he observed Randy taking in their conversation. "Well, I'd better be on my way," he said. "Got some things to do." Of course, he didn't have any idea of what they might be.

He leaned over and clumsily gave Niki a kiss on the cheek.

Redden was confused. The morning sun was just rising over the Lomita rooftops, and he had just gotten out of bed, had breakfast, and was now saying goodbye to a woman and her child who, until last night, had been near strangers to him. What was happening? Where was this all going?

"Well, thanks for the breakfast," he said to Randy.

"You're welcome."

He then slipped into the Porsche, kicked on the engine, and was gone.

No sooner had Redden's car departed when Niki turned to Randy and said, "Okay, honey, go get dressed. Gotta go down and pick up our rental car. Alicia should be up by now."

In the distance, she could see the Porsche slow and then turn at the end of the block. She smiled, silently congratulating herself. Mission accomplished. She reached into the pocket of her robe and pulled out her hand.

In the middle of her palm was the rotor to the distributor of the rental car.

———•—•———

CHAPTER 11

Thursday, September 24

Redden is jogging along a sidewalk adjacent to the beach in Redondo. It is early morning, and a surprising chill is in the air. A marine layer is hanging like a shroud only a quarter mile offshore, and although it is daylight, the sun has yet to break over the buildings to the east. It was 6:40 AM, and he had already been on his morning run for half an hour. Fall must be coming early, he suspected, but of course, he had not been around for a while.

He stopped for a brief moment, unexpectedly winded, and pulled the hood to his sweatshirt over his head. He had heard once that keeping a head warm was necessary to maintaining body warmth. He attributed his labored breathing to the cold and hoped that this adjustment might remedy the problem. His uncovered legs did not appear to be an issue. After he cinched up the hood with a drawstring, he was ran off again.

In truth, what was impacting Redden was that he had not slept well, not last night or even the past several nights. He was wrestling with a dilemma. It had been dogging him for over four years but recently seemed to be occupying most of his thoughts when not working on the handful of cases sitting in his file cabinet.

Fifteen minutes later, Redden was nearing exhaustion but kept pushing and pushing, expecting that the answer to his quandary would somehow appear before him, perhaps as a vision. It was true that Randy Burroughs was an inspiration to cast all caution aside and go for the brass ring – a major verdict in the freeway case would be an ideal jumpstart to his sidetracked career. The jury verdict would no doubt hit the press, and his old public relations firm would make sure of that. But no client is worth risking a suspension or possibly even disbarment. As much as Redden would like to help Niki and her son, there was little question about whether he had made the right decision.

But why did he continue to explore the possibility of pursuing the drug case? Why had his thoughts been overwhelming over the past 5 days? It is a much more difficult lawsuit and most certainly would push Gillingham to seek a full-blown investigation by the State Bar. Why would it even be a consideration?

Redden, like most of the top trial lawyers in the state, carried his ego much like a suit of armor. Ego evolves out of confidence, and when it comes to courtroom skills, very few lawyers have more confidence in their abilities than Mitchell Redden. Born of his natural talent and nurtured by his successes, it both aided and plagued him. In the practice of law, it had been an ally, intimidating opponents and drawing respect from judges and credibility from juries. But in many other ways, it was a curse. In spite of all the rationalizing, justifying, reasoning, reconciling, and every other excuse he could seek out, the ego of Redden always drew him back to one inescapable conclusion: Chester Raymond Gillingham III, his antagonist, adversary, and sworn enemy, a lawyer whose legal skills paled in comparison with his own, has had the ability and power to push him not only out of the courtroom, which he missed with a passion but effectively control the very manner by which he even practiced law.

No one should have such power over his life.

Counterbalanced against this frustration was the equally strong will for self-preservation. Brookhurst Pharmaceuticals was a client of Gillingham's firm, and Gillingham would never tolerate Redden showing up as the attorney of record on a lawsuit filed against it......or would he?

As Redden continued to drive himself along the concrete walkway, he began to explore the possibilities. Perhaps Gillingham had now found sufficient satisfaction to forget the past and look on to crumbling other mountains. Nine years had passed since the first episode, including the four of Redden's self-imposed exile. Gillingham had exacted his blood of vengeance, a body full of it. With the efficiency of a guillotine, he had severed Redden from the firm and brought himself the highly-prized partnership he was after. He also now had the power that few other lawyers in the state could boast about, and he would shortly would enjoy the further prestige of senior partner. What more did he need?

Redden, of course, was well aware of the answer. Life at the top is a precarious one, and the fall from its pinnacle is sometimes swift and fatal. Gillingham would never take a chance at even a stumble. Brookhurst Pharmaceuticals was a big-paying client – a lucrative asset of the firm. Redden had seen first-hand the billing practices employed by Barry, Klein – inflated hours, double billing, dispatching two lawyers on a motion when one would suffice, sending statements at a partner's rate when the work was done by an associate and only initialed by the partner – and also knew that Brookhurst, like many other drug companies, held to the belief that the bigger the bill the stronger the sense it was getting good representation. Unlike the miserly rates insisted by auto insurance carriers, drug companies paid the best, and defending just one case could result in hundreds of thousands of dollars of income for the firm. Gillingham would never jeopardize losing such a client by getting tagged with a major verdict – and by a former member of the firm at that. Then, too, was Gillingham's insatiable appetite for power, enjoyed to its fullest while keeping Mitchell Redden out to pasture. There was little doubt that Gillingham would jump at the opportunity to destroy two careers if Redden's name showed up on a pleading for Randolph Burroughs.

No, the answer was definitely not to be found in a change of heart by C. Raymond Gillingham III. Stone will forever remain stone. The solution had to lay elsewhere – perhaps in the weakness of the evidence held against him.

Redden had never believed that Gillingham could carry the burden of proving the charges against him, true though they might have been. Few witnesses held up under his intense and unrelenting cross-examination, and he doubted that the weasel of a law clerk would have fared differently. All of the weapons for an effective attack were there, including bias, motivation, uncertainty, and little else by way of corroboration. Redden had convinced himself at the time that he could have survived the charges and a full-blown hearing by the State Bar. It was not himself that was the concern. For even if all went bad, he was prepared for the consequences; he would take his suspension and see the world – exactly as he did five years later after the second and final go-around with Gillingham.

It was the likely tragedy to befall Harry Blaylock that stopped him dead in his tracks. After the earlier suspension, a second adverse finding would no doubt result in disbarment, the end of his professional career, and possibly even his life. Harry was hanging by the thinnest of threads in those days; on the brink of financial ruin, his wife recently gone from his life, an emotional derelict, confused, uncertain, depressed. He would never have held up under the pressure during a hearing. Harry would have fallen – and possibly dragged Redden right along with him. At this point, suicide would have seemed a welcome solution to Blaylock. So thought Redden at the time, which facilitated the acceptance of Gillingham's terms, even without debate or attempt at negotiation.

But today was a different circumstance – the terrain had totally changed. Harry was stronger now and capable of bearing up under a State Bar investigation. The evidence was also old and stale after all these years, perhaps no longer sufficient to even justify a hearing. Perhaps the law clerk was no longer around, possibly vanquished by Gillingham back into the ranks of the unemployed, his purpose having been served. Having only once seen his face for a brief ten minutes so long ago, Redden had no recollection of his face and had not even been privy to his name. It was difficult to comprehend him, somehow unearthed again, making a final appearance amid controversy and public spectacle in an attempt to destroy two strangers against whom he held no grievance. More importantly, Blaylock's involvement was only minor, and if the hearing was going bad, Redden would accept full responsibility and exonerate Harry from any guilt.

No, it was the second episode five years later that presented the real problem, the event that had sent Redden to his self-imposed exile and his law practice dismantled and off in pieces to the four corners of the county at the time of his departure. That time around, it was all Harry.

But what about the value of the evidence?

Redden stumbled to a stop and took in the thundering waves of the surf, winded in a state of utter exhaustion. Maybe this was where he would find his answer. Maybe there was something he had overlooked. Maybe if he had not been so impulsive and emotional at the time. Maybe if he had been more analytical of the evidence. Maybe if…. Redden pondered the last meeting with Gillingham.

Had it really been four years?

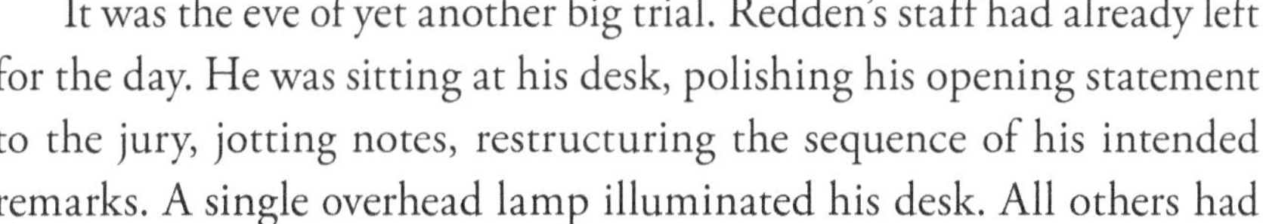

It was the eve of yet another big trial. Redden's staff had already left for the day. He was sitting at his desk, polishing his opening statement to the jury, jotting notes, restructuring the sequence of his intended remarks. A single overhead lamp illuminated his desk. All others had been turned off by Mary Ellen just before her departure. A knock drew him away from his notes and to the man standing at the doorway to his office. It was Raymond Gillingham.

"I hope you don't mind," he began. "The front door to your office was unlocked, so I showed myself in."

It initially surprised him that Gillingham would know he was even there. But then he was well aware of Mitch Redden's habits, and late hours the night before a trial was not unusual for the alumnus from Barry, Klein & Nance. "What do you want, Ray? I'm kind of busy."

Redden, of course, knew the answer to his question. He was about to commence jury selection on a medical malpractice case against a physician represented by the Barry, Klein firm. He was the attorney for the widow of a man who had died during a routine surgery. The case had substantial potential for a large verdict since the victim had been a successful businessman earning several hundred thousand dollars a year at the time of his death. What really drew Redden to the case, however, was the prominence of the physician. He was a famed general surgeon, having operated once on the President of the United States and later on several celebrities in the entertainment business. To top it off, he was also the current president of the California Medical Association. A big verdict would no doubt hit the front page of the *Los Angeles Times*.

Redden had also found a golden piece of evidence. At the time of the operation, the physician had been scheduling a high volume of surgeries to benefit from his recent fame and was heavily into drugs to sustain his five-hours-of-sleep-a-day practice. Although there was some question of whether or not he had been high during the surgery in question, Redden was prepared with expert testimony that such a level of drug usage, along with the limited sleep, would still have affected his performance and judgment. The evidence would unquestionably come in.

Gillingham took a step inside the office. In his hand, he held a large envelope. "I came here to urge you to take the offer on the table. It's a reasonable number."

"It's not your case. Why are you here, and where is Joel?"

"Joel Grayson is at home preparing for tomorrow. I'm here as a representative of the firm to talk about settlement. Take the offer, Mitch."

"It's unacceptable." The surgeon himself had added to the insurance carrier's offer to make it as attractive as possible, but Redden had already talked the widow out of accepting it.

"And if I offered more money…?"

"Not interested."

The case was a reputation builder, and the interests of the client were secondary. He knew when he had a winner, and Redden had convinced himself that the client would financially benefit more from a trial and verdict than any settlement offer. Grayson had previously pleaded that the surgeon was now in a drug rehabilitation program and that publicity of this nature would destroy his career. "He should have thought about that possibility before killing my client's husband," had been Redden's retort.

"You are indeed predictable," said Gillingham.

"Then you know you're wasting your time. This case doesn't concern you, so I would suggest heading back out that door."

"Oh, but it does. It concerns me very much." Gillingham approached the desk and tossed the envelope in front of Redden. "You may want to read these – and perhaps reconsider the offer."

Redden hesitated, then opened the envelope and emptied its contents. And what he read did not make him happy. They were bank records – several pages of them – of Harry Blaylock's client trust account. When he saw the nature of the records, he instantly knew what they would disclose, but still, he read. By following the various entries, he could easily reconstruct what had occurred. Harry had settled three personal injury cases, presumably without the clients' knowledge and consent – which meant forging their names on releases – and then began withdrawing the funds at weekly intervals over a period of three months.

"He's been making weekly trips to Vegas, usually on a weekend," said Gillingham as Redden continued to read. "Not exactly the luckiest guy, that Blaylock. Heavy losses at the tables, as you can imagine."

The more Redden read, the angrier he became, to the point of it becoming masochistic. In a way he could not quite understand, he was now looking for one more settlement, one more withdrawal, anything to become increasingly irate – an emotion he now welcomed. He was enraged at Harry and had he walked in at the very moment, Redden would have thrown him out on the street, wished him luck, and demanded that he never show up in his life again. "So, what are you after, Ray?"

With Redden now under his thumb, Gillingham sat down in one of the client chairs in front of the desk. "Well, for starters, you take the existing offer. No negotiating. Just accept the offer. It's a good number, and you shouldn't have any problem convincing your client to take it. The amount of the settlement and your evidence on drug use, of course, will have to be sealed."

Redden glared at his nemesis without comment.

"Then, of course, there's this little problem of you showing up against BKN clients. Can't have any more of that. You know our carrier clients and corporate clients, so your course of action will be quite simple – you don't take the cases, never again."

"Anything else?"

"Well, just one more thing, a small matter, really." Gillingham waited until he had piqued Redden's interest. "No more trials. No jury trials, no court trials, none, *nada*, zilch. Your trial days are over."

Redden slammed his hands down on his desk. "Fuck you, Chester! No way!"

"You mean, 'fuck Harry Blaylock,' don't you?"

"What possible benefit is it to Barry, Klein if I'm off trying lawsuits against other law firms?"

Gillingham folded his arms and leaned back in the chair. "Call this a personal benefit. The first two are for the firm – this one for me." Gillingham was twisting the knife and enjoying every minute of it.

"You bastard!"

Gillingham nodded. "You know, you're right, I am a bastard." He then smiled as if it was something to be proud of.

"I would suggest again that you show yourself out." Redden was inclined to physically assist him but instead just stood. "You'll have my answer in the morning."

"Of course, I will," said Gillingham, who rose from his seat and walked to the door. "Before ten o'clock." He then disappeared into the darkness of the outer office.

Only when Redden heard the front office door close did he again sit down and begin assessing the situation. Harry would be going down for the final count – full disbarment, no question.

But then that was four years ago when Redden had acted out of emotion and fear for Harry's life, not with a clear mind uninfluenced by intimidation and coercion. There was one glaring question that Redden had failed to consider at the time that today seemed to be so fundamental.

How did Gillingham acquire those records?

The answer to that very simple and basic question could not only unlock the door of opportunity to re-establish Redden's career but perhaps present Gillingham with a whole set of problems of his own. The light of discovery that had eluded Redden over these years was now fully illuminated by a solution to his dilemma. Every motivation held by Gillingham to maintain his seat of power was an even stronger inspiration for Redden to now pursue the suit – Gillingham, the king, toppled from his throne, out the door with the nightly trash.

Randy Burroughs had been the catalyst to open the door, the reasons noble and well-intentioned. But now something deeper, uglier, was seeping to the surface, something lying in wait these many years.

Revenge.

Every skill, every trick, every secret, every resource would be funneled into this one case. Randy Burroughs and his mother would be the beneficiaries, but Gillingham would be the prize.

A small practice with no trial work – the idea had its attractiveness; no pressure, no stress, a simple professional career merged with the pleasures of life at the beach. But in a few more months, he knew he would only find disappointment and unhappiness. Trial work was in his blood, and he had savored the high of victory too many times. Try as he might to convince himself of a Shangri-La existence in Redondo Beach, he remained anguished and unfulfilled – especially after his four-year hiatus.

Back in the office, Redden placed a call with Niki. He invited her over for dinner that evening, and she had accepted. He'd play chef, and she'd have to trust that he knew his way around a kitchen. It was necessary that they meet, he urged, to discuss something of utmost importance. Niki, of course, had little doubt about the subject of the discussion. Everything was going according to plan.

CHAPTER 12

Wednesday, October 7

Mary Ellen is opening the morning mail, something she looked forward to each day, a break in the monotony of routine. Here, she gained insight into the cases she labored over, otherwise excluded by Redden from the confidentialities of stories that sometimes read like a steamy novel or a Greek tragedy. Never one to open up, either about his clients or himself, Redden leaked only enough facts and information needed to carry out his instructions. A man of mystery since the day she met him, Mary Ellen was always scrutinizing each document in hopes of gathering anything anything, about Redden's puzzling leave of absence. After dispensing with the junk mail, the flyers, and the advertisements, deposited by instruction directly into the trash container, each piece is date-stamped and carefully read before being placed on Redden's desk in a neat stack. Denied these confidences, it is with considerable satisfaction that Mary Ellen is the first to know the surprises delivered each day by the U.S. Postal Service. She will frequently verbalize the information first-hand to Redden as she presents his mail.

Mary Ellen Dovinowitz was widowed at 37 and left a very wealthy woman, but not without a lengthy and controversial battle in the courts with the son and daughter of her deceased husband. The marriage had been brief – barely seventeen months – after a substantially shorter courtship. They had met while Mary Ellen was working for a probate attorney in Beverly Hills. Ira Dovinowitz was in the midst of several meetings with Mary Ellen's employer, planning his estate, when he had asked her out for dinner and a show, a play at the Mark Taper Forum. Always an opportunist, Mary Ellen accepted in the face of an explicit directive against dating clients of the firm and having already suffered through the play, which folded in five weeks. She was fired within a week after an unsuccessful attempt by her boss to break it off. Six weeks later, they were wed. She was 35, and he was 62.

The first few months were all that she imagined they would be. He was in the clothing business, with a line of women's sportswear sold throughout the world – "Ira Dove," with the logo of a dove embroidered on each piece to signal its authenticity. To service his business, Ira traveled extensively, following the fashions of the world, visiting his distribution outlets, and negotiating with various clothing manufacturers in Hong Kong and Korea. He insisted that she accompany him everywhere, his constant companion, which was not a hard sell since it was the lifestyle she fancied and sought from the moment of their first date. World travel, with fashion shows in Paris, Rome, and London, suites at all the luxury hotels, limousines, and a wardrobe in keeping with the wife of a man who had achieved something akin to celebrity status in the industry. Their home, a two-acre estate in Bel Air, was more a showpiece than a residence since they both found themselves more often on the road than in town.

Then came the revelation – the catch to the sudden fantasy world of Mary Ellen Dovinowitz. Ira had pancreatic cancer, in remission at the time of their meeting, but with a poor prognosis. He had withheld it from her, as had her employer. But after a half year in the fast lane, his symptoms began to worsen, and the inevitable came to pass. He had possibly six months to live, a year at most. Ira told her the day he had learned the sentence from his physician. It was direct and to the point, but with a profound apology for the secrecy. He had been selfish, he acknowledged, but he wanted to grab as much as he could for the last months of his life. If she had known, she would not have married him, and even if she had, it would have burdened their lives like a cloak of doom. He assured her she would be well-cared for after he was gone, just compensation for the deception and giving him the happiest days of his life. Within eleven months, he had died, leaving her with the majority of his estate after some select charities and a modest bequest to his two children. The ensuing will contest took several years to conclude, resulting in a settlement that left the children with the home and many of Ira's holdings but Mary Ellen with a little over seventeen million dollars after legal fees, costs, and taxes.

Still alive and vital, after a couple years of unsuccessfully trying to fit into the mode of the "idle rich," she returned to her vocation of legal secretary. She had recently entered her forties, attractive and wealthy, yet still without a man. Seeing herself now as a target, much as Ira had been for her, a busy law office seemed the place to lose herself again in activity and a forum to meet someone to share her life as she entered middle age. It had worked before – why not again? It was at this point she was first interviewed and employed by Mitchell Redden.

The attraction to Redden was immediate and deep. In addition to being strikingly handsome, he was engaging, personable, impulsive – almost to the point of recklessness – as well as high-profile and successful. Though recognizing the difference in their ages placed him probably with the unattainable, Mary Ellen accepted his offer of employment without reflection. The years that followed, however, offered little by way of encouragement. Other than an affectionate touch here and there, a friendly kiss on the cheek, a hug of consolation or greeting, nothing had happened to the point of his mysterious disappearance.

Redden's clientele, the lame and infirm, tragedy-stricken, from the low to middle-income strata of society, proved to be even less of a market for the lonely widow. Only an occasional date with a visiting attorney – and the current successes at Ricardo's – gave her the encouragement to remain and not seek more fertile ground elsewhere. When Redden stepped out of nowhere and back into her life, it was a more difficult sell to bring her into the fold. But still, she came, hopelessly attached to a man she knew would always be out of range.

Well into the mail, she sliced into an envelope from Barry, Klein & Nance. It contained a number of legal documents on the case of

Burroughs versus Brookhurst Pharmaceuticals, including a petition for removal from state to federal court. The lawsuit was filed in the Los Angeles Superior Court three weeks earlier. Mary Ellen stamped it in and immediately delivered it to Redden in his office, though she had yet to finish the mail. At the moment, he was deeply into a recently published appellate decision on drug product liability.

"Something for your favorite client," she said, placing the documents on his desk.

Redden tolerated such little remarks, ignorantly writing them off as a change of life. With his dependence upon her skill and knowledge and her unfailing ability to continually protect his hind flank, Redden never gave so much thought to even a reprove for what was now just blending in as part of Mary Ellen's personality.

"Yeah, what you got?" he said, looking up at his secretary.

"Your buddies at Barry, Klein just removed to federal court."

Redden stared at the papers in dismay. "No way!"

"Afraid so, Boss." Mary Ellen offered a sardonic grin, shrugged, and exited the office to complete her review of the mail.

Barry, Klein never, but never, removed to federal court. Not only did Gillingham share Redden's disdain for the more regimented judicial system of the two, it was state court where Barry, Klein – and Gillingham – held their power. State court judicial appointments were made under the considerable influence of Redden's ex-employer. Even judges not beholding to the firm for their positions on the bench knew that any aspirations for the appellate court could be jeopardized by crossing Barry, Klein, at least during the current gubernatorial leadership. Redden's hopes, until now, had rested on the chance assignment to an older appointment from the former governor of the opposition party, what Redden called the "independent judiciary." Even had he been assigned to the "wrong" judge in state court, he still would have retained the right to challenge the first choice and a shot at another – a right not available in federal court. There you got what you got; a presidential appointment for life, a non-elective office unanswerable to anyone other than the Grim Reaper, and the impeachment process of the United States Senate. However, the political connections of Barry, Klein &

Nance were not at the national level. It made little sense that the firm would surrender a chance at such a major advantage. The unexpected had occurred.

The first volley from Gillingham had been fired.

The answer had to be somehow connected with the judge assigned to the case: United States District Court Judge, Roger Langhorne. Redden pondered his name, searching the far reaches of his memory banks, but came up wanting. He recalled the name – Langhorne had been on the federal bench for a number of years – but could not recall any prior association, even the slightest, with Barry, Klein & Nance. Like many trial lawyers representing injured plaintiffs, Redden had avoided federal court as one told it incubated a new strain of the Bubonic Plague. He thus knew little else about the judge.

"Heard the bad news." The voice came from Harry Blaylock, standing at Redden's doorway.

"I'm in shock. It's never happened before, Harry, never. Even when I was defending at BKN, they never removed. It was like an unwritten rule – never remove to the feds unless pushed by the client."

"Well, maybe that's it. Brookhurst must've insisted. Would make sense, with all the conservative judges."

"No, I don't buy it, Harry. There's something else going on here. I know Gillingham. He always covers his bets. There's gotta be a connection with the judge, something."

"Who'd ya get?"

"Roger Langhorne."

Harry shook his head. "You're shitting me, right?"

"That's what the papers say, 'Roger Langhorne.'"

The man with the loud suspenders and no coat dropped onto Redden's couch. "Shit. The guy's a fucking idiot and a feisty old bastard at that. Used to prosecute tax fraud for the US Attorney's office. He was a *tax* lawyer, for Christ's sake. Got no business hearing civil cases."

"Not good, huh?"

"He doesn't know civil law, Mitch. Everything's off the wall. Refuses to read the cases. Doubt there's a book in his library that doesn't have an inch of fucking dust on it. Gets reversed all the time but doesn't seem to give a shit. Won't even use his law clerk – an ego thing, I'm sure."

As Harry rambled, Redden pulled a binder of judicial profiles from the credenza behind his desk. It was published and updated annually by the local legal newspaper. It did little to solve Gillingham's perplexing move . Nothing about Langhorne's history prior to the bench gave as much as a hint as to why he would be wanted on the case. Seven years in the Los Angeles District Attorney's office and another twelve with the U.S. Attorney, prosecuting tax fraud cases; nineteen years of practice, all criminal, before selection to the U.S. District Court. Barry, Klein & Nance never involved itself in criminal matters – exclusively a civil firm – so what was the connection?

"Nothing here either," he said as he tossed the binder onto his desk.

"I'm telling you, Mitch, he tries everything from the seat of his pants – unless, of course, you've got a criminal or tax matter. But civil, forget it. Defense guys don't like him either."

What this told Redden was that no civil litigant or his attorney would ever feel secure upon learning that his case had been assigned to Roger Langhorne – a further reason to question the wisdom of Barry, Klein in rolling the dice and seeking removal.

Gillingham wanted Langhorne on the case, and Redden was convinced of this. But why and how did he pull it off? In federal court, judges were assigned by random selection. Tampering with this system could mean criminal prosecution and severe discipline by the State Bar. It would be an act of considerable desperation for one to even attempt such a maneuver.

"So why don't we take a shot at remand?" suggested Harry. "Let's amend the goddamn complaint and add a California defendant. There's gotta be someone we can add." The primary prerequisite for removal to federal court was diversity. At least two of the parties to the action had to be domiciled in different states. The grounds for removal could be broken, however, if just one defendant was a resident of the same state as the plaintiffs: California.

"But who, Harry? Phenatol issold over the counter. No prescribing doctor. That knocks out malpractice."

"Then, how about the pharmacy? Who sold the drug?"

"LoPrice Drugs."

"There you go. Let's amend in LoPrice and go for the remand."

"Can't do."

"Why not? They're part of the chain of sale."

"No strict liability. That only works in product cases with strict liability and no strict liability in drug cases. We'd have to show some form of negligence on the part of the pharmacy, and there's just no way we could pull it off."

"Why not?"

"Because LoPrice Drugs had no more knowledge about the risks of Phenatol than Niki Burroughs did, back when she was pregnant with Randy."

"But maybe there was a memo floating around seven years ago. Maybe one of its pharmacists had done some research. Let's amend the goddamn complaint, allege negligence for LoPrice, then move for remand. Who knows? Maybe we'll turn something in during discovery. At least we'll be in state court during discovery."

"Tell you what," offered Redden. "Let me make a phone call. This may all be a waste of time."

And it was. A quick telephone call to a local LoPrice drug store finally laid the question to rest. LoPrice was a chain with its corporate headquarters located in Chicago, Illinois. It was not a California corporation. Even if they could establish negligence, diversity could not be broken.

They were helplessly mired in federal court.

Redden began to parade the unpleasantries through his mind as he toyed with the stack of papers from Barry, Klein & Nance. Conservative juries are generally limited to six men and women, require a unanimous verdict, no questions by counsel during impaneling of the jury, the pace of the trial controlled tightly by the judge, re-educating himself on a wholly different set of rules and procedures, and worst of all – the outcome likely hinging upon the whims of an unpredictable tyrant.

"So, what's up next?" asked Blaylock.

"A status conference. It's set in 30 days, November 6." Redden lifted his calendar and stared at the date, but his mind was elsewhere, contemplating an event one month into the future.

"I'll check my calendar, Mitch, but I'm sure I can cover it."

"No need. I'm going."

This came as a shock to Harry, as the announcement brought him into a fully upright position on the couch. "To hell you say!"

Redden took in Harry's look of astonishment and grinned. "You heard me right," he said. It felt good to express the confirmation out loud.

"No shit! We're talking a courtroom now – you know, one of those funny rooms with a big desk at the far end mounted by a man in a black robe pretending to be God, one of those kinds of rooms. You're actually gonna walk into one and give your name?"

"With a briefcase in my hand. I may even wear a suit."

"I'll be god damn. I can't tell you what this does for these old bones." Could this signal a return of Mitchell Redden, trial lawyer extraordinaire, the only meaningful legacy of Harry Leonard Blaylock? Perhaps, thought Harry, who perceived a glint in the eyes of his younger colleague he hadn't seen in four years.

"I just might get a little bit out of this myself," noted Redden.

To Mitchell Redden, the time had come to test uncharted waters, to assess the reaction of Gillingham, and take a first-hand look at the judge who was about to have a major influence on the future course of his life and those of his two clients.

Was he going to be ready for the task? He would soon find out.

CHAPTER 13

Friday, November 6

Redden approached the front steps of the Federal Building in downtown Los Angeles. A good 12 years had elapsed since he last ascended the steps into the aging building, an unpleasant day he always carried with him like a bad dream refusing to fade away. He had inadvertently failed to comply with a minor procedure unique to federal court and had received blistering criticism from the judge, who was totally indifferent to the fact that Redden's client was seated next to him at the time. Humiliated and embarrassed, he pledged never to set foot again inside a United States District Court, a pledge he had managed to adhere to up to this very moment. Yet here he was, and the episode of over a decade earlier only added to the anxiety that was churning away inside.

He quickly proceeded through the security system, then up the elevator to the third floor. Although it was early – 8:20 AM – the hallway was alive with counsel, their various clients, and miscellaneous court personnel scurrying about their tasks, creating a sense of chaotic madness as the 8:30 and nine o'clock calendars fast approached.

Redden had held to the now-dwindling hope that returning to a courtroom – the primary environment of his professional life for so many years – would ease the tension and aid a quick transition to the mode of the experienced and confident trial lawyer as he had once seen himself. Any such hope promptly vanished as he opened the door and took in the formal and stately atmosphere of Roger Langhorne's domain. The bench loomed prominently at the end of the room, the throne of the little kingdom. Even absent the king, it seemed to demand homage from all who dared to stand before it. Redden needed little encouragement to step back outside into the active hallway and find a seat. He had 40 minutes to kill, and although a status conference demanded little skill and far less preparation, it seemed wise to review his handbook on federal court procedures.

At exactly 8:45 AM, Redden could sense the presence of two figures standing nearby and looked up from his handbook, having just reviewed it for the third time. It is Gillingham and Rothenberg.

"You look out of your element," quipped Gillingham.

"Just a quick refresher course," said Redden as he rose, taking in Gillingham in a quick assessment. As he might have expected, the eyes were the same, with a hint of smugness, Gillingham's arrogance beaming like a beacon to all within reaching distance. How the look used to grate at Redden. He had almost forgotten but now found comfort in the reminder. Those eyes in front of a jury would be a definite turnoff. But there were also changes. Gray was beginning to sprinkle over the ears, and the hairline advanced much further than before. The face itself was also fuller, with a prominent double chin hanging like the jowls of a bulldog. Raymond Gillingham was a good 20 pounds heavier than Redden had last remembered him.

"We need to talk," urged Gillingham, "privately." He motioned to a vacant area down the hallway.

"Got no time, Chester. Need to bone up on federal procedures," he said, holding up the handbook. "But then I don't need someone to hold my hand. Maybe we're *both* out of our element." Redden pushed on by, with a wink to Rothenberg, and defiantly entered the courtroom. Two lawyers for a status conference – the billing practices at Barry, Klein & Nance were still in high gear.

Gillingham and Rothenberg watched the door slowly close. Rothenberg is bristling. "So, when do we confront him?" he asked.

"He filed on a BKN client and now is showing his face in a courtroom. Isn't it time to let him know where this is going?"

Gillingham contemplated the spot where Redden had disappeared through the door for a moment. "Give it some time," he said. "Yeah, give it some time and a dose of Langhorne. Then we'll see if he's ready for a chat."

Inside, Langhorne's courtroom was filling to near-capacity as Redden casually sat behind the railing like a seasoned veteran of the federal system. But within, he was still alive with anxiety. Four years away from a courtroom had taken its toll. He also knew Gillingham would confront him again before he could escape from the courthouse. He had violated one of the Bulldog's dictates: he had filed on a Barry, Klein client. Brookhurst Pharmaceuticals was off-limits.

And he would not be able to sweep the issue aside as easily as he had with Niki. Niki, of course, was not a problem. He had simply explained that Brookhurst became a BKN client *after* he had left the firm. He never had access to any confidential information of the corporation. It would thus not be an obstacle to representing the two of them in a lawsuit against the pharmaceutical giant. Had he lied to her back in his office? Yes, he had. At the time, he did not want to take her case, and conflict of interest offered a convenient excuse. His reasons for declining her case were personal but no longer relevant. Niki readily accepted this without further debate or questioning. After all, she had gotten what she was after.

Just like all courtrooms, a railing divided the audience section from the area up front where everything happened. To the left was the jury box, smaller than the state court but large enough to seat 6 jurors and two alternates. In the center of the room was a podium, flanked on each side by a counsel table. On the right side was a small desk to accommodate the bailiff, who was also a federal marshal.

As the two defense counsels settled themselves on the opposite side of the room, Langhorne suddenly came charging out of his chambers and took the bench. It was twenty after nine, and he was late, by reputation, a common practice. He was a man in his late sixties, bald, with eyes darting about from his small round face, seeming anxious, unfocused, a man in a hurry. His most striking feature to Redden, however, was his size. Langhorne could not have been a quarter inch over 5'2".

Napoleon had just mounted his throne.

After the bailiff called the courtroom to order, the Burroughs case was called first out of order. This caught Redden somewhat off guard. The three men stood up, paraded in front of Langhorne, and announced their appearances. They then stood waiting while the diminutive judge perused their file. After what seemed an inordinate period of silence, Langhorne contemplatively pursed his lips and then nodded as if he had just arrived at a momentous decision on the case. He then peered down at the trio.

"Counsel, I'm going to set this case for trial in five months," he announced. "Let's see…," he added as he looked over a calendar hidden by the elevated bench. "That will be April five, and discovery cutoff in four months, with expert designations in 90 days."

Redden appears shocked. "Excuse me, your Honor!" His first words uttered inside a courtroom since his unexplained disappearance rang out more loudly than he had intended, prompting a sharp glare from Langhorne. "This leaves plaintiffs with inadequate time to prepare," he continued. "This is a complex case…"

"Mr. Redden!" interrupted Langhorne, equally assertive. "Did I solicit any comments?"

"No, Your Honor."

"In my courtroom, you do not speak unless invited to do so. Are you clear on this very important matter of protocol?"

"Yes, Your Honor, but may I be heard?"

"No, you may not. I have seen drug product cases in this courtroom before, and many of them and counsel always try to make them more complicated than they are. It is my job to dispense justice expeditiously, and these types of cases are clogging my docket. The dates will stand." So as to make a point, Langhorne turned and addressed his clerk as if the three lawyers had already vacated their spot in front of the bench. "Call the next case," he instructed.

Trial counsel on the Burroughs case was quickly replaced and exited into the hallway. Redden's displeasure was obvious as he pushed through the door. His two opponents followed him, each sporting a grin.

"Perhaps now we could have our chat," called out Gillingham from behind.

Recognizing that escape was impossible, Redden stopped and turned – and for a brief moment, their eyes engaged one another in silent battle. "What's on your mind, Chester?"

"You damn well know what's on my mind," responded Gillingham, after first assuring that they were not within earshot of others, save for Rothenberg. The younger lawyer, who had anxiously been waiting for this moment for months, drew closer, not to be denied a word of the exchange. "You have stepped over the line," added the Bulldog. "Violated an express directive of our agreement."

"Actually, not." Redden's response conveyed a sense of finality on the issue. "You see, our agreement has been rescinded – unilaterally, of course, but rescinded no less."

"Then I presume that you and Blaylock are prepared to turn in your State Bar cards?"

"Oh, I don't think that will be necessary." Now, it was Redden who was displaying a grin, enjoying every minute of the confrontation.

"Perhaps the years away have clouded your memory," said Gillingham.

"Not in the slightest. But clarify for me. How might Harry and I lose our tickets to practice law?"

Gillingham briefly contemplated Redden's briefcase and what it might be concealing. He was not about to be drawn into a threat that could be interpreted as extortion. Beginning from the moment he acquired the Blaylock records, he had taken every precaution to eliminate any and all evidence, the least bit incriminating, and was not about to give Redden the upper hand with such a recording.

Not hearing a reply, Redden smiled, "See you in court, Chester" – then added over his shoulder while departing, "The word is 'prejudice.' Maybe you should start doing your own homework."

Prejudice? Redden didn't know how it might play a role in their plight, but it sounded like something that might concern the two BKN lawyers. A little misdirection never hurt. He could visualize

Gillingham and Rothenberg scrambling for the books, Chester barking out his instructions, Rothenberg pledging his undying fealty, spending hour after hour on his computer and in the office library. Indeed, to Redden's considerable amusement, he had just thrown out a word with little thought of how it could fit into any defense.

Authentication. That was his real safety net. It was so basic, so fundamental. The only evidence against Blaylock lay in bank records that could never be legally authenticated. All Gillingham had were copies of hearsay documents. Without the actual records – the originals – they would never be admissible in a judicial proceeding. Not without Harry's permission. Banks were governed by state and federal privacy laws and would only turn over a depositor's records with the written consent of the depositor.

Gillingham, or more likely some investigator he had hired, had paid someone off inside the bank. The records unquestionably had been illegally obtained. Not only would they be inadmissible in a State Bar hearing, but Gillingham could never reveal his possession of those records without being exposed to a disciplinary proceeding himself. There would be no hearing because there was no evidence, and losing money in Las Vegas was not illegal. With help from Redden, Harry had also provided trust fund checks to the three clients after obtaining their "approvals" of the settlements.

"So, what did he mean, 'prejudice'?" Rothenberg inquired of his mentor.

"That's what I pay you for," Gillingham angrily snapped. "I want a complete memo on the role of prejudice in disciplinary proceedings on my desk by this afternoon. Redden has an angle, and I want to know what it is."

As he proceeded down the elevator, Redden savored the short exchange outside the courtroom. It was stimulating and felt good to again lock horns inside a courthouse, even one under the jurisdiction of the federal government.

CHAPTER 14

Wednesday, November 11

With Randy in tow, it was late afternoon when Niki entered her father's room at the Golden Age Nursing Home. It was another random stop, although she had yet to find Stavros as she had on the day of the accident. She had made her point, and no one present that day would likely forget her threat – or the chance she would follow through if justified. In truth, no one in the nursing facility had received better care over the past three months than Stavros Leondopoulos.

Randy enthusiastically yelled, "Hi, Grandpa," and with the help of a stool, climbed up onto his bed to kiss the feeble old man on the cheek. Stavros' incessantly trembling head turned toward the boy with a smile and tried, without success, to express some type of greeting. After a quick kiss, Randy dropped to the floor, pulled a couple toy cars out of a cabinet, and began to play with them.

Stavros' tired eyes gazed up at Niki, standing beside the bed. For some reason, he seemed more aware and more cognizant of his surroundings.

"You're looking better, Steve," she observed. "Yes, you are," she added, looking deeper into his eyes.

Stavros made an effort to speak again, straining, barely moving his lips, but like before, nothing escaped. Niki leaned her ear up to his lips and heard in barely audible Greek, "My little kitten…where have you been, and where's Momma?"

This impacted Niki as she pulled away and inspected his eyes again.

Stavros had not spoken a word in over five months, and the last time he had used that nickname was the very day she had commenced her first menstrual period. Having no mother with whom to share the traumatic day, she had blushingly informed her father of her entry into womanhood. It all now flushed up from her memory as if it had happened that morning. Stavros had let out a hearty laugh and pronounced, first in Greek and then in broken English, "My little kitten, she is no more. Today, I share my house with a woman."

"Momma's gone, Steve, a long time ago. Don't you remember?" Niki then repeated it again in Greek. But Stavros just turned his eyes back to the wall, departing into his private world, his hands trembling, working them together as if rubbing in soap under a faucet.

She verbally tried to reach him several more times, but her efforts were fruitless.

Nikifora Leondopoulos grew up a rebel. Having lost her mother at the age of thirteen, Niki at first resented her father, holding him responsible for her death. Stavros reached out to her, not understanding his daughter's reaction, but all of his efforts were met with rejection. Over time, their relationship improved, but they never reached the closeness enjoyed before the death. Eventually, Stavros began spending more and more time on his trawler to maintain his struggling business, and the distance between them increased even further. The fishing industry was coming of age technologically, but Niki's father refused to abandon his old ways. In Greece, he was to grow up a fisherman, as had his father, and changing the traditions of his life-long vocation seemed a rejection of his heritage. The increasing loss of her father at home brought further resentment, not just for his stubbornness but Niki's Greek ancestry as well. Stavros was an American now, and symbolic of her stand, Niki began to call him "Steve." He wasn't her Pappa anymore, just a man who lived in the same house and provided her with financial support.

Upon entering high school, Nikifora Leondopoulos shortened her name to "Niki Leon" and stopped speaking to her father in his native tongue. When she finally met Scott Burroughs in her senior year of high school, Niki was primed for the dubious relationship that followed.

Niki made a quick check of her father and the room and satisfied herself once again that both had been properly cleansed and maintained. She then launched into her weekly report.

"You know, Steve, I may have mentioned that I've been dating a man for the past couple of months, a lawyer. He's actually filed a lawsuit for Randy and me. We…well, we found out that this pill I had been taking during pregnancy, Phenatol, caused Randy's birth defect. His name is Mitchell, Mitchell Redden….He believes we have a good case."

Stavros continued to fix his eyes on the wall as if his two visitors were not even there. Niki, on the other hand, spoke to her father as if he was fully attentive and digesting every word.

"Mitch…'Mitch' is what I call him. He's a wonderful man really, and very caring. Well, he seems to be, anyway, and thinks of the world of Randy. After all, he was the only lawyer in Los Angeles willing to help us and offer Randy a chance at a future."

Niki continued, but the tone in her voice began to change. "Of course, as I said, he is a lawyer, and I am trying to keep the relationship somewhat professional. After all, I'm sure he has his own agenda, and there is something about his past that he's unwilling to share. And then, of course, he is a man, and men, well, you should know, men are different than women. They can be unfeeling and impersonal, selfish, thinking only of themselves, with their own hidden motives. And Mitchell Redden, like pretty much all men, is no doubt a user of women as well."

Niki is now staring down at Stavros, much like he is staring at the wall. "I'm sure he has his own reasons for taking our case. And I'm sure they have nothing to do with helping a struggling mother and her handicapped child. But of course, he can't really help himself, can he, being a man, as I said? When was the last time you heard of an honest lawyer? Really, when you put the two together – male and lawyer – what else would you expect?"

Niki's anger began to spill out uncontrollably, gaining momentum as she unloaded. "This Mitchell Redden, he…he claims to be a savior of the handicapped, the injured and all, but it's greed, his own selfish ambition that drives him. I could see it the very first day, Steve. But no, not this time. This time, he's gonna find out that he has met his match. He…he thinks he has total control over our case and our lives, but boy, is he in for a surprise. Not with *this* woman. Not with me. He's gonna find out that it is *me*, Steve, not him, not you, no one else. *I'm* the one who is in control, and no man, ever again, is gonna have control over my life."

Blinded by her anger, Niki fails to see that the tremors have stopped, with Stavros' hands in a motionless grip, tucked tightly against his chest. She is also unaware that Randy is now taking in her tirade.

"I've seen it before, many times. The empty promises, the lies, the deceit, offering hope and expectation and then walking away. This goddamn world is filled with Mitchell Reddens, and I am tired of it! Tired and prepared to deal with them. As he's gonna find out, and soon, *I* am the one doing the manipulating here," she emphasized with some pride. "*I* am the one controlling the course of this lawsuit, and Scott Edward Burroughs may think he is sitting on top of the case of his career…"

Niki suddenly stopped as the name of her former husband seemed to rebound off the wall and hit her square between the eyes.

"Did I say 'Scott'? No, I meant to say 'Mitch, Mitchell Redden'.…"

Niki's emotional rambling finally caught up with her, leaving the young woman bewildered and confused. Where had it all come from, and why? She looked down at Randy, who was staring back up at her. Sensing an uncommon stillness in the room, Niki's eyes fell to her father's rigid hands and then moved up to his face.

The eyes of Stavros Leondopoulos were still open, but now they had assumed a certain peaceful appearance, staring at nothing, the anguish gone, and vanished for eternity.

Niki screamed out, "Pappa, no…!" and tried vainly several times to shake him back to life. "No, Pappa, no, not now!"

But Stavros had departed the living, and with his departure, Niki's last opportunity to share a secret that had been so difficult to reveal and explain how it had impacted their relationship.

"No, Pappa, no, not now!" she repeated, but this time with resignation and less emotion. And with those final words to her father, Niki dropped across his lifeless form and began sobbing.

⎯⎯⎯●⎯⎯⎯

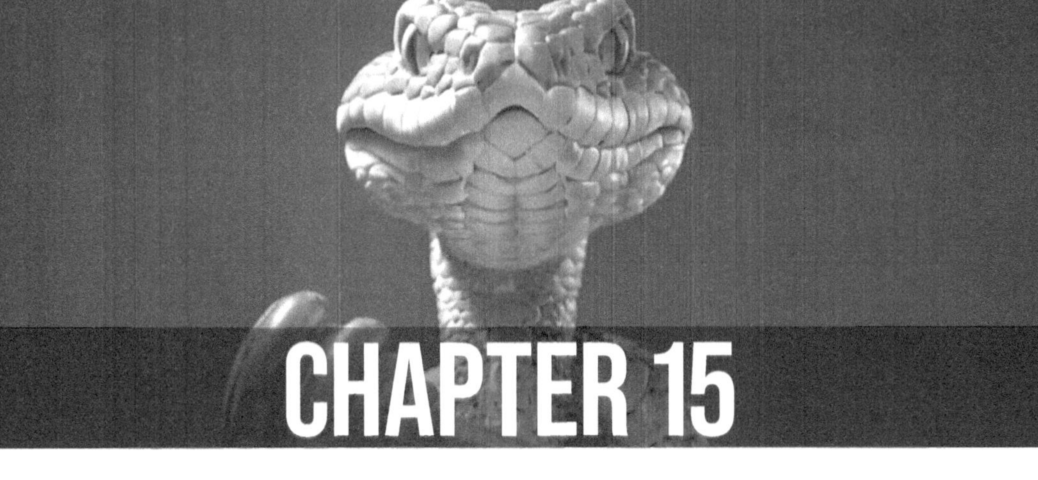

CHAPTER 15

Monday, November 16

It is early morning, and Redden is already in his office dictating when Blaylock ducks his head into the door. Redden's office door was always open, an interview with a client being the rare exception.

"You're at it early," said Blaylock. The sight of Redden at work brought delight to his mentor.

"Interrogatories and request for admissions, but doubt they will be of much help," said Redden.

"You're probably right," said the older lawyer. "Bullshit answers and objections. Standard protocol at Barry, Klein, if not the whole defense industry, don't you think?" Harry entered the office and dropped onto Redden's couch.

"I wouldn't expect anything else."

But that was only part of the problem. Even with candid answers and a discovery cutoff of four months, there was insufficient time for a full document inspection and employee depositions. Redden was at the mercy of Roger Langhorne. Would the federal court judge be prepared to order a postponement of the trial and allow additional discovery procedures? Unlikely. After the experience at the status conference, Redden had serious doubts about receiving any accommodations on the timetable for trial. For whatever motivation, this case was being railroaded to a swift conclusion, and Mitchell Redden would have to grab what he could along the way and hope for the best.

"So where do we go from here?" Harry was in virgin territory. Drug product cases were not part of his resume.

"I need to get a look at the records, the New Drug Application, the 'NDA' it is called." Redden stared off contemplatively for a moment, then added, "Harry, if there is anything to be found, that is where we will find it – the NDA and the internal memos at Brookhurst. All it takes is someone with the time and patience to sift through about 100,000 pages of documents – and know what in the hell he is looking for."

"Well, that lets me out," offered Harry. "Especially the patience part."

"As if I didn't know. It's like panning for gold. If you put in the time and find it – that smoking gun you hope is in there – it can break the case wide open." Redden smiled at his colleague. "But it does take the patience of Jobe," he added. "And that's something you ain't got, my friend."

"Amen to that," Harry acknowledged.

Redden had been down this road a few times before and knew what to expect. The document inspection trip and tour through the company records was where drug product liability cases were either made or crumbled under the sheer weight of the task. Given the time parameters Redden was working under, it also offered their only opportunity for success.

Redden pushed a button to the intercom and spoke to Mary Ellen. "Mary E, I want you to put in a call to Gillingham's secretary. Schedule a document inspection trip to New Jersey. The earlier, the better. Allow for four, no five, days at the company. Tell them I want to look at the NDA….Oh, and the IND as well." The Investigational New Drug application should be part of the NDA, but a separate request would avoid any games with semantics or the description of what was being sought. "Let me know when you have some dates, and I'll dictate a request for production."

Redden seemed to be gaining some enthusiasm for the case, observed Blaylock, seeing for the first time some of the old sparks.

Redden explained his game plan. He would initiate the paper war with interrogatories and request for admissions aggressively, with motions to compel at every turn, but his real target would be the company records. If he had any hope of seeing a high number on a check, Redden would need to turn up with a piece of incriminating evidence that Brookhurst would want to keep under wraps. And if it were to be found, it would be buried deep within the confines of the IND and NDA or internal company memos. Redden was also convinced that there was something there.

The challenge would be in finding it.

"So, let me give you a primer on Drug Liability 101," said Redden to Blaylock. "When a drug company wants to start human studies – clinical investigations – in order to get approval to market a drug, it files with the FDA what is called an Investigational New Drug application or IND. After the initial approval of the IND, as the investigators treat their patients with the experimental drug, they forward copies of their records to the drug company. That's the *drug company*, not the FDA," he emphasized. "And this is where the company can manipulate the findings – cook the books, so to speak. Drug companies are not beyond altering and destroying records and have been caught doing so many times in the past. This is where I'll be focusing my inspection."

Redden continued to educate Blaylock. Although the younger lawyer would be reviewing the NDA and other records, the allotted five-day period would still be insufficient to do a thorough analysis. There would still be large sets of documents that would need to be more closely inspected – some literally with a magnifying glass. These he would simply order, copy and ship to his office – which is when Harry would be of his greatest value.

Notwithstanding his unflattering history, Harry Blaylock had an eye for discovering evidence that could break open a case, an innate sense of picking up a clue to something incriminating that others would overlook. Although Redden would need to dig in his spurs to motivate his old friend, there was no one better at the task, and Redden had every intention of taking full advantage of that talent.

"Rick Hildebrand is here." Mary Ellen was standing in the open doorway.

"Show him in," said Redden.

Hildebrand was brought in and introduced to Blaylock. The two had not met before. Redden began using Hildebrand only a year before his disappearance. Always on the lookout for a better investigator, Mitchell considered himself fortunate for the referral from a fellow member of the plaintiffs' bar.

In Richard Hildebrand's view, he was not a private investigator; he described his vocation as a *professional* investigator. He was college-educated with a bachelor's degree in psychology and a minor in business administration, followed by training by the Los Angeles Police Department, where he spent nine years of his career. He was an impeccable dresser with a full wardrobe of hand-tailored business suits. Ambitious, he now has a growing business with five other investigators working under him. "Efficient and thorough" was how the referring lawyer described Hildebrand.

Redden invited Hildebrand to have a seat. He had already been briefed about the case but had yet to learn of his assignment.

Redden stood. "Okay, here's what I need," he began, pondering the floor as he collected his thoughts. He then rounded his desk to address the two men. "My gut is telling me – and my intuition is usually right – that there is something going on between Langhorne and Gillingham. Chester never leaves anything to chance. He covers his bets – *always*. How can I put this…? It feels like I'm on a runaway train – the status conference was an absolute disaster. Yet I know it's being controlled by Gillingham. Chester is pulling Langhorne's strings, but *how* is the mystery. And how in the hell did he rig Langhorne's assignment on the case?"

Hildebrand could see where Redden was going but wanted absolute clarity on instructions. This would be an involved assignment – involved and expensive and, to some extent, somewhat open-ended. "So, exactly what do you want from me?" he asked.

Redden was quick in his reply. "I want you to dig up everything you can about Roger Langhorne, from the cradle to yesterday's breakfast. His family, what they did, business associations inside and outside the profession, investments and financial holdings, former clients, organizations, and other affiliations, cases before him on the bench – past and present – everything, and all with an eye to any possible association between Langhorne and Gillingham or Barry, Klein, and Nance. Spare no expense and give the case top priority in your office."

"Weekly reports?" Hildebrand wanted to know how tightly Redden would be monitoring his investigation.

"Weekly. But if a question should arise, I want a call...immediately, day or night."

"In writing?"

"Not necessary, but I want you to document anything you might discover. Think in terms of supporting evidence."

Hildebrand, who had been taking notes, gave Redden the assurance he wanted to hear. "Anything, even slightly suspicious, any clue, any piece of information of value, and you will get my call. Promise. Day or night." Hildebrand stands. "Is that it?"

"That's it. Look forward to your calls."

If it was there to be found, he would find it, he promised. And with that, the investigator disappeared through the door.

Redden's engine, lying dormant over four years, was now turning at a higher RPM. He felt energized, even excited, about the challenges he was facing, however uncertain they might be. The bigger the challenge, the bigger the sense of success. And this case might well represent the biggest challenge of his career.

Harry was taking it all in and with considerable pleasure. At the moment, he was witnessing the Mitchell Redden of old, barking out instructions, animated, gesturing, pacing the floor, contemplating his next move. This was the transformation he had been hoping for when he had talked Redden out of retirement.

Harry also wanted to be part of the team. "Got something for me? I wanna be part of this, you know."

"You kidding? You'll be working your ass off," promised Redden.

"You're not going to talk me out of retirement and then stand on the sidelines while I'm busting my buns. No, you'll have plenty to do."

Redden paused, contemplating the crossroads he was at. It seemed to be the appropriate time to enlighten Harry about what might be coming down on them. But, then again, Gillingham had yet to file charges with the State Bar, and Redden now doubted that he ever would. Harry, on the other hand, was still weak and vulnerable in spite of weekly sessions with a psychiatrist; stronger, yes, but still a big question mark.

In some ways, it seemed that the visit from Gillingham had occurred only a week earlier. After his departure, Redden had torn up his office, throwing files everywhere, screaming obscenities, most of them directed at Harry. At one point, he told himself he would turn Blaylock in. In the end, though, he saw it as a sickness and resolved to do something about it in his own way. Then, as now, they shared office space together, and he angrily told Blaylock of his "discovery" while looking for some records in his office. Either he restored the funds to the trust account immediately and sought professional help, or he would report his conduct to the State Bar. Redden must have been convincing since Blaylock embraced the idea with open arms. Harry replaced the funds, in part with a loan from Redden, and began psychiatric counseling. Two months later, Redden told Blaylock he was retiring and closed his doors.

No, the time was not ripe for the candid conversation he knew could not be avoided. Harry would continue to pressure him for an answer. But Blaylock, always unpredictable, at this point in time might just walk out the door and turn himself into the State Bar, an act that might turn out to be totally unnecessary. If Redden's assessment was correct – as he believed it to be – Gillingham was handcuffed to his own devious conduct and would never risk exposing himself to the same discipline he threatened for Blaylock. Redden would continue with his wait-and-see plan. Once he was convinced of Gillingham's permanent silence, he would have his conversation with Harry. But not until then.

"No, we are in this together," added Redden. "But be prepared. Something is telling me we both are in for the ride of our lives."

"I'd walk through hell with you," answered Harry, meaning every word of it.

The sincerity of the comment struck an emotional chord with Redden, as it brought home the bond between the two men.

"I know you would," he said.

CHAPTER 16

Thursday, November 19

There is a bite in the air on an overcast fall day, and Nikifora Leondopoulos Burroughs is seated on a metal folding chair, staring at her father's casket. It is poised over a freshly dug grave, awaiting its final resting place. Niki's eyes, glistening with tears, betray a decade of guilt as a Greek Orthodox priest pronounces the final rites – in Greek by Stavros' earlier request. A throng of 20 to 30 mourners openly weep and sob, most of them dressed in traditional black.

Randy, seated next to his mother, is trying to sort out the significance of what to him was a confusing series of events. Grandpa was gone now, but he could only recall his lengthy illness and the inconvenient visits, and he hardly ever saw him smile. Grandpa must have been very unhappy, so why was everyone so sad now that he was finally in heaven?

However, adults rarely share the same simplistic views of life, and Niki was burdened more than most. Times and events long suppressed are flowing to the surface now like a bubbling spring. Many years ago, her father shared with her his adolescent years and his arrival and growth in this strange new country, a bit of the past at a time, always holding back and capturing her interest until their next session of family history. How she had enjoyed those Sunday afternoons. Stavros, a master storyteller, would narrate the experiences and adventures of this young Greek boy like some fictional character out of a historical novel. As each chapter would close, Niki would again conclude that the boy in the story was her father – although he would never acknowledge it.

Stavros Leondopoulos moved from Greece to the United States with his parents when he was 14 years old. The family had settled in San Pedro, a smaller city fronting a mass of waterways, shipyards, warehouses, and marinas known as "Los Angeles Harbor," and the hub of the local fishing industry. From his early teens into adulthood, he worked on his father's trawler and later took over the vessel upon the retirement of the older Leondopoulos. He then headed his own business, but things got tougher. Unions moved in, driving up the cost of labor, and he found himself competing with larger and more scientifically equipped boats. Stavros dug in his heels, unwilling to advance with the times. He soon was working longer hours and showing less effort. Friends urged him to switch to recreational fishing, but he rejected the idea, even though the adversity served as a constant drain on his family unit.

Stavros had met Jasmine at a Greek wedding and married her after a lengthy courtship. Seven years later, Niki was born following three miscarriages. Her arrival into the Leondopoulos' household was looked upon as a gift from heaven, for Jasmine was never again able to conceive. Her physician considered it nothing short of a miracle that Niki was delivered at all. The three of them had always remained close until one cold day when Niki was thirteen. Her mind drifted back to that day as the priest continued the rites.

Niki had arrived home from school at her usual time and had tried the front door, only to find that it was locked. She knocked several times and called out to her mother but heard no response. She sensed stillness about the house that brought on a chill and a sense of anxiety that choked off her voice as she attempted to call out again. After a quick glimpse through a window, she raced around to the rear of the house and burst through the back door.

No sooner was she inside when she was hit with the acrid odor of natural gas. Her eyes smarted and began to tear as she screamed out for her mother, then gagged as she sucked in the gas, causing her to stumble back outside, coughing until her throat felt aflame. Undaunted, she drew in some air and was again back inside, making her way to the kitchen. On the floor, she found her mother, near the stove, coiled up in a fetal position, as if symbolizing the cycle of life as it had come to a close. Smashing open a window with a chair and her feeble effort at mouth-to-mouth resuscitation had been an act of utter futility, she had later been told. Her mother had been dead a good hour before her arrival. Accidental death from a faulty pilot light in the stove had been the final conclusion from the coroner's office. The stove, old and obsolete, was pulled out of the kitchen and sent off to the trash yard.

Stavros had fallen into a deep depression, vocally finding fault with the sources of his financial despair that kept him from replacing the stove, but within blaming himself. Niki, too, found difficulty in dealing with the death of her mother. She refused to talk, other than uttering what was necessary to get by, and left the house only to attend school. No longer interested in friends or a social life outside her house, Niki's focus was now only on her studies, refusing to open up about the events of that fateful day. "I don't want to talk about it," she would say whenever Stavros would ask.

The father and daughter grew more distant from each other over the following years, also shutting out relationships with all outsiders and limiting their social existence to those few relatives who shared their grief. Niki became a surrogate wife to her father, cooking the meals, cleaning the house, and shopping for food and other needs, while Stavros worked and provided the necessary maintenance around the house. But their continued isolation began to stimulate rumors of an unnatural intimacy, all brought home to Niki when her father was deposited at their door one day by a local police officer. Stavros had been pulled off by a neighbor at a San Pedro hardware store short of killing the man. Neither would talk about what prompted the fight, but Niki found out later that evening. Before retiring to bed, she spent an hour sobbing, standing in the shower, and washing and rewashing long after the water turned icy cold. Only her father's pounding on the door brought her to finally shut off the water.

Stavros began to work even harder, encouraging Niki to focus on her education. A college degree for his daughter became not just his hope but his obsession.

Through her junior year of high school, Niki was named to the Honor Society, and hopes of a scholarship at a prestigious university seemed within reach. It was at this point that Scott Burroughs walked into her life.

Niki became immediately infatuated with the outgoing and gregarious Burroughs, spending more and more time with him and less with her studies. By the end of the first semester of her senior year, Niki's grades began to fall, and with them, any chance at a scholarship. Stavros complained and tried to reach her, but it was futile. Niki was as strong-willed as her father – and in love. The father and boyfriend became estranged, and Scott was prohibited from entering the house, driving a deeper wedge between Niki and Stavros. Then came pregnancy and marriage two months before graduation.

Stavros refused to attend the wedding and became increasingly despondent over the ensuing months, a condition from which he never seemed to fully recover. Even after the divorce, when Niki and Randy returned to the Leondopoulos household, it became apparent that Stavros had lost his will to live, sitting for hours staring out the window as if waiting for someone to return after a long journey.

One night, Niki sat talking to her father, pleading for his forgiveness. There was nothing to forgive, he assured her, but tears flowed down his cheek as he continued his fixation on the window and the large olive tree he and Jasmine had planted after their wedding. It was the first day she had ever noticed a tremor in her father's hand.

After the casket was lowered into the ground, Niki approached the open grave and tossed in some dirt. "My secret dies with you, Pappa," she said in Greek. "No longer do I bear this heavy burden. It is now buried forever."

CHAPTER 17

It was late in the day when Redden arrived at the Newark airport for his document inspection trip. After a prolonged delay, waiting for luggage, he secured a rental car and was off through the rolling green hills of New Jersey. Redden and darkness arrived at the same time in Princeton, where he checked into his hotel and collapsed on a bed after ordering room service. Brookhurst was only a twenty-minute drive away in the morning, and it is one of a number of major pharmaceutical companies that call New Jersey home, including Bristol-Myers Squibb, Johnson & Johnson, and Bayer.

Lying on his bed, awaiting dinner, Redden tried to organize his thoughts about the prodigious charge awaiting him. The light next to the bed was turned low, adding to the relaxed atmosphere, and he closed his eyes. Would he be up to the task? Had too many years passed him by? What had been his approach last time? Had he turned the evidence just by chance, or did he really know what he was doing? The uncertainties raced by as he drew upon his memory, pulling up pieces from the past, trying to structure his search over the next few days.

He would first concentrate on the NDA, trying as much as possible to follow the individual volumes in the chronological sequence in which they were prepared and forwarded to the FDA. This had a number of purposes. First, it would be easier to trace and understand the documents and their importance; second, depending upon the content of earlier comments or communications, he would have a clue of what to be on the alert for in later volumes; and third, it would be easier to spot records that were dated out of sequence, a red flag that a letter, memorandum or other communiqué had been individually removed, altered and returned or intentionally misplaced in the records to avoid discovery. By following this practice, he would also learn earlier in the inspection trip if volumes or sets of records were missing.

Facing the prospect of reviewing up to 100,000 pages of documents, or even more, Redden knew it would be impossible to read all but a few select records. Instead, he would scan each page, hoping to pick up buzzwords, such as "birth defects," "malformations," "anomalies," "fetus," "teratology studies," and others, and to assure himself that nothing appeared out of order.

Certain categories of records, however, would be reviewed more slowly and carefully than others. Adverse Experience Reports, or AERs, were one such group. Here were post-marketing reports of possible adverse reactions from the drug trickling in from the medical profession and the general public. Maybe complaints of congenital malformations might show up in these records. Correspondence between the FDA and Brookhurst might also be revealing, especially those in the letters addressing the results of the recently published study associating phenylpropelene and limb-reduction birth defects. Interoffice memoranda, any of them discussing the issue of birth defects remotely, would also be closely scrutinized.

However, the principal target – at least initially – would be the designs and protocols of the pre-marketing clinical investigations, as well as the statistics and conclusions of the results reported by Brookhurst. Had the drug been used on pregnant women at all? If so, was any effort made to document the time during gestation when the drug was actually ingested? Were examinations of newborn infants ever performed?

Redden expected that the answers to these questions would demonstrate that the study was never designed to evaluate the pharmacological effect of Phenatol on a developing embryo or fetus.

The statistics would also be of little assistance in developing his case other than to provide a baseline of what was reported to the FDA. Against this data, he would compare his own computations drawn, not from the individual case reports prepared by Brookhurst but from the original records created by the clinical investigator and his or her staff.

It was here that Redden hoped that he might strike gold…his last thought until he heard pounding on the door, pulling him back to an awakened state in his dimly lit room.

Redden rose from the bed. "Yes?" he inquired.

"Room service," he heard through the door.

Redden began to open the door, then stopped. For the first time, he experienced a twinge of anxiety, prompting him to peer through the security hole in the door. Only after confirming who was present did he open the door and invite the young man from room service inside.

"Sorry, I must have dosed off."

"No problem," the server smiled while setting up the meal on the portable table.

On earlier inspection trips, Redden had considered his vulnerability. On each occasion, he was alone and, at night, often away from his hotel, either walking to a nearby restaurant or simply for the purpose of exercise. He was also the enemy, someone looking to do damage – to locate an incriminating document that could result in costing the drug company millions, maybe even billions of dollars. Such a discovery could foster an explosion of litigation, as others followed suit upon learning of the evidence through the media. At risk for the defendant was not only the high cost of litigation, including settlements and potential judgments but also the cost of lost revenue. Yet Redden took no precautions for his own protection. Justified or not, he believed that he was dealing with professionals in his own little war, that everything with a major corporation, whether a drug company or a manufacturer of some product, was reduced to a dollars-and-cents issue and would be fought exclusively on that plane.

But in this case, something felt different. At a visceral level, he sensed a need for precaution. Gillingham could be ruthless, but was he capable of violence – not personally, but was he beyond soliciting others to act on his behalf? To Redden, that was an open question, especially if Gillingham's career was at stake.

Redden thanked and tipped the young man, then secured the door both with the deadbolt and the security latch as he showed him out of the room. Was he being paranoid? Perhaps. But then again, maybe not.

Redden quickly consumed the small meal and arranged a wake-up call before retiring early, looking forward to the challenges of the next day.

CHAPTER 18

Monday, December 7

By 7:45 AM, Redden had already showered, dressed, and eaten a full breakfast in the hotel coffee shop. Per the agreement, the inspection days were to last from 8:30 AM to 4:30 PM. He would not be late.

Thirty minutes later – at precisely 8:15 AM – he arrived at the Brookhurst parking lot, ready to go to work. This would be his routine for each of the five days. He would not waste a minute of the allotted time.

The entrance and grounds of Brookhurst Pharmaceuticals would have impressed even the most sophisticated and successful of businessmen. Situated on 220 acres, the three monolithic stone and tinted glass structures rose out of the low-lying countryside like an oasis of modern architecture. A green undulating lawn stretched between the abutting road and the front parking lot, a good 300 yards back, adding to the stately appearance of the three buildings. The first, to Redden's left as he drove up the private drive, was a six-story edifice designated the International Building, accommodating the business offices of the corporate staff involved in foreign sales, promotion, and marketing, as well as foreign regulatory affairs and international law. To his right was the Administration Building, his intended designation, rising above the grounds the same number of stories. Beyond and adjoining administration by an enclosed walkway was the laboratory, a lower and sprawling two-story structure extending toward the rear of the property, and a security-enclosed parking lot.

Redden parked and entered the Administration Building and was at once equally taken by the interior design and décor. The entrance area stood three stories high, with two levels of mezzanines on both sides and ended 150 feet distant at a large semi-circular information booth where he signed in and received a badge. In the adjoining waiting area were several comfortable upholstered chairs and couches, as well as a large glass case displaying the various drug products manufactured and sold by Brookhurst. Phenatol enjoyed a prominent location in the center of the display.

As the clock above the information booth struck 8:30 AM, a young woman entered the lobby from an adjacent door and approached Redden. She wore glasses and a dress suit and had a somewhat impersonal air about her. Her dark brown hair was pulled back into a bun; her features were hard and all business. "Hi, I'm Rachel Ordman," she said, extending her hand.

Redden stood and shook her hand. "Hi, Mitch Redden." He smiled, but the gesture was not reciprocated. The message was clear: This was all taking place under the threat of a court order, not by invitation. She would be professional and accommodating, but that was all.

"I'm from corporate legal," she said, "and will be your contact person for the week. If you have any questions, I'm the one you want to talk to. Actually, we'd prefer that you not speak with anyone else other than to ask for me."

"And if I need a glass of water?"

"Water, coffee, paper clips, rubber bands, items to assist you in your inspection, anything of that nature, sure, you can ask the girls overseeing your document inspection. But nothing else, okay?"

"Agreed."

"Good. Follow me," she said. "I'll take you where you'll be inspecting the records." With that, she turned and was off to their predetermined destination, her guest following closely behind.

From the reception area, Redden and his guide proceeded to an elevator, ascended to the third floor, traversed two long hallways, and entered through double glass doors labeled "Regulatory Affairs." Along the way were a number of strategically placed security cameras, reminding Redden again that he was there only by legal mandate.

Inside Regulatory Affairs, the uninvited guest was taken to a small room and introduced to Arlene and Judy. By dispensing with last names, Rachel was communicating that the two young women were there strictly to observe – and nothing else other than to see that he was comfortable and had a hot cup of coffee and an ample supply of paper clips. Again, in the event there were any questions, they would know how to reach Ms. Ordman.

In the center of the 14 by 24 room was a conference table surrounded by chairs. In the middle of the table sat two large plastic containers, one filled with metal and plastic paperclips and another with large rubber bands. For each document or set of records he desired to copy, Redden had to paperclip or wrap it with one of the rubber bands. Stacked neatly around the perimeter of the room were perhaps 50 to 60 storage boxes, purportedly holding the individual volumes of the IND and NDA – the reason for his presence in hostile territory.

"Anything else?" asks Ordman as she turns to exit the room.

"Yes, do you have an index to these boxes?" Redden inquired but knew what response would be from prior experience.

"Not that I know of."

"Nothing to assist the company in quickly locating a document?"

"Not that I know of."

"So if Brookhurst wanted to find a given animal study or an investigator's report, someone would have to start digging without a clue to where it might be?

"As far as I know. Of course, everything is pretty much in chronological order…Anything else?"

"Yes. Do I have your assurance that all volumes of the IND and NDA are present in the room?"

Ordman scanned the many boxes surrounding her in the room and then took a fix on Redden's eyes. "As far as I know," she repeated, this time with a barely detectable smirk.

The seasoned lawyer thought of confronting her but knew it would serve no purpose and did not want to give her the satisfaction of witnessing an emotional reaction to her comments. He was the enemy, and she had her marching orders.

Let the games begin.

Ordman promptly left, along with Arlene. From his experience, Redden determined that the two girls would alternate shifts. Judy was the first with the baton and would probably hand it off at the noon hour break. Food would be brought in from the cafeteria if requested, although, on one prior occasion, he was directed to the facility and ate with corporate personnel. His hunch was that there would be no commingling on this trip. Isolation was the order of the day.

Redden next took a tour around the room, inspecting the various boxes and their labels. Each container was identified with either the Phenatol IND or NDA number, along with a supplemental numbering system that allowed him to ascertain the earliest container and the order of those that followed. He grabbed a box bearing the earliest date of the IND, plopped it next to a chair at the conference table, sat, pulled out the first binder, and looked at his watch. It was 8:52 AM.

As he was about to open the binder and peruse the first page, he looked over at Judy, who sat at the other end of the table. At the moment, she was observing him, as was her assigned task. In front of her, she is holding a current edition of *People* magazine. Next to her sat a couple more magazines and a paperback novel. Redden smiled, more out of a desire to break the ice with his companion for the next five days than any type of test. And unlike Miss Personality, who had just exited the room, she smiled back.

"Something tells me that you're going to enjoy your reading material more than I am," he said. Judy, an attractive woman in her early twenties, smiled again. There would be no conversations, not even small talk. As with Ordman, she had her instructions on what was allowed and what was prohibited. With those final words, Redden opened the binder and began his task.

Throughout the remainder of the morning, as Redden perused each volume, Judy continued her vigil as a watchdog, first trying to observe his every move to ensure nothing was removed or altered. This, however, only lasted for about an hour. As time slowly passed, she became more engrossed in her magazines than anything Mitchell Redden was doing at the other end of the table. After all, he seemed to be only interested in reading and taking notes. And if the truth be known, she really care much about what information he was able to extract and how it might impact her employer. Brookhurst was not paying her a lot of money. and she had recently given thought to looking for another job.

By late morning, Redden had become quite aware that the room had gotten progressively warmer and had already removed the coat to his suit. A complaint was lodged with Judy, who, after a call, explained that they were having a problem with the air conditioning but that they should have it repaired by the next day. Redden saw it as nothing more than another tactic but again resolved not to complain.

At noon, he announced that he work through the lunch hour, removed his tie, and rolled up his sleeves. He ordered a sandwich and a soda, which were brought to him in the room a short time later.

Over the morning hours, he had also become aware of an annoying habit of his companion. She was a gum chewer – and seemed to have an ample supply to keep her jaws moving and the gum occasionally popping. Again, Redden decided that he would not complain. Each obstacle – the lack of an index, the room temperature, the gum popping – would be cataloged and, at the appropriate time, would be presented as a formal complaint. If he had placed a call to Ordman as each issue surfaced, he would have seemed to be nothing more than a chronic complainer. The heat and the gum-popping were also no longer intruding on his thoughts, becoming as much a part of the surrounding environment as the storage boxes and furniture. After the first three hours, he was now finally getting up to speed and totally focused on his task.

At 12:30 PM, Arlene – the more cerebral of the two – replaced Judy and became the corporate sentinel for the afternoon session. She was the older, perhaps by 6 or 7 years, bespectacled, with harder feature, and dark, closely cropped hair. After getting settled, she retrieved some college textbooks from a backpack and dove into her studies, although spending more time observing Redden than reading. It seemed that

Arlene took her job more seriously than the co-employee she replaced, a fact Redden noted and something he would use over the next four days if needed. Yet, all things considered, everything had gone pretty smoothly the first half day.

But at 12:50 PM, Redden ran into a significant stumbling block – the first of many he was sure. A large number of volumes from the IND were not in the room, perhaps as many as 20 boxes of them, maybe more.

"There are some boxes missing," he announced to Arlene. "Several of them. I need an explanation as to why they are not here."

"I'll put in a call to Ms. Ordman," she said.

Arlene placed her phone call and could be heard explaining the problem. She then hung up and said, "She'll give me a call as soon as she has an answer."

Over the next two hours, Redden continued his routine of reviewing each binder, waiting to hear from Ordman and growing angrier by the minute. After completing his review of each volume, he would note its number and title on his legal notepad, along with its date and a description of each document he clipped for photocopying. But his anger was increasingly breaking his concentration, slowing his pace, and enhancing the risk of overlooking something important. Finally, he stopped, poured himself a glass of water, and walked over to a window, staring out at the countryside. It was time to slow himself down, take a breath, and grab hold of his emotions. He had been playing into their hands, and it was not going to happen anymore. If necessary, he would wait until he got his answer, even if it meant spending another day in New Jersey.

At precisely 3:00 PM, as if on cue, Ordman and two of her staff entered the room, wheeling in two carts full of boxes.

"I am sorry," she said. "There was a huge misunderstanding. It is all my fault. As it turns out, all of the records had not been produced because there was inadequate space in the room to accommodate the entire set of records."

Redden nodded his head, doubting the sincerity of the apology.

"The remaining volumes will have to be delivered in sets," she continued, "and those you have reviewed removed. It is quite impossible to have the entire IND and NDA in the room at the same time."

"And about the heat…?"

"I apologize for that as well. But I'm sure Arlene has explained we are having a problem with the air conditioning unit that services this area of the building. We should have it fixed by tomorrow." With that, Ordman and her staff leave, along with the boxes already reviewed by Redden.

Over the remaining hour and a half, Redden became increasingly sleepy and started loading up on coffee. His back was also aching, and the words on the documents seemed to be running together. Arlene, who had apparently completed her homework assignment, began to occupy her spare time through a series of personal calls on her cell phone.

His patience stretching thin, Redden finally put down a binder he had been reviewing and decided it was time to make a request. "Excuse me!" he barked, interrupting one of many calls.

Arlene pulled the cell phone away from her ear and looked over at Redden.

"Your calls, are a bit of a distraction," he said. "Perhaps you could save them until after 4:30."

"Oh, I'm sorry," she said, acting somewhat surprised. "Of course."

Redden condemned himself for his shortness and revealed the effectiveness of their latest ploy, as he is convinced that everything occurring that day was all out of design and strategy. This was not the first visit by a lawyer engaged in civil litigation with the company, nor would it be the last. Everything was no doubt standard operating procedure and initiated for the express purpose of minimizing the efficiency of the inspection.

Toward the end of the day, Redden observed that Arlene was compiling notes on the documents he was paper-clipping and wrapping with rubber bands. These were the records he found important – though certainly no "smoking guns" in the bunch – and no doubt would be the subject of intense review by the medical and legal staffs of Brookhurst Pharmaceuticals, even before he left New Jersey.

Approaching the final quarter-hour, Redden decided it was time to have a little fun. Suddenly, he reacted as if he had discovered a note identifying the current location of the Holy Grail, enthusiastically scribbling notes, flipping pages, paper-clipping, then reading again, and finally punctuating the revelation of a lifetime by standing, with a mischievous smile, announcing as he wrapped the entire binder with a rubber band, "Oh hell, just copy the whole volume."

No sooner had he handed it over than Arlene had the band off and frantically read the paper-clipped pages. In sharp contrast to the behavior of his overseer, Redden calmly closed his briefcase, put on his coat, and said goodbye.

It had been a frustrating, nonproductive day, but Mitchell Redden, in the end, enjoyed the last laugh.

CHAPTER 19

Tuesday, December 8

The clock in the clerk's office of the United States District Court is invariably sitting at 7:55 AM when Reese Harrelson enters each day, unloads his coat, and settles at his desk for the day's tasks. It is *always* 7:55 AM when Harrelson arrives, and it has been rumored around the office that the clocks would be reset if he ever arrived at a different time. Punctual and dependable, Harrelson arrives on time, does his job, and then leaves at 4:35 PM, disappearing each day to a life unknown. He is a loner who speaks little of his personal life but is devoted to his job. During his twelve years in the office, he has yet to miss a day of illness, a fact he relishes with considerable pride.

Upon returning from his lunch break, the same five messages from Rick Hildebrand were still sitting on his desk – three from the day before and two from that morning. Each message identified Hildebrand as an investigator from the law offices of Mitchell Redden. He inspected each of them nervously through his wire-rimmed glasses one more time, as if they would somehow change. How could this all be happening? Chaos had thrust its ugly head into the orderly world of Reese Harrelson, and he was ill-equipped to deal with it. He was in bad need of guidance, yet to this very moment, all of his efforts to seek it out had run into a stone wall.

No sooner had Harrelson sat behind his desk than another clerk, who had been working the front counter, approached him.

"There's a Mr. Hildebrand out front," she said. "He would like to talk to you."

"He's here?" The walls began to close in even further.

The middle-aged clerk with rosy cheeks sensed the anxiety in Harrelson's voice, something she had never witnessed before – not from "Mr. Promptness," as the rest of the clerks referred to him.

"Yes. He's at the counter. Said it would only take ten minutes. Something about the Burroughs case and Judge Langhorne."

Harrelson removed his glasses and ran his hand over the slender, pointed features of his troubled face.

"Tell him I'm busy," was the curt reply, wishing now more than ever he had never accepted the position as assignment clerk two and a half years earlier. At the time, it seemed a reward for his years of devoted service and one of the few jobs available in the clerk's office to at least grant him some semblance of power.

And why had he taken the money?

Upon the filing of a lawsuit or a petition to remove an action from state to federal court, Harrelson would oversee the random assignment of the judge to the case, a process now done exclusively by computer. Yet, even with the program's safeguards, he had discovered a way to beat the system. Initially, he had explored the possibility simply as a challenge, a grasp at real power, to have true control over the direction of every case reaching his office.

But now it was all turning into a nightmare.

Within five minutes, the clerk with the rosy cheeks returned, enjoying every minute of her experience as the go-between. It was something she would soon be sharing with a couple of her friends in the clerk's office. Controversy was surfacing from the secret life of Reese Harrelson, and she could hardly wait to hear what it might be.

Her return message did nothing to relieve his anxiety.

"He said he would be back tomorrow morning. Ten AM. He said you should find the time to talk to him. He said it would make matters…How did he put it? Oh yes,… 'less complicated.'"

"Anything else?"

"No, that was it. He said if you would chat with him, it would make matters less complicated," she said, finding delight in repeating the message.

"Thank you, Amy," Harrelson said.

No sooner had Amy left than Harrelson was on the phone to Langhorne's clerk. "Burt, it's me again. I need to talk to the judge."

"He's on the bench."

"This is urgent."

"Yeah, well, he's on the bench and can't be interrupted. That's his standing order. But I will give him the message at the break."

"Thanks, Burt. Stress again the urgency..."

"Will do," he said, followed quickly by a dial tone.

The brief talk between Harrelson and the judge the day before did little to allay his concerns, and now Harrelson was after more definitive directions. Hildebrand was showing up at his office and had communicated some kind of a veiled threat.

A second and third call to Langhorne's private secretary did little more than draw her ire and an admonition that the judge was still tied up with counsel and the call would be returned as soon as he could break free – not a minute sooner.

"He requested that you not call again," she emphasized.

But the message about meeting with counsel had been a lie. Langhorne had no more desire to confront the issue of his assignment to the Burroughs case than did Harrelson. He was well aware that he had stepped over some legal boundaries and had yet to resolve how to deal with any form of an investigation. He simply needed more time. The issue had just come up the day before, and the current case before him consumed all of his time, both in and out of the courtroom.

He would think about how to deal with the investigator overnight and get back to Harrelson in the morning.

Preliminarily, Langhorne had considered that he would not be dealing with a formal investigation. This only involved a private investigator, and he would have little difficulty avoiding and insulating himself from any questioning by a private investigator. He was, after all, a federal court judge, cloaked with all the privileges and power that went with the appointment.

The problem was not staving off some questioning initiated by the law offices of Mitchell Redden. The problem was in the form of an assignment clerk named Reese Harrelson. He was the weak link. And the flurry of calls and their discussion the day before did nothing to satisfy his concern. Perhaps he needed direction from someone else, someone who benefited from the accommodation.

Perhaps a phone call was in order.

━━●━━

Harrelson stared up at the clock on the wall. It was 5:37 PM, and everyone else had gone home. He had also given up any hope of receiving a call from Langhorne, at least for the day. He would call the judge shortly after arriving in the morning. Langhorne was an early riser and was always in his chambers by 8:00 AM. And if he got the same runaround, well, he knew how to deal with that, too. He would leave a message that no doubt would capture his attention. He was scheduled to speak with an investigator at ten and needed to have a talk with him before the meeting.

Harrelson exited the clerk's office, walked down the hallway, and descended in the elevator to the courthouse underground parking lot. Other than security personnel at the ground level, he figured everyone else had gone home.

As the elevator doors opened, it seemed that the garage was a little darker than usual. Perhaps it was because he could not recall ever leaving this late before. With all of the budgetary cutbacks and the need to conserve electricity, nothing would surprise him. He could, however, see his car in a shadow from the closest light, about 150 feet away from the elevator. It was the only vehicle remaining on this level.

While walking toward his car, he felt a chill run up his spine. He pulled the collar up on his coat and quickened his pace, eager to get home and savor a taste of his favorite brandy. It seemed an ideal night for it. It was the perfect stress reliever; that and his classical music, which had now become his routine. He would pour himself a drink, turn on the music, grab a book he was into, and then ease back into his recliner. As each day came to an end, he would look forward to the experience, but never more than tonight.

Harrelson approached his car only to find that his left rear tire was flat.

"Damn it!" he cursed.

He had recently replaced all four tires at Costco. He must have picked up a nail on the way to work that morning. "Damn it!" he repeated, then popped open his trunk and began to retrieve his jack and spare tire. He could not remember the last time he had changed a tire, as he had always been conscientious about maintaining his car. At the first sign of a problem or need for replacement, he was on top of it. Always. It was a way of insuring against future problems.

Five minutes later, he had removed his coat and pumped up the left rear of the car with the jack.

Since his divorce seven years earlier, Harrelson had lived alone, which was the way he preferred it. It gave him the independence to do what he wanted and when he wanted to do it, something that was denied to him during his marriage, even though it had become stale and no longer met the needs of how he wanted to spend his life. At the time, both were leading separate lives anyway, other than having to answer to one another, and the divorce only formalized that which had already taken place.

After removing the lug bolts and pulling the flat tire, Harrelson spied something under the car, caught by the spill of light over his shoulder. He crouched to get a better look. It appeared to be money, but he could not determine with any certainty, so he got down on one knee and leaned even closer to the concrete floor. Upon closer inspection, he discovered that not only was it money, but it was also a one-hundred-dollar bill.

He first tried to reach for it with his extended arm, but it was under the axle and about 18 inches out of reach. He thought of grabbing the lug wrench for assistance, but he had tossed it into the open trunk and figured he could just as easily crawl a foot or so under the car and grab the money. After all, this was one hundred bucks, and his pants were already soiled from removing the tire. So under the car, he went and within a moment was clutching it in his hand – and saw a second one-hundred-dollar bill only twelve inches further.

So, with little consideration, he crawled the extra foot and secured the second bill as well. Of all the luck, he thought.

But he could not have been more wrong.

Just as he reached the seond-century note, Harrelson spied a pair of shoes near the right rear tire, which quickly traversed the short distance to the rear of the car where the jack held up the left corner of a vehicle lacking the support of a wheel and tire. At the moment, he could not have felt more foolish.

"Hi, there," he said, pondering what else to say to explain his current situation.

But there was no reply. The stranger, apparently a man, stood silently next to the jack. Maybe he had not heard his…

At this very moment, Harrelson fully appreciated what was about to happen and was overcome by the sheer terror of what he was facing. "Oh, no, oh no," he cried out just as he heard something metallic strike the jack and felt the brake drum drop with a muted thud onto his back, immediately fracturing his spine and collapsing his lungs.

Harrelson now had neither sensation below the waist nor any movement of his legs. He tried to draw in a breath but was incapable of expanding his lungs. His mouth filled with something warm, trickling down his chin and onto the concrete floor of the garage. As death began to close in, he now felt numbness throughout his body, seeming almost like a dream.

How could he have been so foolish not to see this coming? Perhaps it was the frustration of waiting for a call that never came. Perhaps it was the anger at finding the flat tire. Perhaps it was the lure of money found under the car. Perhaps he would awaken in the next few moments and laugh it all off.

Harrelson's final vision was the image of a hand, not much more than a blur, reaching beneath the car and extracting something from his grasp. He offered no resistance as both one-hundred-dollar bills slid away.

Mercifully, death quickly followed – the final and ultimate anesthetic.

CHAPTER 20

Thursday, December 10

Redden was still in his isolated room at Brookhurst Pharmaceuticals, growing increasingly frustrated. Days two and three went pretty much as day one, with little to show for the effort, other than a few letters missing that had been referred to in other correspondence. It might be something of significance, but it is more likely just misplaced and would probably show up in a cross-check of a duplicate set at the FDA.

It was now day four, and Redden was feeling the strain of bending over the conference table for hours on end, meticulously reviewing thousands of documents. Each day, the aching in his lower back seemed to be starting earlier than the day before. By 10:15 AM, he had completed his review of the Adverse Experience Reports. Still, he had found nothing of use; one report of umbilical hernia, one of metatarsus varus – a form of club foot, and another involving a congenital heart defect. None of the reporting physicians expressed concern about a possible association between the anomalies and the ingestion of the drug but felt it was of interest and should be reported. More to the point, none of the AERs contained a history of a limb-reduction type birth defect.

As Redden was starting the next storage box of binders, he discovered a new problem – and a significant one. For some time, he had been getting a sense of familiarity as he had been reviewing the forms, but

179

he passed them off due to fatigue and the duplicative nature of the information he was reviewing. But now he was certain he had seen the very same report earlier – perhaps as early as day two. A quick check of his notes confirmed it. The report had the same date, author, and subject matter.

Unquestionably, it was the same document.

A further review of his notes and surrounding boxes disclosed that at least twenty-five percent of them contained material he had already reviewed – some now a second time. Redden finally explodes.

"Goddamnit!" he exclaimed.

Judy dropped her magazine and looked up.

"This time, your boss has gone too far! I wanna see Ms. Ordman and without delay!"

"Yes, Mr. Redden. Right away." She had witnessed some irritation on his part over the past three days, but nothing like this. She immediately got on the phone and conveyed the message to Ordman. Her eyes found Redden's as she repeated, "Without delay, he said."

What *had* Ordman and her staff pulled this time? Her curiosity was exceeded only by her embarrassment. At the moment, she wanted to be somewhere else, anywhere else, just not in the middle of another battle. It was not what she had hired on for, and Judy was more determined than ever to seek out another job. In fact, it would be at the top of her to-do list next week.

Five minutes later, Ordman entered the room, knowing what was coming but underestimating the intensity of how it would be delivered. As she entered, Redden rose from his chair, and she could see that he was fuming.

"I can put up with the air conditioning thing, the cell phone calls and the gum popping," he began. "I can even deal with the lack of an index and the gamesmanship of what is or is not in the room. That's par for the course, and I've been there before. So go ahead and play your little games because what you will find is that *this* lawyer will only dig in his heels and be more determined than ever to find what there is to find. Count on it!"

Ordman sensed that a bubbling volcano was about to erupt – and she was right.

"But I have now spent a good day and a half looking, as it turns out, at the same records I had already spent hours reviewing before." His voice was now louder and sprinkled with a trace of emotion. "And these kind of games are gonna stop! And I mean now!"

"I assure you there was no…"

"Don't!" said Redden, holding up his hand like a traffic cop. "I don't want to hear your bullshit excuses." He was pacing now, somewhat like a caged animal, animated and gesturing as he made his points. "All I want you to do is listen! Because the next time something like this happens – *anything* that intrudes on my ability to do my job – we'll be breaking this off, and I'll be on my way to federal court for sanctions, and I'm talking about *major* sanctions. *Got it?*"

The last point was more for effect, as he had little confidence that Langhorne would do more than give Brookhurst a slap on the wrist.

Ordman, stone-faced, just calmly accepted the abuse and nodded her head. "Anything else?" she said, as if he had just requested more paperclips. She had been the brunt of angry lawyers before – though never at this level – and was developing a thick skin to the experience.

Redden stopped pacing and stood, facing Ordman, pondering the question while gathering his emotion. "No," he said more calmly. "Just give me the rest of the records, and let me do my job."

"Segregate out what you have reviewed," she said, "and I'll have them removed and replaced with the balance of the IND and NDA. Promise. I'll also implement safeguards to ensure that this doesn't happen again." With that, Ordman turned and promptly exited the room.

Confused about his outburst, Redden assessed whether he should feel more like a victorious prizefighter – or a fool. Probably the latter, he concluded.

Within fifteen minutes, all of the previously reviewed boxes had been replaced, and Redden was back on pace, a little wiser and much more alert. He was also assured that the balance of the documents to be produced, including the interoffice memoranda and correspondence, were now in the room.

Tomorrow was getaway day, and Redden had already booked flight reservations for early evening, allowing himself sufficient time to complete a full day of review by 4:30 PM and still have sufficient time to reach the Newark airport. By calculating the number of boxes yet to be reviewed, along with the length of time it took him to scan each box of binders, Redden was beginning to feel comfortable about completing his assignment well before closing time, and by 11:45 AM, he had seriously considered taking a lunch break. A more cautious man now, he quickly discarded the notion and decided to order a sandwich and work on through.

It turned out to be a wise decision.

At 12:25 PM, Redden ran into the final hurdle of the trip. A whole series of boxes were missing. He had just completed his review of seven binders, identified on the outside of the box as "Volumes 1-7 of 112," but nowhere in the room could he locate any boxes for volumes 8 through 112. Yet it was not that there were boxes missing that excited Redden – he had been through this once before.

It was the nature of the records that were missing.

The absent boxes purportedly contained raw clinical records prepared by two investigators, involving a total of over 500 case histories, including many women who had ingested Phenatol *during pregnancy.* These were the records initially created by the two physicians as they were treating each patient, from which the pertinent data and other information were later transposed onto printed forms prepared by Brookhurst. Volumes 1 through 7 contained the printed forms, along with various summaries, statistics, and reports analyzing the data; volumes 8 through 112 contained the original raw data from which the printed forms were compiled – and the only means to verify the accuracy of the forms.

Redden re-examined volume 2 before voicing his protest. It set out the various protocols of the studies conducted by the two investigators. Four specific studies were designed by Brookhurst and later approved by the FDA, each with a separate and distinct goal toward evaluating and assessing the possibility of different types of adverse reactions, or side effects, to the drug. Although three others appeared to be of little significance, the fourth seemed to jump out at him like a beacon of light: The offspring of 328 patients who ingested phenylpropelene during pregnancy were to be evaluated at birth for congenital malformations. Conducted between 1983 and 1987, the FDA requested the study out of deference to the thalidomide tragedy of 1961. The resulting incidence of birth defects was then compared to those of an equal number of births from the same hospitals over the same period of time from pregnancies not exposed to the same drug. If an increased incidence was found, the figures would be evaluated by an epidemiologist for statistical significance. Volume 7 reported only 9 case histories of birth defects – none involving absent or reduced limbs – and 7 cases from the control group, a meaningless difference.

The real question was whether these statistics represented an accurate reflection of what was contained in the missing original records.

Redden motioned to Arlene, the afternoon watchdog, and quickly caught her attention. "I'll need to see Ms. Ordman," he said. "I have another issue that needs to be addressed." He spoke calmly, determined not to repeat his earlier display. In fact, it was not anger he was experiencing; it was pure unadulterated excitement.

"We're missing a few records," he told Ordman, who arrived within minutes of Arlene's call. "Actually, about 105 binders of them." He then explained how he had made the determination, being very explicit in his explanation to avoid any claim of a misunderstanding.

Ordman was pleased, even surprised, at Redden's change in demeanor. She was well aware of the missing records but had only learned of it the day before. "I will look into it right away and get back to you as soon as I have an answer," she said, following instructions from above. By design, there would be more foot-dragging.

The answer did not arrive until 2:30 PM.

"The missing volumes are apparently at another facility," said Ordman upon her return. "This is where we keep the raw data, the investigators' records, I'm told."

"And you just learned about this?" asked Redden.

"Just an hour ago. The records can be retrieved, but it will take a couple of days, which means not until next Tuesday. So if you're willing to wait…"

"Can't do. Got commitments in L.A. next week, but I have all day tomorrow. So, why can't this be given a priority? We're only talking about moving boxes here. Why should it take two days?"

"I'm sorry. There's a process involved, and it takes two days to complete," she said, without explaining what the process might be. "However, Brookhurst *will* pay for your return trip to New Jersey."

"So that's it?"

"That's it."

Redden nodded, then sat without further comment and continued his review of the remaining binders. He had nothing further to say on the matter and, in fact, needed to determine his next course of action.

Sensing that their discussion had concluded, Ordman left to give her report.

Friday, December 11

By 4:30 PM, Redden had concluded his review of the remaining available records. Among them were reports on several teratology – birth defect – studies performed by Brookhurst personnel on pregnant rats and rabbits. No congenital malformations were reportedly found in the offspring. Redden had demanded to see the original bench books maintained by the scientists as they were feeding the pregnant animals and then sacrificing and dissecting the offspring. His request had been refused. These documents were not part of the IND or NDA and were not part of the formal request, which had been Ordman's argument. If Redden had wanted them, he should have asked for them.

Actually, even now, Redden had little interest in their production, as he was convinced that they would be pretty much "sanitized" by the time he would get to see them. The real prize would be in the original records prepared by the two investigators conducting the human studies. If a case could be developed: unreported birth defects, falsely transposing findings and data to the company's forms, comments of concern about a risk to the fetus – any of which could add up to the infamous "smoking gun" and none of which showed up in the reports to the FDA – that was where it would be made.

Redden had left at the end of the day with a threat to be back with a court order – and a lot more time.

CHAPTER 21

Monday, December 14

When Redden returned to his office on Monday morning, Mary Ellen casually informed him about the death of Niki's father. In truth, she had read about it in an obituary three weeks earlier, but as far as Mitchell was concerned, she had only picked up the news over the weekend and just by chance. A friend had a relative who had shared the same room with the old man, a fabrication Mary Ellen knew would never be checked. Redden reacted with surprise, which pleased her, as it suggested that the lawyer and his client were not really that close. Sexually active, yes, but nothing beyond Redden getting his horns trimmed once or twice a week.

Redden attempted to call Niki – three times over the period of an hour – but was unsuccessful. No one answered the phone, and the voicemail was apparently been turned off. Since he would see her Tuesday evening, he decided to postpone any discussion about withholding news of the loss. Besides, it would be better if it took place in person. She would have difficulty reading over the phone.

"So, how did it go?" Redden still had the phone in his hand when he looked over at Harry standing in the doorway.

"About as expected," Redden replied as he hung up the phone. "Roadblocks at every turn and tens of thousands of pages to look at, some with words I had never heard before. It was a blast, Harry. You should have been there."

"You sound a little frustrated."

"You might say that."

"Pissed?"

Redden nodded as he mentally revisited the confrontation with Ordman. "Yeah, you might say that too."

"Good! That's exactly what I wanted to hear."

"You did, huh?"

"You bet I did. 'Cause that's when the Mitch Redden I know is at the top of his game. And that's what it's gonna take to come out on top of this case." There was nothing but delight in Blaylock's eyes as he strolled over and plopped himself in one of the client chairs. "So, a big waste of time, huh?"

This was the moment Redden had been waiting for as his stern face transformed into a broad smile. He loved playing games with Harry, whose emotions could run the gamut in seconds. "Nope," he said.

"You son of a bitch! What did you find?"

Really nothing, but Redden had the senses of a canine. His gut instinct rarely failed him when it came to breaking open a case. "Just a lead," he said. "I found a door, but I don't know what's on the other side. Not yet, anyway."

For the next half hour, Redden recited in detail what had occurred during his five days in New Jersey, frequently referring to his notes and avoiding nothing. He was intent on sharing the total experience with Harry, not so much to educate but to pick the senior lawyer's brain. After four years out of the loop, he could easily overlook something significant, and brainstorming with Harry had always been productive in the past. They were a team now, working together as they had several times before.

It was also an opportunity to elevate Blaylock's self-esteem. And if there was anything more important to Redden than winning the case, it was restoring his old friend to respectability, if not within the legal community, at least in the mind of one Harry Leonard Blaylock. At one point in time, many years earlier, Blaylock had given direction and purpose to the life of Mitchell Redden. Perhaps the favor could now be returned.

Redden had saved the best for last: the original records from the two clinical investigators who followed up on infants born to women exposed to phenylpropelene during pregnancy. These were records that were part of both the IND and NDA, yet were not included in the production. Why not? Why were they stored at a different facility? Why would Brookhurst segregate them from the rest of the IND and NDA records? Why would it take two full days to retrieve a couple dozen boxes, at most? Would they be seeing original records or only copies? Were the originals with the investigators or with Brookhurst? If copies were produced, had they been altered or otherwise manipulated? Who transposed the factual information from the investigator's records to Brookhurst's forms, the investigators or the drug company? Had the investigators retained copies of their own records?

A parade of questions was thrown out and kicked around by the two lawyers. They would need a game plan – and an effective one at that – since neither knew what the answers were and they did not have the luxury of time.

But first things first. Harry was to prepare and file a motion to compel the production of the withheld bench books and missing clinical data. He would request monetary sanctions as part of the motion – ten thousand dollars was suggested by Redden. Harry would also prepare and file a motion for continuance of the trial, to delay it for at least three months, although they were sure it would be an act of futility. In fact, they would not be counting on any help from Langhorne on either motion. Therefore, Redden would focus on other sources to get the records.

Mary Ellen was called into the office and stood in front of Redden's desk, her pen poised over her notepad.

"I want to overnight a letter to the FDA," Redden said. "A formal demand under the Freedom of Information Act. You've done them before, so use the same format. I want the clinical records from two investigators. I'll get you their names and the NDA and IND numbers." Redden had copied down their names and last known addresses while in New Jersey. "It'll probably take too long to use this method, but I want to cover every base. Maybe I can pull a few strings."

"Anything else?" she asked.

"Yeah, as I said, I have their addresses, so I want you to locate their phone numbers and get them to me as soon as you can. I'll make the calls. Oh, and get Hildebrand in here ASAP. I need an update on what he's got and have some additional work for him."

"You got it, Boss," said Mary Ellen as she disappeared through the door. She was followed by Harry, who promised to be spending the afternoon on both motions. He should have drafts to him no later than Tuesday morning.

⬤

Fifty-five minutes later, Rick Hildebrand was sitting across the desk from Redden, bringing him up to speed on his investigative efforts.

"One more thing," said Hildebrand after completing the rundown on all of his efforts to date, none of which had been productive. He had purposely held some troubling news until the end, as he had wanted to get everything else out of the way. "You recall wondering how Gillingham could have pulled off getting Langhorne assigned to your case?"

"Yeah, it's done by a computer, as I understand."

"Yes, it is. I confirmed that with the court. I was also able to learn the name of the clerk who was overseeing the assignments. A fellow by the name of Reese Harrelson. I was going to interview him but ran into a problem."

"What was that?"

After pausing a moment, Hildebrand responded, "He's dead."

"That *would* make him inaccessible," said Redden. "What, a heart attack or something?" Redden saw it as just one more obstacle fate had thrown at him – and another convenience for Gillingham.

"No, he was killed."

Redden's interest in Harrelson's demise now moved from cursing the fates to one of curiosity. "Killed. How…and when?"

"Some kind of bizarre accident in the federal court garage. I've already talked to the LAPD. They've written it off as an accident, but I don't buy it."

This now has Redden's full attention. "Okay, what don't you buy and why?"

"Well…here it is. This happened just last Tuesday. And get the timing of this. It followed two days of phone calls from yours truly and happened only *four hours* after I visited the clerk's office. Got that? *Four hours* later, he's off with the Grim Reaper. He had also refused to come out and talk to me. But get this. Security found him at about 6:00 PM. He was underneath his car. His left rear tire was flat and had been pulled off, and the brake drum was sitting squarely on top of his back. His jack, which had apparently slipped off the car, was lying on its side about two feet from his body. Now, what would have possessed him to crawl beneath the drum of a car held up only by a jack?"

"You make a good point." Redden was now stunned.

"And here's the kicker," said Hildebrand. "I checked with a friend of mine in Homicide. There was nothing wrong with the rear tire – it was simply out of air."

Redden was skeptical. If it was a homicide – and it certainly might be – he doubted that Gillingham would be implicated in a murder. There had to be some other explanation. Not even Gillingham would take such a radical step. It wasn't that he didn't lack the morality; it was simply an unacceptable risk for the potential benefits.

Hildebrand responded that he was only reporting what he had found and concluding that what he had found was quite apparent. Of course, it could be someone other than Gillingham. There could be any number of things going down on the other side that they had no knowledge of, involving persons unknown in ways they could not possibly imagine. Then, again, perhaps Gillingham was not the same man he knew before. Perhaps there were factors entering into the equation that were hidden. Ray Gillingham, for some unknown reason, maybe a desperate man. And what about the drug company? What undiscovered fact might someone at Brookhurst want to be concealed?

Upon concluding his report, Hildebrand left, promising to take a deeper look into Harrelson's background. He would have a further report for Redden within a week.

Mary Ellen buzzed Redden over the intercom.

"Yeah, what ya got?" he inquired.

"Nothing helpful. Both clinical investigators are no longer available. One died 12 years ago, and the other has Alzheimer's."

"Figures." Redden thought for a moment. "Well, maybe it's not another dead-end. Wait thirty minutes and then get Rick on his cell phone. I've got another assignment for him." Maybe Hildebrand can locate their records. Maybe they're in storage somewhere. They are, after all, medical records of patients.

Redden wandered over to Harry's office. Blaylock was sitting behind his desk, dictating the first of the two motions. Redden promptly unloaded the report about Harrelson's death and then stared at Harry for a reaction.

Blaylock just shrugged it off. "Gillingham's an asshole, but murder…? Mitch, you know him better than I do, but taking out someone to help you defend a case…that does seem to be a stretch."

"Well, this does go a bit further than that. We're talking about judicial manipulation and a possible cover-up, which could lead to disbarment, maybe even criminal prosecution."

"Hey, I'm just a foot soldier," said Harry. "I'll leave the theorizing to you."

• • •

CHAPTER 22

Tuesday, December 15

Mitchell Redden was lying in bed watching Niki dress, with the moonlight through the window highlighting the curves of her naked body as she methodically put on her clothing. In many ways, it was as sensuous watching her replace each item as it was when they were removed. She was truly a beautiful woman in every particular, more attractive than any he had ever seen.

But for the one flaw, she would be a perfect package.

Increasingly, with each passing week, Redden was coming to the conclusion that Niki hated men, not just some of them, but every human mortal possessed of the Y chromosome, Randy being the sole exception. Some, of course, more than others. In the past, it had been well concealed, but now it was becoming more and more evident as their dating had stretched out over a period of three months. Recently, it was slipping out in her comments and conversations. "What would you expect? He's a man," was one; "All men think alike," was another; "He can't help himself, he's got a penis," was yet another. At first, finding amusement in her assault on the masculine gender, it was now occurring so frequently that Mitchell began to appreciate the depth of the flaw and wondered if it was fostered by something more than her failed marriage.

Earlier that evening, they had enjoyed dinner and a play at the Music Center. On the way back to Mitchell's, Niki had made yet another comment about the male character in the play. "Well, *I* have a penis," had been Redden's response. "What about me?" Niki smiled, "No, you're different. You have a *good* penis. I *like* your penis," she said, trying to make light of the subject. At that point, he had let the subject drop. From prior discussions, he knew it would lead to nowhere. For the moment, the issue would remain unresolved.

At dinner and on the way to the Music Center, Redden had given a full report on his trip to New Jersey but avoided any reference to Niki's father, hoping that she would bring it up on her own. That, however, had not happened. To Redden's growing agitation, she had failed to mention a word of her father's passing – and would shortly be on her way home after touching up her makeup in the bathroom. Niki had driven her car over to Redden's before the two had left for dinner and had her own means of transportation back to her house.

Redden was still lying in bed when Niki walked over and gave him a peck on the cheek. "Well, I'll be on my way," she said while starting for the door.

"Why haven't you said anything about your father?"

She had taken two steps when the question stopped her in her tracks. Redden's inquiry came out of nowhere, as Niki had no reason to believe he had any knowledge about the loss. After a moment to think about her reply, she turned and said, "You never met the man. It didn't occur to me that you would want to know."

"He was your father; of course, I would want to know."

She stared at the floor, searching for the right words. "Look, Mitch, I really don't want to talk about this. My relationship with my father, well, it wasn't the best, and the last several years have been rather painful."

"All the more reason," he said, intent on breaking through the wall.

As he was discovering, Mitchell wanted more out of whatever it was they had. But Niki was holding back, resistant to any intimacy beyond sex and rejecting all overtures at anything more serious. Redden, on the other hand, had recently entered his forties and was now looking for something meaningful, for someone who would be his companion, to share his everyday goals and challenges, someone to grow older with. Mitchell Redden had finally concluded he no longer desired the lonely road he had been traveling. He also wanted children – a void that could be immediately filled with a child by the name of "Randy." But above and beyond all of that, with each passing week, he found his feelings growing deeper and deeper for Nikifora Leondopoulos, a woman who was increasingly dominating his thoughts.

As Redden should have seen, their relationship was on a collision course.

"It was all a personal matter and doesn't concern you," she said.

"But it does."

"Well, it *shouldn't*," she stated with conviction. "He was an old man who had suffered a long time. Now, he is at peace. Just leave it at that, Mitch."

Redden sensed a coldness in her voice, but he pushed further. "Maybe I never met your father," he said, "But I care about you and Randy and would have liked to have been there to support you, both of you."

"Your support was not necessary, and Stavros' death has nothing to do with the case, so let it go."

"My interest goes beyond what is or is not relevant to the case," he said, now sitting upright and asserting his position as if arguing an issue in court. "As I said, I happen to care about you, or perhaps you didn't notice."

She had but was not inclined to acknowledge it. "I want to keep our relationship casual and uncomplicated," she said.

"I think it's progressed beyond 'casual,'" Redden pointed out. "And I cannot imagine a more complicated relationship."

Niki took a step toward the bed. She had seen this coming, and it was time to take a stand. She was also confident that Redden would not abandon her case. "Don't spoil it, Mitch. All this is about is good sex and a little bit of fun. And that's all it'll ever be. So, if you're expecting anything more than that, maybe we should break it off right now."

Redden shook his head. "No need," he said. "No need at all. You're absolutely right. All we are is a good fuck for one another, so why not just leave it at that."

CHAPTER 23

Wednesday, December 16

Ray Gillingham sat behind the large oak desk of Morris Klein, staring out at the city below and feeling the power that had only been a dream earlier. He had finally arrived – or would next month, right after the first of the year. Klein would be retiring at the end of the year, vacating the corner office Gillingham had been seeking since the day he joined the firm. But the office represented more than the plush trappings of a highly prized position. To Gillingham, the fully-paneled room was the symbol of prestige and achievement, and it had become his obsession.

Only the bothersome George Armbrister stood in his way. Both had arrived at the firm during the very same month, thirteen years earlier, and both would be up for senior partner after year's end. Though the two men were actively seeking the same position – the title and points held by Morris Richmond Klein – no one in the firm doubted the outcome of the final vote, including Armbrister himself. Since the announcement of Klein's forthcoming retirement, Gillingham had aggressively, through connivance, promises, intimidations, and outright threats, sought out a commitment from every voting member of the firm and had a virtual lock on the position – barring anything unforeseen, such as a major verdict against Brookhurst Pharmaceuticals.

Not only did Brookhurst receive the firm's highest billings, but as an industry leader it drew to Barry, Klein, and other pharmaceutical companies seeking representation in the Southern California area. For the very reason his close association with Brookhurst had brought Gillingham added power in the firm, losing the same client would likely be fatal to any aspiration for senior partnership – or retaining it once it had been awarded.

Gillingham spied a framed photograph sitting on the credenza behind him and picked it up for a closer inspection. It was of Klein and his wife. He had seen it before – many times – but not with the same satisfaction. Never having visited the office or attended any of the firm's social gatherings, Helen Klein had become no more than an image in a photograph, a mystery woman without history or personality. This apparent effort at privacy had led to speculation and rumor that the reclusive Mrs. Klein had been shipped off to a mental institution many years ago and perhaps was now even deceased. Mysteries and secrets in the world of Raymond Gillingham were there to be solved and discovered. They were the fuel that drove his career, and the true fate of Helen Klein was no exception.

What he had unearthed only seventeen months earlier brought the influence he needed to precipitate the early retirement of Morris Klein.

"A little premature, don't you think?"

Klein stood in the doorway, not exactly enjoying the sight of Gillingham sitting behind his desk. "The photograph is off limits as well," he added, stepping into his office. The resentment was obvious but restrained.

"My apologies," said Gillingham, only slightly embarrassed, an emotion rarely allowed by his arrogance. Not in any hurry, he replaced the photograph, stood, and came out from behind the desk. "Sorry. Just thinking ahead," he said, lacking any sincerity about the apology. Gillingham saw Klein as no more than a lame duck senior partner who would be no more than a historical note in another three weeks.

"If you don't mind," said Klein, "I'd like some privacy."

"Sure," replied Bulldog, who then slowly walked out of the office, his leisurely cadence making a statement as much as an exit.

Klein, who was only in to inspect his mail, was nearing his sixty-second year and hid it well. An advocate of a rigorous exercise program and several matches of tennis a week, he radiated health and fitness and, with his tanned face and silver hair, seemed a natural for the bench. Yet to Gillingham, this healthful exterior belied the true character of the man, whom he saw as weak and who had little to contribute to the future of the firm. Though at one time a stalwart of Barry, Klein, and principal moving force in its growth, Klein had grown mild and passive over recent years and now was only extra baggage, making his weekly visit to review his mail and dictate a couple of letters.

Seventeen months earlier, the two had shared a conversation, which resulted in Klein accelerating his retirement by several years. Since that day, the two had rarely spoken to one another, which did not go unnoticed by the office staff and any lawyer who pulled his head out of a book long enough to see what was happening on the political front in the firm. The fact that Gillingham could take down one of its senior partners only added to his reputation of ruthlessness and was seen as a graphic demonstration of his power.

Halfway down the hallway, Gillingham ran into Rothenberg. "What's up with Morris?" queried the younger lawyer. "Seems a little uptight."

"Doesn't he," was the curt reply, as the two of them continued walking. "The man's only happy on a tennis court," added Gillingham. "Lost interest in practicing law some time ago."

Rothenberg's question had been posed only to get Bulldog's reaction and hear his contrived explanation. As with everyone else in the office, he knew that Klein was being pushed out onto the street and who was doing the pushing.

"Good job in New Jersey," said Gillingham. "My contact there said you had Redden running in circles."

"I made my suggestions, and they made theirs," said Rothenberg. "I guess Redden wasn't happy about it either." This brought on a smile, although the whole experience smacked of dirty tricks right out of Watergate. It was not exactly how he envisioned spending his time when he signed on with the firm — and it definitely offered nothing to build a reputation as a trial lawyer. He also had a concern. "What's with the missing records?" he asked.

"Just a delay tactic," was the reply. "Don't worry about it. Just another way to get Redden spinning his wheels into another dead end." This was not exactly the truth. Gillingham had been recently informed by the company that they needed to have a conversation about the records. This conversation that could only take place at a secure location within their corporate offices. This was nothing he wanted to share with Rothenberg, however, who did not seem fully on board with his game plan.

"Why not let Redden have the goddamn records?" said the young lawyer, who wanted nothing short of Redden's scalp hanging from his belt. "Our experts will blow him out of the water, so why are we dancing around it?"

Bulldog pulled Rothenberg from the hallway into his adjoining office. "What do you think this is? A fucking joust of honor?" Gillingham was irritated and could see it was time to put his young protégé in line and educate him on the realities of the business they were in. "A trial is a game of odds, in case you didn't know, and the bottom line is who will step into the winner's circle. Winning is everything. Everything! And if you want to be there, and I hope you are listening, you will use everything at your disposal, at any cost, every trick, within the rules, outside the rules, it doesn't make a fucking bit of difference. If you want to win, you will do whatever you have to do without giving it a second thought. So, are we on the same page here?"

Rothenberg, a little shaken, said, "Yes, I am. I'm committed, Ray. I am."

"Because if you're not prepared to go all the way…"

"I am. I am."

"Do not underestimate Redden," continued Gillingham. "You do not want this man in front of a jury, not on this case. Not with a malformed child and a single parent trying to cut it on her own. He'll eat us alive."

CHAPTER 24

Redden stood in front of the bench, silently waiting for Langhorne to finish his review of the court's file on the case and communicate his approval to begin the argument. They were back in front of Langhorne on Redden's motion to compel production of the missing records and the bench books. Finally, the judge looked up and said, "Proceed."

"Per the prior agreement and a formal notice to produce," began Redden, "defendant was to produce the entire NDA and IND during my inspection trip to New Jersey. And I emphasize that it was to be the *entire* NDA and…"

"Excuse me, Your Honor," interrupted Bulldog.

"Yes, Mr. Gillingham," responded Langhorne cordially.

"This motion, well, it was absolutely unnecessary."

"Continue," said the judge.

"Brookhurst has already offered to produce all of the records and to pay for Mr. Redden's trip back to New Jersey as well. Everything. Hotel, airfare, everything. They've even agreed to produce the bench books, which are not part of the NDA and were not part of the original production request. The problem back in New Jersey was nothing more than a misunderstanding. My office communicated this to Mr. Redden *two weeks ago!*"

Langhorne, with a look of astonishment, turned toward Redden. "Is this true?" asked the judge.

"Your Honor needs to place this in context with what was happening while I was in New Jersey. Throughout my entire week, Brookhurst was playing games…"

"No, I want you to answer my question; that you are not wasting the court's time. Is it true that Brookhurst has offered to produce everything *voluntarily?*"

Redden hesitated. He could sense where this was all going. "Well, technically, yes, but I knew that if I went back to New Jersey armed with anything less than a court order…"

"Technically!" Langhorne was doing little to hide his irritation, and Redden braced himself as the wrath of Napoleon was about to come down on him. "Technically! What you're telling me is that two weeks ago, Brookhurst invited you back as the company's guest – *at its own cost* – but that it was more important to you to waste the court's time than to accept this very generous invitation."

"That's not the way it was," responded Redden, although recognizing that his position was hopeless and that the decision had already been carved in stone before he had ever stepped into the courtroom that morning.

Langhorne had absolutely no interest in hearing him out.

"It appears to this court that that is *exactly* the way it was," said the judge with the small round head and darting eyes. "Motion denied. Mr. Redden, you are to pay defense counsel $5,000 as sanctions for bringing this motion and for the undue consumption of time by the court and counsel. Your motion for continuance of the trial is also denied," added Langhorne.

"Your Honor, irrespective of the defendant's offer to produce the records two weeks ago, there has been a delay occasioned by Brookhurst's failure to produce records on my first trip."

"I'll repeat. Your motion to continue is denied. Counsel, you could have been back in New Jersey weeks ago, and a delay of a few days is no reason for me to rearrange my entire trial calendar. It strikes this court that you are not too eager to bring this case to trial."

Langhorne directed his attention to Bulldog. "Mr. Gillingham."

"Yes, Your Honor."

"Perhaps you might want to explore whether there are any true factual conflicts in this case, whether there's sufficient evidence to get this case to a jury."

Before Redden could react to the not-too-subtle invitation to file a motion for summary judgment, Langhorne announced, "Defendant to give notice," and was up from the bench and off to his chambers.

For a moment, Redden stared up at the empty throne, absorbing what had just taken place, and then began stuffing papers into his briefcase. He was livid but unwilling to reveal any sign of emotion. "Well, Chester, looks like you've got more work to do," he said, referring to the invited motion.

"It would appear so," said Gillingham, with his trademark grin of superiority. "Looks like your case will never get to see a jury, counselor." A motion for summary judgment, filed by a party and ruled upon before a case gets to trial, is granted when a judge concludes that there is insufficient evidence to have the case decided by a jury.

"We'll see about that," said Redden as he walked off and out of the courtroom.

Rothenberg had been taking this all in and knew railroading when he saw one. A motion for summary judgment was normally reserved for the weakest of cases. It was used to weed out lawsuits where the plaintiff's evidence lacked sufficient substance to present any issue for a jury to decide, which was exactly what bothered Rothenberg.

Langhorne did not have a clue about the strength of Redden's case.

Rothenberg could only conclude that Langhorne was never going to let this lawsuit go to a jury and would efficiently dispose of it in a pre-trial motion. Whatever Bulldog was holding over Langhorne, it was quite effective. The case would be over well before trial, and there was nothing Redden could do to alter that inevitable course.

❖

Later in the day, Redden was at a local gym pushing weights and trying to purge his anger and frustration. In many ways, it seemed to have started an eternity ago. So much had happened in the intervening years. Yet some fragments of the episode still lingered – an episode which would ultimately have an impact on the direction of his career.

When Redden was initially employed by Barry, Klein & Nance, he had signed a confidentiality agreement with the firm, including a provision that prohibited his involvement in a case handled by any former firm he had previously worked for or with. Blaylock, at the time, was having considerable financial problems, which Redden later learned were due to gambling losses. Harry had difficulty meeting his bills and was in danger of going under. He believed that his financial survival was dependent upon a personal injury lawsuit pending against a client of Barry, Klein & Nance. Because of his prior relationship with Blaylock, Redden had been isolated from the case and had been admonished about steering clear of the file. As Blaylock became more and more desperate, the pressure mounted on Redden to bail out his old friend and mentor.

One late night, shortly before the scheduled trial date, Redden was at the firm office and pulled the case from the file cabinet. He initially found the amount that the insurance company had set on the reserves, as well as the settlement authority given to Barry, Klein & Nance, which at the time was even higher than the settlement demand being made by Blaylock. But he really struck gold when he located the name of a *nondisclosed* witness, who could finger an employee of the defendant corporation as the operator of a bulldozer that had dropped the blade onto the plaintiff's leg, causing immediate amputation. The defendant had previously denied any knowledge of how the accident occurred and contended that none of its employees were anywhere near the vehicle at the time the blade was dropped.

During a casual conversation with Blaylock the following day, Redden mentioned that he might want to hold out for $900,000 without revealing that this was the exact amount of settlement authority granted by the insurance carrier. He also dropped the name of the witness and suggested that Blaylock may want to chat with him. Blaylock inquired why, but Redden only responded that he should just talk to him. The following day, Blaylock increased his settlement demand to $900,000 and subpoenaed the witness for trial.

When Gillingham, who was trial counsel on the case, learned of this recent turn of events, he went through the roof. His explosion was overheard by a new law clerk, employed only days earlier, who had observed Redden going through the file. At the time. he did not place any significance in his observation, although he knew that the file cabinet contained only files assigned to Gillingham. Now, he saw the association and approached Gillingham with the information.

Gillingham, an opportunist, had finally found an answer to the problem of Mitchell Redden, a rising star in the firm and next in line to make partner. He initially confronted Redden about his disclosures, holding back his ace-in-the-hole for shock value. The reaction was as expected; with outrage and a stinging attack on Gillingham, he could even *contemplate* such a charge. Right on cue, in walked the young law clerk who nervously, but with conviction, related his observation. Redden immediately responded that he was simply looking for the name of an expert witness Gillingham had disclosed to him a couple weeks earlier. He had not even touched the Blaylock case, a credible reply since the conversation had, in fact, taken place.

But Gillingham had also anticipated it. Pursuant to the scripted encounter, the law clerk, without a moment of hesitation, related that he had been curious about Redden's presence at the file cabinet and had pulled the file when he left and noted the name on the case. A lie, but Gillingham was shrewd enough to know he would need this extra "evidence" if he had any hope of getting a confession. That the clerk had been working with Gillingham at the time also added to his credibility. And he had been easily convinced that this ruse would work to his long-range benefit in the firm.

Without admitting guilt, Redden simply asked what Gillingham was after. His immediate resignation was the reply. Redden stared for a moment at the two and then walked away without uttering another word. The following morning, he resigned, citing his desire to jump to the other side to open his own practice in plaintiff's personal injury litigation.

The same day, Blaylock's case was settled for $900,000.

As Redden strained on the last of his repetitions with the weights, Harry Blaylock approached him, looking much like a fish out of water. A gymnasium was the last place one would ever expect to find Harry. "You wanted to see me, Mitch?"

"Got fucked again by Langhorne," Redden replied, replacing the barbell onto its rack. "Motions denied; both of 'em."

"Sorry to hear that."

"Yeah, he then sweetened it up with $5,000 in sanctions."

"The bastard. So, what are you gonna do?"

"Pay it, of course. Got no choice. But that's not the worst of it. The prick invited Gillingham to file a motion for summary judgment."

"What! Just like that?"

"Just like that. And unless we turn something big, and soon, you better believe he's gonna grant it." Redden headed over to a treadmill machine, turned it on, and then stepped onto the rotating belt at the pace of a brisk walk.

"So, what can I do, Mitch? Just name it," said Harry, who, at this point in his life, was not burdened by ethical considerations. He also shared Redden's anger. If asked, Blaylock would have no problem breaking into an office and tearing it apart in search of some evidence, anything that would help the case.

"No, I want you staying out of this," said Redden as he turned up the speed on the treadmill. "You're a lawyer. I want legal work, nothing more. Got it?" The last thing Redden needed was Blaylock off, creating a whole new set of problems.

"Got it."

"But I do need you to get a hold of Rick Hildebrand. I want him to turn this town upside down. Not a detail of his life is to be spared. Langhorne is in Gillingham's hip pocket, and I want to know how and why."

"You've already given him that assignment," reminded Harry.

"I know, I know. But I want you to stress the urgency, that, and thoroughness. Let Rick know what we are facing with Langhorne. There is always more that can be done. I want nothing left to chance. Not a detail of Langhorne's life is to be spared."

"Got it."

"Assignment number two. I want you to call my expert, Alan Donner. He's a pharmacologist/toxicologist with expertise in teratology and a birth defects expert. I used him once before. Mary Ellen has his phone number. Send everything to Donner that has come in from the inspection trip, along with Randy's meds and the study that appeared in the *Times*. A motion for summary judgment is coming down the pipe, and we need to be putting our case together now."

Harry nodded. "Sure thing, Mitch," he said, then stopped and turned after taking a couple of steps. For a few moments, he stared at his old protégé jogging on the treadmill until he caught Redden's attention. "Kinda like old times, ain't it?"

"Just like old times," smiled Redden as his shoes pounded the treadmill.

During those early years, Harry had told Redden that he had the knowledge, the training, and the scars from years in the trenches but never the talent. With both men working together, using Harry's experience and Redden's presence in front of a jury, they would be unstoppable. In the few cases they worked up together, this assessment proved to be true. In a courtroom, working shoulder-to-shoulder, they had been quite successful. However, Harry's caseload was not large. When the cases began to dry up, Redden decided to move on and back into defense work, where a larger volume of lawsuits and valuable trial experience was waiting for him.

Now, they were again working together.

"Next time in court, I'd like to be there," said Harry. "If you wouldn't mind, of course."

"Just waiting for you to ask," said Redden. "Just waiting for you to ask."

CHAPTER 25

"You're late," was Niki's cold greeting at the front door. She was pissed. Redden had been expected a good hour and a half earlier.

"Yes, I know. I'm sorry, Niki," said Mitch as he eased his way through the door, carrying two wrapped Christmas gifts.

"A call would have helped."

"It was inexcusable, I agree," he responded as he made his way over to the illuminated Christmas tree and placed the gifts beneath it. "I've been overwhelmed with work on the case, and the time just got away from me. An explanation, not an excuse."

Randy had already been served and sent off to bed. The living room, alive with Christmas décor, could have been a set straight out of Macy's, while Bing Crosby entertained with his seasonal classic, "White Christmas." The dining table, fully set for an intimate dinner, was displayed by two flickering candles. Niki had clearly gone out of her way to make this a special evening – a fact, only adding to Redden's guilt.

"It's beautiful, and I feel awful."

"You should," she said, but now managing a slight smile. After all, the case was the number one priority in their relationship, as she had convinced herself and that his absolute commitment was exactly what she wanted. "But you're forgiven," she added as she reached up and gave him a peck on the cheek, then walked over to the table and poured two glasses of cabernet.

One hour later, they had finished dinner, sustaining themselves with small talk and both purposely avoiding any discussion about litigation. That came later when they retired to the living room to prepare Niki for her deposition on Monday.

At first, Redden had considered updating Niki on the federal court disaster earlier in the day but disregarded the thought. After all, it was Christmas Eve, and there was plenty of time to unload the bad news over the next few weeks. Besides, Hildebrand might just turn up something and motivate Langhorne to cut himself loose from the case – not likely, but it could happen.

Redden gave Niki the standard admonition for a deposition. She should answer all questions as briefly as possible, not volunteering any information, nor guessing or speculating on any testimony, and answer a question only if she understands it. If he should object, she is to immediately stop speaking and wait for his instruction on whether to give an answer. She will be under oath and should only tell the truth, but what is truthful can be subject to different interpretations. She should thus think carefully before giving any answer to a question.

Redden probed more deeply into the facts than he had before. When she was 14 or 15, Niki began to get headaches each month shortly before the onset of her menstrual period. These headaches were severe, much like a migraine, and so debilitating that she would frequently spend a day or two at home from school. This happened so often that her friends began to tease her. They would needle, "Everyone in school knew when she got her period." It was at this point that Niki began to take Phenatol. It provided her with immediate and complete relief, and she jokingly called it her "wonder drug." She "wondered" how she ever got along without it before.

They were sitting together on Niki's couch, but Mitch took precautions to ensure they maintained a comfortable distance. This was to impress upon Niki that, for the next couple of hours, their relationship was only that of attorney and client – nothing more. One mistake on a major issue while testifying under oath could be an absolute disaster for the case.

"Do you recall reading the label on the bottle of Phenatol?

Niki pondered the question momentarily. "Not really. I was young and not in the habit of reading labels on nonprescription drugs, like aspirin."

Potential disaster number one. "Okay, let's think about this a moment. Cases against drug companies are based upon a failure to warn the consumer of the dangers and risks associated with the use of the drug. If one did not read the labeling, then all of the warnings in the world would not have made a difference – the consumer would have still used the product and suffered the adverse reaction, the injury."

"I see your point."

"I'm not suggesting that you lie. You just have to give it a lot of thought before coming up with your answer. It just seems that in all the years you were using Phenatol – before you conceived Randy – that you would have developed some curiosity about the content of the label on your 'wonder drug.'" Redden knew he was manipulating Niki's testimony but convinced himself it was justified. After all, the odds are that she did read the label and has just forgotten. He also was not about to let the case go down in flames simply because she chose not to read the labeling.

"You know, you're right," she said. "Once I knew I was pregnant, there was no way I would have popped one of those pills in my mouth without reading the label. I was almost obsessive in protecting my baby."

Redden could see she needed another push.

"You were also having sex without any protection, right?"

"Yes...."

"And knew you could conceive well *before* you knew you were pregnant."

"So, you're suggesting that I would have read the labeling even earlier?"

"Only if that would be your testimony."

"It makes sense. Yes, that would be my testimony." Niki was beginning to see how this was going to go and was totally on board; anything to present the strongest case.

"Another important question; what would have been your reaction if you had read the Phenatol labeling, and it warned that there was an increased risk of birth defects if taken during pregnancy? What would you have done if you had a raging headache and either knew or suspected that you might be pregnant? Would you have still taken the drug to get relief, to eliminate the pain?" Mitchell did not want the question to be easy.

"No, I don't think so," she said as she considered the debilitating pain.

"Your answer sounds equivocal, uncertain."

Niki was tempted to say, "Well then, just tell me what to say, and that will be my testimony," but instead amended her response. "No, I definitely would not have endangered my baby, no matter how severe the pain."

The two of them then explored other options. This line of inquiry might well be pursued during her deposition, and she would have to be prepared in her reply. She would have sought out ibuprofen or aspirin or some other risk-free tablet. Before Phenatol, she had also found some degree of relief in resting her head on a hot-water bag. And if none of these options were effective, she would have suffered from the headache.

Redden then explores an even more critical question. Why was Niki so certain that she had taken the Phenatol during pregnancy? Her headaches had only come on at the onset of her menstrual period. Since all her periods had stopped with her pregnancy, hadn't the headaches stopped as well?

This causes Niki to pause; she had never thought about this inconsistency before. But there was absolutely no doubt in her mind that the headaches had continued beyond her periods, and she had always taken her pills to get relief. At the time of her pregnancy, she was taking Phenatol almost daily. She was positive about this and had even told her doctor. Perhaps there might be a notation of this in her medical records.

"There is. I have those records and checked, although it is simply noted as 'headache pills.'"

"Then why are you questioning me about this?"

"Because you're going to be aggressively tested on every critical fact in the case, and I have to satisfy myself that you will be up to the challenge."

Over the next hour, Redden continued throwing question after question at Niki, assessing each response, driving home when his client needed to be firm about her answer and when uncertainty would be more appropriate to avoid risk credibility. When hitting on a fact critical to the case, Redden would emphasize its importance and explain why the case could collapse without it.

Finally, shortly before midnight, Redden announced that he was through. Christmas day was almost upon them, and it was time to enjoy a glass of eggnog and rum.

It was also time to retire to the bedroom.

CHAPTER 26

Monday, December 28

Niki arrives at Redden's office and checks in with Mary Ellen, who asks the client to have a seat in the reception room. Niki complies as Mary Ellen makes her way down the hall, taps twice on the door, then opens it and ducks her head inside.

"Miss Business and Pleasure is here," she offers, dripping with sarcasm. She is clearly bothered by Niki's intrusion into Redden's personal life. She has made little effort to conceal the agitation from her boss, who passes it off to menopause and Mary Ellen's lonely lifestyle. "Oh, and I just got word back from the FDA. It will take at least 90 days before they can send the requested records. They say they are backed up and short on personnel." She then closed the door and returned to her desk.

Redden stares at the closed door for a moment, contemplating the remark about Niki. He is tempted to approach her about the matter, but in the context of everything else that is going on, he decides that it is not worth the aggravation.

Redden collects Niki and heads for the conference room. Upon arrival, he is surprised to see that Gillingham and Rothenberg are both present, along with the court reporter.

"Of course, you know only one of you will be asking questions." The warning is directed by Redden straight at Gillingham.

"Mr. Rothenberg is only here for assistance. He will not be directing any inquiries," responds Bulldog.

After the standard admonition and a few preliminary questions, Gillingham launches into an unanticipated subject. Niki is sitting directly across from Gillingham, next to Redden.

"You were previously married to a Scott Burroughs, is that correct?"

"Yes."

"And he is, in fact, the father of the plaintiff, Randolph Burroughs?"

"Yes, he is."

"During your marriage and prior to the plaintiff's conception, did Mr. Burroughs ever use illegal drugs?"

"Yes, although I did not know it at the time." The response was blurted out before Redden could react as he assessed the possible relevancy. He decided to let it play out.

"Heavily?"

"Objection, vague and ambiguous. Don't answer the question," he admonished.

"How frequently?"

"I Don't know."

"When did he first start? How long had he been using before you conceived the plaintiff?"

"I don't know?"

"What were the drugs?"

"Grass and coke, I understand. But I never saw him use them, myself."

"How did you discover this?"

"A mutual friend."

"Who is this mutual friend; his or her name?"

Finally, Redden jumped in with an objection. Such evidence was irrelevant and immaterial, and there would be no further testimony on the subject. His initial hesitation was due to the simple fact that he had no idea if a father's use of a drug could cause a birth defect in his offspring. He was also certain that Langhorne would grant Gillingham a free rein on wherever he wanted to go on the subject. But it was time for damage control, as he did not have a clue where this was all leading – and needed to speak with his client.

"This is relevant testimony, counselor. Or do you need to have Judge Langhorne enlighten you on the law?" asserts Gillingham.

"It's irrelevant, and there will be no further questions or testimony on the subject of paternal drug use. We are also gonna take a short break while I speak with my client."

At this point, Redden whisks Niki out of the conference room and into his office. He is quite upset and is making no effort to hide the fact.

"How is it possible that you never brought this up? Niki, I specifically asked you if you could think of anything else that might be related to the pregnancy?" They are both standing, facing one another.

"Why???" she snaps back, reacting to his agitation. "Because I was the one carrying the baby, not Scott! And if this was so goddamn important, why didn't *you* ask me about it! You're the lawyer!"

Her rebuke hits home. She is right. Causes of birth defects – it's an issue he should have explored with his expert before Niki's preparation on Thursday.

It is time to de-escalate.

"I'm sorry, Niki. You're right," Redden says as he takes her by the hand, and they both sit down on the office couch. Once again, he finds himself apologizing. "As I told you before, I've been away from the practice of law too long, and the rust is still showing.

"Do you think we have a problem?" she asks.

"I'm sure not." They do, but for an entirely different reason, Redden is still not ready to share with his client. "We have a peer-reviewed study associating limb reduction birth defects with the maternal ingestion of Phenatol, and I'm sure no one is going to find a similar study implicating the paternal use of cocaine and pot." He adds, "This questioning, however, brings home something else."

"What's that?"

"Gillingham has obviously done his homework. This was not a fishing expedition – he knew exactly where he was going. As expected, he is well prepared and should not be underestimated." But there will be no more testimony on the subject, Redden assures Niki, not unless and until he is faced with a court order and has explored the issue with his expert.

They both return to the conference room to conclude the deposition. The remainder of the day, however, pretty much goes without incident or surprise. Unknown to Redden, the query about Scott Burroughs' drug use had been nothing more than a shot across the bow. Bulldog was simply giving notice that Redden should expect more of the same. When it came to surprises, Redden's old nemesis at BKN was loaded with them.

Rothenberg lingers behind in the conference room and approaches Redden as Gillingham exits the office suite. Niki has retired to Mitchell's office and is awaiting his assessment of her testimony. Rothenberg seems to be on a high from what he has seen as a successful deposition, and cannot resist a final dig.

"You really don't remember me, do you?"

Redden has no idea what he is talking about.

"You once called me an insect. Said I'd never get any taller. I guess we'll see who's the tallest when this thing is over."

"So, it was you!" Suddenly, it all comes back to Redden, who can't help but smile. "Actually, the description was 'worm,' but why argue the point. So, it was you who crawled out from under those file cabinets. I'll be damned!"

Rothenberg will not let it go. For the past five months, his last visit to Redden's office had been eating away at him as he waited for the right opportunity to exact some form of revenge.

The time had now arrived.

"You should have remained in seclusion," said Rothenberg. "But I guess your ego got the best of you. You just had to throw down the gauntlet right at the feet of BKN. Big mistake!" he adds. "Very shortly, everyone will be writing you off for good."

"Wow! You're right. That would be quite impressive. Chester pulls a few of Langhorne's puppet strings and runs off with a summary judgment. Yeah, that will really impress all of the trial lawyers in town – assuming, of course, that judicial manipulation is the coin of the realm."

This seems to stop Rothenberg in his tracks. But Redden is not through.

"If you really want something to crow about, then why not stop the fucking games and meet me head-to-head in front of a jury. Gimme the goddamn records I am entitled to, and let the chips fall where they may. But of course, that is not going to happen because you and Chester are terrified of facing me. No, you will continue to engage in their deceptions and dirty tricks because that is the only way you know how to play the game."

Redden is still not through. He has one final point to make.

"But you wanna know something?" Redden says, poking his finger on the younger lawyer's chest, "No matter how this case goes down, you will be the loser. You will be the loser because you have absolutely no idea in the world what really is important, the value of integrity and character, and the meaning of the oath that you took when you became a lawyer."

Rothenberg is stunned and shaken from the experience, now wishing that he had left with Gillingham – and promptly exits the office suite without further comment.

Niki, who overheard the last part of the exchange as she was making her way back down the hallway, approaches Redden.

"What was that all about?" she asks.

"Oh, nothing," he assures her. "Just getting something off my chest."

CHAPTER 27

Wednesday, January 27

Snow flurries greet Redden as he arrives at Brookhurst Pharmaceuticals. The procedure now is feeling much like a ritual as he again enters, registers at the desk, greets Ordman, and is led through the same hallways and elevator to the same small room, which is occupied by the same two sentinels – neither of whom appears happy to be there.

The new set of boxes is also waiting, considerably smaller in number than before. It appears that Arlene and Judy have switched roles this time, with the gum-chewer exiting with Ordman. Arlene sits resolute and emotionless at the far end of the conference table. As before, there will be no cordial chit-chat.

Redden hastily launches into his search. Within the first twenty minutes, he discovers that a chart is missing, but he decides to avoid confrontation until he has completed his review. With only 18 boxes to inspect, he was not expecting a lengthy stay.

By 1:45 in the afternoon, he has the full story. Sporadically, throughout the thirteen boxes containing the raw data, he learns that 53 out of the 507 case histories have completely vanished as if they had never existed. Only by use of the sequential numbering system placed there by the clinical investigators could one determine that anything was missing.

As Redden is systematically thumbing through the pages from a volume in one of the few remaining boxes, something catches his eye. While rapidly scanning a series of graphs and charts, the typewritten pages were no more than a fleeting change in the pattern of lines and numbers and easily could have been overlooked – but they weren't and turned out to be the find of the day.

It was a copy of an internal memo from Roland Kupperman, Vice President of Regulatory Affairs. It was addressed to the head of the Medical Department, which oversaw all clinical investigations on the drug. The memo began routinely, summarizing a recent submission for the New Drug Application and complimenting the work of the department. What caught Redden's attention, however, was a paragraph midway down the second page, which read:

> "Your criticism of the results of most of our investigators is well taken, for I must agree that all of those whose cases are included in the NDA are not of the highest standing as medical investigators. However, the Food and Drug Administration tends to pay attention to the number of reports as much as quality, and no doubt when Ed Thomas set up the studies, he had this in mind and included a number of investigators who would get some quick clinical reports to make weight and bulk, though, of course, we at Brookhurst do not regard them as being of the greatest scientific and clinical value."

After writing out the pertinent passages from the memo, Redden presented the document to Judy and invited her to read it. When the afternoon guard was finished, she looked up at Redden, awaiting his next direction.

"Judy…You don't mind me calling you 'Judy'?"

She shrugs.

"Judy, I hate to drag you into this – I know you are just doing your job – but I want to caution you that if this memo does not show up in the copies that I order, you will be subpoenaed for a deposition and interrogated about its content under oath."

Judy seems somewhat stressed by the threat but avoids making any comments.

"Something else. Could you have Ms. Ordman join us? I have a request to make."

Redden overhears the call being made to Ordman and then waits – for over two hours. When she finally arrives, Redden's emotions are at a slow boil, but he is determined not to give Ordman the satisfaction of witnessing a reaction.

"Sorry for the wait," she says, "but your request caught me in the middle of a meeting. How can I help you?"

"I've gone through all the case history boxes now, and there are 53 of them that are missing. Vanished. All of them."

"Really! Are you sure about that?" Redden sees the appearance of surprise as nothing but a feigned reaction.

"Positive."

"I'll have to look into it, convey your inquiry to corporate counsel, and get back to you." Ordman inspects her watch and says, "I can see we are about at the end of your day, so hopefully, I can give you an answer tomorrow morning."

"I will look forward to your explanation," said Redden, who then gathered his briefcase and coat and followed Ordman out the door.

After an early dinner back at his hotel, Redden decides to take in a movie. Although he does not have proper clothing for the weather, there is a theater only 5 or 6 blocks away, and the distraction offers a welcome escape from the tension that continues to mount. Not thinking, he had come to New Jersey without an overcoat. But he has a raincoat and resolves to walk the few blocks rather than wait for a cab.

Redden is walking briskly down the street, his shoulders humped forward and his hands stuffed in the unlined pockets. Although the street is clear, snow lines the sidewalk, and he trembles slightly from the sub-freezing temperature. The neon lights of the theater can be seen now only about three blocks away.

Suddenly, he hears the sound of a muted ricochet and is sprayed by snow.

Momentary confusion is replaced by the terrifying realization that someone has just taken a shot at him. He crouches and stares off into the darkness, not knowing the direction of the shot, hoping to pick up a figure or some form of movement.

Within seconds, another shot hits the ground, this time only a couple feet away.

Redden starts to run, slips on the icy sidewalk, and falls, scraping his hand. Then, is up again running and stumbles into the alcove of a nearby building.

A third bullet shatters the window next to him, setting off an alarm. Shards of glass are everywhere; in his hair, over his crouched torso, and scattered on the ground around him.

He crawls on his hands and knees further into the shadows, waiting for yet another shot. There, he waits for a couple minutes, with the alarm blaring away above him. But there are no further shots. It seems that the gunman may have fled.

With a siren now being heard in the distance, Redden decides to leave, not wanting to hang around and answer any questions.

Back at the hotel, Redden rushes through the lobby, into an awaiting elevator, then down the hallway into his room. Safely inside, he stares down at his shaking hands, the realization brought home that someone had tried to kill him.

He sits down on the bed and begins to devise a plan to ensure his safety. At this point, it is mandatory that he thinks clearly, and panicking might be a fatal mistake. Redden changes rooms under an assumed name after slipping the desk clerk $100 in cash and instructs him not to give anyone any information about the change.

Thursday, January 28

Determined not to be intimidated, Redden returns to Brookhurst the following morning. It is 9:15 AM, and he had been waiting in the reception area for 45 minutes. Finally, Ordman arrives with her scripted marching orders. Early in her employment, she recognized that she was the buffer between visiting attorneys and corporate counsel but never enjoyed the gamesmanship and deception frequently practiced, as she was the one often faced with the resulting ire from its victims.

"Sorry again for the wait," she said. "But here's the final word. There was a fire that destroyed some of the NDA records a number of years back, and apparently, these 53 case histories you are after were the ones that were destroyed."

"So, these 53 cases had been previously segregated out of the 507 total, isolated to a separate location, then set ablaze by an unfortunate fire for which Brookhurst had no responsibility."

"I don't know that I would describe it that way, but that's pretty much what happened…as I've been told."

"When did this happen? I'm assuming it was not last week." The sarcasm was intentional. Redden wanted it understood that he was not buying the story.

"As I said several years ago. I believe prior to market approval." After waiting a moment for further comment, she adds, "If you want, I'll show you upstairs to your room to complete your inspection."

Redden nodded his agreement, and the two were off for his final visit.

Over the next two hours, Redden completed his review of the remaining boxes, containing summaries and statistical information from the study. Methodically, he would review each folder, turning page by page, rapidly scanning the text, focused on possible buzz words, such as "birth defects," "malformations," or "congenital anomalies," or anything else that hinted at an examination of the offspring of women who had ingested Phenatol while pregnant.

Close to finishing his task, something struck Redden as odd, inconsistent with the text and quality of the writings for the time they were created. Almost all the summaries are typed carbon copies, typical of the time, and the summaries that set forth the statistics and conclusions of the evaluation of birth defects are photocopied. Running short on time, he decides to store this information away and determines not to raise a red flag – not now, not until he has discussed it with Blaylock and Dr. Donner. As a former FDA employee, Donner should have valuable insight into the creation and maintenance of IND and NDA records.

Upon completing his inspection of the boxes, Redden is finally handed the bench books prepared by the scientists conducting the laboratory animal studies. Although he could find nothing inconsistent with the findings and conclusions set forth within the written reports, upon close examination, he does detect that two pages appear to have been severed out of the bound volume at the spine. Since there was no numbering system, it would be difficult, if not impossible, to confirm that the two pages had been removed. It is also a professional job; the language on the following pages does not appear to be out of context.

He does note, however, that the sentence at the end of one page appears to conclude at the top above the scored lines on the next page, but apparently in the same handwriting and with the same pen. Redden writes down the names of the scientists and leaves Brookhurst Pharmaceuticals – although making a change in his plans, adding another stop before returning home.

Friday, January 29

After a short flight to Dulles Airport, Redden rents a car and drives to the FDA in Rockville, Maryland. Before leaving New Jersey, he had placed a call to Donner. As a former employee of the FDA, with one call, he was able to pull a few strings and facilitate quick access to the FDA's set of records of the Phenatol IND and NDA. One hour after arriving at the federal facility, Redden sat in another small room, meticulously scanning thousands of pages of documents through a microfiche viewer.

As expected, the same 53 case histories of the original physician-generated records are likewise missing. It appeared that the FDA had the identical file that was shown to him at Brookhurst. Though more difficult to detect through microfiche, the summary of the study on congenital malformations was also distinctly different than the other three, with sharper and more defined print. Whoever had made the changes had been thorough. Every alteration made at Brookhurst was duplicated in the FDA set of records – except for the incriminating memo from Kupperman, which was missing from the FDA's records. And although he had hope, Redden was not surprised to learn that the bench books were not part of the IND or NDA.

As a final act, Redden notes the name of the medical officer assigned by the FDA to review the file, Dr. Martin Radcliffe.

Redden inquires around to see if he can locate Radcliffe – an obvious person to talk to. He shortly learns that he no longer works at the FDA and hasn't for some time. After questioning several staff members about the current whereabouts of Radcliffe, Redden is ultimately referred to one of the old-timers.

Ronald Armbrister, MD, PhD, would seem an anomaly at the FDA and certainly a rarity. Following completion of his doctorate in pharmacology, he went straight to the FDA and never left. Unlike so many of his colleagues, who saw the agency as a launching pad for lucrative positions in the drug industry, Ronald Armbrister was a lifelong public servant who saw his work at the agency as his higher calling, to ensure not only that the public benefited from safe and effective drugs, but was also protected from their inevitable hazards with adequate and proper warnings.

At the age of 64, Armbrister was approaching retirement age with considerable resistance, although resigned to that fate due to a very insistent wife.

Redden located Armbrister and approached his desk in the Office of Surveillance and Epidemiology. "Yes, sir, how can I help you?" asked a smiling Armbrister.

"I'm looking for someone who used to work here, and I'm told that you might be able to help."

"And you are?"

"Mitchell Redden, an attorney doing a little research here," he said, extending his hand. Armbrister stands, and they shake.

"Who might that be?" he asks.

"Martin Radcliffe, a medical review officer."

Armbrister squints as if necessary to access his memory cells. "Hmm…Radcliffe…Radcliffe…so many have come and gone…hmm."

Sensing that the doctor needed a little stimulus, Redden reaches into his pocket and holds up a one-hundred-dollar bill.

Armbrister reacts as if it was infected with a lethal virus. "No, thank you," he said. "I only get one paycheck, and it's from my employer."

"Sorry," said Redden, as he immediately shoved the bill back into his pocket. "I was just trying to stress the importance of this information."

"This is a public service facility, and if I can provide you with what you are after, I will do so. No charge."

"Again, I am sorry."

This seems to satisfy Armbrister as he again begins to search his memory. "Hmm…now wait a minute…Marty…. yes, Marty Radcliffe. I remember him. Left about 10, 12 years ago. A good man. One of the more devoted to work in the review section."

"But where did he go?" urges Redden.

"Off to one of the companies," Armbrister replies. "Sooner or later, they all do, don't they?"

"What kind of company?"

"Pharmaceutical, of course. Old Marty did well for himself. Some high position. VP, I think."

Even before asking the question, Redden would have laid ten to one on picking the right answer. "Do you know the name of the company?"

"Not positive, but I think Brookhurst."

Redden thanks the Armbrister with an enthusiastic smile and shake of the hand. This is a major lead, and he will schedule Radcliffe's deposition as soon as he returns.

Outside, Redden stares back at the FDA building for a few seconds before entering his rental car. He momentarily assesses what it represents. He sees a giant dinosaur moving slowly forward but unable to keep pace with an ever-developing society that is outdated and, behind the times, perhaps well-intentioned but plagued with a pervasive infection and no antibiotics in sight. Only major surgery could save it, and no one could afford to have a surgeon without help from Congress.

Redden enters the car, exits the parking lot, and checks the rearview mirror to ensure he is not being followed. He is off to Dulles on his late afternoon flight. Changes must be made now: changes in patterns, habits, and how he approaches even the simplest of tasks. Perhaps yesterday's episode was a warning, but then again, maybe it wasn't. Without question, the agenda for the day was one of extreme caution.

CHAPTER 28

Monday, February 1

Redden descends the stairs from his second-story condominium and enters the door to his office suite. As he approaches Mary Ellen at the reception window, she plops a thick legal document on the shelf in front of him.

"Well, here it is," she announces. "The Brookhurst motion for summary judgment – all four inches of it. The hearing is set for 30 days. Got an order shortening time."

She looks up, awaiting his reaction, but sees no emotion.

"As expected," he offers, then picks it up and heads for his office. His world seems to be collapsing on top of him, and he is running out of options. His earlier career had enjoyed multiple successes, with few disappointments, and had come seemingly with ease. But then, it was the rare case that did not find him in front of a jury, where his natural talents and appeal were on display. Only twice before had a judge stood between him and 12 members of a jury, and that was early in his march to fame.

As Redden places the motion on his desk and drops into his chair, Blaylock appears at the doorway to his office.

"I saw," said the older lawyer. "Well…it's not as if it was unexpected, given the invitation." Harry continues inside and grabs one of the client's chairs.

"Yeah, I know. But it's not that we'll have a problem putting together a strong opposition. It's the sense that it will be meaningless, no matter what we shove in Langhorne's face – that Bulldog has him by the balls and won't let go until this case is tossed out the door."

"But we still need to make our record," said Harry.

"Yes, we do. So, have you talked to Donner? We're gonna need a strong declaration from him. Both on causation and standard of care."

"Yeah…that. The declaration…." Harry stares at the written motion for a moment, telegraphing that it was not good news.

"Okay, let's have it," said Mitchell. "Why the doom and gloom?"

"Causation is not going to be a problem. Regarding the NIH study and the timing of exposure, Donner is totally on board, and Phenatol is the probable cause. But…," Harry shakes his head as he finds Redden's eyes. "It's the standard of care if you can believe. He said he will help as much as he can, but he's struggling with it."

"Struggling, but why?"

"Well, for starters, the rat and rabbit studies were not helpful. The offspring did not have malformations. The drug…as they say, was not teratogenic in animals, so no red flags there. Then, there are the clinical studies with humans. Only a handful of kids with birth defects – none with a limb-reduction defect – and no significant increase over controls. So…" Harry shrugs, "as Donner put it, 'how do you require a warning if there's nothing to warn about?'"

"Got a point," agrees Mitchell. "But how do you find a problem if you're not looking for it? Or build a goddamn bonfire out of what you did find?"

"Yeah, but how do we prove it?"

Redden chooses to ignore the question, recognizing that it may be an insurmountable problem. "You say Donner indicated he can help. How?"

"You just mentioned it. How do you find a problem if you're not looking for it? He says he can attack the design of the study. He will say that if the study had been properly designed, they would have come up with the same results as the NIH study. But...."

"But what?"

"He said, 'between you and I, it's a stretch,' that he would be vulnerable on cross-examination, that there are weaknesses."

"Well, there will be no cross-examination on his declaration, at least not before the hearing. So, work with him on the wording and show it to me before sending it out for his signature."

"Anything else?"

"Yeah, I might be onto something." Redden filled Harry in on his trip to the East Coast – the missing 53 case histories, the questionable explanation for their absence, the identical set missing at the FDA, and the final shocker – the ultimate destination of the same FDA review officer responsible for assessing the quality and completeness of the clinical studies.

"Brookhurst!" Harry is shocked. "No fucking way!"

"Yeah, and just before market approval. Quite a coincidence, huh?"

"So, how are you gonna play this out? What's the move?"

"Get him under subpoena; get his testimony under oath. I'll fly to New Jersey and take his deposition."

Redden is beginning to get energized. Just talking to Harry brings back an earlier time together – the tandem, once again working as before – just one more time. He fixes on Harry's eyes and senses a sparkle he has not seen in years. Yes, maybe, just maybe, Harry Leonard Blaylock might just be another beneficiary of the lawsuit.

"You know," offers Harry, "on its face, this smells of blatant conflict of interest. Maybe Langhorne will now back off and cut us some slack."

Redden tells Blaylock not to bank on it. People leave the FDA for industry all the time and often even return. It's nothing more than a revolving door. Langhorne will never see the connection between the missing records and the shift of employment.

"What we will need is solid testimony," said Redden, "and Radcliffe is the key. We'll see how strong of a witness he is when he is forced to testify under oath, especially when presented with the multiple discrepancies appearing in the records…records that he was responsible for reviewing and evaluating – and apparently green-lighted."

After discussing a few additional assignments, Blaylock was out the door to work with Donner on his declaration while Redden began a thorough review of the motion.

⸺ • ⸺

A good two hours later, Redden places a call to Gillingham. After the initial receptionist screening and a lengthy delay, Bulldog finally picks up.

"Yes, Mitchell, what do you need?"

"I need to take a deposition, a depo of a Martin Radcliffe."

A long silence. The name came out of left field, although Gillingham knew exactly who he was and how he fit into the puzzle. Corporate legal at Brookhurst had filled him in on all the uncomfortable details.

"Hmmm… Radcliffe…. I'm not sure I know who that is," said Gillingham, with all the contrived sincerity he could muster.

"Think hard, Chester. Martin Radcliffe, as in Vice President Radcliffe, formerly of FDA."

Another pause.

"Oh, yeah. Now it comes to me. So, why do you need to talk to Dr. Radcliffe?"

"Show up at the depo, and you'll find out. But for now, I need some available dates. Sometime in February."

"I'll do what I can," said Gillingham, not meaning a word of it. "But I may not be able to help. Radcliffe retired a few years ago and may no longer be available. As you might guess, he's no longer within the reach of Brookhurst."

"Look, either you find Radcliffe, or we will. Either get back to me within two days with a mutually agreeable date, or we'll find Radcliffe through their own means and, who knows, maybe just have our own private chat with him. As you so clearly pointed out, he is no longer with Brookhurst."

No sooner had Redden hung up the phone than he realized his

mistake. Of course, Radcliffe was a free game. And a quick check could have confirmed that. Now Bulldog gets a first shot at him before Hildebrand can corner Radcliffe and tie him down with a written statement. Once again, Redden is reminded that he is still not up to speed – and the mistakes are starting to pile up on him.

Redden next gets Hildebrand on the phone. After the investigator updates Mitchell on the Langhorne investigation – "still running into a series of dead ends" – he turns to something more urgent. Rick is to drop everything else and locate Radcliffe. This must be done as soon as possible, hopefully before Gillingham can reach him. The former FDA medical review officer and Brookhurst VP is no longer with the company, so he is "available." He is to be found and a statement obtained, if possible. Redden then proceeds to explain exactly what he needs.

CHAPTER 29

It is late evening, and Mary Ellen is at Ricardo's, feeling no pain. She is high but not stumbling drunk, although her condition is quite apparent as she, at the moment, is getting a little loud. She attempts to make a hit on one of the younger men in the bar, being somewhat suggestive but without success. He is not interested.

Richard Smith, the owner, approaches her. "Mary Ellen, my favorite customer. How ya doing?" As one of his regulars, the two of them have been on a first-name basis for a couple of years.

"Well, it's Richard Ricardo. Como estas, mi amigo?" she smiled. Her state of inebriation had been called to Richard's attention by a bartender a few minutes earlier.

"Do me a favor," he said. "Let me buy you a cup of coffee and then call you a cab. I don't think you should be driving tonight."

"That's very kind of you," she said as she began sizing up the situation, her eyes telegraphing an obvious interest. She had always viewed Richard as attractive but generally unavailable. However, she now had his attention and an apparent sense of an obligation to be of assistance to her. Maybe, just maybe….

"Better idea. Why don't *you* take me home, Richard Ricardo?" Mary Ellen always called him by that nickname, her continuing dig at his attempt to be theatrical with his otherwise common name.

"I'm afraid that would not be possible. Too many obligations," he said, waving his hand as if to remind her where they were and his related responsibilities.

"C'mon, there's lots of people here who can cover for you. Besides, there are side benefits, you know," she said, leaving little doubt what they might be.

"You tempt me," he graciously smiled as he held up his left hand to display a gold wedding ring. "But I've got other obligations too."

"It's just one night," she pleaded, her eyes beginning to well with tears. Mary Ellen is a lonely and desperate woman in need of someone.

"Sorry," he said, then firmly added, "I'm gonna have one of the waitresses take you home. No debate."

━━●━━

Niki and Redden are making love in the bedroom of his upstairs living quarters. As usual, it had started slowly, then progressively became more and more physical, and now was reaching the point where both seemed out of control.

Suddenly, Redden brought them to an abrupt stop – and then slowly eased himself deeper into her. But this time tenderly, with a deliberate and measured drive, until he was so deep within her he felt overwhelmed by the oneness they had become. Their act of sexual gratification had become almost impersonal, and to Redden, this was no longer acceptable.

Niki tried to move, to reactivate the gyration that had brought her to the brink of ecstasy. Redden, instead, embraced her tightly, locking the two of them together. "What are you doing?" she asked. "What's wrong?"

Redden shook his head, uncertain himself. Nothing was wrong. He just wanted to remain this way, immobile and attached.

"Why did you stop?"

He does not answer but instead caresses her cheek and stares deeply into her eyes, caught by the moonlight through the window. Then, like a sudden eruption, the words were out, impulsively, laid out before reason or good sense could take over control.

"I love you, Nikki."

Niki's reaction is immediate, as she pronounces a defiant "No!"

This was not supposed to happen. She is confused. This had not been expected. For what seemed an eternity, they stared at one another, locked by their emotions, neither prepared to take the next step nor certain what it should be.

The utter silence is suddenly broken by a slight but distinct metallic sound, apparently coming from the adjacent room through the open door to his bedroom. Redden realizes that someone is placing a key in a lock, his lock, to his own living quarters. And before he can react, this is followed by the equally discernible sounds of his deadbolt shifting and a door swinging open.

Redden pushes Niki off to the side and rolls from the bed to the floor, reaching and grasping for the bat beneath his bed. It had been placed there upon arriving home from New Jersey, although he had never anticipated calling upon its use. After groping several times, he grasped the handle and stood as a figure approached and stopped in the doorway to the bedroom, silhouetted by the light behind. For a moment, everything is frozen until he sees the figure sway, and then drop a piece of clothing.

"Don't stop," orders the vaguely familiar voice emanating from the silhouette.

Redden reaches and further opens the drape to the window, revealing Mary Ellen, as she unsnaps her bra and drops it to the floor. She is now standing there, only in her panties.

"Don't stop," she repeats. "Let's make it a threesome," she slurs, then takes a few steps closer, inspecting Redden and his equipment – including the bat. Through thick and barely understandable words, she adds, "I pro…pre…fer whips ma'self, but, ya know, whatever ya two are into is..is fine with me."

Redden, still confused and indecisive, only stares as she leans over and begins to remove her panties. At 48, her figure is still quite well preserved, and Redden is taking this all in when Niki finally screams at him, "Do something!"

This seems to break the spell.

Redden reaches for his pants, throws on the lights, and grabs a nearby blanket. For the briefest moment, he takes in the scene. Mary Ellen is standing there in all her nudity, the trail of clothes behind her leading back into the living room. The face is much older now than in the flattering moonlight, the features harder, with makeup smeared from the earlier tears.

Redden steps over and cloaks Mary Ellen in the blanket.

"I'm gonna take her home," Redden tells Niki, who is sitting up in bed with the sheet pulled around her neck.

Niki nods her acknowledgment. "You'll understand if I'm not here when you get back."

"Of course," he said after a few moments of reflection, then turned and ushered Mary Ellen through the bedroom door, gathering the trail of clothing on his way out.

It would be an uncomfortable drive to Mary Ellen's home.

Tuesday, February 2

Rothenberg is finishing breakfast in his 12th floor apartment near the beach in Santa Monica. The décor is contemporary, with chrome and glass, accented in whites, grays, and blacks. One got the sense that he was no longer in a Technicolor world when visiting the Rothenbergs. The dining area, like every other room in the apartment, is immaculate and uncluttered, a testimonial to Rothenberg's wife, a woman whose obsession with order and organization is slowly driving Rothenberg up the wall.

Carol Rothenberg, quiet and slight of figure, is pretty, but in an artificial sort of way. Her makeup case is never far away, and she will not start a day without first spending a good half hour in the mirror. At the moment, she is picking up Rothenberg's clothes, which he dropped onto the couch in the living room. The night before, he had arrived late – long after Carol had retired – and had undressed outside the bedroom, not wanting to awaken her.

Rothenberg spies Carol in the living room. "What are you doing?" he demands.

"Just straightening up," she answers defensively.

"Leave them be! I dropped them there, and I'll pick 'em up."

"No big deal," she said, not to be deterred.

"Stop!" he commanded as he stood up from the table. This time, he was drawing a line in the sand. She abruptly stopped, then dropped his shirt back onto the couch. "Why are you angry at me?"

Rothenberg takes a few steps closer. "I'm not angry. It's just that you pick up after me like I was a teenager. Quit being a codependent!"

The accusation was nothing new. Carol had been raised by an alcoholic father and did not leave his home until she married at 27. Rothenberg was initially happy with the relationship, with all of the attention and patronizing, but it gradually began to wear on him. Along with the frustration of where his employment was taking him, each time she would pick up after Rothenberg, his sense of helplessness would be a stinging reminder of how he was floundering in his career. In many ways, she was ideal, always tolerant and understanding of his late nights, but Rothenberg was hungry for altercation and battle, even if it came from his spouse. But today, he seemed more agitated than ever.

"What's going on, Geoff?"

"What do you mean, 'what's going on'? I'm tired of you picking up after me."

"I know I have a problem. We've talked about it. But you're always snapping at me. You're impatient. Everything I do seems to irritate you. You're changing, Geoff."

This seems to ring true. She is right, and he knows why.

"You're right, honey," he said, then approached Carol and gave her a big hug. "I'm sorry," he added. "You deserve better, and I'll work on it. Promise."

Rothenberg knew exactly where this was coming from. He was frustrated. His game plan had been to build his reputation by knocking off the heavyweights of the plaintiffs' bar, and Redden had always been at the top of that list. This was his biggest opportunity, and Gillingham was denying it to him. If the case went to trial, it would be Rothenberg who would be trying the major part of the case. Gillingham had been away from trial work too long. Although Rothenberg had assisted others in the firm in cases involving severe injuries, this was to be his first major breakthrough. When the jury publications would report on the verdict, perhaps some would see Gillingham's name and assume he was responsible for the verdict. Still, word would quickly spread that it was Geoffrey Rothenberg who knocked off the great Mitchell Redden.

"You promise?" she inquired, seeking further confirmation.

"I promise. And again, I'm sorry."

Rothenberg kissed his wife goodbye. He was to meet Gillingham at a house in Beverly Hills and promised he would be home that night at a decent hour.

•••

Rothenberg is driving through the Sunset area of Beverly Hills in a light sprinkling rain. He had returned from New Jersey over the weekend, but this was his first opportunity to give a report on the trip to Gillingham, who at the time was looking at expensive homes with a real estate agent and would be spending the entire day doing so.

Eventually, Rothenberg's car pulls up behind Gillingham's black BMW and parks. They are sitting in front of a large two-story Spanish-style home, and the real estate agent is opening the gate to the property. Spying Rothenberg's arrival, Bulldog motions for the agent to go on and yells that he will join him in a few minutes.

Rothenberg slid into the front passenger seat of the BMW.

"We've got some problems," the young lawyer said with a tinge of anxiety.

"What might that be?" By contrast, Gillingham was calm and added even a slight smile. It was an image he had developed over the years, notwithstanding what was going on inside. Nothing ever seemed to ruffle Bulldog.

"Records are missing, a lot of them, not just a letter or a report here and there. Corporate counsel says it happened in a fire, but I don't buy it."

"You shouldn't." Then, with a slight smirk, Gillingham adds, "They were – how should I put this – they were *lost* about a dozen years ago."

"But what if Redden goes to the FDA?"

"He won't find them there either. Everything that matters is gone. Don't worry about it."

"But… what's in the records?"

"It is not our concern. Our only responsibility is to protect the interests of our client – at all cost, whatever it takes."

Rothenberg is bothered by this, and it is not lost on Gillingham.

"Apparently, someone felt that the records might be damaging to their efforts to market the drug," Rothenberg said to his young protégé. "Remember that Brookhurst spent tens of millions of dollars developing this drug. It is our firm's job to protect that product and not question motives or morality. Brookhurst was under an entirely different management team back then. The president has retired, and so has everyone else involved in the matter."

Rothenberg nods his understanding, and they both exit the car and begin walking up to the house. The light rain has also momentarily stopped.

Rothenberg adds, "By the way, Redden knows about a memorandum incriminating Brookhurst's own clinical studies."

Gillingham seems unconcerned as they continue to walk toward the entrance.

"You're not at all worried about this, are you?" asks Rothenberg.

"Not really."

"But if a jury gets wind of the memo and the missing records, they are gonna have some problems with that, don't you think? I mean, juries don't like big corporations that manipulate records. Isn't that a given?"

The two of them stop in front of a large glass door framed in wrought iron. For obvious reasons, this conversation would not be continued inside.

Gillingham shrugs. "Look, there will be no problem because Redden will never survive the motion for summary judgment."

Rothenberg is intent on making his point. "Are you sure about that? Langhorne may not be happy about this records thing, and he's notorious for being unpredictable. They also have the New England Journal of Medicine study. Shouldn't we be stacking up a big list of the top experts for trial?"

For the first time, Gillingham takes a fix on Rothenberg's eyes. "Let me make my point again. This case will never see a jury."

It finally sinks in on the young lawyer. "You've got this case wired, don't you?"

Preferring to ignore the question, Bulldog said, "Don't let me down, Geoff. I'll be over the top tomorrow at the firm meeting and I want to take you with me. I'm talking about junior partner. But then again, maybe that's not what you're after."

"Of course, it is," assures Rothenberg. "But we can beat Redden, and we don't need any help from Langhorne."

Gillingham is intent on making his point. "It is not going to happen," he said. "Not this time. And nothing is wired. I just know my judges." It's a lie, but he knows it won't be questioned.

Rothenberg looks out toward the street, not attempting to hide his obvious frustration. But for Bulldog, a moment of truth has arrived.

"I need to know, Geoff, are you on board or not?"

"Of course I am," said Rothenberg, recognizing that he may have been a bit too confrontational. "Totally committed," he added. His career as a trial lawyer might need to be put on hold, as a BKN partnership was a front-and-center priority. At the very least, he owed that to Carol. "Just let me know what you need, and you've got it."

"Good. I need you to track down Dr. Martin Radcliffe. He retired from Brookhurst a couple of years ago. Go through personnel and get his current address and telephone number. Call Radcliffe and get some available dates for a deposition here in L.A., then set it up with Redden. In the meantime, let Radcliffe know that I'll be calling him tomorrow, and that it's very important we have a chat."

"Something I should know about?" Notwithstanding his expressed commitment, Rothenberg sees himself as an outsider, shielded from a set of facts about the case he might never be privy to – a dark side destined to never reach the light of day. Perhaps it might be in his best interest to leave well enough alone. It was not lost on Rothenberg that Gillingham had a reputation around the office of frequently stepping over the line when it came to the Rules of Professional Conduct, the gold standard by which all attorneys were bound to live by, and strictly enforced by the California State Bar.

"Not really," said Gillingham. "I'll be in the office tomorrow. I have a few more homes to look at."

Rothenberg decides to give it one more shot. "Just as an insurance policy, maybe I should be putting in a few hours toward trial prep, maybe line up a few top-notch experts."

Gillingham smiles. "That won't be necessary," he promises, then disappears through the door.

CHAPTER 31

Located in the northern mountains of New Jersey, Lake Hopatcong is the largest freshwater lake in the state and covers an area of four square miles. It also teems with pickerel, walleye, largemouth and smallmouth bass, muskies, hybrid stripers, and more. An avid fisherman, when Martin Radcliffe was approaching retirement age, he knew exactly where he would be heading – living a dream in a lakefront home with rod and reel in hand. By the time he made his final exit from Brookhurst, Martin and his wife had purchased a house on the water, nestled in a cove, with a thick backdrop of oak, sycamore, white oak, and dogwood trees and the privacy they afforded. Extending from the shoreline was a 50-foot boat dock. The final touch was a 31-foot Sea Ray, added within two weeks of Martin and Mabel's move-in and, at the moment, was tied up alongside the boat dock.

It was late morning, and Radcliffe was gathering fishing gear in the garage of their home when he heard Mabel call to him through the adjoining doorway.

"Hey, Marty! You just got another call. A Mr. Rothenberg."

Radcliffe is digging through a metal case filled with fishing gear. "What's he want?" he asked, more preoccupied with the object of his search.

"He needs to set up a meeting. Something about a deposition. Why are you so popular all of a sudden?"

"Beats me.... Oh, here it is." He pulls out his favorite lure for bass.

"So, what do I tell him. He says it's about Phenatol."

This caught his attention, so he stopped and stared at the lure.

"He says he's from the company," continued Mabel. "He says it's important."

"Get his number. Tell him I'll have to call him back."

"But...."

Radcliffe now turned and faced Mabel, who was still standing in the doorway. "Tell him I will have to call him back," he repeated firmly, communicating that it was not open for debate.

Never one to engage in arguments, Mabel simply nodded, closed the door, and then left to end the phone call. Early in their marriage, Radcliffe made it clear that all decisions related to his profession would be made by him and him alone – unless, of course, he solicited her input, which only rarely occurred. What made this arrangement tolerable – barely – was that conversely, every decision related to their home, including the style of the house, the furniture, and all of its décor, even the neighborhood, would be in Mabel's domain, the singular exception being their retirement lakeside home, which was a joint decision. Surprisingly, accepting where each of them stood on these two major issues had led to very few altercations over the period of their 42-year marriage.

But now Phenatol was rearing its ugly head again, something Radcliffe had hoped would be buried in the past, a blemish on an otherwise exemplary record. First, this Hildebrand person over the past two days, and now this deposition thing. He needed time to think this through, to organize his thoughts, to follow the best path forward. But what path should that be? What would be best for him economically, or...should his conscience be his guide? Yes, he had to think. He was coming to a fork in the road, and he was certain about that. And the path he should decide to take – in either direction – will no doubt bring with it a consequence he will have to live with over the remainder of his life.

Yes, he needed to drop a line in the lake and think. Fishing had always brought clarity to his life and had frequently given him guidance before – the singular exception occurring when Phenatol and Brookhurst entered his life.

Radcliffe grabbed his rod and reel, and a few other essentials, exited the garage, and began his trek down to the boat dock, a couple hundred feet away. Upon arrival, he pulled up a chair, previously positioned at the end of the dock, hooked up the lure, then cast his line in an area of the cove that had brought him some luck recently and slowly began reeling it in.

Martin Radcliffe had always seen himself as a scientist, even when he was studying for his M.D. degree. He was quiet and methodical, always deep in thought, and could stick to a task for a thousand years if necessary. He was well-suited for research and went straight to the FDA upon completion of his residency in pharmacology and toxicology and a short stint at a university doing research. In a university setting, there were too many people to answer to, and he had no desire to participate in education. At the FDA, he would review data on experimental drugs from all over the pharmaceutical industry, which is at the forefront of pharmacological medicine. This was where he belonged – or so he thought at the time.

After a few years as a medical reviewer, Radcliffe began to experience frustration. He was overworked and understaffed. He would wait for months to get his reports typed and often would end up typing them himself. Frequently, he shared a desk with another reviewer. Budget cuts were making matters even worse, resulting in outdated equipment and further cutbacks on staff. Several times, drug companies offered to have his reports typed by their own staff, but he refused and typed them himself to maintain integrity in the established procedure.

Many times, inadequate data came in on clinical studies, which he refused to accept and would routinely reject. When supplemental data were returned, he suspected the studies were being misrepresented. However, pressure from above to sign off on the studies was frequently there. And the message was clear: reject the studies – especially after one or two revisions by the drug company – and they would simply be reassigned to another reviewer who would give them a pass. It would also have an impact on his ability to move up the ladder.

Rumors among Radcliffe's colleagues in the review department were that others had even accepted bribes and had then moved on to better jobs in the industry. With long hours and low pay, he faced a persistent dilemma of whether or not to succumb to the temptations. Increasingly, it was a strain on his marriage, and he was at his weakest state when the Phenatol study had been laid on his desk.

Over a thirteen-month period, he reviewed the studies and the compiled data thoroughly and finally dictated a report. Then he waited. The typists were overloaded, and no one could get to it for months. He was also in the middle of typing two other reports himself. Brookhurst inquired about the holdup, and he relayed the problem. The company offered to have it typed by their own staff, which he promptly refused. Then, it offered to pay for an independent typist, which he could select himself. He had resisted this offer from other pharmaceutical companies before but now was quite tempted, even though he knew his assessments and conclusions would not please Brookhurst. These studies were poorly designed, especially concerning teratogenicity. His recommendations were for additional and extensive studies.

Then came the conclusions from the two clinical investigators: their data was inconsistent with their findings. Radcliffe had a strong suspicion about possible manipulation by Brookhurst – and had even considered making a direct call to the investigators. But this time, he relented. He called up a typist who had previously worked for the FDA and was out freelancing in the D.C. area. Arrangements were made, and she was given the tapes.

When the completed report was finally returned to his desk, awaiting his signature, it contained numerous statements he had never dictated. It concluded that the studies were sufficient and recommended approval.

An angry Radcliffe immediately called the typist, but she would not accept his calls. He then called Kupperman, head of Regulatory Affairs for Brookhurst. Kupperman refused to discuss the matter over the phone but suggested they meet privately. A telephone call is not where such delicate matters should be discussed. Kupperman suggested that he fly to New Jersey – at their expense – and meet at the company facility.

Radcliffe refused, stating that he would think of another location overnight and call him back in the morning. Over the remainder of the day, Radcliffe seriously considered reporting the whole matter to his supervisor but rejected the idea. It would entail acknowledging that he had violated FDA policy by forwarding his confidential dictation to an outside source – and would be a serious mark against his exemplary record at the FDA. That night, he and Mabel had a drag-out battle about their current financial situation, and the die was cast. The following morning, he called and made arrangements to come to New Jersey.

Upon arriving, Radcliffe was put up in a suite in a local hotel and then met with the top brass of the company. Even before the subject of the report could be addressed, he was being flattered about his exacting standards and scientific acumen. He was the kind of man they were after to improve and upgrade the quality of their clinical studies. If he was interested, a high-level entry position was available – a vice president – at a salary and benefits commensurate with the title. Radcliffe returned to Rockville and signed off on the report.

Three months later, he left the FDA and began working for Brookhurst. After an additional four and a half months, the Phenatol NDA was approved for marketing.

However, on the very day that the Phenatol approval was reported in the Federal Register, Radcliffe received a call from one of the two clinical investigators whose conclusions did not match the statistical data within the summaries. How could he have possibly approved the drug? How could he have ignored his report?

The magnitude of the problem, potentially affecting thousands of users, demanded a full hearing and….

Suddenly, a fish struck the lure, and his pole bent almost in half. It was a big one, maybe the biggest he had ever hooked up with – maybe even a record. Radcliffe jumped up from his chair. The fight was on as he first pulled back, securing the hook, then let the fish run. After a few moments, Radcliffe began to reel him in, first slowly, then with increasing aggression. The tug on the line was strong as the fish fought back, darting in different directions. These were the moments he lived for, man against fish, a blending of skill, determination, and the stamina to stay with the challenge.

So absorbed was the elderly fisherman in the excitement of the catch that he failed to notice a shadow that had just cast over him, at which point his line abruptly snapped!

"Shit!" He shouted. "Dammit!"

He now sees the shadow and turns into the glare of the sun, shielding his eyes.

"Mabel, is that you? I just lost the biggest son of a bitch…"

He now catches a glimpse of a rock coming down on him an instant before it slams into his skull. He is immediately stunned, with no balance or sense of up and down, and stumbles backward into the lake.

Radcliffe is now gagging, gasping for air, his body gripped by total weakness. He gasps for air one last time before feeling something heavy on his head, forcing him down, deep under the water. He opens his mouth, sucking for air but only swallowing more water.

Gradually, his senses become numb, and with total resignation, he succumbs to death.

✦

CHAPTER 32

Wednesday, February 17

Mary Ellen had refused to show up for work now for two weeks. Redden, understanding the situation, had accepted her claim of illness without debate. After all, in many ways, she was right. She was no doubt an emotional wreck, and time away would have some medicinal benefits. So, he had gone with temporary help – five girls in 11 days – only to find himself backed up on dictation and up to his neck in a number of administrative problems. By mid-morning, not even the temp had shown up.

Redden is now sitting at his desk, first listening to the phone ring and then Mary Ellen's familiar voice-mail message. Upon hearing the beep, Redden began his plea.

"Mary Ellen, I know you're there, and I know what you are going through. You are embarrassed and, and…well, so am I. Really. But you and I, go back too far, and we know each other too well. Please, just hear me out. You are like my alter ego around here and I am totally lost without you. This case is coming down on top of me, and I need you by my side…Please, please, pick up…."

After a pause, he finally hears a live but somewhat distant voice say, "Yes."

"Thank you," said Redden, then hesitated, fishing for the right words, sensing that this would be his only opportunity, and he did not want to blow it. "Mary Ellen, we need to talk, face-to-face, here in the office, just you and me." He pauses once again, hoping to hear her jump in and offer a few words, but no such luck. "Look, it is absolutely essential that we talk, and the sooner, the better. Avoiding the topic and postponing a discussion will only increase the tension between us, making it more difficult to resolve – and it needs to be resolved." Still no participation from the other end of the line. "Don't you understand? You are my friend, and friends do not abandon friends. They reach out to help them. And that is what I am doing right now. I am reaching out."

This seems to do it. "I'll be in later this afternoon," she said, then hung up the phone.

⸺●⸺

At promptly 2:00 PM, Mary Ellen entered Redden's office suite and approached the receptionist's window. Observing that her old chair was unoccupied, she continued down the interior hallway to Redden's office, where the door was wide open.

"No receptionist?" she asked.

"A no-show."

"Sorry," she offered. True to her unwavering commitment to the office, she could not avoid a sense of guilt about Redden's plight.

"Not your fault. Please have a seat."

As she made her way to one of the two client chairs, Redden noted, true to form, Mary Ellen was professionally attired and fully color-coordinated, including her purse, belt, and shoes. Redden's secretary had an expensive taste in clothing, which always showed, even today. As always, she appeared to be on her way to an interview for a top executive position – except for the pair of dark sunglasses she had yet to remove.

Mary Ellen sat in the chair, her purse in her lap, which she viewed contemplatively for a few moments, then looked up at Mitchell.

"Could I ask you to remove your glasses?" he asked.

"I would prefer not."

"Please."

At first, resistant to the idea, she relents and places the glasses in her lap. Mary Ellen's eyes are glossy and reddened, and her best effort to mask her emotional state with makeup proved to be woefully inadequate. For the briefest moment, Redden wanted to rescind his request regarding the glasses. Maybe he was in way over his head; that is if he had any hope to rescue Mary Ellen from her obvious state of depression. But notwithstanding his perceived ineptness for the task, he knew he had to give it a try.

"Look, Mary Ellen, let's face it. You had too much to drink that night. No, that does not describe it. You were ripped! Blitzed! And when people are drunk, they do stupid things, things they would never do when they were sober. And don't I know that? I have done things when I was drunk that, believe me, I wish I could forget. Hey, I have even engaged in behavior that I *can't* remember. How scary is that? …."

"Can we at least agree on this?" he adds.

"Of course," she softly replied as she looked straight at Redden.

"And when people are in a state of intoxication, their actions are really beyond their control. So,…so, what happened that night was really beyond your control. And…and, as such, there is absolutely nothing for you to apologize for, assuming, of course, you have convinced yourself that there is some need to apologize, which there isn't, but assuming you felt that way, well, I am herein accepting your apology, which again, is unnecessary."

Redden now realizes that he is just rambling, searching for the words, any words that might have some impact on Mary Ellen, who continues to stare at him. "Does any of this make sense?" he adds as she continues to stare at him.

"Of course," she said again.

"What I'm asking is, can't we just say that what happened that night was nothing more than a product of too much to drink and something we can both put behind us and move on with our respective lives?"

"Of course," she said one more time, not for a moment taking her eyes off his.

"Really?" Was this really going to be this easy? Redden was still skeptical.

"I'm in full agreement," she adds.

"So, then, you would have no problem coming in tomorrow to kind of get up to speed on what is happening around the office?"

Mary Ellen nods her head. "Yes, I'll come in tomorrow. But I will be giving you thirty days' notice. I'll give you a month to find a full-time replacement."

"But…I don't understand. I thought we were in agreement."

Mary Ellen rises from the chair and replaces her dark glasses. Now, *she* is searching for the right words. "The problem, Mitch, is not what I did after I got drunk a couple weeks ago. I'm prepared to move on from that."

She looks down at the floor momentarily, then up again.

"It's why I got drunk to begin with." With that, she began to exit the office and added, "I'll see you in the morning."

Mary Ellen did not want to unload about the emotionally distraught reject she saw herself to be. She owed Mitchell the thirty days but would not stay a day longer.

He was so fucking blind. Even now, he could not see what had been staring at him in the face since the day they met. Right up to her surprise visit that night, Redden had never even contemplated a sexual liaison between the two of them. She was an older woman who had always handled her job with professional detachment. But after that night, one would have to be at the imbecilic level and not appreciate her interest. Maybe it was something he felt uncomfortable talking about, and perhaps his appearance of perplexed mystification seemed the safest route for him to take at the moment. Yes, maybe insulating himself with ignorance was the safest course to follow.

Redden stared for a moment at the empty doorway as he heard the door to the suite snap shut, conveying a sense of finality to the visit — maybe even to their relationship. Women! Whatever drove them and triggered their behavior was one of the great mysteries of life that had always eluded him. Two failed marriages had convinced him of that. What was the secret that prompted Mary Ellen to turn to the bottle?

Well, he had thirty days. There was still time.

⸺•⸺

It seemed to be a day for reaching resolutions about that night – at least to make the effort. Although it had not gone well with Mary Ellen, perhaps a dose of good fortune might look favorably upon him and come to his rescue. All his recent efforts seem to be nothing but a series of dead ends, so maybe it was time for some old-fashioned good luck.

He knocked several times at the door without an answer but was certain he had seen movement through the window when his Porsche had pulled up in front and parked – so he continued to knock.

"C'mon, Niki, I know you're inside. Answer the door!"

Again, he knocked several times without a response.

"Look, I'm gonna stand here until you answer the door…hours, if necessary."

A minute later, the door slowly opened, and Niki appeared on the other side of the screen door – a locked screen door, as Redden found out with a subtle tug.

Before her stood Mitchell, with a bouquet of flowers in his hand. "Delivery for a Ms. Niki Burroughs," he announced. "Valentine's greetings from Mr. Mitchell Redden."

"I can't be bought with flowers. Besides, you're three days late."

"Better late than never."

"And your lines are a bit dated."

Another challenge is to find the right words.

"Unlock the door, Niki. We need to talk…. Please."

"I don't want to talk. I want to be left alone."

"No, you don't."

"Yes, I do, Mitch. Our relationship needs to be put on hold, maybe permanently."

"Look, Niki, I am really sorry. I never should have said it. I know we had an agreement. But the words, they just kind of jumped out, you know, in the heat of passion, without any thought."

"So, you didn't mean it?"

Had he actually boxed himself into a corner? This was a no-win question, and for the second time of the day, Mitchell Redden, the hotshot lawyer with a history of mesmerizing juries, found himself wanting. Try the truth, idiot.

"I certainly did at that moment. In point of fact, Niki, I have never experienced an emotion like that in all my forty years, not even close. So, was it love? Yeah, I think so. And the way it kind of snuck up on me that night certainly created some confusion, I will have to admit. But having had a couple weeks now to digest what happened between us that night, I will have to flat out say, yes, I'm in love with you," he firmly announced as he stared at her through the screen that separated them.

"And if there is any possibility that you might feel the same way," he continued, "I'm begging you, please give it a chance."

So, there it was, laid at her feet. No more uncertainty, no ambiguity. Mitchell Redden was in love with her, which was an unequivocal distraction to her goals, not to mention the impact it might have on his representation in the lawsuit. No, this could not possibly be a good thing.

"I'm sorry, Mitch, but I'm not going to change my mind. We need to give ourselves a break, a separation."

"Okay," he said reluctantly. "I'll accept that, but could we possibly talk inside without a screen between us? I'm also your lawyer. Unless. of course, it's your intent to end that as well."

After a brief moment, Niki unlocked the screen door and backed away as Redden entered the living room. "Have a seat," she invited. Redden seated himself on the couch, hoping Niki would join him there, but instead, she positioned herself across the room on a chair.

"Okay, say your piece," she said, although confident that it would not alter her resolve for a much-needed separation.

Redden saw himself at a crossroads in their relationship and knew what he was about to say could send Niki off in the wrong direction with little hope of bringing her back. Yet, at the same time, he felt that the issue was at the core of her resistance to anything meaningful between them.

"I am not Scott Burroughs," he announced as if it was something that needed clarification.

"Of course, you're not. What's that supposed to mean?"

"It means that I know that he hurt you deeply, I'm sure, and I would think you are still carrying the emotional scars from that relationship."

"I still don't get your point."

With some trepidation, he decides to push forward. "All males are not as calloused and self-centered as Scott Burroughs. Your experience with one man should not set the standard by which all others are categorized or judged."

"I have never compared you with Scott if that's what you're suggesting."

"I'm sure that's been your intent, but…." Redden sees himself sitting on a precipice at this point, not knowing whether the next statement will send him falling into the abyss. "It's been my perception, over the past few months, that deep down, maybe unconsciously, you are…." Should he say it? Is it worth the gamble? " …Well, that you are anti-male, that you've closed off the possibility of a relationship, a meaningful relationship with *any* man, because…because you don't want to be hurt again." There, he said it and sat, almost holding his breath, waiting for the explosion.

"Maybe you should go," she finally said.

"Can you hear me out?"

She doesn't respond but sits and mentally debates whether she should show Redden out the door – or maybe hear him out. She knows he is right, of course, but does she want to be dissuaded from a view firmly entrenched in her psyche over the past several years.

Hearing no resistance, Redden decides to push on. "I agree, there are a lot of jerks out there, but all men are not created equal, not on this issue."

"All men are alike," she said. "And it wasn't just Scott. It's every man I have ever had contact with. They are all users and lack even the slightest trace of feelings."

"Putting me aside for the moment, your father was a man. There can be exceptions."

Suddenly, in a rush of emotion, Niki leaned forward in her chair and blurted out, "My father…," said Niki, as tears filled her eyes, "…

my father drove my mother to suicide. I found the note…next to her body." She now started sobbing. "I destroyed it so no one would ever know. So, don't tell me about exceptions."

So now it was out, the secret she had carried for a decade. Not once, not even with her best friend, Alicia, had she shared this burden that had tormented her from the day she had found her mother and the note.

As Niki sobbed, Redden got up from the couch and crouched down in front of her. "Niki, I am so sorry." He reaches for her hand, but she pulls it away.

"No, Mitch," she said. "Let's keep this professional."

"Of course," he reassured her. Niki was fragile, and this was not the time to push. Perhaps in time, but words right now would have little meaning. Only his actions might have an impact on her, and he was unsure even about that. But there was still time, as long as the case was pending. Redden placed a handkerchief in her lap, stood, and returned to the couch.

"Professional it is," he concurred. "So, I want to bring you up to speed on the case."

Niki dabbed her eyes with the cloth and said, "I'm listening."

With some hesitation, Redden launched into the upcoming motion for summary judgment, explaining what it was and the profound consequence if they lost.

"You seem concerned," she observed. "Is there a danger of the court granting this motion?"

"I'm not going to sugar-coat this. Yes, there is a serious risk that we may lose. And it's not because we have a weak case. We don't. But we are getting signals, comments from the judge, and an attitude. Something smells, but we have yet to figure out what it is. But without hearing or seeing one piece of evidence, no testimony, no documents, he is communicating that he does not like our case."

"Is this possible?" she asked incredulously.

"It is."

"So, can't we get rid of him? If a judge is biased, can't he be removed?"

"It is not that simple? If a judge doesn't admit his bias – which they rarely do – then you've got to have some evidence – which we don't have. This is also the federal court system, where judges are appointed for life, and great deference is given to their denials of bias. Absent any evidence, and I mean strong evidence, we are stuck with Judge Langhorne."

"Well, there must be something we can do."

"Of course, we always have the recourse of appeal, but that is nothing we want to rely on. I have my investigator on this, and he is turning over every stone he can. He is also one of the best I've had the pleasure of working with. If something is out there, I have every confidence that he will find it. But the reality, Niki, is that there may be nothing to find."

"You don't seem very optimistic about the outcome of this motion."

"I could lie to you, but the reality is that your case might well end in two weeks. I am doing everything that I can, but in the end, it may not be enough."

Redden was about to fill his client in on the frustrating trip to the East Coast but thought better of it. The dose of bad news he had just delivered was enough for her to absorb for the day, and it would not serve any purpose to burden her with yet another problem. That would have to wait for another day. And who knows? Maybe something might actually break their way over the next few days.

Redden stood. "I am going to head on back to the office, Niki. I still have a lot of work to do, as you might guess. But know this. You have my total commitment on your case. Between now and whenever this case might end, you will get nothing but my absolute best effort."

He had hoped that she would approach him with a casual kiss on the cheek or even a hug, but it was not to happen, so he simply said, "Goodbye, Niki. I'll stay in touch," then exited through the door. A few moments later, she could hear the Porsche rev up, then head down the street.

While still seated, she looked over at the couch and saw the bouquet of flowers, Mitchell Redden's calling card, and his fruitless attempt at bribery. Yes, she had set him straight – left little doubt about her resolve. There would be no further intimacy, although the sex had been great and filled a long-frustrated need. But especially now, with these new challenges presented by the judge, she wanted Redden laser-focused on the lawsuit, nothing else. From this date forward, he would see nothing but a wall – and it would start right now with dumping those damn flowers into the trash.

Niki rose from the chair, stepped over onto the couch, and picked up the bouquet. But after taking no more than three steps toward the kitchen, the unmistakable fragrance of plumeria brought her to a complete halt. Plumeria! How could he possibly have known? Well, of course, he couldn't have since she had never revealed to him that plumeria flowers were her absolute favorite and carried an aroma that sent her off into dreamland to faraway places she had hoped to one day visit.

No, that was not going to work! Again, she pushed on toward the trash container in the kitchen – and again stopped. Oh, what the hell! Mitch will never know, she assured herself, as she reached for a lead crystal vase in the cupboard and began filling it with water. No, he will never know.

⸻ ● ⸻

Redden arrived back at his office and dropped down into his desk chair. It was already 6:30 PM. Harry had left for the day after opening his mail and placing it on his desk. Included was a written status report from Hildebrand.

It contained nothing but bad news.

Both Langhorne and the clerk were clean, at least as far as his investigation had taken him. He had a few leads left but nothing promising. He also had more bad news. Martin Radcliffe, the former FDA medical examiner, had been killed in some kind of a freak accident. He had slipped and struck his head while fishing and had fallen into a lake and drowned. He was discovered about two or three hours after his death by his wife. Hildebrand was certain that the drowning was not a coincidence, except that the county coroner was still reporting it as an accident. It appeared that the case was leaving a trail of blood all the way back to New Jersey.

Hildebrand had also checked with the offices of the two clinical investigators. As expected, all of their records on the clinical studies had been destroyed years earlier. The originals, of course, had been forwarded on to Brookhurst. Thus, they were again close to another dead end.

Redden had one more assignment for Hildebrand and placed a call to his cell number. As always, the investigator was quick to respond.

"Hi, Rick. It's Mitch."

"Yes, Mitch. How can I help?"

"Got your report."

"Yeah, sorry about that. Still a few leads, so don't give up hope."

"I won't. Hey, I want you to locate a nurse who completed the Phenatol report for one of the two clinical investigators. Her name is Roberta Blanchard, and she worked in the investigator's office in Philadelphia during the clinical investigations. Track her down and report back whenever you have a good address. Locate her as soon as possible, as she may be our only hope on the motion for summary judgment."

— • —

CHAPTER 33

Wednesday, March 3

Tomorrow is judgment day – summary judgment day. It is early evening, and Redden has resigned himself to what he sees as inevitable: the case is going south in the morning at the hands of Langhorne or, more likely, the hands of his puppeteer, Chester Raymond Gillingham III.

Two weeks had passed, and still nothing on Roberta Blanchard. "It's as if she has disappeared off the face of the earth," had been Hildebrand's words, communicated to Redden only about two hours earlier. As Rick had explained, this only happens when someone does not want to be found, when they are actively hiding, often changing their name, even their vocation.

Redden scanned the notes for his argument one last time, then dropped them into his briefcase. Following his usual routine, he headed to the entrance door to his office suite to exit, then climbed the stairs to his second-floor condominium. But as he opened the door, he spied a manila envelope on the threshold, obviously left there by someone who did not want to be identified.

There was no addressee on its face, although the envelope was sealed. Intrigued about the surprise delivery, he opened it but found only a blank piece of stationery. It was discolored and torn in a couple of locations, suggesting that it had been around for several years –

although this could have been established by the firm name on the letterhead: "Barry & Klein."

On the left side at the top were the names of only five attorneys – and on the right side, a single name listed "Of Counsel" – was *Roger Langhorne.*

⸺●⸺

Thursday, March 4

Redden looked at his watch as he and Blaylock sat together behind the railing in Langhorne's courtroom. It was 8:44 AM. True to form, Langhorne was running late for his 8:30 calendar. On the outside chance that the judge might be on time, the two of them had arrived 15 minutes early, not wanting to draw the ire of little Napoleon. The challenge they were facing was significant enough without facing an agitated judge.

Riding together to the courthouse that morning, Mitch and Harry had discussed the "gift" left at Redden's door the prior evening. Neither believed that, by itself, the piece of stationery would be sufficient to motivate Langhorne to recuse himself. The effectiveness of the evidence would depend upon the argument presented, and multiple ideas were kicked around by the two lawyers during the one-hour drive. And as they sat awaiting the arrival of Langhorne, Redden had yet to decide what that argument might be. As was often the case, Redden's oral presentation would be dictated by the defense counsel's argument and the comments coming from the bench.

Also behind the railing, but on the opposite side of the courtroom, sat the tandem of Gillingham and Rothenberg. The older of the two sat calmly, exuding the confidence of one who had little doubt about the forthcoming decision. Rothenberg, on the other hand, had mixed emotions. Although he was looking forward to Redden going down to defeat – an ordained result, according to Gillingham – he also wanted his day in court.

"All rise," said the bailiff, proclaiming the arrival of the judge, who quickly ascended to his throne, then just as quickly held up his hand and said,

"Be seated, be seated." Langhorne left little doubt that he wanted to move forward as expeditiously as possible. "Call the first case," he instructed the clerk.

"Yes, Your Honor. Case number one, Burroughs versus Brookhurst Pharmaceuticals."

Both sets of attorneys promptly rose, passed through the swinging gate, made their way to their designated locations at the counsel table, and then announced their appearances for the record.

Langhorne is direct and to the point. He wanted this whole matter behind him, and the sooner, the better. "Counsel, I have read all of the papers, both the motion and the opposition, and it will not be necessary to repeat what has already been written. So, please confine your argument to anything that you might want to add."

Gillingham, as counsel for the moving party, addressed the court first. His comments were succinct and to the point. As expected, his focus was on the standard of care for pharmaceutical companies, and in that regard, "Brookhurst's conduct was exemplary, as demonstrated by the FDA's stamp of approval."

"Regarding the issue of causation, the only published study referred to by Dr. Donner in his declaration was the one conducted by Rhoden and colleagues, appearing in The New England Journal of Medicine. That study, although reporting a statistically significant increased risk, reported an increase only at 87%, a percentage less than double and thus failing to meet the legal standard, namely that it was more likely than not the drug was the cause of the alleged injury. Because plaintiffs have failed to meet their burden of proof, plaintiff must lose." Gillingham, having concluded, sat down next to Rothenberg, who managed to force a smile of approval.

Langhorne quietly nodded his head, suggesting that he likewise was impressed by the argument.

Redden slowly rose, contemplating the words he would use on this delicate matter. He had to raise the issue of recusal first, for launching into his argument on the merits of the motion might result waiving of his right to excuse the judge.

"Your honor, there is a preliminary matter which needs to be first addressed before delivering any argument on the merits," he began.

Langhorne's reply was sternly stated. "Mr. Redden, either you argue the motion or you don't."

"But…"

"Either you argue, or you waive. What's it gonna be? Counsel, I don't want to drag this out. I have a large calendar this morning, so, again, What's it gonna be?"

Recognizing that the ruling had been decided long before he had walked into the courtroom, Redden didn't hesitate in his response. "Your Honor, the plaintiff will be moving this court to recuse itself." Redden's voice was quite firm.

"On what ground?" Langhorne angrily demanded.

"On this ground," said Redden as he held up the blank stationery and handed a copy to Gillingham.

After a nod from the judge, the clerk retrieved the original from Redden and handed it to Langhorne.

"When did you receive this?" asked Langhorne after examining the document.

"Last night."

After digesting the issue for a moment, Langhorne invited counsel into his chambers – lead counsel only – and the two men followed the judge into his private office. The court reporter remained in her seat. Nothing would be on the record. All three men remained standing.

"What's the significance of this?" demanded Langhorne.

"It establishes a professional relationship between Your Honor and counsel for the defendant."

Unless called upon for comment, Gillingham opted to remain silent.

"This was 28 years ago, and no relationship with defense counsel has existed since. There is absolutely no factual basis for recusal. I have never represented Brookhurst Pharmaceuticals and was never "of counsel" during any period when Barry, Klein, and Nance represented that party."

Redden's voice is now even stronger. "28 USC 455(a) demands a judge to disqualify himself where impartiality might reasonably be questioned."

Langhorne's voice is also now louder as emotions begin to boil. "Might *reasonably* be questioned is the key, Mr. Redden. There is nothing reasonable about questioning my impartiality after this length of time."

"Is the court going to represent that there has been no professional or social relationship with any member of the Barry, Klein firm since you went on the bench?"

Langhorne angrily states, "I am not here to be cross-examined, and if you have further evidence on the subject, you should present it now."

Although separated by 5-6 feet, Redden is essentially standing toe-to-toe with the judge, both as to his conviction and his anger.

"I have no additional evidence at the moment, but if this case goes down on the wrong side of the motion, there will be a full-blown investigation into the entire matter. You can bank on it!"

Langhorne explodes. "How dare you threaten a federal court judge! This whole matter will be brought up to the California State Bar. And you can bank on that!"

"Fine. Be sure to tell them that you refused to represent and that you have not had any personal or professional relationship with BKN since you were of counsel. Oh, and if you want to put this all on the record, I would be happy to invite the court reporter into chambers."

"Get out of here!" demanded Langhorne.

Gillingham, who has not uttered a word throughout the matter, quietly follows Redden out of chambers and back into the courtroom.

A good 10 minutes elapsed while Langhorne apparently composed himself. When he finally entered the courtroom and took the bench, he appeared in full control of his emotions and knew exactly what he wanted to say on the record.

"After giving due consideration to the plaintiff's argument on his motion for recusal, I am going to deny that motion. There is absolutely no factual basis that would disqualify me from proceeding with this case. However, notwithstanding the weak defense in opposition to the motion for summary judgment, in the interests of justice, I am going to deny that motion and allow the plaintiff additional time to attempt to develop the needed evidence to meet his burden of proof at the time of trial. Thus, the denial is without prejudice to be renewed as a motion for nonsuit at the time of trial."

With that, Langhorne pounded the gavel and added, "Plaintiff to give notice." Whereupon Langhorne abruptly left the bench, stating over his shoulder that there would be a 15-minute break in the morning's calendar.

Redden secured the original stationery from the clerk and left the courtroom with Harry. Once they were sufficiently alone, Blaylock asked, "What in the hell went on in there?"

"Not here," said Mitchell. "I'll fill you in on the way home. Suffice it to say, Langhorne is scared shitless about this of-counsel thing. No way does he fold on the MSJ unless he has something to hide. Everything was set to go down this morning, and it didn't. We need to find out why."

— ● —

Upon returning to his office, Redden placed a call to Niki and reported the outcome of the motion. He cautioned her, however, that this was only a reprieve. Langhorne will never let the case go to a jury for a decision.

Niki is perplexed. "But why, Mitch? Why?."

"I can't prove it," he began, "not yet. But I believe defense counsel has the judge by the balls, and every time he hears something he does not like, he gives them a big squeeze. After today, I am more convinced than ever. But whatever it is, I am absolutely committed to digging up all the dirty laundry and displaying it for the world to see – assuming, of course, that it is there. We also got a big break last night, a strong lead. We just learned that Langhorne was associated with the defense firm several years ago. He claims no further affiliation has existed since then, but I don't believe him. I've turned over our evidence to my investigator, and we'll just have to wait and see what he can turn up."

"And if he doesn't? If he comes up empty? What then?"

"Then your case goes out the door with the evening trash. Langhorne will grant the defendant's motion for nonsuit, and a jury will never get to hear my brilliant argument."

"I appreciate your candor…and your commitment," she adds.

"You deserve nothing less," he said. "After all, you are my client."

CHAPTER 34

Wednesday, March 17

Alan Donner, MD, stared across the conference table at Gillingham. They are at the law offices of Barry, Klein & Nance. He appears passive and casual with his loosened tie and coat thrown across a chair behind him. A seasoned veteran, he has had his deposition taken in excess of 200 times over the years. His once-dark hair is now totally grey and thinning above his forehead. At 68 years of age, the etched lines on his face underscore not only his years of mileage but the maturity they accumulated. His rimless glasses are often guided down his nose, allowing him to peer over the top of the lenses. Professorial in appearance with a closely-trimmed beard, Donner could have been pulled straight out of central casting.

To Gillingham's left sat Rothenberg, there to only take notes, not to mention to continue the firm's practice of double billing. To Donner's right sat Redden.

To complete the ensemble, Trisha O'Brien, the court reporter who had enjoyed Redden's entertainment at his office back in July, sat at the end of the table, poised over her stenographic machine.

Gillingham first questioned Donner about his education, training, and experience. Donner recited his background with exquisite detail as if he were reading directly from his curriculum vitae. He was initially trained as a pediatrician, serving his residency at a small but respected hospital on the East Coast. After successfully completing his boards, he turned to pharmacology and toxicology. Donner also related the dates and positions of all employment he held over the years, including a seven-year stint with the FDA.

"Are you an epidemiologist?" asked Gillingham, knowing exactly what his response would be, having previously reviewed his CV and a number of his earlier deposition transcripts in preparation for this day.

"No, I am not."

"Then isn't it somewhat presumptuous of you to express expert opinions assessing the epidemiological merits of the Rhoden study?"

Redden was about to object to the argumentative nature of the question but caught himself. Alan Donner was quite capable of taking care of himself.

"I stated that I was not an epidemiologist, not that I lacked expertise in the field." "Do you have any formal training as an epidemiologist?"

"No."

"Have you ever worked as an epidemiologist?"

"No."

"Then, from what enigmatic background have you gathered such an array of knowledge?"

Donner was too smart and savvy to be drawn into an angry exchange. Instead, he smiled. "During my undergraduate years, I took a number of classes involving higher mathematics, including three different courses on statistics. In fact, if you had taken the time to read my CV, you would see that I had a minor in math."

"Anything else?"

"Well, yes. I have read numerous texts on epidemiology. As a matter of fact, since becoming a pharmacologist, I have spent a good part of my practice assessing the epidemiology of various published studies, literally thousands of them. When one studies pharmaceutical products, both their side effects and their efficacy, one necessity must understand epidemiology because that is how they are evaluated. Perhaps you didn't know, but epidemiology is an integral part of pharmacology and toxicology."

Gillingham's face was now a shade redder than it was before. "Well, the Rhoden study only found an 87 percent increased risk, correct?"

"Yes, but I wouldn't minimize an 87 percent increased risk. That means against a control population of ten thousand babies with 300 birth defects, a similar population treated with Phenatol would have 561 babies with birth defects. I find that quite significant."

"But it was less than double the incidence, correct?"

"Of course."

"You understand that in a court of law – in this specific case – you must prove that it is more likely than not, a 51 percent probability, that Phenatol was the cause of Randy Burroughs' limb-reduction birth defect?"

"I do understand that legal standard."

"So, assuming that you get by all the flaws in the Rhoden study, and a jury concludes that the drug is capable of causing limb-reduction defects in humans – which we will call *general* causation – you still must prove *case-specific* causation, namely that Phenatol was the cause of this *specific* birth defect suffered by the Burroughs boy?"

"Aside from your comment about flaws in the study, yes, I would agree with your statement. It must be proven in court that there is at least a 51 percent probability that Phenatol was the cause of Randy's birth defect."

"You would agree, would you not, that there are children born with limb-reduction birth defects from mothers who never ingested Phenatol?

"Yes, I would agree with that."

"Then, limb-reduction birth defects can also be caused by factors *other* than Phenatol?

"Yes."

"In fact, would you also agree that over 95 percent of all pregnant mothers who ingest Phenatol during pregnancy have children that are totally normal, in other words, without birth defects of any kind?"

With this series of artfully drafted questions, Redden is beginning to sense that his expert witness is being painted into a corner. He was also painfully aware that he had not spent any time with Donner on this line of questioning, which at the moment was creating a slight sense of anxiety – and again reflected on his lack of recent experience. He would have to rely upon Donner's many years in the trenches.

"Of course," responded Donner, who knew exactly where Gillingham was going with his questions.

"So, even assuming that Phenatol was a human teratogen, just because a pregnant woman has ingested Phenatol and subsequently delivered a baby with a limb-reduction defect, does not automatically establish that the two were related?"

"I would agree with that."

"And if out of one thousand pregnant women exposed to Phenatol during pregnancy, 10 children were born with limb-reduction defects, you could not take the results of the Rhoden study and tell me which child's defect was caused by Phenatol, could you?"

Donner hesitated before giving an answer, inducing even more anxiety in Redden. Conversely, Bulldog's barely visible smirk conveyed the image of a cat playing with a cornered mouse – about ready to make the kill.

"I don't disagree with that," Donner finally responded.

"In fact, taking the results of the Rhoden study, one cannot state with reasonable medical probability – a 51 percent or more probability – which child's defect was caused by Phenatol, can he?"

Redden momentarily held his breath as he awaited the answer that might be the death blow to the case.

"If one *only* looked at the Rhoden Phenatol study, that would be true. But if you should choose to bury your head in the sand and ignore all the other related factors in assessing the etiology of the anomaly, that would be your choice – but it is not mine."

Redden could not have been more delighted at the response, especially the zinger that targeted Gillingham's ego. Now he could breathe again.

"Explain," demanded an agitated Gillingham.

Donner removed his glasses and placed them on the conference table. This was the moment he had been waiting for. "The Rhoden study leads me to conclude, with reasonable medical probability – in fact, with at least a 95% certainty – that Phenatol is a human teratogen capable of causing limb-reduction birth defects; 'general causation,' as you refer to it. However, to determine which of the ten children, if any, had a limb-reduction defect caused by Phenatol – case-specific causation – I would be looking at a multitude of other factors. First, of course, would be that the mother ingested a drug capable of causing the same limb abnormality suffered by the child. In addition, the next biggest issue would be the timing of the ingestion – when was the drug ingested by the mother? If it was ingested too early or too late in the gestational period, then the drug could be eliminated as the etiological factor. Third would be eliminating all other known factors that can cause human congenital malformations, such as heredity, exposure to radiation, maternal illness, physical trauma, and, of course, other teratogenic drugs."

Donner momentarily paused, seeming to do so for the dramatic impact. "In assessing all the medical records and medical and personal histories identified in my report, I can conclude with reasonable medical probability that Phenatol was the cause of Randy Burroughs' limb-reduction birth defect. Preliminary to doing so, I determined that Phenatol was ingested right at the critical period of time and was able to eliminate all other known causes of birth defects in humans."

For the remainder of the morning, Bulldog continued to flush out as many details as he could, pinning Donner down on all his supporting reasons and facts on the issue of causation. By the time they broke for lunch, he was ready to launch into the doctor's opinions on the propriety of Brookhurst's clinical studies – whether or not they met the industry standard of care. Over the one-hour break, he would also solicit input from Rothenberg on any "clean-up" questions related to the morning session.

Redden also had a lot to think about over the lunch break. He would spend some time revisiting some of the morning's testimony to ensure nothing would be said that would weaken Donner's earlier opinions, as well as to strengthen some of the doctor's statements that Redden felt could have been testified to with less equivocation. It was also not lost on Mitchell Redden that notwithstanding Bulldog's time away from the judicial arena, he was still quite skilled at his craft and unquestionably a formidable opponent who should not be underestimated.

— • —

The afternoon session began promptly at 1:00 PM.

"Have you ever reviewed the actual premarket clinical studies conducted by Brookhurst – either the originals or copies of them?" began Gillingham.

"You are speaking of the raw data, the original records, and reports by the clinical investigators?"

"Yes."

"No, I have not."

"Then, in assessing the quality of those studies, you are relying upon the summary reports, setting out the data and the conclusions regarding the studies?

"Studies prepared by your client and submitted to the FDA as being factually accurate, yes. However, my review was not limited to those summary reports. I also reviewed discovery responses in this lawsuit, responses to questions answered under oath."

"So, the summary reports and discovery responses provided the factual basis for your opinion that the clinical studies did not comply with the standard of care in the drug industry, correct?"

"Well, not totally. I also reviewed a memo from one of your guys, Roland Kupperman. He was Vice President of Regulatory Affairs, as I recall. He apparently shared my view of the studies. I happen to have a copy here," said Donner as he pulled the memo from his briefcase. "I'll be happy to read the language I am referring to," he added.

"That won't be necessary," said Gillingham, holding up his hand. He was quite familiar with the memorandum, which had been attached as an exhibit in opposition to the motion for summary judgment.

"Oh, another fact that should not be overlooked. There is the matter of the missing 53 case histories. That is quite a significant number to be missing. One certainly needs to wonder what the content of those documents might reveal."

"You, of course, were advised that they were accidentally destroyed in a fire?"

"Yes, indeed, I was told that. However, I do not necessarily have to accept that explanation since one would wonder why these 53 case histories were segregated from the balance of the premarket records. I have also not seen any fire report or any other evidence of a fire destroying these records. Let's just say that I am quite suspicious, especially when I see what a properly conducted study by Rhoden and colleagues unearthed several years later."

Gillingham next went through a series of questions, tying down each criticism Donner had with the Brookhurst premarket study, information he would eventually feed to his own set of experts, although presuming they would never be called to testify at the trial. Finally, late in the day, Bulldog arrived at the moment he had been relishing since he began his preparation for the deposition.

"You no longer practice medicine as a pediatrician, correct?"

"Correct."

"And you haven't for many years?"

"True."

"You no longer practice medicine in the field of pharmacology and toxicology. Isn't that also true?"

"Well, I occasionally do consulting work, but that is generally true."

"In fact, you are pretty much a full-time expert witness, aren't you?"

"Pretty much."

Donner knew where this was all going but gave little concern about the innuendo. Was he looked upon as a maverick in the industry? Indeed, he was, and Alan Donner relished the role. Most of his peers were tied in with the drug industry, either as employees or consultants, and many others were working under grants funded by one or more drug companies. Still, others worked at the FDA. Very few offered their services to victims of dangerous drugs. He thus saw himself as filling a void.

"And have you been a full-time expert over the past ten years?"

"Pretty much."

"So, you're a hired gun?"

Redden again fought, jumping in with an objection and giving Donner free rein on how he wanted to address any of the questions, something else they had discussed over the lunch break.

"I don't own a gun."

"Okay, so your opinion is for sale."

"Is that a question?"

"Yeah, it's a question."

"No, I am a forensic expert. My testimony is for sale – at a reasonable fee – but not my opinion. My expert opinions are what I sincerely believe based on the facts I review, along with my education, training, and experience in the field of pharmacology and toxicology over the past several decades. My services are equally available to the drug industry."

Gillingham now reaches down to a lower level.

"Is it true that you have been investigated by the Internal Revenue Service?"

Redden is about to jump out of his chair with an objection, but Donner grabs him by the arm.

"Yes, that's true."

"In fact, there were charges against you for receiving cash from plaintiffs' attorneys and not reporting it as income?"

Donner grabs Redden's arm again. "That's alright, Mitch. I want to answer this." The anger is now brimming over as Donner takes a fix on Bulldog's eyes. "Yes, Mr. Gillingham, those charges have been leveled at me, all prompted at the instigation of several drug companies – a clear form of harassment. In fact, I have been the subject of personal harassment by pharmaceutical companies over the past ten years – many times." Donner picks up his glasses from the table and waves them at Bulldog as he continues. "But you want to know something, Mr. Gillingham? I am still here and will be for the next ten years, God willing. As you no doubt already know, the IRS never pursued the matter because it quite simply never found any evidence to substantiate those charges."

Redden finally jumped in. "Ask your next question," he demanded, making it clear there would be no further questioning about the IRS or any other related issue.

Donner's questioning continued for several hours, not concluding until 6:35 in the evening. Throughout the questioning, Donner was still unwavering in his opinion that Phenatol was teratogenic and the probable cause of Randy Burroughs' proximal femoral focal deficiency.

Upon conclusion of the deposition, Gillingham was quick to leave, frustrated by the ineffectiveness of his interrogation. Rothenberg is more contemplative about what has taken place, recognizing the impressiveness of this key witness and what impact he might have on a jury.

As Rothenberg slowly loads up a briefcase with his accumulated notes, he is approached by Redden.

"I know it was you, Geoff." It was the first time Redden had referred to the younger lawyer by his first name.

"I have no idea what you're talking about!"

"Sure, you do. The Barry and Klein stationery."

"You got *nothing* from me!"

"Of course not." Redden senses a degree of uncertainty in Rothenberg, perhaps confusion or a moral dilemma about where he is going.

"Get out, Geoff, while you still have some integrity."

Rothenberg snaps back. "Assuming that I had slipped you the stationery, which I emphatically deny, my only motivation would have been to take you off at the knees, nothing more."

"*That* I would admire," said Redden. "And who knows, maybe you might just get your chance."

CHAPTER 35

Friday, April 2

Redden is at Ricardo's and intends to drink some seriously. And why not:?It is Friday night, with the trial scheduled to start on Monday; there is still no lead on Roberta Blanchard, no evidence of a contemporary tie between Langhorne and BKN, and an inevitable nonsuit waiting in the wings by the end of next week at the latest. In addition, Niki still has their relationship on hold and will only discuss issues regarding the case. Working on his second beer, Mitchell is prepared to move to a libation more suited for the occasion.

"Billy!" he called out to the bartender. "Time for a change. Tanqueray on the rocks. All gin, no Vermouth."

"You got it!" is the reply.

After Donner's impressive deposition testimony, there was little doubt that Gillingham would be yanking every string at his disposal – each of them firmly attached to Langhorne. Alan Donner would be a disaster for Brookhurst, Gillingham no doubt concluded after the deposition. Juries loved him, and now Bulldog knew why.

Just as Redden's drink arrives, he is tapped on the shoulder by someone from behind and turns to find Hildebrand. Harry had told him where to find Redden.

"Rick! What are you doing here?"

"Just got some good news and wanted to deliver it personally."

"I'd pretty much given up hope. What is it?" he anxiously asked.

"I found Roberta Blanchard."

"Great!" Instantaneously, Redden's spirit elevated several notches.

"I traced her through five different cities and 8 different jobs, but I had found her. She works at UC Medical Center in San Francisco and currently resides in Sausalito, just north of San Francisco. She lives with her sister." Hildebrand handed Redden a slip of paper with the two addresses and their phone numbers.

Redden read the names and addresses on the memo and held it up. "Do you have any idea what this might represent?"

"Something important, I presume."

"Important! This woman knows the content of clinical records destroyed by Brookhurst. She holds the key, Rick, the key!"

"Well, if you're heading up to the Bay Area, my friend, I'd be watching my back."

"As if I need to be reminded," noted Redden, who then turned to the bartender. "Billy, give this man anything he needs, and I mean anything. Put it on my tab."

"Oh, and something else," Hildebrand added. "I don't want to go into it now, as it may be nothing, but I have a new lead on Langhorne. Won't know for a couple days, though."

"Let me know if you do. ASAP. I'm almost out of time."

Redden thanked Hildebrand again and promptly left. He would be catching an early flight to San Francisco in the morning.

Saturday, April 3

Not wanting to waste even an hour, Redden caught the first flight out of LAX to San Francisco International Airport, then rented a car. But rather than taking a straight route to the Golden Gate Bridge and over into Marin County, he took a side trip into the downtown area. Originally from the Bay Area, Mitchell Redden knew "The City" as well as any tour guide – and, at the moment, was taking full advantage of that knowledge, making multiple turns, heading generally in one direction and then in another. It was still relatively early on a Saturday morning, and traffic was light, making it easy to detect anyone who might be following him.

Once he was satisfied it was safe to proceed to his intended destination, Redden made his way back to US 101, then over the bridge and the short drive into the city limits of Sausalito. With his GPS, he quickly located Blanchard's home and parked in front of a small duplex overlooking San Francisco Bay. At the moment, there is a strong wind blowing in gusts, but no rain. It was 10:15 AM.

Redden knocked at the door and then anxiously waited. He had not called ahead to set up a meeting, not knowing how she might react. If unwilling to discuss anything related to Brookhurst or Phenatol, she might quickly disappear again, and with a trial only two days away, he did not have the luxury of time for another search. It was also a Saturday morning, and the odds were that she might be at home.

After a short wait, a woman answered the door.

"Good morning, I'm looking for a Roberta Blanchard," said Redden.

"Who might you be?" she asked.

"My name is Mitchell Ridden. I'm an attorney," he said, handing her a business card along with his state bar card."

The woman looked them over carefully, then handed them back. "I'm Roberta," she said. "How can I help you?"

Roberta Blanchard had blonde hair, was slightly overweight, and appeared at the door as a woman in her mid-50s with a pleasant smile. According to Rick, she was a career nurse and now worked in the obstetrics unit at the UC Medical Center in San Francisco.

"I'm involved in a lawsuit against Brookhurst Pharmaceuticals down in Los Angeles. I represent a malformed child by the name of Randolph Burroughs. We are contending that his malformation was caused by one of its drugs, a drug called Phenatol."

Redden detected a slight reaction by Blanchard upon hearing the name of the drug. "Come on in, Mr. Redden," she invited. As they entered the living room, she offered him a cup of coffee, which he declined. "Have a seat," she said. Redden grabbed a convenient chair, as did his hostess. "I am familiar with the drug, and I have no great love for drug companies," she said, "but I don't know how I could possibly help you."

"My understanding is you used to work for a physician, Carl Shelton, back in Philadelphia."

"Yes, I worked for him for 12 years until he retired. I then followed my husband's job around the country until he passed away a couple years ago."

"I'm sorry." Redden is trying to ease his way into the subject, not knowing what approach would be the most effective. "I also understand that Dr. Shelton was a clinical investigator."

"Yes, for several companies on a number of drugs."

"As I mentioned, this case involved Phenatol, which I understand was one of the drugs Dr. Shelton worked on." Again, the same reaction, as Blanchard seemed slightly more distressed about the subject, staring off as if looking for a lifeline to rescue her.

"In my work up on the case, I have had access to the Phenatol NDA and have reviewed several clinical reports that you apparently typed up from Dr. Shelton's charts."

This time, she does not give him the confirmation that he is seeking. For a moment, she only stared at him. "Maybe you should go, Mr. Redden. Everything involving that drug is either confidential or a matter of public record," she said. "I really don't believe that I can help you."

Blanchard rises from her chair and proceeds to the front door. Redden reluctantly followed. As she opened the door, Redden recognized that it was desperation time. Blanchard had a weakness, as revealed by her current employment in obstetrics, and it was time to exploit it. "Please, Mrs. Blanchard…Roberta, please. I really need your help." Using her given name would help bring their meeting to a more personal level.

"Again, Mr. Redden, I don't know how I could help you. There is nothing I know that could possibly be of any assistance to you."

Redden's voice sounded slightly more desperate. "Look, Roberta. I am representing a boy – a 6-year-old boy – crippled by a drug, a limb-reduction defect, and a trial date on Monday with one big hole in our case. The reason for that hole is that the company destroyed every incriminating piece of evidence. Apparently, Dr. Shelton's study demonstrated some teratogenic effects from the drug, and the company covered up that evidence."

"No, you are wrong, Mr. Redden, totally wrong. Dr. Shelton's study had nothing to do with birth defects. That wasn't the design of his study."

Redden is stunned. He had been so certain he had found the answer, and now the case was sliding through his fingers like a bucket of sand.

"Then what *was* the design of the study?"

Blanchard is still reticent about discussing anything regarding the Phenatol study. It had been a secret she had held inside for over a decade, something buried in the past she had committed to never reveal. Finally, she shrugged her shoulders. Maybe it was time to open up. After all, Dr. Shelton could no longer be impacted, so why is there a need for secrecy?

"Dr. Shelton was a toxicologist. He was studying the *addictive* aspects of phenylpropelene. Phenatol is addictive – and at low doses. Withdrawal of the drug produces more headaches, which in turn prompts the user to use more Phenatol. All one had to do was to look at the sales, which exploded after the first year the drug was on the market. Within three years, it was the number one headache medication in America. The company has made billions in sales. And the reason, quite simply, is because it is more addictive than prescription-strength codeine."

Redden is trying to process what he has just heard. "But why wasn't this reported to the FDA?"

"It *was* reported to the FDA. It was in Dr. Shelton's report. I typed it myself, and then mailed it to Brookhurst, just like all his case reports. He even called the FDA and spoke to one of the doctors assigned to the drug."

Those reports, thought Redden, had been altered by Brookhurst, but how could Shelton or Blanchard have possibly known that?

Blanchard continued, now intent on unloading the whole story.

"Dr. Shelton also complained to the company shortly after he read about the market approval. But Brookhurst threatened him. Said that if his study went public, they would ensure that all his research grants would be pulled."

Blanchard's eyes begin to glisten from accumulating tears. "Dr. Shelton was a good man, committed to his research. He was a toxicologist and dependent upon the drug industry for his research. This was his career, and Brookhurst threatened to destroy it, so he remained quiet…but it destroyed him…" Tears were now trickling down her cheeks that a few minutes earlier had been supporting a smile. "…gradually and insidiously, over a period of time." The attachment with Dr. Shelton was obvious. "They say he developed Alzheimer's, but I think this all took its toll on him. The last time I saw him, he didn't even recognize me."

"What about you? Why didn't you step forward?"

"I made a promise to Dr. Shelton. I couldn't. They said if this went public, they would destroy his career. I could not do that to him."

Redden is about to leave as he steps outside through the doorway. "There are hundreds of thousands who are addicted to this drug. Someone needs to blow the lid off this thing, and you are the only one who can do it. I might be able to use you in the trial if you are willing. What do you think?"

Blanchard nodded her willingness.

"Good. I will call you on Monday and let you know if and when."

The two said their goodbyes, then Redden turned and headed down the walkway toward his car, as Blanchard closed the door.

Inside, the nurse sensed an enormous relief at being relieved of the burden she had been carrying for over a decade, which had now been passed on to this lawyer. She had just purged the guilt that began the day she had made the pledge to her employer. Testifying would not be something she would relish, but it would be the right thing to do – something that would have the blessing of Dr. Shelton if only he was capable of giving it. Yes, she was certain of that.

On his way back to San Francisco International Airport, Redden began to explore what had just been dumped in his lap. It would be explosive testimony, to be sure, but how could he possibly get it in front of a jury on the Burroughs case? What would be the relevance that Brookhurst destroyed records about its addictive drug in a lawsuit about its ability to cause birth defects?

Well, there was one theory.

Had Niki Burroughs not become addicted to Phenatol – which she unquestionably was – she would not have been taking it during her pregnancy. It was certainly a reasonable argument, but Gillingham would be all over it because the plaintiff had never raised it in pretrial discovery – the contention had not been previously presented with sufficient time to allow Brookhurst to develop its defense to the contention; that it would be highly prejudicial to the defendant.

Of course, the fact that this was only discovered over the weekend would not carry much weight on a judge hell-bent on dismissing the lawsuit. Redden would make the argument that taking Blanchard's deposition after hours or, better yet, a short continuance of the trial would solve the prejudice argument, but again, it would fall on Langhorne's deaf ears. This case was destined to end in a nonsuit.

So, the goal here was to secure and preserve Blanchard's testimony, something that would likely force Brookhurst into making a significant settlement offer. The absolute last thing that the drug company would want would be any form of a public record of testimony from Roberta Blanchard. But how could that happen?

Well, there was a way. An offer of proof.

When a trial judge excludes testimonial evidence during a trial, the proponent of the evidence must make a record for the appellate court to assess its relevance and whether its exclusion was prejudicial to the party seeking to introduce it. Although Gillingham would no doubt argue that the plaintiff's counsel could verbally make an offer of proof, whether or not such testimony would have been *prejudicial* could only be determined by hearing testimony and cross-examination of that witness.

By the time Redden pulled into the rental car agency at the SFO airport, he had concluded his analysis and had settled on his argument.

And if everything went as expected, the lawsuit would end in a major settlement on Monday morning.

But, when was the last time anything went as expected in this lawsuit?

CHAPTER 36

Monday, April 5

Roger Langhorne sat stern and all-business on his high throne as he looked down at the legal representatives who had become a major thorn in his side. The quicker he could put this case behind him, the better. Both sets of counsel were still outside the railing, waiting to be called. The judge's support staff were all in place, ready for their various functions. A no-nonsense judge, Langhorne's attitude had likewise been taken up by his crew. This would not be a fun-filled trial.

"Burroughs verses Brookhurst Pharmaceuticals," Langhorne called out.

The two sets of lawyers rose, made their way through the gate, and approached the counsel table, aligned with their traditional spots. The small sign designating "Plaintiff" was closest to the jury box, and the more distant sign stated "Defendant."

"Good morning, Your Honor. Mitchell Redden and Harry Blaylock are appearing for the plaintiff," announced Redden. Blaylock, standing next to him, was nervously biting his lip, uncertain about the direction the case would be taking and the potential consequences it would have on his future.

"Good morning. C. Raymond Gillingham and Geoffrey Rothenberg appearing for the defendant." Rothenberg stood with his eyes anxiously fixed on the judge, hoping that Redden would pull something out of the bag that would push Bulldog back on his heels.

He would not be disappointed.

"Will there be any matters for the court preliminary to calling in a panel of jurors?" Langhorne's inquiry was strictly routine, with no expected affirmative response.

"Yes, Your Honor," announced Redden. "Plaintiff moves to add a name to his witness list, a Roberta Blanchard."

With a theatrical display of shock, Gillingham provided his response. "Defendant strongly objects! This is a surprise witness who has never been deposed and for whom there is inadequate time to prepare for her testimony. It would be highly prejudicial to the defense to allow her to testify at this time."

Langhorne turned to Redden to hear his justification.

"We were only able to locate this witness on Friday night and speak to her on Saturday. She is a critical witness who can reveal the content of records Brookhurst claims were destroyed in a fire over a decade ago and can also testify about altered reports on those records. And there is little doubt that Brookhurst knows very well what her testimony will disclose."

"Pure unsubstantiated allegations," said an obviously agitated Gillingham, apparently caught by surprise. "Those records were destroyed by a fire! The plaintiff wants to bring in a witness to give hearsay testimony about the alleged content of records last seen over a dozen years ago. The defense would have no way to rebut her testimony."

"This is *not* hearsay," countered Redden. "She will not be reciting what she *read* but what she recorded herself as the author of the records and reports. It is a means of authentication of the defendant's own business records, an exception to the rule even if it was hearsay."

"Why wasn't her name disclosed earlier?" asked Langhorne.

"Your Honor, I have spent days examining thousands of pages of the NDA, an inspection trip conducted at the earliest possible time. It was only on my second trip to complete that review that I learned about the alleged fire. I even spent a good part of a day at the FDA, only to learn that the federal agency likewise did not have copies of those records. When I learned that the investigators involved in the studies were not available due to death and illness, I then sought out a nurse who had worked with one of them. And here," he said, holding up a declaration signed by Hildebrand, "is a detailed report on all the efforts made by my investigator to locate that nurse. I can assure the court that it would have been *impossible* to locate this witness prior to this last weekend."

The clerk took the declaration from Redden and delivered it to the judge while Mitchell handed a copy to Gillingham.

Langhorne appeared to be having some difficulty with the motion as he poured over the declaration. Finally, he began shaking his head and said, "I am sorry, Mr. Redden. I do appreciate the effort you have made, but I cannot allow a new witness without giving the other side an opportunity to conduct discovery. It would be too prejudicial."

Redden was not about to give up, although he knew where this was all heading, even before he made the motion. After all, Bulldog was still in full control. At this point, it was more of a matter of making a record for a possible appellate court. "Then let's schedule a deposition of the witness. I could have her available after court hours tomorrow."

"I'm sorry, Mr. Redden. I have never favored conducting depositions in the middle of a trial. It is too disruptive, and invariably, the testimony leads to the need for further discovery. That request is also denied."

"Then I would move for a continuance of the trial. Just a short continuance," urged Redden, knowing well it was a lost cause. In reality, everything was going pretty much as expected.

"That motion is also denied. My trial calendar is set for the next year, and I am not going to disrupt my calendar. Nor am I willing to put this trial off for another year. Again, the motion is denied."

"I have one more matter, Your Honor," said Redden, who simultaneously noticed that Hildebrand had recently arrived and was motioning to him. "If the court would give me a brief moment."

"Of course," said Langhorne.

Redden stepped over to the railing and met with Hildebrand, who said in a barely audible voice, "We lost your witness." He then handed Mitchell a small article from the *San Francisco Chronicle*. It identified

Roberta Blanchard as the fatal victim of a hit-and-run accident. She had been struck in front of the UC Medical Center while crossing the street for work Sunday morning.

The news hit Redden like a Mack Truck, as he was immediately overwhelmed with guilt. He turned toward the bench and softly stated, "Nothing further for the plaintiff, Your Honor."

Gillingham then echoed the same for the defendant.

With no further motions, Langhorne announced that there would be a 15-minute break while the clerk called up a jury panel and then left the bench.

Stunned, Redden made his way past Niki – who had arrived a half hour earlier without Randy – through the double doors to the courtroom and into the hallway, found a convenient bench, and sat, staring at nothing but visualizing the face of Roberta Blanchard, as he had last seen her on Saturday morning. Sensing that something was wrong, Niki rose and followed Redden to his bench, then sat next to him.

"What's wrong?" she asked.

"I killed her," he responded. "Roberta Blanchard. She agreed to testify, and now she's dead. Struck by a hit-and-run driver yesterday morning."

"I don't understand. How could that possibly be your fault?"

"It's complicated."

Niki placed her hand on Mitchell's cheek and turned him to face her. "Try me."

"Two others related to this case have died since I filed this lawsuit, each under very suspicious circumstances. Now, a third. This could not be a coincidence…. Something else I never told you. When I was in New Jersey two months ago, someone took a shot at me. Three of them, actually."

"What?"

"That's right. I later convinced myself that it was just a warning. But someone, maybe several, maybe even Brookhurst itself, does not want this case to go forward and is prepared to kill to ensure that it doesn't…. And now I know why."

"But why? Why would someone commit murder over a drug that

causes birth defects? It makes no sense. The news is already public knowledge and published in a respected medical journal. So how could our lawsuit change anything?"

"Niki, it has nothing to do with birth defects. It's bigger, much bigger."

"Then what?"

"I can't tell you."

"Why not?

Redden had taken every precaution to protect Blanchard, but it had been useless. As soon as Hildebrand had found her, she had been marked for death, and there was nothing they could have done to alter that outcome. And Niki Burroughs was not going to be the next victim.

"Because, Niki, if you knew, it might place you in danger, and that is not going to happen. Not as long as I'm alive."

The life and death discussion they were having had seemingly transported Niki into a different world, as if watching a fictional account of a story in a movie and then suddenly joining it in real-time. This could not possibly be happening because the reality of what she was hearing was terrifying. And it was not lost on her that Mitchell Redden was right in the middle of it. The man she manipulated to pursue this very same lawsuit was apparently facing real danger. He was a man committed – committed to her cause and facing unimaginable challenges.

For a moment, Niki wanted to express her admiration and searched for the right words. But just as she was about to speak, Redden spied Gillingham and Rothenberg exiting the hallway and excused himself.

"Stop for a moment," Redden called out. "I have something to say," he announced, still reeling from the emotional impact of Blanchard's death. It was in such a state that common sense taught him not to vocalize his thoughts. But at the moment, he was intent on expressing his feelings and throwing caution aside. It was time to make a statement to his principal nemesis. A war had been started, and he, Mitchell Redden, would be up to the task.

"You may have succeeded in excluding the evidence from the trial," said Redden, glaring at Gillingham, "but the whole world will know about Shelton's studies – the true studies. And I will make sure that happens. Count on it!"

Redden had his doubts about Bulldog's involvement in the three deaths – it was not his nature to take on the risk associated with such a drastic act – but Brookhurst had billions to lose, literally. Those at the top might very well see it in the company's best interests to eliminate all risks of exposure to what had been carefully concealed.

"The whole world will only know what it already knows," smiled Gillingham, who continued to move with his associate further down the hallway, passing Hildebrand on the way.

The investigator approached Redden, sensing his need for some moral support. "You all right, Mitch?"

"Roberta Blanchard died because of my obsession with ringing the victory bell in a courtroom. And for what purpose, a fucking lawsuit for damages – for money."

"I don't see it that way," offered Hildebrand. "Something someone told me several years ago – and it made sense to me then and still does."

"And what was that?"

"Okay, yeah, you're after some money for a needing client, but there's something bigger here, something a lot bigger. You are holding people accountable. Who else is gonna bring Brookhurst to task, if not you? It hasn't happened yet."

Redden digests the words of encouragement. "But at what expense?"

"Sometimes at an extreme cost, but in the bigger picture, thousands, maybe millions, may eventually benefit."

Redden shook his head, still unwilling to forgive himself.

"Makes sense, doesn't it?

"Yeah, I guess…"

"It should. It was you who said it."

"Well, don't despair," added Hildebrand. "I should have something on my Langhorne lead by this evening."

This gave Redden some rejuvenation – but only slightly.

At the same moment, they both heard a crowd of prospective jurors approaching from down the hall, several chatting with one another, all representing a cross-section of the community, young and old, professionals and nonprofessionals, as well as a mixture of Asians, Hispanics, African-Americans and Caucasians, some dressed in suits and others with less formal ware, all to shortly be exposed to questions designed to elicit any form of bias or prejudice toward the facts of the case.

As if on cue, shortly before arriving at Langhorne's courtroom, the bailiff opened the double doors, and all 25 of them marched inside.

"Time to go to work," said Redden as he nodded to Niki to join him.

Hildebrand bid his goodbye, reminding Mitch he would be in touch that evening, then was on his way down the hall.

Redden and Niki entered the courtroom and were followed by both defense attorneys. All prospective jurors were seated outside of the railing, and now, counsel and the parties would join them in their chairs at the counsel table. Voir dire examination of the jury panel was ready to commence.

All would wait another twenty minutes before being joined by the judge.

It was a common practice employed by Langhorne, which was seen by most observers as an issue of control. The courtroom was Langhorne's kingdom, and no one was to forget for a minute who was in charge.

Jury selection was not completed until 4:35 PM.

⬥

At 8:30 PM, Redden received a call from Hildebrand. He had never heard such enthusiasm in Rick's voice before. "I have something, and I think you are going to be very pleased," was Hildebrand's introductory comment.

"No, wait!" was the response. "Nothing over the phone. I'll meet you at nine-thirty, as planned." Both had agreed to a mutually convenient location while at the courthouse.

"See you then," said Rick, who then hung up the phone. Both would also take every precaution to be sure that neither was being followed.

⬥

At promptly 9:30 PM, Redden's Porsche pulled up next to Rick Hildebrand, leaning against his remodeled 1964 Ford Mustang in a public parking lot in Century City. It was a multilevel parking structure, and by agreement, they were on the second level. Only a handful of cars were scattered around the large structure, most cast in shadows due to the limited lighting. In Rick's hand was a large manila envelope, and on his face was a smile. It was moments like this that Rick Hildebrand lived for.

As Redden climbed out of his car, Hildebrand handed over the envelope, which was quickly opened. He had yet to know the nature of this new evidence other than it related to Roger Langhorne. He would not be disappointed.

To assist in his viewing, Mitchell pulled out his iPhone and turned on the flashlight. As he reviewed the document, he, too, was struck by a rush of excitement. It had been scanned and e-mailed to Hildebrand only three hours earlier. A photograph was to be electronically sent tomorrow morning to provide even stronger evidence.

"I knew you wouldn't let me down," smiled Redden. "How in the world did you locate this?"

"You don't wanna to know. I pride myself on results. But the methods, well, let's say they are proprietary and my secret."

"Gotcha."

Through the corner of Redden's eye, he thought he saw a man duck and disappear behind one of the parked cars. Maybe it was just someone leaving for the evening – but then, maybe it wasn't. It was time to leave.

Without further discussion, they split up and left in their individual cars. They would both meet at the courtroom in the morning.

Redden decided to spend the night at a motel and go straight to court without returning to his office or residence. He had the Burroughs' file and his briefcase in the Porsche. Over his cell phone he telephoned Niki. She was to meet him in front of the courtroom at 8:00 o'clock.

He had a breakthrough that would turn the case upside down.

CHAPTER 37

As planned, Redden and Niki met in front of Langhorne's courtroom at 8:00 AM. Randy, who was with his mother, was to be their first witness after opening statements. The doors were locked and would remain so until 8:45 AM. The trial was scheduled to commence promptly at nine.

"Does this mean what I think it means?" she asked while reviewing Hildebrand's recent discovery. They are both sitting on a bench adjacent to the courtroom doors.

"Yes, but the clincher is the photograph, and Rick had not received it yet when we last talked. He is running late. So, I may have to start my opening statement before renewing my motion for recusal."

"Is that a problem?"

"I don't think so. I hope not. But..."

"So, it *is* a problem."

"Well, here it is. I've known for a couple months that a motion for nonsuit was inevitable, not to mention the ordained result. It's a motion that basically says, notwithstanding all of the plaintiff's evidence, the case is too weak to be decided by a jury. It could be as a result of the plaintiff lacking evidence on a given fact that must be proven or because of a legal requirement that cannot be met."

Redden is educating his client, who is intently listening. What is about to happen over the next hour or two could have a major impact on her future, including the needs of her six-year-old son.

"Traditionally, this motion is made after the plaintiff has presented all of his evidence to the jury and has rested his case. But on a rare occasion, it can be granted after the plaintiff makes his opening statement, in that he is telling the jury what his evidence will prove from the witness's stand. Something happened yesterday that made me concerned. After picking our six jurors, Langhorne refused to add any alternates."

"Why does that concern you?"

"Because once we begin putting on evidence, if we should lose just one juror, without an alternate to replace him, Langhorne would be forced to declare a mistrial, which would effectively give us our one-year continuance….I just don't see him taking that chance."

"Meaning?"

"Meaning, I believe Gillingham and Langhorne have set it up to grant a nonsuit motion after I finish my opening statement. Appellate courts tend to view recusal motions made *after* a ruling on the merits of the case as having been waived. In other words, if I am right, I need to make my motion before giving my opening statement – and I still don't have my best piece of evidence, the photograph."

"So, what are you gonna do?"

"What I always do – wing it!" he smiled.

At that moment, Harry Blaylock arrived, and Mitchell spent the next twenty minutes filling him in on all the recent developments.

Their timing was perfect. Just as the two lawyers finished their discussion, they heard the doors to the courtroom unlock – and all of them filed in and took their seats.

"All rise," announced the clerk. It was 9:00 AM, and Langhorne was taking the bench, a further confirmation that the case was moving toward a hasty conclusion after the plaintiff's opening statement. Rarely did the judge arrive on time after a break. The six jurors were in the box, and all parties and their counsel were present. A representative from Brookhurst was even at the counsel table with her attorneys.

"Be seated," said Langhorne. "I presume we are ready to proceed with opening statements?"

Redden nervously checked the courtroom, hoping the entry doors would suddenly burst open. But still no sign of Hildebrand. "Your Honor, could we possibly take a short ten-minute break? I'm waiting for someone due any minute. He has some information that I would like to include in my opening." Creative but hopeless, thought Redden.

"You've had plenty of time to prepare your opening statement, Mr. Redden. Please proceed."

Redden paused, picked up his legal pad, and scanned it as if refreshing his memory on his introductory remarks. Anything to delay. He then decided to give it another shot. "You know, judge, I am waiting for this information; I only learned about it last night. Could you just give me another five minutes?"

"Counsel, either you proceed with your opening, or I will deem it waived."

Redden wanted to address the recusal matter before proceeding with his opening. He did not want to argue his motion without the photograph – he wanted to go in with his strongest hand. But at the moment, there was no Hildebrand and no photograph. No other option was available.

For a brief moment, Niki's and Redden's eyes met, and upon giving her a well-here-it-goes glance, he said, "Excuse me, Your Honor, but I have another matter to address with the court."

The judge is now clearly agitated. "Mr. Redden! Either you proceed with your opening or waive. There will be no other matters!"

"Your Honor, I have a matter that needs to be addressed in chambers."

"Okay, you have waived your opening, so sit down!"

Redden was now openly defying the judge and remained standing, his determination evidenced by his clenched jaw and his glare back at Langhorne.

"Mr. Redden, you will sit down, or I'll hold you in contempt of court."

At this point, Redden's anger begins to boil, and armed with what he holds in his hand, he feels quite comfortable with what next comes out of his mouth. "That would be quite appropriate since that would aptly reflect the feelings of counsel right at this moment."

Langhorne explodes and slams down the gavel. "That outburst will cost you $10,000, counselor and another word will get you jail time."

Redden is not about to give a quarter. "I want this court to recuse itself and declare a mistrial."

"Five days, counselor. Upon conclusion of the trial. Wanna try for more?"

"We'll see who's sitting in jail after we start digging into your little soiree at the Royal Hawaiian Hotel," Redden announced for everyone's benefit. If this did not get him into chambers, nothing would. Instinctively, the bailiff rose from his chair.

Langhorne stopped the bailiff. The jury was enjoying every minute of this – which did not go unnoticed – and Langhorne sent them back into the jury room. He then ordered lead counsel into chambers.

Before retiring, Redden took a quick look for Hildebrand, but he had yet to arrive.

In chambers, the three men stood facing one another in a repeat of what had taken place only one month earlier.

"I want the court reporter," demanded Redden.

"You'll get your chance," said Langhorne, fighting to control his emotions, "but you now have your in-chambers audience. So, state your accusation. But I will caution you, if you are not prepared to back up everything you have to say, I will see to it that you are run right out of the legal profession."

Like Vesuvius, Mitchell Redden, the trial lawyer extraordinaire who prided himself in always maintaining control over his emotions, erupted. "So, you're gonna drum me out of the legal profession, huh? Well, fuck your threats, and fuck you…*and* your co-conspirator!" he yelled as he turned toward Gillingham. The multiple obstacles of the lawsuit, the associated murders, and the current stresses of the trial had all coalesced and had finally taken their toll.

The bailiff, hearing the loud voice, came charging in. "It's all right,

Jake," said Langhorne. "We're fine. Please close the door." The bailiff complied as the judge directed his comments again to Redden. "Get on with it, counsel."

Redden slammed copies of registration documents from the Royal Hawaiian Hotel in Waikiki onto Langhorne's desk. The registration sheets, dated just eight months earlier, revealed that Langhorne and Morris Richman Klein, soon-to-be-retiring senior partner of Barry, Klein & Nance, had registered in adjoining rooms. This took some steam out of Langhorne, but not all of it.

Gillingham stood silently, taking in the incriminating display. It did not come as a surprise beyond Redden's knowledge of its existence.

"This proves nothing," said Langhorne, sounding unconvinced himself.

Seeing the impact on Langhorne, Redden continued. "You can drop the act, judge. I know that you and Klein are lovers and have had a closet relationship for over 20 years. I also know that Chester has been pulling your strings and that you've been playing a role scripted by counsel for the defendant – and that this whole case has been nothing more than an elaborate scheme of deception, suppression of evidence, judicial manipulation, and murder."

At this point, Gillingham jumped into the fray. "Murder? Are you out of your mind? Who in the hell has been murdered, and what ungodly evidence could possibly lead you to believe that his honor and I are involved in it?"

Gillingham had now taken over the fight, Langhorne having collapsed in his chair with little else to say. "As usual, your argument is built on nothing more than supposition and innuendo. All the registration sheets prove is that the two of them, coincidentally, were at the hotel at the same time, nothing else."

"I have corroborating evidence," said Redden, "and if it is not in the courtroom now, it should be shortly."

"Either produce it now or begin serving your 5 days." A quick look by Gillingham at Langhorne produced only a nod of approval. Bulldog's directions to the judge were now out in the open.

"Be glad to," was Redden's curt reply, who then exited the chambers.

How had matters escalated so quickly? The idea of going into chambers was to drag it out. Not only was Redden now out on a limb, but he was actively cutting it off – with a chainsaw!

Thank God, thought Redden, as he spied Hildebrand sitting next to Niki in the courtroom. "Where's the photo?" he eagerly asked as he approached them. It was time to put this whole matter to bed. Langhorne would now have no choice but to recuse himself and declare a mistrial. A full investigation by the California State Bar would undoubtedly implicate Chester Raymond Gillingham III, followed by his disbarment – all about to be set in motion by a simple photograph.

"I gave it to Harry," said Hildebrand. "I believe he put it in his briefcase, just before he took Randy to get a drink of water. It's in a large envelope."

Redden spied Harry's old briefcase, sitting on the floor next to his chair. Its years of use and abuse were reflected in its discolored leather and scuff marks. It had been in Harry's possession since his graduation from law school, and he often declared that it would be with him on the last day of his career as a lawyer. The two were forever inseparable. To Redden, the briefcase seemed to symbolize the downtrodden life of its owner, although, at the moment, it gleamed like a beacon of promise.

Quickly, Redden picked up the briefcase, placed it on Harry's chair, pulled back the leather flap, reached in, and pulled out an envelope – and from it was the photograph. It was a picture of Langhorne and Klein, both with Aloha shirts and leis, with their arms around one another at a luau. Redden then displayed it for Niki's view, and they shared a smile. It was everything that Rick Hildebrand had promised.

But something else caught Redden's attention. It was a piece of paper that had inadvertently been withdrawn from the briefcase along with the envelope and had dropped onto the counsel table. Curious, Mitchell picked it up for a closer examination. It was a receipt for an airline ticket in Harry's name for a roundtrip flight to San Francisco, arriving only last Saturday and returning on Sunday afternoon. Harry had flown to San Francisco the same day that Mitchell Redden had returned from the same destination.

But why? And why had Harry not mentioned it to him?

Perplexed, Redden dug again into the briefcase, this time pulling out receipts for two more flights, both to the Newark Airport in New Jersey, arriving on January 26th and returning January 28th, and the second arriving on February 2nd and returning February 4th.

Again, the same questions: Why? And why had Harry not mentioned it to him?

He looked again at the dates. Why were they familiar to him? Why were they…..? It then hit him. In a flash, it all came together. The first trip to New Jersey coincided with his second inspection trip to Brookhurst and the second flight….."Oh, my God," he said out loud. "That's when Radcliffe died!"

Niki, perplexed at the remark, stared at Redden.

But before she could ask a question, Mitchell continued, "And earlier, the gunshots. Then in San Francisco, Roberta Blanchard…. Oh, no…no."

As Redden was stood there in shock, grasping the airline receipts, Harry entered the courtroom holding Randy's hand. Redden looked up at him pleadingly, extending the receipts, standing next to Harry's open briefcase.

"My God, Harry, why?"

Harry began shaking his head. "It is not what you think, Mitch."

Redden began walking toward Blaylock, whose reaction was to back away – with Randy in tow. "You don't understand! You don't understand!" pleaded Blaylock.

Redden took another step. "Then tell me, Harry, tell me why?"

"It was Gillingham, he was pressuring me…"

Blaylock backed up against the courtroom doors – and panicked. Whatever was left in his world had now unraveled. He was outed by his own protégé, and his dark deeds over the past couple of months were discovered by the one person in the world whose respect he had treasured.

In a flash, Harry's instinct for self-preservation took over as he grabbed Randy by the arm, burst through the doors, hoisted the young boy onto his shoulder,and then took off down the hallway.

Almost simultaneously, Redden screamed out, "Harry, no!" and began his chase.

It had all happened so fast that Blaylock did not have a full appreciation that he had involved Randy in his impromptu escape plan. This unwilling prisoner, at the moment, was both terrified and confused as to what was happening.

In pursuit, Redden pushed his way through the double doors, followed by Niki, who momentarily assessed Harry's escape route, then took off after him, with Niki screaming out, "My baby, my baby!"

Two federal marshals, having heard the commotion, appeared out of a courtroom down the hallway, between Harry and the elevators, prompting Blaylock to change his intended course and charge into a stairwell and up the stairs to the roof. Within seconds, the alarm to the rooftop door was triggered, just as Redden and Niki reached the stairwell – and continued their pursuit, with the two marshals, Langhorne's bailiff, Hildebrand, and a few spectators drawn to the unfolding drama, not far behind.

Moments later, Redden and Niki – and their entourage – stepped through the doorway and onto the roof. Harry was standing next to the low railing, tightly holding Randy by the wrist, who was now standing on the roof deck, tears streaming down his face.

"Stand back!" screamed Harry, appearing desperate and somewhat confused, with his back against the wall, both figuratively and literally. Immediately, the two marshals began backing everyone up, save for Redden, who stood only 20 to 25 feet away from Harry. "Let him go, Harry, said Redden as he slowly moved forward. "Don't hurt the boy."

"I would never hurt Randy. I just want everyone to stand back. I...I just need to think...Please stop!"

Redden complied, stopping only 9 or 10 feet from Harry, whose shoes were up against the low railing bordering the roof. Niki is a short distance behind him. Mitchell turned toward her, motioning with his hand for her to step back, which she did for a couple steps. An emotionally unstable man is standing on a precipice, tightly gripping the wrist of her son. If the confrontation were not effectively dealt with, his life could be over in seconds. It was time to place all her trust and faith in Mitchell Redden, the only one who could possibly reason with Harry Blaylock.

Redden took another step closer to Harry and stopped. "Let him go," he repeated.

"You just don't understand, Mitch. There have been pressures, Gillingham, his demands, his threats. I just wanted you back the way you were, just like we were, our old allegiance, the two of us fighting our battles together. That was a good thing, wasn't it?"

"Of course." Nodded Redden.

"But Gillingham said he had proof that we would both be disbarred. I mean, me, I didn't give a shit about me, but there was no fucking way I could let him take away your career. Again, he said he had all the proof; he had a witness and documents. He also knew the details. If this case went to trial, everything would go public, and the state bar would see it all. Don't you see, I had to put up roadblocks? I couldn't let this happen."

"I understand, Harry," said Redden as he took another step closer.

"No, I don't think you do. Not really. It was you, Mitch. It has always been about you. In my whole lousy fucking life as a lawyer, you were the one bright spot. It was you who gave meaning to my existence. You were blessed with all this natural talent but had not realized your potential. Then, I came along and provided you with a little direction and some polish. Don't you see, Mitch, you are the one thing, the only thing in my life that I can point to with some pride – and I was not gonna let Gillingham take that away from me, not that… It was all I had left."

"I know, Harry, I really do. You were desperate." Redden took another step closer.

"Stop!" demanded Harry, as he partially put his hip on top of the railing while still clinging to Randy.

Redden complied. "But murder, Harry."

"Gillingham said if the case went away, so would the evidence. He didn't want to know how. He just wanted results. These people who died were all part of the scheme, Mitch. These were bad people, and

I only fired the shots to scare you away. I never would have hurt you." Tears are now streaming down Harry's face.

"I know, but not Roberta Blanchard," Redden reminds. "Not her, Harry. She was a good woman just trying to survive."

Harry nodded, momentarily staring down. "Yes, I know, but it was still necessary."

"None of this was necessary," said Redden. "I would never have filed this lawsuit if I thought Gillingham's claims would hold up. But they won't – they can't. All of this was for nothing. His evidence never would have held up to any level of scrutiny."

This impacted Harry and he instantly released Randy, who ran to Niki and was embraced by his mother. He then seated himself on top of the railing and threw a leg over the other side.

"Don't, Harry! This can all be worked out. You are sick. You need treatment, not this!"

Harry shook his head and, with a weak smile, said, "Sorry, old friend, I'm beyond help," and slipped his other leg over and began to push off. At that exact moment, Redden leaped and grabbed Harry by the arm just as he disappeared over the side.

For a brief moment, Redden stared down at Harry and Harry back at him, the younger lawyer tightly gripping his arm with one hand and holding onto the railing with the other. Harry pleaded, "Let me go, Mitch, let me go. It's what I want."

With Harry's weight working to his advantage, he slowly slid from Redden's grip and dropped to his death 100 feet below.

For a few moments, Redden stared at the lifeless body of his friend, still trying to grasp what had just taken place over the past twenty minutes. Had this all been a dream, a nightmare from which he would shortly awaken? How could something switch from good to bad so rapidly, denying all the opportunity to adjust to such a dramatic and irrevocable result?

Redden pulled himself back onto the roof and saw Gillingham stepping onto the rooftop through the doorway – followed by Rothenberg. Instantly enraged, he charged at his nemesis and landed a solid blow to his face, knocking Bulldog flat on his back while the two marshals grabbed and restrained him.

"Let him go," said Gillingham as he was Rothenberg assisted him to his feet. "I have other ways of dealing with this," he threatened, then made his way back through the doorway along with his colleague.

Redden was immediately released, made his way over to the wall adjacent to the doorway, and dropped down into a sitting position as the crowd began to disperse in the direction of the marshals. Tears welled up in his eyes as he pondered his loss.

Niki sat next to him with Randy and put her arm around his shoulder.

"*Se agapo*," she said, staring into his eyes.

"It's all Greek to me," he said, forcing a smile.

"It means that I love you," she said. "It means that you are the most wonderful man in the world, and I'm sorry it has taken me so long to see it."

EPILOGUE

Saturday, May 29

Mitchell and Niki sat on beach chairs, taking in the view of Randy playing with a couple of other children on the beach, building high mounds of sand. His prosthesis had been left in the car, and after satisfying their curiosity, neither of the other two kids seemed to pay any attention to his handicap. Above the couple is a large umbrella stuck in the sand, affording them some protection from the mid-day sun. A light trade wind, blowing in from the northeast, kept the late spring temperature at a comfortable level, while the fresh salt air seemed to have its own therapeutic benefit following their high-stress experience over the preceding months. Tunnels Beach, on the north shore of the island of Kauai, was a popular location for tourists and locals alike.

The three of them had arrived 3 days earlier for a short one-week vacation. Mitchell had wanted Niki and Randy to see where he had spent three years of his life before Harry Blaylock had sought him out. Randy had also just started his summer vacation.

"So, are you gonna tell me, or do I need to pry it out of you?" asked Niki. Earlier in the day, Redden had received a call from Rick Hildebrand.

"About the best restaurants on Kauai you're asking about?" He, of course, knew exactly what she was after.

"So, you want to play it that way, do you?" Niki reached into a cooler, extracted a can of beer, popped it open, and was about to pour it on top of Mitchell when he responded, "Okay, okay!" as they both laughed. "Come on, Niki. No need to waste a good can of beer."

"Your choice."

"Okay, here it is. As you know, the FBI investigated Harry's death, including an interview with yours truly. Apparently, everything was turned over to Congress and the federal court because while facing almost certain impeachment by the House, Langhorne, just two days ago, permanently resigned from the bench. It was reported by the media, I think, today. And here's the shocker. Apparently, after a decade of separation, Mrs. Klein has just filed for divorce. Motivated, I guess, by the fact that her husband recently moved in with the now former judge Langhorne."

"You're serious?"

"It's the gospel, according to Rick. He verified everything. I guess both men are no longer concealing their affection for one another."

"What about your old buddy, Raymond Gillingham?"

"Oh, Chester? Yeah, I saved the best for last. Bulldog's been indicted. I guess the feds frown on judicial manipulation. There's a warrant out for his arrest as we speak. He will also be facing a disbarment hearing in one month. According to Rick, I've been asked to be a witness, which I okayed. But here's the final touch. Chester's partners have also voted him out of the firm. His most cherished goal – senior partnership in the firm – is not only gone, he is no longer even a member of the firm."

"Will he be disbarred?

"If convicted by the feds, a certainty."

Niki handed the beer to Mitchell, pulled another out of the cooler for herself, opened the can, and then held it up in a toast. "Here's to Chester," she said.

"And his well-earned future," added Mitchell.

⟶ ● ⟵

Following the declared mistrial, both sides had decided that it was best to put the case behind them. Neither wanted another go-around. Redden knew the case had its challenges, especially absent the clinical records and the inability to present a strong case that the drug company should have known from its own studies that the drug was a human teratogen. But after the emotional roller coaster ride he had experienced, Redden needed little convincing that it was time to move on – to settle the case and forget the nightmare it represented.

Brookhurst, on the other hand, did not want to give Redden another shot at locating any of Shelton's studies on chemical dependency – a motivation having little to do with the merits of the lawsuit. In fact, Brookhurst had sought to suppress the information received from Roberta Blanchard as a condition of the settlement. But neither the client nor the lawyer would agree to those terms, and in the end, Brookhurst caved and withdrew the condition. The last thing upper management wanted was to have Mitchell Redden digging through their Phenatol records again – at least before they could have another shot to further sanitize their files.

The funds from the seven-figure settlement were placed in an interest-bearing trust account. By the time Randy reached 18, he would have a substantial nest egg for a college education or to train himself in a vocation or career of his choosing. In 12 years, the technology in the development of prostheses might be such that his dream of being a fireman might even become a reality.

Niki and Mitchell have a wedding planned in late June, but a honeymoon will have to be delayed. They had both worked together to create a new website. It began: "WARNING! PHENATOL MAY BE DANGEROUS TO YOUR HEALTH. It has recently been discovered that *phenylpropelane*, the active ingredient in Phenatol, is highly addictive. Upon withdrawal from the drug, many users develop debilitating headaches that can only be reduced or eliminated by returning to Phenatol. Acetylsalicylic acid (aspirin), naproxen, ibuprofen, and acetaminophen have little effect on relieving headaches. If you should fail the withdrawal test, it is strongly recommended that you contact your physician." It was signed by the Roberta Blanchard Foundation with the permission of Blanchard's sister, June. Redden had provided the necessary funding to establish the legal entity. The website had received over 100,000 hits in its first two weeks.

The problem: many had sought out the phone number for the Roberta Blanchard Foundation and were telephoning its director, June (Blanchard) Whitman, for more information.

All of the calls were being forwarded to the Law Offices of Mitchell Redden.

In anticipation of the need to supply information, Niki and Mitchell had prepared a pamphlet explaining who Roberta Blanchard was and how the studies about addiction had been discovered. Although it was never his intention to pursue new lawsuits, many of the callers were seeking out representation.

Redden at first resisted, but Niki pressed him to take on any cases that appeared meritorious. These people needed help, which was another way to get back into the Brookhurst facility and its Phenatol records.

As the lawsuits began to line up, Redden was in desperate need of some legal assistance. One or two lawyers, at least. Next week, he was interviewing a young lawyer with promise, someone whose skills only needed a little bit of polishing from a seasoned veteran. Mitchell had gotten a call from him just before they left for Hawaii.

His name was Geoffrey Rothenberg.

As to the possible conflict of interest, well, they would figure out some way of working around the problem.

9 781965 687109